Acknowledgements

To Mr Malcolm A. Loudon, M.B.Ch.B., FRCSEd., M.D., FRCS (Gen), Consultant Surgeon and NHS Grampian Lead Clinician for Colo-rectal cancer, with great gratitude.

This novel was written during 'interesting times'. The first third was written in CLAN Haven, Aberdeen, during five weeks of radio- and chemo-therapy after a diagnosis of bowel cancer. Thank you to Mr Samuel, Janette, and the oncology and radiotherapy teams; thank you, the kind housekeepers at CLAN, the therapists, the staff, Bill the bus driver, and thank you, my fellow cancer sufferers, all of you far worse than I was, for all your companionship, cheerfulness, care, and kindness.

After that I was sent home to recover, and finished the first draft before the Big Op. The cancer bit went fine, but I developed an infection. Thank you, to the surgeons, nurses, and orderlies of Ward 1 in the Gilbert Bain Hospital, Lerwick, for your care; thank you, Mr Mikolajczak and Miss Weber, for putting me on that emergency flight to Aberdeen Royal Infirmary before it was too late. I think Miss Weber would approve my independent heroine, Cass!

My next thank you is to Mr Loudon of the ARI, and his staff in Ward 31. The operation he perfomed there, on what should have been his Queen's Jubilee holiday, saved my life.

I managed to stay out of hospital for all of two weeks before being re-admitted to the Gilbert Bain with acute dehydration. I spent five weeks on a drip –

which left my writing hand free for improving my first draft. Thank you, once more, to the wonderful staff of Ward 1.

The editorial copy of *The Trowie Mound Murders* arrived in my in-box as I was lying in the renamed Ward 501, Aberdeen Royal Infirmary, after the stoma reversal operation which we feared might not be possible. Thank you once more to Mr Loudon, for putting Humpty Dumpty back together, and to John Graham and all his team in Ward 501 for their care during my recovery.

Finally, thank you to all my friends who sent cards, letters, and flowers, who brought communion to me in hospital, and remembered me in church services and prayer groups – your support was truly appreciated. Thank you to my wonderful agent, Teresa Chris, who phoned with news of a publisher at last on the day I'd had my first chemo blast, and encouraged me to keep writing through it all. Thank you to my editor at Accent, Cat Camacho. Most of all, thank you to my husband and family, for all their support through two difficult years.

Now, *please*, can I get back to normal life …?

Monday 6 August
Tide times for Brae:
Low Water 06.32   0.4m
High Water 12.58   2.1m
Low Water 18.41   0.6m
High Water 01.03   2.3m
Moon waning gibbous

Two days after it was all over, I set out for Bergen.

The salvage boats were out before me, one on each side of where the Rustler had gone down. I watched them as I sailed *Khalida* down between the low green hills of Busta voe, with the township of Brae receding behind two solidly built, catamaran-hulled metal hulks with the power to raise a thirty-six foot yacht from the green depths of Cole Deeps.

I wasn't going to stick around to watch. I knew how the water would already have damaged her immaculate interior: gleaming varnish clouded white, tendrils of weed and clawed sea-creatures creeping over her willow-green cushions and into her closed lockers. Her electrics would be beyond repair, her rigging starting to rust. She was a salvage job now, if anyone cared to buy her – someone who hadn't had to identify the dreadful things that had lain on the cabin floor down in the depths, for the crabs to scavenge.

Four people had died, and three were in custody. It was over.

I tacked *Khalida* round, and turned her nose to the open sea.

A silk Monenday maks a canvas week.

(Old Shetland proverb: a week that begins too well can end badly)

Chapter One

Monday 30 July
Tide times for Brae:
Low Water 01.08   0.7m
High Water 07.22   1.9m
Low Water 13.30   0.8m
High Water 19.39   2.0m
Moon waxing gibbous

'I know how you got that scar,' the boy said, eyes travelling along the ragged indentation that ran across my cheek.

I wasn't going to let him see any reaction. He was in his mid-teens, sturdily built, with the tan of someone who's rarely indoors, glossy black hair, and a seaman's earring dangling from his left ear, a gold hoop with a cross. He had grey-green eyes, set close together over a beaked nose, and very dark lashes, half-lowered at the moment so that he could watch me slantways from behind them, like a cormorant keeping an eye on a dangling fish.

I was still trying to place him. I was getting to know most of the children in the area, and his face was familiar. Not one of the club's sailors – then I remembered this face smiling insolently at me from under a helmet. He'd come to fetch his little brother on a quad. His brother was Alex, a keen sailor who was still working his way through the wind-still in the marina's rocky entrance behind me. Olaf Johnston's son – Norman, that was his name. I remembered Olaf from school, and wasn't at all surprised that he'd turned into a parent who let his children charge around the roads on the quad; he likely considered that making them wear a helmet was discharging his duty to health and safety.

He wasn't a parent who'd be much help in the present situation.

It was a bonny, bonny evening. Even though it was almost nine o'clock the sun shone steadily on above the hill to the west and glinted on the water. The tide had turned an hour ago, and was just beginning to sidle down from the warmed concrete of the slip. The silver ghost of a three-quarters moon gleamed above the eastern hills. The force 3 southerly had kept the pink-sailed Picos scudding briskly around their racing triangle, and we'd all been having a really good time until there was a high-whine engine roar from the jetty below the clubhouse, then this boy bounced out on his jet-ski, curving around the dinghies to rock them, and flipping in between them to send water glittering over them. I'd resolved to have a word with him once he came ashore again.

'Look,' I said, 'I know this is a public slip, but there's no need for you to be driving your jet-ski so close to these beginner sailors.'

He ignored that. 'Your boyfriend shot at you. Then you pushed him overboard and left him to drown.'

Alain ... It felt as though he'd slapped me. He must have seen my eyes widen in shock, for his thin lips spread in a mocking grin.

'That is enough,' a voice said over my shoulder. There was a heaviness about the t, a guttural note to the vowels, that made the speaker Norwegian. A young man had come up from behind me to stand at my shoulder. He was half a head taller than I, and broad-shouldered with the muscles that come from spending the day hefting engines about.

His silver-gilt hair was covered with a cap that sent a dark shadow across his brow, his eyes were the cold blue of the sea on a winter's day, and his mouth was a hard line between the fair moustache and neat Elizabethan beard. He took a step forward. 'I see you here again, you won't be on a jet-ski for a couple of months.'

I made a protesting movement. He stepped in front of me, squaring into the boy's space. 'Not until the plaster comes off. You understand?'

'You can't –' I began. They ignored me, staring at each other like two foredeck hands playing poker. The boy wasn't going to show he was intimidated, but his defiant stance shifted and the eyes meeting mine so boldly slid away. He wasn't going to take total defeat though.

'Like she said, it's a public pier. I can use it if I want.' He surveyed the Norwegian, then that unpleasant smile curled his mouth again. 'My dad's Olaf Johnston. He wouldn't want you to be bothering me.' His eyes shifted to my face, then back to the Norwegian.

Anders wasn't having it. He took a step forward, spoke very softly. 'This is nothing to do with your father. I am talking to you. Don't come anywhere near our dinghies.' He gave the boy a last hard stare. 'Or me.' Point made, he turned to me as if the boy wasn't there, and jerked his head up towards where our pupils had finished hosing down the dinghies and moved on to splash suits, lifejackets, and each other. 'Shall we go, Cass?'

I could tell he wanted to get out of there while he still had the advantage. He'd taken only two steps away when his left shoulder bulged and moved; the lump travelled along his front and slid upwards. A pink nose and a set of quivering whiskers appeared in the neck of his checked shirt, then Rat wriggled out to sit on his shoulder, tail coiled around Anders' neck. Pet rats are sizeable animals, and Rat was a well-grown specimen, nearly 60 cm long from nose to tail. His fur was gleamingly white, with one glossy black patch on his starboard side, and another over his port ear and cheek. I liked him; he was clean, agile, and generally trustworthy aboard a boat, if the ship's biscuit container was screwed closed, and the light airs sails kept in the stern locker. All the same, I could see why Anders had wanted to keep him under cover; he would definitely have spoiled the hard man image.

Anders strode off up the slip; I paused to help haul the last dinghy up. The water was warm around my ankles.

'We got stuck in the mouth of the marina,' the skipper explained. It was Alex, our jet-ski maniac's brother. He was an under-sized ten-year-old with lavender-blue eyes set in a round face, and gold-rimmed glasses held on with elastic. His fair hair was cut fashionably long, and straggled damply round his neck, like the tendrils of a jellyfish.

'I saw you,' I agreed. 'What were you doing wrong?'

He thought about it. 'Waggling the tiller.'

'Yes.'

'Going into the no-go zone?'

'That was your main problem,' I said. 'Next time, free off a little and get your boat speed up. Never mind if it takes more tacks.'

'Okay,' he said. He looked up at the day-glo-pink triangle flapping above us. 'Do I have to hose the sail too?'

'Did it go in the water?'

'No.'

I gave his wet hair a pointed look. 'How come you did then?'

'Oh, yeah, I capsized,' he conceded.

'Then hose the sail.'

We backed the dinghy into its place in the row below the Boating Club. The club itself was a seventies concrete cube, one of the legacies from when Shetland had suddenly found itself the oil capital of Europe. During the building phase of the huge terminal ten miles north, at Sullom Voe, there had been over four thousand men in the accommodation camp, and so the bosses had had to find ways of keeping them amused. The cinema and sports hall had long since decayed into sheep fodder stores, but the boating club had been embraced with enthusiasm by local folk. Shetlanders were traditionally fishermen with a croft. In the eighties, this voe (the dialect word for a long sea-inlet like this one) had been white with the sails of the traditional Shetland Models, or Maids; youngsters had been encouraged in the red-sailed Mirrors. Now the older sailors extended their sailing range with yachts, heading off to Faroe and Norway at the drop of a shackle-spindle, and slaking their competitive instinct with hotly contested points races. The younger sailors spent their time in the Picos, something like a flattened bath tub with a mast. I wasn't taken with them from a sailing point of view, but had to concede that they were virtually indestructible, even in the hands of nutters like Alex, who spent as much time in the water as on it.

By the time I got up to the clubhouse, most of the children had hung their dripping blue splash-suits and scarlet lifejackets up in the drying room, and (from the noise filtering through the windows) were busy in the showers: the girls showering at length in a cloud of smelly bubbles, the boys splashing each other as much as possible. It's worrying how predictable genders can be.

I sat down on the bench to wait for them to finish. My hair was damp; I loosed it from its normal plait and let the dark waves curl over my shoulders. To my right, the green curve of Ladies' Mire stretched along below the standing stone that raised a rough back to the sun and cast a bulky shadow down the daisy-sprinkled field to the dark seaweed on the shore. Behind it was darker heather hill, the

9

scattald. Crofters had been working with sheep there all day; there was a row of parked pick-ups below the hill gate, with black and white collies snarling defiance at each other through the rear portholes. Every so often I'd looked up to see a clump of indignant, nervous sheep moving across, with two or three dogs wheeling around them. Clipping, dipping, checking on feet, and spraying them purple, there was no end of things that needed to be done to sheep. These hill sheep huddled together so nervously in a multi-coloured clump were proper Shetland sheep, half the size of the muckle-nosed Suffolks that paced majestically around the green parks by the houses. They roamed the heather hills in summer, and in winter they came down to eat seaweed on the shore, and lick the salt from the roads. They were black, grey, and moorit in colour, with the occasional piebald or white one. The 'black sheep of the family' proverb didn't work here.

A hay-filled Berlingo rattled along the main road between the new houses on this side and the older ones opposite, traditional croft houses built after the Viking pattern, long and low, with grey-tiled roofs and a sheltering thicket of bronze-leaved sycamores. To my left, the shore curved around to old Brae, where each house was set in its own strip of land that reached up to the rough hill grazing, and down to where the boat waited in its noost. Even the minister's house had a stone landing point, and the former shop stood proud above a substantial jetty, from the days – not so long ago, either – when goods and shoppers all came by sea. Shetland's history was always with us, the old patterns continued.

The shore ended in the point of Weathersta. I'd dreamt last night about the selkie wife who'd lived there, one of those dreams that left you with a sense of foreboding that clung like a dark mist for the rest of the day. I'd been that selkie wife, born a seal and delighting in the roughness of the waves, yet shedding my skin to be a woman on shore, and dance on human feet in the moonlight – until a young fisherman had hidden my skin and kept me for himself. In the dream, I'd loved him, and melted into his arms. I wasn't going to give the face a name, not even to myself. But my selkie wife had grown gnawingly, achingly, heartsick for the sea, and I'd searched for my skin in the bare house with its driftwood furniture, in the cluttered byre under the old dogskin buoys and tangle of lines, until I'd become frantic, thinking he'd destroyed it, and I'd be trapped on this heavy land until I died of longing. I'd run into the sea, leaving my baby wailing in its cradle, and awoke gasping as my mouth filled with water –

I knew where the dream had come from. My friend Magnie had been telling ghost stories, and one of them had been of the wailing baby, the selkie wife's deserted child, which had sickened and died without her. I knew why too. It wasn't hard to analyse. After a dozen years at sea, as yacht skipper and dinghy instructor, I'd decided to go for a commercial qualification at the North Atlantic Fisheries College in Scalloway, Shetland's ancient capital. I knew it was a sensible idea – no, better than that, it was what I really wanted, to be eligible for a paid job aboard a tall ship, instead of being volunteer crew for my bed and board. All the same, I was dreading it, a year of school, of being trapped day after day ashore, stuck in this northern climate, with no chance of tiers of white sails above my head, and the southern cross bright before the prow in the blue-black night. I was afraid that I wouldn't be able to do it, that the call of the sea would be too strong; that I wouldn't know myself in a classroom, with my hair neat in its plait, and a shore-patterned jumper, and shoes instead of sailing boots or flip-flops.

My brooding was interrupted by movement at the end of the voe: a motorboat coming in. I ran an eye over the pontoons, looking for gaps. The yellow one belonging to the noisy young couple was missing, but this wasn't them returning, thank goodness. This boat was white, with a high bow. At the speed it was coming down the voe, it'd be with us in five minutes. I was just wondering if they'd phoned ahead to book a berth when there was a scrunch of tyres on the gravel slope from the main road down to the slip. An ancient mustard Fiesta spattered past me and halted at the metal gate. It was Magnie himself, the marina's guardian, come to take their warps and give them a key to the club-house.

He'd dressed for the occasion. The sun picked up the dazzling white of his traditional Fair Isle gansey, knitted by his late mother and patterned with upright lines of cable and anchors on a dull-blue background. His reddish-fair hair was sleeked back, and his ruddy cheeks shone as if they'd just been shaved. They had to be visitors; Shetland residents enjoying a fine evening would have got the traditional blue boiler suit and yellow rubber boots.

The motor-boat was a forty-five footer, with a long foredeck for sunbathing in port, and a high wheelhouse opening into a sheltered cockpit. The engine roared as she curved round outside the marina, then quietened to a purr as the driver brought her round to the pontoon where Magnie was waiting.

Below me, on the slip, Norman watched open-mouthed as she gleamed her way across the water. There was a churning of water at the bow, then she stopped dead. Magnie threw the aft warp and the man at the wheel made it fast; a hatch opened in the foredeck and a woman came out, hand extended for Magnie's second warp. A pause, while they made her fast on the other side too, then Magnie clambered aboard. I wondered if he'd got a welcoming bottle in his hip-pocket.

Norman wasn't the only one staring. Anders breathed, in Norwegian, 'That's a Bénéteau Antares.'

I shrugged one shoulder at him, with the sailor's traditional contempt for power-boats.

'She'll do thirty knots,' Anders added.

'Without getting her crew wet,' I conceded, looking at the flared bow. She looked almost half as broad as she was long. 'She must be huge inside.' I turned my head to smile at Anders. 'We'll likely get a look later.'

Having to throw your boat open to all and sundry is a perennial hazard of mooring in marinas.

'They might want to look inside *Khalida*,' he mourned.

'Show them how the other half lives,' I agreed. *Khalida*, my yacht and our shared home, was only 8 m.

A thump of feet on the stairs announced that our youngsters were out of the showers at last. Anders went upstairs to dole out hot juice and chocolate digestive biscuits, and I took a quick recce into the talc-scented air of the lasses' changing room. It was pretty good: a minor flood on the floor, two splash-suit coat-hangers, and the perennial single sock. Then I followed Anders up to do the debriefing and sign their RYA log-books: *27 July, activity: race practice, 2 hours helming, force 2-3, Cass Lynch*. At last they rode off on their bicycles, or were collected by their parents in muddied pick-ups with a barking dog in the back, and Anders and I could go home.

Norman hadn't given up. As we came out of the clubhouse door there was a whine and a roar from his infernal machine, then he sped off in two wings of oily water. A pause, a spin to spray some of it over *Khalida*, with a look back over his shoulder to check we'd seen, before he roared off down the voe to make sure that nobody in a three-mile range could enjoy the quiet of a summer evening.

We watched him go. I wanted to thank Anders for sorting him out, yet I hadn't really needed the intervention, and I wasn't at all sure that threats of violence would improve the situation. Nor did I want to leave it there. *You pushed him overboard and left him to drown ...* Anders and I had never talked about Alain's death, and I didn't want him left with Norman's twist. I gave him an uncertain look, which he didn't see. He was too busy drooling over the newly arrived Bénéteau.

'It has twin 500 horse-power Cummins.'

Clearly Cummins out-ranked *Khalida*'s clanky Volvo Penta. I gave in.

'Let's go and say hello, then.'

Chapter Two

We sauntered along the pontoon. The woman had gone below, but the man was standing with Magnie on the foredeck, demonstrating a sizeable electric windlass. I felt a twinge of envy. Hauling *Khalida*'s anchor up could be back-breaking work, especially when the tide was pulling the other way.

Magnie nodded once we were ten metres away, and gave us the traditional Shetland greeting. 'Noo dan.'

'Now,' I replied. I nodded to the stranger. 'Hello, there. Have you come far?'

'From Orkney,' he said. He was in his late forties, and dark-avised, a tan that gave him a leathered hide, a glossy black moustache, and bristly brows shielding brown eyes. He was beginning to go bald on top, you could see, in spite of the peaked yachting cap, his black hair receding from the front, but still thick at the back, and worn rather long in compensation. He was hefty, too, with a thick neck running down to broad shoulders and a bulky waistline that swelled his white jersey under the navy jacket. There was something familiar about him, but for the moment I couldn't place it; I was sure I'd never seen him before. He came forward to shake my hand with a no-nonsense grip.

'David Morse.'

'Cass Lynch,' I said, 'of *Khalida*.' I jerked my chin backwards. 'The Offshore 8 m there.'

He looked, picked her out straight away. 'Van de Stadt.'

'Yes, the Pandora's big sister.'

'He was a great designer. We had a Pioneer, oh, way back, must be twenty years ago.' I couldn't place his accent; educated Scots, east coast rather than west, with a corporate feel about it. Maybe a boat like this was what bankers did with their bonuses; she was split-new, and must have cost a packet. 'Wonderful sea-boat, wonderful. Come aboard.' He motioned me forwards, turned to Anders, held out his hand, stared, and raised the hand in the air, palm forwards. 'Well, now, I thought for a moment I was seeing things. Your pet, young man?' He held his hand out again. 'David Morse.'

It was the repetition of his name that did it. Suddenly I was five again, turning the pages of a French picture book, *Capitaine Morse et le Dragon de la Mer*, marvelling at the detailed pictures of the green and red sea-serpent, and the fishing boat belonging to 'Captain Walrus'. Here he was in the flesh, genial smile, moustache, cap, and all. For all the bonhomie, though, if I'd had the placing of him, I'd have given him either an older male watch leader who could pull rank, or a young, efficient woman who'd catch him off guard. Otherwise, he'd be too inclined to take charge, even when he didn't quite know what he was doing. You could see he was used to getting his own way.

'Anders Johansen.' Anders raised a hand to Rat, who was whiffling his whiskers in expectation of being allowed to explore a new ship. 'You do not mind him? He is house-trained.'

'Not at all, but I'll warn my wife.' He turned and called down into the cabin. 'Madge? Madge, visitors, including a pet rat.'

There was a muffled shriek from below, a clatter of dropped mug. 'Oh, my.' The voice was unmistakeably west-coast, the posher end of Glasgow. She peered round the doorway. She had hair the colour of a crab's back, cut in a flicked-up bob, and a pink-powdered, plump face. Her grey-green eyes were fringed with mascara. Her eyes crossed me, reacted to the snail-trail scar across my cheek, moved too quickly on to Anders' face and slid to his shoulder. Her mouth fell open. 'Goodness me, that's more like a small horse. It doesn't bite, does it?' The Glasgow accent was still strong, but, now I heard more of it, it was overlaid over something else, the north of England maybe.

Anders shook his head, and gave his best Norse god smile. 'Rat has never bitten anyone.'

'Well, well, that's the first rat we've ever had aboard this ship. Go on up, the kettle's just boiled.'

We stepped over the gleaming fibreglass side and into the cockpit. David motioned us upwards. 'It's far too fine a night to be indoors.'

The high top of the wheelhouse framed an upper level with a table and chairs upholstered in white leather-look PVC, a little sink, a pale wooden worktop, and a double-bed-sized sun-lounger. *Khalida*'s whole cabin would have fitted into this bit alone. Her dashboard was like a car's, with a wheel, gears, and instruments. Just this array of screens and knobs was worth twenty thousand. I recognised a fish finder, a radar, a chart plotter, and an Automatic Identification System, along with the usual radio, echo sounder, wind instruments, barometer, tide clock, and log. I paused by the AIS.

'I'd like one of these, particularly out at sea. If you're single-handing, it must be great to get early warning, and the chance to call them up personally.'

Not that it always helped. That liner, *Sea Princess*, who'd passed us just before Alain had gone over, hadn't responded to my call; she'd just kept on sailing away. She had a schedule to keep.

David reached over my shoulder to switch it on. 'It has an integral alarm, too. Anything comes closer than, well, you set it, ten miles, twenty miles, it warns you.'

17

'Cool,' I said.

'Well, well,' Magnie said. 'It's amazing what they can do nowadays.'

I shot him a sideways glance. He'd been mate on a whaling ship in the Antarctic for many years before taking charge of a fishing vessel nearer home, and what he didn't know about boat gadgetry wasn't worth knowing. I'd ask him later why he was playing the yokel.

'Now you just put that off again,' Madge called from below. 'I know what you sailors are like.' There was a stomping noise on the stairs, then a tray appeared in the hatch, was set on the floor, and her crab-orange head appeared after it. She was wearing a jade velour tracksuit underneath a floral print apron, colourful and homely, the chairman's wife relaxing. The hands that reached for the tray were encrusted with rings. 'Switch one gadget on,' she continued, 'and you need to demonstrate it thoroughly, then the next one, and before we know it we're back out at sea, looking for fish. No, thank you. Switch it all off, David, and let our guests drink their coffee.'

It was real coffee, the aroma mingling with the suggestion of freshly baked chocolate cake. I slid my legs under the table, sat down on the cream leather settee, and admired the array on the tray: a cafetiére, bone-china mugs, milk jug, sugar bowl, and a plate with a neat pyramid of chocolate brownies. Bone china wouldn't last ten minutes on *Khalida*.

'Milk and sugar?' Madge asked.

'Just black,' I said. I waited till she'd finished pouring, then held out my hand. 'I'm Cass Lynch, of the *Khalida*, the little white yacht over there. First mast on the right.'

'Madge Morse.' She made a face. 'I know, it sounds awful. Not only the short sound, but the two ms together. If we were marrying now, I'd keep my maiden name. Madge Arbuthnot sounds much more dignified.'

'What's your Cass short for?' David asked.

It seemed an odd question.

'Cassandre,' I said, pronouncing it French style. His brows rose. 'My mother's French,' I explained, 'and an opera singer. At the time she was in a production of *The Trojan Women*.'

'Well, that's exciting,' Madge said. 'I'm afraid we don't listen to much opera, I'm a Radio 2 person, although we do love Andrew Lloyd Webber – has your mother ever sung in any of that?'

I smiled, envisaging my mother receiving a phone call from Sir Andrew. *You wish me to take part in a musical?* She'd sound like a captain being asked to scrub the decks. *You have the wrong number, monsieur. I am Eugénie Delafauve* ... And then laying the phone down, *It was some person who wished me to sing light music. I must talk to my agent.*

'No,' I said, 'she's a "court of the Sun King" woman. Costumed performances in stately chateaux.' At the moment, she was rehearsing a Rameau chief villainess, Erinice in *Zoroastre,* for a massive production at Chinon at the end of August. In keeping with their so-far-effective reconciliation, before Dad had headed down to Edinburgh to bully the Scottish Government into backing his company's wind farm, he'd booked tickets for us both to fly over and see it.

'That sounds fun,' Madge said. She turned to Anders, still looking wistfully at the engine hatch. 'I didn't catch your name.'

He hauled his thoughts away from cylinders with a visible effort, and introduced himself.

'Milk, sugar? Would your rat like a biscuit?'

Anders looked doubtfully at the cream leather. 'If you permit, I will give him some of mine, on the floor. A whole one to himself would be too much.'

19

We settled down in the C-shaped curve of the sofa: Magnie forrard, the Charles Rennie Mackintosh mug looking dangerously frail in his gnarled hand, then me, Anders, Madge in the widest space between table and couch, and David completing the circle in the driving seat. I took a brownie and bit into it with appreciation. It was still warm, and very good.

Anders asked Madge, 'May I set Rat down to explore?'

'Be our guests,' she said. 'Does he keep himself so white, or do you have to wash him?'

'Oh, he keeps himself clean,' Anders said. 'Rats are very particular animals.' He set Rat on the floor, spread-eagled, with tail waggling, and offered him a piece of brownie. Rat considered it, pulled his transparent toes under him, curled his tail, and tucked in.

'You're from Norway, then,' David said. 'Just visiting?'

'At the moment,' Anders agreed. 'Cass brought me over to be engineer on a film ship.'

'Oh,' Madge said, surprised. 'I took you to be a couple, now.'

We both shook our heads. I was surprised to see David give Madge a steady look, as if this was somehow significant. Magnie spotted that too; I saw his fair lashes lift from his mug and fall again.

'I have engineering work here at the moment,' Anders said.

He didn't mention that he and his nerdish mates were also engrossed in a sword-and-sorcery intergalactic war, played with intricately painted figures on a model railway landscape that took up an entire basement, and that nothing would induce him to leave until it was over. I suspected he was winning too; he'd had an air of confidence this last week – the way he'd dealt with young Norman, for example. If it had been anyone else I'd have

20

deduced a willing girlfriend, but with Anders it was far more likely that he was now Warlord Ruler of the planet Krill. I managed to suppress the smile brought on just by thinking about it.

'There is no hurry to go home, although my father is beginning to be impatient. He runs a yard near Bergen – do you know Norway?'

David said, 'No' at the same time as Madge said, 'Yes.' David looked annoyed, shook his head at her. 'Not really,' he temporised. 'We've had one holiday there, but further south than Bergen, touring around from Stavanger. We keep meaning to go back. From here we'd get over to Bergen in seven, eight, hours.'

It had taken thirty on *Khalida*.

'Stavanger was lovely,' Madge said wistfully. 'All so clean, and the wooden houses with their red roofs around the lake.'

'Is Stavanger the one that has the little wooden houses right down at the water front?' Magnie asked guilelessly, as if he didn't know every Norwegian port as well as he knew Lerwick.

David shook his head. 'That's Bergen, I think, the Bryggen. Where did you say your father's yard was, Anders?'

'It's just behind the marina in Bildøy,' Anders said, 'the Johansen yard, and if you are ever out there and need work done, they will make sure it is done well, at a reasonable cost.'

'I'll write that down,' David said. 'A good contact's always useful.' He pulled out an iPad and got Anders to repeat the address and phone number, then turned to me. 'And where are you from, Cass?'

'This is my home area, here – I grew up just over the hill, there.' I pointed towards the green curve of Muckle Roe. 'That island there – it's joined by a bridge, but you can't see that from here.'

My dad had been one of the construction workers overseeing the building of Sullom Voe terminal; the house I'd grown up in had the Atlantic pounding the beach alongside and flinging salt at my bedroom window. This long finger of sea had been my playground, two miles to the widening turn that became the Atlantic (off-limits: next stop the remote island of Foula, then the tip of Greenland). I'd crossed the Atlantic several times now. In my mind's eye the blue ripples hemmed so neatly to the brown shore by lines of mussel floats became a waste of grey water, with great breakers rolling across. A man who went overboard mid-Atlantic wasn't easy to find again. I'd never found Alain.

'A lovely area to sail in,' David agreed.

'A lovely place to grow up,' Madge added, 'although there maybe wasn't much to do here.'

'Well, I don't know about that,' I said. 'I was lucky that my best friend Inga lived just a hundred yards further along our road, so either I was at hers or she was at mine, or she and I and her brother Martin were roaming the hills and beaches together. It was a fun childhood. We made hoosies in the old crofthouse, and fires on the beach, and we swam in the loch and cycled along to the shop for sweeties. And of course I sailed. I had a Mirror, and Martin crewed for me. We went all round the regattas.' The only thing I'd hated was being kept indoors. Maman had had a shot at turning me into a pretty little girl with long, dark plaits and frilled dresses. It hadn't worked. 'And now of course, bairns have the leisure centre and swimming pool right on their doorstep, as well as all the stuff in Lerwick.'

Madge still looked unconvinced. 'What about school, though? Did you have to travel to your main town for that?'

I shook my head, and pointed. 'That's the school there, with the leisure centre, right next door. We had a good education. Computers, and PE, and foreign trips. The teachers all knew us, and we knew them.'

'You took your exams there?'

'No. My last bit of schooling was in France.' I was beginning to share Magnie's suspicions. Any Shetland person would ask these questions, of course, to 'place' me, and the conversation would end, 'Ye, ye, I ken wha du is noo.' But Madge wasn't Shetland, so the names wouldn't mean anything to her. Maybe she was just nosy, and too new to boating to understand the unwritten rules about privacy – yet she'd made the bow rope fast like a pro. I decided to make it their turn. 'How about you, did you say you're from Orkney?'

Neither of the voices suggested Orkney, that lovely lilting accent, like Scots spoken by a Welsh singer, but they could be retired there. Orkney had a much higher incomer population than Shetland.

David shook his head. 'Central belt, us, but Orkney was where we'd just come from. Beautiful place, and we found a little hotel that gave us the best steaks I've ever tasted. We had a couple of days in Kirkwall, then came up via Fair Isle.' He looked at his watch. 'Ten o'clock already! I'm not used to the light here yet. It's barely dimming. Excuse me, I must check on the news.'

He snicked on the radio, and we had five minutes of headlines: crisis in the euro, a charity worried about falling donations, the chancellor announcing another austerity measure. I was rich at the moment, as the film job had paid well, but I was keeping that for going to college, so Anders and I were living on our day-to-day wages: his job as an engineer for cash, mine teaching sailing for the club in exchange for free mooring. Belts were being worn tight this summer.

At the end of the headlines, David switched the radio off, shaking his head. 'I'd got all interested in the latest of these robberies, but there's obviously nothing new.'

Robberies didn't ring any bells, but I wasn't a great news watcher. I set my jaw to suppress a yawn. 'Excuse me – I've been out on the water all day.'

Magnie came to my rescue. 'The ones with paintings and things from Scottish houses? No grand houses particularly, no' the big ones like Glamis. Lairds' houses.'

'There's been a bit of coverage about it,' David said. 'Anders, come and admire our engines.'

Anders didn't need asking twice. He put Rat back on his shoulder, and they disappeared down the ladder.

'They've recovered one of the Epstein bronze heads, in Faroe,' Madge said.

'That's good,' I said. This yawn wouldn't be suppressed. 'I'm sorry!' I rose. 'Thank you very much for the coffee, and I hope you have a pleasant stay in Shetland. Do you plan to be here long?'

'Oh, a week or so, touring around,' she said. 'Probably not in Brae, though; we'll just stock up on fresh supplies and fuel, then move on.'

'Well, good journey,' I said. Magnie put his mug down and stood up.

'Just post the key in the boating club letterbox,' he said. 'Have a good stay in Shetland.'

'I'm sure we will,' Madge said, smiling.

'They're up to something,' Magnie stated, when Anders had returned, with the dreamy air of a man who'd seen a vision, and we were all safely ensconced in *Khalida*'s much smaller cabin, with the candle in the lantern sending flickering shadows round the varnished wooden walls. She had a traditional layout, my little home, with a blue-cushioned seat along the starboard side, running from the wooden bulkhead forrard to the quarterberth aft, and the cooker, sink, and chart table on port. Past the bulkhead was the heads, which we didn't use in the marina, with a hatch amidships, and a hanging locker opposite it, to starboard, and past that again, with a curtain for privacy, was the v-shaped forepeak berth where Anders and Rat slept. The settee was interrupted by a prop-legged table. Anders sat behind it, his fair head tilted against the bulkhead, with Rat balanced beside him on the wooden fiddle that kept our books in place at sea. Magnie sat opposite and I was on my usual place on the steps that doubled as the engine cover.

'You over-did the country bumpkin act a touch,' I said. 'No fisherman would be surprised by AIS, they've had it for years.'

'They didna ken I was a fisherman,' Magnie said. 'And,' he repeated stubbornly, 'they're up to something. I doot they're police.'

'Police?' I echoed.

Anders looked alarmed. 'Why would the police be here?'

'Service. Something like that,' Magnie insisted. I looked at him doubtfully. 'That boat was just too fancy,' he said, 'and they just didna fit it. I dinna ken for south folk, of course, but there was something no' right. She was over young to be old riggit.'

I considered that one. 'The apron?'

'What age would you say she was, now? Forty-five?'

'Around there,' I agreed.

'Well, now, I'm no' seen a pinny like that on a body under sixty, no' for years, nor face-powder like that either. She was pretty spry too.'

'Forty-five's not exactly rheumatism age,' I said.

'She still moved like a younger body,' Magnie insisted. 'If you went by the way she pranced up and down that ladder wi' a tray in her hands, well, you'd have guessed she was thirty.'

'Maybe she goes to the gym,' I said.

'If she went to the gym she'd no' have all that ply on her.'

'Yes,' I agreed. 'She was plump. They both were.'

'It was the robberies,' Anders said suddenly. 'Before that, they were just asking questions, the way people do, on boats. Below, too, the man kept talking about them.'

'Too many questions,' I said.

'Not too many for passing in harbour,' Anders said. 'That is different. As crew on a ship, yes, it would be far too many, for people you will be living with for a month.'

I nodded. Privacy was jealously guarded with seven of you in a forty-foot yacht.

'I thought that too,' Magnie said. 'Finding out whaur you grew up, Cass.'

'They were odd about Norway,' I said, 'as if they were checking up on you too.'

'But when David came to the robbery, he was watching you. He was suspicious, especially when you yawned.'

'I've been on the water all day,' I protested. 'Fresh air and all that.'

'If one of these head things has turned up in Faroe,' Magnie said, 'well, maybe they're suspicious of private yachts that could go between Scotland and there.'

I looked across at Anders, leaning back in his corner, with Rat drowsing under his chin, and the lantern casting amber shadows on his hair, then down at my own paint-stained jeans. 'Do we look like people who'd know a Leonardo from a lighthouse?'

'We'd know the lighthouse,' Anders said.

'It was odd, too, their name,' I said. 'I know people's names do often suit them, but I thought he looked a bit like a walrus, he had that blubbery look, you know, with power under the fat, and then I suddenly remembered this book I loved as a child, about 'Captain Morse', and he looked just like the pictures.

'Where are they from?' Magnie asked suddenly. 'I never looked at the stern o' her.'

'There was nothing on her bows,' I said.

Anders put Rat on the table, took one step forrard, raised the hatch, and stuck his head up. 'This is very odd.' He reached up, put one foot on his bunk and swung himself out, fluid as water. Magnie and I looked at each other, brows raised, then came out through the companionway into the cockpit. The moon had intensified to a silver penny, bright in the pale blue sky; the water had fallen halfway down the slip and swirled out of the marina towards its gathering in the deep of the ocean.

'She does not have a name,' Anders murmured. 'And I think there was not a call sign by the instruments.'

'No,' I said, remembering, 'there wasn't.'

Magnie shook his head. 'That's aye by the wireless, standard practice.'

We looked across *Khalida*'s bows at the gleaming transom making a broad figure 8 with its reflection. Above it the cabin lights shone orange, darkening the clear night. The white sweep of fibreglass was unmarked. There was no name, no port, just the red ensign, hanging in folds in the still air.

We stood for a moment, looking at her. I tried to think if I'd ever seen a nameless boat before, and decided that I hadn't.

'No SSR number either,' Anders murmured.

'Illegal,' I agreed.

Dublin, Edinburgh, Newcastle, Portsmouth. Norway, Faroe, Germany, Poland. The Viking road was open to her here. David and Madge were Scottish, but they could have arrived from anywhere.

Chapter Three

'I'm telling you,' Magnie said, 'she's police, or undercover services.' He stumped forrard and took a long, slow look down the voe. 'Well, if this other boat doesna come soon I'm away to my bed.'

'Other boat?' Anders shook his head and lapsed into Shetland. 'Boys a boys, this place is coming like Waterloo station in the rush hour.'

'Two at once is good going,' I agreed. 'They must have heard about the boating club hot showers.'

'The Mid-Brae Inn's stock of Shetland real ale.'

'Frankie's fish and chip shop.'

'Britain's most northerly Indian takeaway.'

'A yacht,' Magnie said. 'She phoned around dinner-time. She's making her way under sail down from Hillswick, the man said, and they hoped to be in Brae before it got dark. I told her to knock you pair up if I wasn't there.'

'No problem,' Anders said. He came back along to the cockpit. 'I will still be awake, even if Cass is out cold. Much good knocking her up would do, I can tell you.'

'I can sleep on a clothes rail,' I agreed.

'It's fine,' Magnie said. 'This'll be her comin' now. Listen.'

We listened to the soft lap of water on the pebble shore, and the chittering of the tirricks, settling their chicks for the night; a car driving around the curve towards the boating club; a sheep, calling its lamb; the houb-boub-boub of a snipe on the hill. Once our ears had filtered those noises out, there was the soft throb of an engine in the distance.

'Unless it's the party boat, the yellow one,' I said. 'Kevin and Geri's.'

Anders shook his head. 'It's a yacht engine.'

Magnie looked into the distance. 'That's her lights now, coming round the headland.' He swung over *Khalida*'s side onto the pontoon. 'Thirty-six foot. I'll put her in nose-on to the other one.'

I slipped below to put out the lantern, then joined Magnie on the pontoon. 'I'll help take her lines.'

We watched as the light approached, until it was close enough to see the slender mast above a dark green hull, sloped gracefully in at each end. 'Why,' I said, eyeing her up greedily, 'she's a Rustler. They're amazing boats, real ocean crossers. If ever I'm rich –'

'A well-kept engine,' Anders said, as she curved into the marina.

'Look at her lines,' I breathed. 'That lovely stern.'

'A long-keeler, though,' Anders said. 'I bet you'd need a bow-thruster to reverse.'

'Is she staying long, Magnie?'

'Twar-tree days. Are you pair helping with these lines or just pier-head skippering?'

We grabbed a warp each, ready to throw. There was a couple aboard, moving with the ease of long practice, the man in the bows and the woman steering. She cut the engine and reversed to stop the boat an exact metre from the Bénéteau's stern; the man stepped unhurriedly on to the pontoon as she came in, rope in one hand, and steadied her before taking a turn around the pontoon loop. Then he turned to us and smiled. 'Thanks.' He tossed the two aft warps to his companion and went forrard himself to secure the Rustler's bow. 'Well, that was a good sail round. Hope you haven't been kept waiting for us –' He considered Anders, moved his gaze to Magnie. 'Mr Williamson, is it?'

'Magnie.' They shook hands.

'Come aboard – can I tempt you to a nightcap?'

'I'm no' wanting to keep you up,' Magnie said.

'Night's young yet,' the man said cheerily. 'A dram's always fine after a long sail. Come in.'

'Yes, do,' the woman echoed from the cockpit. 'We want to pick your brains about the neighbourhood, so you'll be doing us a favour.'

We tramped aboard.

I hadn't been inside a Rustler before, and I wasn't disappointed. There was a fibreglass canopy over the companionway, protecting the nav. instruments and the helmsman; you could go through a gale in this boat without getting your hair wet. I ducked below it and came down into the cabin. The layout was the same as on *Khalida*, with forepeak berth, saloon, chart table, and two quarter-berths running under the cockpit (very old-fashioned these days, where you'd expect at least one aft cabin on a thirty-six footer), but the depth of her keel meant there were four steps down, so it was like coming into the cabin of a tall ship. She was lined with pale wood whose varnish gleamed in the light of the oil lamps, and where Anders' curtain was on *Khalida* there was a substantial bulkhead door, open to show a jazzy blue and green downie spread on the triangular bed. The saloon had the table offset to give a clear gangway, and the green-cushioned couches each side were backed by closed lockers and a well-fiddled bookshelf. Just by the steps, the chart table had a row of screens and a laptop, and there was a neat galley opposite, with a cooker, sink, and workspace. She was immaculately clean, and tidied for sea, with all loose items stowed or secured.

'Peter and Sandra Wearmouth,' the man said. 'Have a seat. Whisky?'

'We've earned a dram,' Sandra said. 'We've just come round Muckle Flugga.' It was Britain's most northerly point, a lighthouse perched on jagged, slanted rock and surrounded by large breakers and cross-currents.

'No' for me,' Magnie said. Anders and I stared. Magnie reddened. 'I'm drivin',' he added. Given that I'd seen him drive when he was barely able to stand, I didn't buy that one.

'A cup of tea then?' Sandra asked.

'That'd be most splendid,' Magnie said, and slid behind the table.

'I'd prefer that too,' I said, and joined him. Peter raised one eyebrow at Anders.

'Whisky, please,' he said. 'Thank you.'

Once we were all installed round the table I got a proper look at them. Peter was in his early fifties, with a smooth cap of gleamingly silver hair and shrewd eyes under level brows. His skin was that plump pink you often see in office workers, overlaid now with a seaman's tan, and he wore a Mike Aston striped jumper in eye-hurting colours. My impression was of someone who'd been in the services; he had that air of command. Sandra was a little younger, late forties or just fifty, with ash blonde hair cut in a fringed bob, and grey-green eyes that reminded me of someone else, though I couldn't quite place the memory. She was dressed with corporate neatness under her sailing oilskins, in a dark green jumper with matching slacks and a contrasting orange scarf that somehow combined smartness with motherliness. They were from Newcastle; Peter spoke London English with the occasional flattened Geordie A or heightened U, Sandra was still pretty broad.

We'd just sat down when there was a cracked squawk

from the forepeak, and the oddest-looking cat I'd ever seen jumped down from the berth, shimmied across the bathroom floor, and leapt, light as a gull's breast-feather in the wind, to Peter's shoulder. It was starvation-skinny, with long chocolate-brown legs, a whiplash black tail, and ears borrowed from something twice its size. Most surprising of all, it had eyes as blue as my own. It gave that strange call again, turned around in Peter's lap, then sat bolt upright, those astonishing eyes fixed on us. I'd never seen anything like it.

Magnie laughed at me. 'It's a Siamese, Cass.'

'A cross between a cat and a monkey,' Peter agreed. 'She's our mascot.'

'Yours,' Sandra said. 'She doesn't talk to me.'

It was just as well Anders had left Rat aboard *Khalida.*

'So,' I asked, 'what brought you to Shetland?'

'The archaeology,' Peter said. He handed Anders a whisky in a cut-crystal glass.

'Peter got hooked on the past through watching *Time Team,'* Sandra said, shaking her head at his jumper. 'I put my foot down about the Phil hat, though, didn't I, pet?'

'I've got one on order from eBay,' he retorted. 'Seriously though, it got me interested in what's all around us, the heritage that we don't even notice. Shetland's an amazing place. Those, for example.'

He waved a hand across at Magnie's cottage, tucked in its own bay. 'The cottage?' I asked.

'Built on a Norse site with stones from a Pictish broch,' Magnie said.

'The big stones running up the hill behind it.'

'Trowie stones,' I said. 'Bad luck to go shifting those.'

'Neolithic field boundaries, five thousand years old.'

'Really?' I said, amazed. 'Five thousand?'

'Perhaps not those actual stones, though the big ones

probably are. But the boundary would have stayed, once it was first marked. And you can't see it from here, but I'm sure there's a chambered cairn on the back of the hill there.' He waved a hand north towards the Nibon skyline.

We gave him a blank look. 'I do not know what this is,' Anders said. 'Do you mean where you put a stone, to show you have climbed the hill?'

'Bigger than that,' Peter said. 'It looks like a grassy hillock now, but there are built walls under the grass. It's not quite up at the top of the hill, on a flat platform looking out over the bay. Look, here.' He spread the chart between us, and indicated the Atlantic coast they'd come round, a mile across the north-sheltering hill, drawing his finger up from the opening under Muckle Roe brig to the long voe of Mangaster, a real Norwegian fjord with steep, green hills rising straight from the sea. The finger stopped on the hill.

'Oh,' I said, 'you mean the trowie mound.'

'Trowie mound?' Sandra echoed.

'Trows are the Shetland fairies,' I said. 'No, not fairies, elves. Puck and all that, plaiting the ponies' manes in the night. Trolls, that's the English.'

'Norwegian,' Anders interjected.

I ignored him. 'They're little hairy people who live in green mounds like that one.'

Peter's eyes lit up. 'You see, that's folk memories of the Picts. They lived in wheelhouses that looked just like a green mound from outside.'

'They like music, particularly fiddle music,' I continued, 'and Magnie's got a story about a fiddler – go on, Magnie, you tell it.'

'This folk are no' wanting to hear me yarning all night,' Magnie protested.

'Yes we are,' Sandra said. 'I want to enjoy your accent.

34

Go on.'

'Well,' said Magnie, with a nicely judged air of reluctance, 'this is one of me grandmidder's stories, and I can vouch for the truth of it, for she met the man himself when she was joost a young lass –'

It was Magnie's best story and he told it well, from the midsummer-eve opening by that green hillock, when a local fiddler was asked by a small, brightly clad man if he'd come and play at a wedding, through the description of the trowie celebrations to the man awakening by the knowe again, to find the landscape changed around him, old houses gone and new ones grown. 'And he went back, that man, to his ain hoose, and the folk there stared at him, until the auld man by the fire minded tales o' his own grandfather, who'd disappeared one night and never been seen again, and that was this very man.'

'And what happened to him then?' Sandra asked.

Magnie's rare smile wrinkled up his weathered face. 'You're thinking he mebbe withered up in front of their eyes? Na, na. Well, they asked him to bide, he was their own kin, but he never settled. There was naebody he kent, you see. In the end he spent day after day ida kirkyard, joost lookin' at the graves. Then, when midsummer came round again, he said he'd had enough. The trows would be glad o' a good fiddler, he said, and midsummer eve they'd be out and about, if ever they were. He'd go up to the knowe and ask to be taken in. So that night up he went and that was the last they ever saw o' him. But sometimes you'll hear – and I'm heard it myself – you'll hear a strain o' fiddle music coming out of that very mound, or see lights moving around it, and I'm seen that too.'

He left a nicely judged pause, then turned to Peter. 'O' course you're fairly right, it's a cairn, as you say, mid-Neothlithic, maybe three and a half thousand years old.' I didn't bother being surprised at his knowledge; what a Shetlander didn't know about his home turf wasn't worth knowing.

'But what is it?' Anders persisted.

'It's a Neolithic burial chamber,' Peter said, 'not very big, because they did sky burials first, you know, exposing the bodies for the birds to pick, then once or twice a year there would be a big ceremony to take the bones into the house of the ancestors. What d'y say, Sand, shall we take a walk up there tomorrow? A nice stroll, to take the fidgets out of our legs.'

'It's further than it looks,' I warned them. 'You can't go straight from here; you'd need to walk along the road, here, five miles or so –' I turned the chart towards them. 'Here, you'd go north from Brae, then strike out into the hills, towards the coast. If I remember right, there's a house here –' I indicated just below the trowie mound hill '– and it'll have a track to it, from the head of the voe, here. Then you'd go straight up the hill to the trowie mound.'

'A good way,' Peter agreed. 'A ten-mile walk. What d'y say, Sand, shall we take the tent? Camp up beside this cairn and give it a good explore. Can you get inside, d'y know, Cass?'

'I have a vague memory,' I admitted, 'that you can. The boy from that house, just below it, well, he was at school with me, here in Brae, three, four years older, and I seem to remember him bringing in a carrier bag with a skull, and trying to scare us with it.'

'A skull?' Peter almost shouted.

'He said it was full of bones,' I said. 'The other boys thought it sounded cool, but I don't know if any of them could ever be bothered walking all that way out there to look.'

'You mean,' Peter said, his voice quivering, 'that it hadn't been excavated? That the bones of the people buried in it were still there?'

'After five thousand years?' I said. 'Surely no.'

'They could easily be,' Sandra said. 'We went to this amazing place in Orkney, the tomb of the eagles, and that had loads of skulls excavated from it. They could tell you all about the people – a young girl, and a man who'd had a broken arm, and a grandmother with arthritis.'

'It could have been a sheep skull, though,' I said, not wanting to get them too excited on the basis of my ignorance. 'I really don't know, and I bet Brian – that's the boy whose house it was – I bet he didn't know either. His mum moved away from there when he started school, they just used it as a holiday home.'

'Tomorrow?' Peter said, looking at Sandra. 'We could get provisions in the morning, then head off – a picnic stop once we're off the road – explore in the afternoon, and be home here before dusk.'

'Okay, pet,' she said.

2

Da stane at lies no' in your gait braks no' your toes.

(Old Shetland proverb: a warning not to interfere with things that are none of your business.)

Chapter Four

Tuesday 31 July
Tide times for Brae:
Low Water   02.06   0.5m
High Water   08.25   1.9m
Low Water   14.23   0.7m
High Water   20.35   2.1m
Moon waxing gibbous

The sheep-workers began early the next morning. I was woken by a fusillade of beeeh-ing from the hill up above me, and when I poked my head out of the hatch into the warm sun, sure enough, there was the cluster of pick-ups, a flock of sheep huddled together in the cro, with men in neon-orange overalls or navy boiler suits shoving between them, and the smell of Jeyes Fluid tainting the air. There was a quad in among it too, swooping around the hill, driving the loose ewes towards where the dogs could pick them up. The driver was slight and black-headed, in a dark blouson that inflated with the wind: Norman, the jet-skier from yesterday. I hoped he'd be up there all day, and give us peace.

It was another perfect sailing day, with a light, warm breeze from the south and the sun dazzling through the cabin windows. The tide was not far off the top of the slip; almost full moon. I hauled my jeans on over my night T-shirt, picked up my washing gear, and headed off round to the showers. Sandra was already there, brushing her hair in front of the mirror. 'Nice morning,' she said.

'Just what the forecast promised,' I agreed, and headed for the shower. I'd only just got my clothes off when the outer door opened again, and I heard Madge's voice: 'Hello, there. Are you the lady from the Rustler?'

More questions. I wondered if Magnie had been right, and they were undercover police. All three of us ending up in the showers together seemed a bit of a coincidence; no, more than that. Given that the pontoon quivered to each walker, you knew pretty well who was where, when, and you wouldn't choose to go for the one shower cubicle when you knew there were two people already in the changing rooms.

'Sandra Wearmouth,' Sandra replied. 'We're from Newcastle. And you?'

'Madge. We've just come up from Orkney.'

No point of origin again. I waited for a moment, but there was silence, a chinking sound as if Madge was laying out bottles, then her voice again, 'Are you going far today?'

'The boat's staying in the marina,' Sandra said, 'but we were thinking of taking a walk up into the hills. My husband's spotted a bit of archaeology he needs to investigate.'

'Archaeology,' Madge echoed, sounding startled, then she laughed. 'Mine's talking about testing his fish-finder. Me, I just make sure I've got my sun-tan cream and a good book.'

'The best way,' Sandra agreed. 'Well, see you later –' and the door opened and closed again. There was a short silence, then Madge said 'Fuck,' softly and clearly. There was a sound as if she was rummaging in her bag.

This was beginning to get awkward. I dropped my shampoo bottle noisily on the floor and pushed the button on the shower. The hot water gushed out. I soaped myself thoroughly, and even washed my hair, although it being capsize drill day meant it'd get wet again.

When I dripped out, towel wrapped round me, Madge was just taking her top off, jade green again, with a sky-blue velour suit laid ready on the slatted bench. I said, 'Morning', and was going to sidle past without looking, in the tactful way one does in communal changing rooms, but she turned with the air of one ready to chat. 'Good morning, Cass. Lovely morning, isn't it?'

'Superb,' I agreed.

'Are you teaching here all day, then?'

'Till five,' I said. 'How about you? Are you heading off again?'

She gave a vague shrug. 'David was talking about going further north, but we're not in a hurry.' She reached her left hand out for her purse. There was something wrong about the gesture, but I couldn't analyse exactly what. 'Do I need a coin to operate these showers?'

'No, just push the button,' I said. I expected her to go straight in, but she was still lingering, folding her top un-necessarily precisely, given that it was probably going straight in the wash.

'It's an interesting place here. Anything we need to explore while we're in the area? You know, ancient chapels, or old burial sites?'

'Oh, yes, we've got one of those,' I conceded. Her pebble-grey eyes were suddenly shrewd. I turned my back towards the trowie mound and pointed in the opposite direction. 'The church on the other side of the voe, the graves in the kirkyard there go back to sixteen-something, so I've been told.'

Her eyes went cold, and sharpened with mistrust. 'That sounds interesting. We could stroll over there this morning. Anything else?'

I turned my back and began drying my hair. 'Not that I know of.' I could feel her eyes boring into my spine, but I focused on teasing out the wet strands, and after a few seconds she went into the shower.

When I came out I saw that David and Peter were already in conversation on the square pier in front of the clubhouse. David had the Bénéteau over, and was fuelling up, head lifted above the heavy plastic hose. Peter had one arm swept forward, pointing up towards the hill where the trowie mound was. David was nodding, eyes flicking from the hose to Peter's face. I puzzled about it all the way back round the marina. Why were David and Madge so keen on keeping tabs on us all? Were they really police?

Peter and Sandra set off just as I was setting up the whiteboard to demonstrate today's wind direction and no-go areas. Each had hiking boots and a little rucksack.

'Have fun,' I called as they passed.

'We will,' Peter said.

Sandra rolled her eyes and laughed. 'See you later.'

They were just going out of the marina when Alex arrived, skidding around them on his bicycle, blond hair flying. He slid down to me in a slither of gravel and got off the bike by the simple method of dropping it. 'Hey, Cass. Was that two the ones on the motorboat, then?'

'No, the sailing boat,' I said.

He gave them another long look, then turned to consider the Rustler. 'Bet you could go to America in that.'

'Bet you could,' I agreed.

His lavender-blue eyes focused on me again. 'Who's in the motorboat, then?'

I shrugged. 'Dunno.'

Suddenly, surprisingly, he looked anxious. 'Yes you do. You were in there, talking to them.'

'Just a cup of coffee,' I conceded.

'Well, then, who are they?'

'Just folk,' I said. 'They've come up from Orkney.'

His face swept itself clean, became innocently guileless. 'See, I ken them. I'm seen them before, anyroad, when I was down at Brian's. You ken Brian, my dad's pal, that he worked with when he was south. They were at the school together. He's up –' He gestured up at the group of men clustered around the pen of sheep. 'Well, we were haeing a holiday down there, where he lives, and that's where I saw them.' A pause to make up detail. 'I mind the man.'

That would have been plausible enough if he hadn't just asked who Peter and Sandra were. I remembered how his big brother had stared at the motorboat yesterday evening, and wondered if it was Norman who wanted to know.

'I'll even mind his name, if I think about it,' Alex said. 'It began with a B ...' He was watching my face intently, tacked quickly. 'No, no, an M.'

'Good guess,' I agreed.

'Morrison,' he said. 'No, that's not quite right. Mackay.' He waited for a second for me to correct him, then shook his head. 'It'll come back to me.'

'Tell me if it does,' I said. He kept staring at me. 'If you go and rig your boat now, before the others arrive, you can get one of the new sails.'

Diverted, he ran off towards the boat shed. Now why on earth, I wondered, would Norman set Alex to find out about these two strangers? It was possible of course that they were police, and he knew it; maybe he'd seen them in uniform. I wouldn't put it past Norman to be involved in something dodgy: drugs, for example.

I remembered the feeling I'd had this morning that there was something wrong about Madge's reaching for her purse. I tried to see it again in my mind's eye; the plump hand, ringless now, moving across the white basin.

Was it just the lack of rings that had made it look different? Yes, but that wouldn't nag at my memory. She'd taken her wedding ring off too – was that significant? Yes, that was what it was. Her hand was evenly tanned, and there was no sign of rings on any of the fingers, not even a white band or a dent where her wedding ring would normally have been, which meant, I reasoned, that she didn't normally wear it.

Which, I supposed, meant that they were only pretending to be married. I remembered Magnie speculating about her age, that she was younger than she looked: a younger colleague and an older one, trying to pass for a middle-aged couple. What I wondered was what had brought them here to Brae.

We got a lot done by teatime. Anders had work to go to, and Rat decided to spend the day sleeping in a patch of sun in *Khalida*'s cockpit, but Magnie joined me in the rescue boat for a companionable day. We got the bairns organised into pairs and played follow-my-leader, with the rescue boat drawing them in zig-zags up towards Linga, then sailing goose-winged back towards the shore. Once they'd done that twice we drew the rescue boat back a bit and rocked gently, watching them and giving advice as each passed us. The sun was warm on the rubber decks; I leant back on my elbow and felt the rubber give squashily.

'Must pump this boat up a bit.'

'It wouldn't hurt,' Magnie agreed. He passed me over the pump and watched the bairns, eyes narrowed, as I set to work. 'Alex, Graham, you're pinching. Come off the wind a bit and you'll go faster.'

'Feels faster tilted,' Alex called as he skidded by.

Magnie shrugged as he flapped his way around the bouy. 'That's Olaf o' Scarvataing's boy, isn't it?'

I tried to remember the name of Olaf's house. 'Olaf

46

Johnston, who was at school with me.'

'Aye, Olaf o' Scarvataing. He married a sooth lass, and I doot he didn't treat her very well, for the word was it would have been divorce if she'd no' been religious. They came back up here to mend matters, but he'd need to change a bit. He would never be told either, nor his father before him – he was at the school wi' me, Steven. Ah, well, we'll keep telling this boy and maybe he'll change the family tradition.'

'His older boy is being a total pain,' I said. 'Someone's given him one of those jet-skis. He was weaving in around the dinghies, splashing everyone.'

'That makes a change,' Magnie said, 'from charging about the hills on that quad o' his.'

'I saw him helping this morning,' I said.

'Helping?' Magnie echoed scornfully. 'No he! Scattering the sheep to the four winds, more like, and getting them that wild the dogs can do nothing with them. And if it's no' the quad, then he's out wi' a shotgun.'

'There's no shortage of rabbits,' I said soothingly. I enjoyed watching them, first thing in the morning, grey humps with alert ears, nibbling the grass in the early sun.

Magnie snorted. 'Rabbits! If it moves, he's blasting off at it. I heard him yesterday evening, up by the trowie mound.' He added thoughtfully, 'He was in a bit o' bother at the school too, wi' things going missing, although there was nothing proved – you ken how careful they have to be these days. The other bairns kent fine it was him.'

I remembered that I'd wondered earlier if he was involved in something dodgy. 'Any word of him being involved in drugs?'

'He could be,' Magnie said. 'There's an awful lock o' this young eens are. I'll no' take his character away though. I'm no' heard that he is, just that the mothers are no' keen on their lasses being onywye near him.' He

47

leaned over the edge of the rescue boat and roared loud enough to make me jump. 'Boy! Wid du stop using these boats to play dodgems wi'!' Alex tacked hastily away from Graham's stern.

'It couldn't have been him shooting yesterday,' I said. 'He was hassling us with his jet-ski all evening.'

'He goes along to the old Nicolson house below the trowie mound.' Magnie sat upright again and glanced over to the marina. 'You'd better get that whistle going. There's someeen coming out – it'll be that motorboat.'

The unmarked white nose was peeping round the rock corner of the marina. I signalled the bairns to cluster around the rescue boat, and David steered in a wide circle past us at a cautious pace. Madge waved from the cockpit. I watched where they went: to the right, out through the Rona and towards the Atlantic. The sea road was open to them now: Norway, Scotland, Faroe, America.

A thump behind us warned me the bairns were getting restive. I trailed them back inside the marina by scattering balls from the rescue boat for them to pick up, with the prize of two nearly-out-of-date Mars Bars from the boating club bar for the crew which picked up the most. The water had gone far enough down the slip to show the rummle of mud and green algae after the concrete ended, so we left the Picos bobbing from the pontoon, and ate our picnics sitting in the sun. After lunch we had another session going around buoys, and finished with capsize drill in the marina, with one dinghy tethered to a long line. That was the highlight of their day, in spite of the shrieks of horror as they felt the cold of the water. I timed them getting the boat sailing from upside down, and Alex won that one by twenty seconds. Then I chased them off home, damp and laughing, peeled myself out of my wetsuit, and headed over to *Khalida*.

Someone had been in her. I knew that the moment I opened the upper washboard; there was something in the air, not so definite as a perfume, and when I looked around everything was just that shade different – the angle of the log book on the table, the tilt of the green and yellow cushions, the hang of Anders and Rat's curtain. Rat himself swarmed up out of his bolt-hole under the tool-shelf; that he'd taken refuge there was further confirmation that somebody, a sly unknown somebody, had been aboard and meddling about. I took careful stock. My bunk; yes, they'd not only checked in my bed, but they'd lifted the cushion to inspect the locker below as well. They'd had the pots and pans out, and even, I thought, given the engine space the once-over; the brass hooks that held the cover weren't quite as I'd have left them. I couldn't tell what they'd done forrard. My temper was rising, and if Madge or David had been about I'd have spoken my mind pretty bluntly. They had no right to come aboard without my permission, no right whatsoever to search my ship. If they were police, they could come back with a warrant.

I wasn't worried about anything being stolen; there was nothing to take. Then I had a nastier thought. Suppose that, rather than taking, they'd added something. There were a dozen places in *Khalida* where they could stow an illegal cargo – drugs, say, or even one of the paintings that David had talked about. All they had to do then was tip off the police, and we were in serious trouble.

Searching *Khalida* was the last thing I felt like doing. I wanted a cup of tea in the sun, with Rat draped around my neck, in the peace of the marina, without a dozen kamikaze Picos circling me.

I sighed, and braced myself. *Khalida* was, for these purposes, a mercifully small ship, and I knew every inch of her. Unless it was something really exotic, like diamonds painted to resemble fibreglass lumps stuck to her hull, it wouldn't take long to make sure there was nothing planted aboard.

It took three-quarters of an hour. I cleared every locker

and re-stowed the contents, I shook out and re-folded my clothes and I shone a torch round every inch of the engine. I even took Rat's paper nest apart, much to his disgust. The only thing I didn't search was Anders' forepeak. I'd leave that to him. Everywhere I'd gone there were signs, faint but unmistakeable, that someone else had been there first, but, as far as I could see, nothing had been taken, nothing left.

I settled at last in *Khalida*'s cockpit with a cup of tea, watching the black-capped arctic terns swooping and diving for sand eels in the still water ten metres from me. The sheep-workers up above must have finished, for the dogs were being loaded into the pick-ups, and the last sheep were scampering in relief across the hill, calling their lambs and escorting them to the safety of the scattald. The pick-ups rattled over the cattle-grid, the quad roared off, and silence flowed back. The smell of flowering whitebeams drifted down from the garden above the marina, the terns chittered at each other, and the water washed gently up the boating club slip again.

There was nothing added to Anders' kit-bag, but for someone usually so laid-back, he was surprisingly annoyed about the search.

'They have no right.'

'No,' I agreed. 'And what were they searching for?'

'The paintings they talked about. I think Magnus is right, they are police, and they think we are the robbers they are chasing for.' He waved his fork in the air. 'I do not know why they should think this, unless they have a description of the real robbers that we fit too.'

'No description of us would fit anyone else: small, dark, half-French girl with scar, Norwegian man with pet rat.'

'This is true.'

'They're suspicious of couples,' I said. 'They were checking out Peter and Sandra too, as if they know it's a couple in a boat they're looking for, but no more than that – no description of us would fit them too, the ages are way different.'

'It is all very odd,' Anders said. He went pink, then crimson, the kind of flush that begins at the root of the neck and swells up to the hairline, with the speed of a tide reaching a flat place. 'Cass, I have been meaning to ask –'

I waited, intrigued.

'I was wondering what are the laws on, you know –' he gave an uneasy glance over his shoulder '– on films of sex in this country.'

I gaped at him. He'd never shown any particular signs of being a sex-movie addict, but what did I know? He had his own laptop, and could watch what he liked. 'Blue-movie DVDs?'

He forked a very large mouthful of stir-fry in and concentrated on chewing it, the blush rising again. He nodded, not looking at me.

'I don't know,' I said, 'but I suppose if it's Norwegian stuff that's not been passed by the British censors they might not be happy.'

He finished his forkful and opened his mouth to speak, then closed it again, shaking his head gloomily. I didn't want to ask any more.

It was a points-race evening. I didn't take *Khalida* out for these – she was my home, not a trophy-winner – but I enjoyed crewing on one of the other boats, a new Starlight. The owner and most of the crew were Magnie's generation, and I enjoyed the sociability of sitting on the foredeck chatting, interrupted by the occasional piece of jib-or spinnaker-wrestling. It felt like returning to my roots, listening to my granny and her mates in Dublin holidays, hearing all the gossip of what was going on in and around Brae – and where women got the blame of being gossips, I can't say, for the men were equal to Granny Bridget any day. We worked through someone called John o' Easthouse, who'd been caught drunk-driving, and a row between Bill and Maggie of the Hoyt, because she'd had a dram too many at their silver wedding: 'You'd a thought he'd be used to it be noo,' Jeemie said – and round to yesterday's sheep-caa.

'Robbie o' the Knowe let his mouth open a bit wide while they were up on the hill,' Jeemie said. 'He was speaking about the goings on at the old Nicolson house, and Brian was standing right ahint him.'

'Aye?' Magnie said encouragingly.

'He didna say ower muckle, but enough, I doot, that Brian might be taking a look at what's going on there.'

Of course, the old Nicolson house was the one below the Trowie Mound, where Brian had been brought up. I supposed he still owned it.

'So what's going on there?' I asked. Magnie reddened, and Jeemie took a sudden interest in the set of the mainsail.

'Dir a bit of meeting up going on,' Magnie said. 'Now don't you ask any more, Cass, lass.'

'Aye, Brian'll maybe be asking for his keys back,' Jeemie said. He gave a relieved glance at the bouy fifty yards ahead. 'Now, folk, are you ready with that kite? Peter o' Wast Point is on my stern, so see how slick you can make it.'

I glanced behind. *Renegade* had her usual full complement of crew, including Olaf Johnston, back in the cockpit with a beer can in one hand, and Alex, perched on the foredeck. He waved. 'Hi, Cass, we're catching you.'

I slid astern, ready to take the sheet and guy; Magnie lifted the pole up, and Jeemie leant forward to haul it up. I pulled the guy tight and fastened it off, then Magnie went to the mast and began hauling the crumpled spinnaker. It came up fast, billowing out, and I hauled the sheet, taming the sail to a beautiful curve. The boat surged forwards.

'That's good,' Magnie called back from the foredeck, 'Hold her at that.' He sat down on the cabin roof. 'How about your walking folk from the yacht, Cass, any sign of them?'

'None,' I called back, over the flapping of *Renegade*'s spinnaker. 'But it's early yet, and light all night. It's a good walk to the trowie mound, too. They'll turn up.'

Renegade got her sheet in, so that the last words echoed over silence. I saw Alex's head turn. He gave me a long look, then, when he saw me watching him, turned away again. I could see, though, that he had it noted; he'd tell Norman. I'd have liked to know why Norman was so very interested in the comings and goings at the marina.

Chapter Five

Wednesday 1 August
Tide times for Brae:
Low Water 02.56   *0.4m*
High Water 09.19   *2.0m*
Low Water 15.09   *0.6m*
High Water 21.25   *2.2m*
Moon waxing gibbous

Peter and Sandra had mentioned camping, and although I hadn't noticed a tent as they'd set off, one of their backpacks could have been a state-of-the-art fold-tiny. I kept glancing across at the boating club drive as the bairns sailed around me in the sunshine the following day, and when there was still no sign of them as Anders and I were sharing a post-work cup of tea, I was uneasy.

'I know they're responsible adults,' I said, 'but all the same, I'd have expected them either to be back by now, or to have called the boating club and asked if we could keep an eye on *Genniveve*. And what about their cat? It's still aboard.'

'If they are weekend sailors,' Anders said, 'they would not count it odd to leave her alone overnight. You are used to being in your boat every day.'

'True,' I conceded, 'but it's a strange berth.'

'They tied her up very carefully, and Peter checked her over before they left. Maybe they are having fun hitch-hiking round Shetland, or have taken the chance of a night in a B&B. Somewhere,' he added with the air of one dreaming of wonders, 'with a cooked breakfast and hot showers, and a comfortable double bed.'

'Maybe,' I said. 'But they left me with the definite impression they were just going for the day. How about you taking the car up along the road way, to see if there are any signs of them, and I'll sail *Khalida* round to the old Nicolson house, anchor up, take the dinghy ashore, and climb up to the trowie mound?'

Hearing myself say the words reminded me of Magnie, yesterday. He'd been talking about Norman – mothers didn't like him near their lasses – and then he'd added, as if it were a clincher, *He goes along to the old Nicolson house.*

Dir a bit o' meeting going on ... Brian'll maybe be asking for his keys back. I said the last phrase aloud, and Anders jumped like a startled sheep.

'What do you mean?'

'It's something Magnie said, yesterday, that Norman, the jet-skier, went along to the old Nicolson house, as if that told me all I should know about him. Alex and Graham started playing dodgems, so I didn't ask what he meant.'

Anders looked sideways at me. 'You are too young, Cass. You are hopeless at seeing the world.'

'What am I missing, then?'

Anders went pink again. I watched with interest as the tide rose, and subsided. But he changed the subject. 'I suppose it would not do any harm to look for them. But if we do not see them?'

'Let's look first,' I said. I glanced out of the window at the tide, inching its way up the slip, and reached for the navy tidal atlas for Orkney and Shetland that lived above the chart table. Low water had been just after three, so it was now high water minus four, an hour to get out into the

Atlantic, high water minus three, then plus two to put it back to high water Dover – I flicked through the pages and considered the arrows. The tide in the sweep of St Magnus Bay would be against me going, but not by much, a knot or so, and it'd help me coming home. With the wind still a southerly force 3, I could sail all the way.

It was a bonny sail. *Khalida* tugged impatiently under my hand as I trimmed the mainsail, glad to be out on the water instead of being used as a houseboat. We surged steadily down the two-mile long voe and around the corner into the deeper Rona, the channel between the red cliffs of Muckle Roe and the island of Vementry with its World War I guns, twenty-foot barrels protecting St Magnus Bay, where the British fleet was anchored before the battle of Jutland. Beyond them was the Atlantic. Already *Khalida* was rising and falling to the larger swell. Gulls swooped and dived at the water just ahead of me. I hooked the autopilot chain over *Khalida*'s tiller, and got out the handline. It would be a shame to waste a shoal of mackerel. By the time we left the Rona I'd caught five medium-sized ones, glinting green and iridescent silver as they came up through the water, flapping tiger-striped in the bucket. We'd have grilled mackerel for supper. I was hungry now, though. I filleted two and put them under the grill. I'd eat one right away, and have the second in a roll up by the trowie mound, looking out over the bay.

I sailed on around the corner. Papa Stour was out to my left; beyond it, the distant three-shelved smudge of Foula, and after that nothing but sea for two thousand miles. I turned right and headed up the coast, keeping a wary distance from the red cliffs with their gaping underhangs, like shark mouths. There was a white motorboat in the distance, a good two miles away, anchored just off where I was headed. I reached for the spyglasses, and focused. Yes, it was David and Madge's boat, right enough, with its high, flared bow, and someone in a red Musto jacket messing about with a couple of rods in holders on the stern. There was no sign of Madge on the foredeck, but it was more exposed out in the Bay here, and too chilly for sunbathing. I watched for a bit longer, but there was no sign of movement from below. I wondered where they'd spent the night. There were pontoons at both Aith and Voe, as well as sheltered, isolated bays if you wanted a night under the stars, although they hadn't struck me as night-under-the-stars people. They'd want their shore power to run all those gadgets.

He stayed put until I was within five cables, then upped anchor and roared off, still with no sign of Madge. I wondered where she was, if she wasn't on board.

The trowie mound headland was much as I remembered it: a steep, green hill on three sides, with the pimple of the mound itself at the top. The fourth side, looking seaward, was a cliff, falling sheer to the sea in a glitter of pink granite. Our ancestors gave their dead the best view of their territory, so that the 'old ones' could keep watching over them. The green was good; Peter and Sandra's red jackets would stand out like a lighthouse beam on a dark night if they were in trouble there. Curving behind the hill, the long voe of Mangaster ran into the land, and there were houses at the far end of it, but the crofts at this end had been abandoned in the fifties, as road transport took over from boats. Only one looked habitable still, the seaward one, 'the Nicolson hoose'. It was tucked into its own little bay, with the isles of Egilsay and Cave protecting it from the Atlantic and hiding it from the houses on Muckle Roe; an isolated spot, too lonely even for me, although I reckoned that nowadays you could bring a pick-up along the walking track by the shore. There was a mooring bouy bobbing in the bay, bright orange, with a ring on the top. Presumably Brian had renewed it for visiting the cottage by boat. *Dir a bit o' meeting up going on ...*

I shoved that thought away, and hauled the anchor chain up from its locker in the bow. The bouy probably would hold *Khalida*, but taking a chance on a strange mooring wasn't seamanlike.

I dropped anchor in three metres of water just off the cottage. It didn't look as if it was used much. It had that dead look houses get, with windows black and empty, and the door shut as if it would never open again. The evening sun tinted the white walls, picked up the cracks in the window paint, and gave the cottage a long, sinister shadow. The strip of beach in front of it had boulders rolled to a line, to make a landing place, and I rowed my rubber dinghy in there, sploshed ashore, and made it fast.

The cottage was of traditional Shetland pattern, just like Magnie's, with the house, barn, and byre all in one line. There was a porch in the centre, with one square window on each side, and three skylights in the roof. Within, there would be a room on each side, with a steep stair in the middle leading up to two rooms above. I caught a glimpse of a double bed, with some kind of black metal tripod standing out against the white bedcover. There was no garden in front, just a rectangle of grey feather-headed grass sprinkled with coral-pink ragged-robin, then the beach, with the waves whispering among the pebbles. It was very still; only the waves sighing, the peep-peep of an oyster-catcher down at the water's edge, and the murmur of the wind broke the silence.

For all that, I had that nasty 'being watched' feeling as I walked past the cottage: a prickling in my shoulder blades, and a wish to turn around. I wondered if it had a reputation for being haunted; I'd ask Magnie next time I saw him. *He goes along to the old Nicolson house ...* Maybe they held those teenage Satanic rituals there, with all the daftness of Ouija boards and table-turning, and Norman dressing himself up as chief priest, or whatever devil worshippers called themselves.

I tried to remember, as I trudged up the hill, when the house had last been used. Brian's mother had been Barbara. Her face swam into my mind, a thin woman with sandy-coloured hair, a sour expression, and pouncing movements, like a curlew on the beach, stabbing its beak into the sand, and coming up with a worm. Now what had happened to Brian's father? He'd gone off in some way, whether with another woman, or just left. I wasn't sure if Barbara had turned sour after that, or if the sourness had driven him off. He'd been a fisherman. Maybe he just hadn't liked living at the back of beyond. This had been her family home, she'd been brought up here, and I had a vague feeling her mother had been alive and living here too. Anyway, Barbara had lived here with Brian until he'd come to school, then she'd been offered a council house, because she couldn't bring him to school by boat every day, and it was too far for a five-year-old to walk to the end of the track for the school bus. Brian had been – let me see, two, no, three years older than me. When he'd been in primary seven I'd been in primary four.

They'd come back here in the holidays. I remembered that. It had been after school went back at the end of summer that Brian had come in boasting about the skulls he'd found in the trowie mound, and trying to scare us by thrusting the open-mouthed carrier bag at us. The grandmother had died twelve years ago, just before I'd left Shetland, in one of the rash of cancers that had afflicted people in Shetland after the first Gulf War, when the wind blew low-grade radiation to us.

Twelve years. I paused and looked down at the house. It still had the traditional tarred roof, black and sticky, needing yearly re-painting, and this one certainly hadn't been left for that long. Brian must be keeping the house up. There would probably be grants from the SIC for re-using an old house site, rather than opening up a new one.

Maybe he planned to move back. I tried to think what had happened to him. An electrician was my impression, working south, on the Scottish mainland. Magnie would know.

I was almost at the top of the hill above it, the Hill of Heodale, rather out of breath, and with the grass-covered walls of the trowie mound looming imposingly above me, when I found a dead kitten. I took it to be a baby black rabbit at first, too visible for its own good, then my brain registered the blunt ears and stubby tail. It lay in a hollow of heather, white paws spread in mute protest. A feral one, I supposed, that had strayed from the rest of the litter and been caught by a black-back gull. They were vicious birds. Fifty metres further, I spotted a second one. Perhaps the mother cat had been killed, and hunger had driven them from the nest. They had to be very young, for neither was bigger than my hand. Poor peerie things.

I climbed the last ten metres to the platform and leaned back against the trowie mound to look around. The sun was still warm on my face, and glittered gold on the water. To the west was the sweep of open sea, with Papa Stour crouched just short of the marmalade horizon, and the faint smudge of white that was the Ve skerries, where, in 1930, the men of the trawler *Ben Doran* had waited, tied in their rigging, for the help that couldn't reach them across two hundred metres of rock-toothed sea. To the north was the hunch of Ronas Hill, made red by the granite gravel and boulders of its wind-blasted arctic tundra. To the south was my own island of Muckle Roe, and behind it stretched the long spine of the Kames, three lines of hills separated by slices of sea. Continue those, and you'd reach Scotland's Great Glen. To the east were the green hills to the north of Brae. The old ones would be able to bless all their world.

There was nothing moving on the green of hill, blue of sea, seaweed-rust of shore. There were no red sailing jackets marching up a slope or lying ominously still at the foot of a bank. I stood up and did a long, careful sweep with my spy glasses. No sign.

I leaned back on the trowie mound, biting my lip. Reasons for reassurance: Peter and Sandra Wearmouth were extremely capable adults, and well used to walking rough terrain. They could easily have decided to stay a night ashore. They were on holiday up here, after all, and could please themselves. Their cat could have been left double-rations and a litter tray. All the same –

All the same, the sea wasn't a safe habitat, and every sensible skipper made a plan before setting out. That plan included a port and time of arrival, so that shore back-up could investigate further if there was a no-show. Peter had told me their plan of a day's walking, and that made me their shore back-up. They hadn't arrived back at their boat, and they hadn't called to say the plan had changed. Granted, they didn't have my mobile number, but the club number was in the book, and they could leave a message.

I slid down the green grass of the trowie mound to sit on the sheep-cropped green turf at its base. There was a great slab of stone behind my back, and I wriggled against it until my back was comfortable, then took my mobile out from my backpack and was surprised and pleased to see a signal; three bars, even. Contacts; Anders; call.

He answered straight away. 'Yo, Cass.'

'Hiya. No sign of them here.'

'None here either. I have driven all the way to Ronas Hill, in case they decided to go and climb that too, but I did not see them, and I have asked several people on the way.'

'Nothing?'

'No. I'm now back at the marina, and they are not here. Nor has there been any word to the club, to say they are delayed, or have changed their plans. Do you think we should call the coastguard?'

'Yeah –' I said reluctantly. 'I'll call them from here. See you back at the marina.'

The coastguard number was programmed in my mobile, although I'd normally call them on the VHF from *Khalida*. It was Hilary who answered.

'Hiya, Hilary,' I said. 'It's Cass here, Cass Lynch. We could have a problem.'

'That handsome Norwegian of yours not servicing your engine well enough?' she riposted. I could hear her colleagues guffawing in the background.

'Men,' I said, rather lamely. I wasn't feeling up to bright back-chat. 'No, it's something quite different – we maybe have a couple of missing people.'

She went serious. 'Who, where, how long?'

I explained, hearing her scribbling at the other end of the phone. 'And you've had no word? No word at the club either?'

'No. And they were older people. I know it's only one night, but they knew we knew their plans –'

'And a night's a long time to be in trouble on the hill,' she finished. 'Okay, Cass, I'll talk to the chopper boys. They could do a sweep over. Descriptions?'

'Nice, spottable scarlet sailing jackets,' I said. 'He's tall, getting on for six foot, with white hair, and she's that peat-ash colour, a reddish blonde. Maybe five five.'

'We'll get the search underway,' she said, and rang off. I sat down against the trowie mound once more. I couldn't do any more now. I dug in my rucksack for the bottle of water and mackerel rolls I'd made back on *Khalida*.

I'd just bitten into the first one when I heard a furtive, scraping noise beside me, from within the trowie mound.

Chapter Six

I froze in mid-bite and listened. It was a very faint noise, yes, scraping. Was there any chance that Peter and Sandra had somehow got stuck inside the mound? I shoved my roll back into its paper and stood up. The sound ceased.

I called their names and my voice bounced off the stones. There was no answer. I began walking slowly round the mound, looking for the entrance.

From the outside, it was simply a circular grassy mound maybe two metres high and ten across, set in a flatter space on top of the hill. It wasn't obviously artificial; these hills were knobbled all over with outcrops of rock. When you looked at the lower sides, though, here and there the outer wall showed through, boulders the size of my body set flat-face outwards and fitted together like crazy-paving. Above one of these, a strip of turf had been torn away to show the first layer of dry-stone wall; torn away recently, too, for the exposed stones were still dark with earth, and the strip of turf lay at the base of the wall.

There was one of these chambered cairns, excavated in Victorian times, above my favourite anchorage on Vementry Isle. I frowned, trying to visualise what it was like. My impression was of a small, square chamber, set with shelves for the bones. It was mostly a rumble of stones, but you could still see the crawl-through entrance. That faced south, down the spine of Shetland towards Fair Isle and Orkney, the stepping stones their ancestors had used to get to Shetland. I came slowly around the mound until I'd got a quarter of the way round.

The rustle came again, from behind me. I jerked my head around. My rucksack was wriggling as if there was something inside it. I turned and crept back, but the vibration of my feet on the soft turf must have been sensed, for just as I got to it a tiny grey-striped kitten backed rapidly out, and vanished under the stone I'd been sitting beside.

I knelt to look. The smooth turf had crept up the stone, but at the side of it the grass was scrabbled into bare earth beside a hole, like the mouth of a rabbit burrow. Perhaps this was where the dead kittens had come from. This one could be the last survivor of the litter, and starving. I spread some bits of mackerel and buttered roll in a line coming forward from the hole, sat back, and waited.

The kitten came out straight away, bolting the crumbs ravenously. It could only have been a few weeks old, staggering on its little paws, with its high-domed head seeming too heavy for its tiny body. Its eyes were that opaque colour of sea-washed blue glass found on the tide line, and its stubby tail was tucked in under its body. It was grey above, cream below, with darker over-hairs on a cloud-grey undercoat, and its white paws were grubby with earth, as if it couldn't quite wash itself. Its ears were flattened, its eyes alert on me as it gollopped the food. As I moved to get the second roll out, it flinched, froze, then dived back into safety. There was a pause, then the little moon face peered out again from under its rock, hoping for more, but ready to retreat.

I sat very still, thinking my next move through. A feral kitten wouldn't take kindly to being carried, but I'd have to try. I couldn't leave it here to starve. It watched nervously as I pulled off my fleece and put it in my rucksack, curling it into a nest and adding a few pieces of the buttery roll. Then I laid out another trail of mackerel. The taste of food had made it bolder; it came almost to my hand as I laid the first piece, and followed it forwards, so that it was easy to turn my hand and lift it, tiny paws scrabbling helplessly in the air. I put it straight into the rucksack. The kitten gave one protesting mew, then crouched there, sniffing, found the pieces of roll, and began eating again. I pulled the drawstrings almost closed and carried the rucksack in front of me as I made my way carefully down the hill.

The dinghy was going to be the worst bit. The kitten had to stay in the rucksack for that. I felt the prickling sensation again as I tightened the drawstring and put the bag on the dinghy floor, but I was too busy to worry about phantoms just now. I shoved the dinghy afloat, rowed out to *Khalida,* handed the rucksack up into the cockpit, and climbed aboard after it.

Boats aren't like houses; you don't have an under-stairs cupboard or back room where you can stow cardboard boxes that might come in useful some day. The best I could manage was a blue plastic mushroom box that kept tins out of the leak in the mid starboard locker. I dried it off and wound my woollen scarf inside it, making a kitten-sized nest. It would have to do for now. I put a dribble of milk in a soup bowl, and I even had a little cooked mince to offer, from remnants intended to make the base of tomorrow's tea.

I slid the washboards into their groove, so that the kitten couldn't bolt on deck, but when I opened the top of the rucksack it showed no signs of wanting to escape. The cream belly was comfortably rounded, the milky eyes opened and shut again. I tried stroking its head with one finger, and was touched to hear the rumbling of a purr. Maybe it wasn't totally feral; maybe someone had dumped an unwanted litter out on the hill, saying: 'Oh, cats can take care of themselves,'. People can be unbelievably cruel.

Well, if it was happy in the rucksack, that was fine. I rolled the top down and wedged the bag in my bunk, with the bowl of milk beside it, then clambered over the washboard and stowed the dinghy. I was just hauling up the mainsail when I heard the drone of a helicopter in the distance. It was the Coastguard chopper, Oscar Charlie. I waved as its red and white chevrons came overhead. If Peter and Sandra were anywhere on the hill, they'd be found.

Then I weighed anchor and sailed out of the bay. *Khalida* made much better speed under sail than under engine, and the noise might frighten my little passenger. The sea was flat, so the kitten wouldn't be too jolted. I wondered if cats got sea-sick; hoped not.

As I rounded the corner into the Atlantic, I glanced back at the old house. There was a flash from the window, sun reflecting on glass, as if someone had hastily lowered a pair of binoculars. I watched, but it didn't come again.Somebody had indeed been watching me as I'd gone up, and come down again, a surreptitious somebody who hadn't come out to say hello.

It wasn't a comfortable thought.

Anders was waiting at the marina for me, back leaning comfortably against one of the bollards. His blue cap lay on the ground beside him, and the sun gleamed in his pale gold hair and glinted off his neat, Elizabethan-seaman beard. Rat was curled around his neck.

Cat and Rat didn't sound a good combination. I hoped it wasn't going to cause too much trouble.

As we came in the marina entrance under jib, Anders rose, picked up his cap, and strolled around to take my mooring warps. 'Are you showing off, or is there diesel bug in the fuel again?'

'Showing off,' I said, 'but for a good reason.'

'Still no sign?'

'None,' I said. 'But –'

'I saw the chopper go over.'

'Hang on,' I said, as he made to swing himself down into the cabin. 'We've got an extra passenger.'

He turned, fair brows raised, and I explained about the kitten. 'I couldn't leave it there,' I said. 'The poor thing was starving. It can't be more than a few weeks old. But what's Rat going to say?'

We went down into the cabin. Rat hopped nimbly out of Anders' shirt-neck, leapt to his usual spot perched on top of the fiddle that held our books on their shelf and began washing his whiskers. Suddenly he looked rather sinister. I had a horrid feeling that I'd once read an account of pet rats killing a baby. My tiny kitten wouldn't last ten seconds.

Anders looked gloomily at the little curl of grey fur. I curved a hand down over it, felt the tiny muscles startle and tense, then relax again. The little head came up, the milky eyes opened. I sat down on the couch beside it and picked it out of the rucksack. The rumbling purr came again, impressively loud.

Rat balanced along the fiddle to see what was going on, whiskers forward and twitching, body elongated. The kitten raised its head to watch, purring louder, then, with a scramble and a scrabble, leapt up to the fiddle too and balanced there, stubby tail waggling wildly. Rat froze, whiskers twitching; I put out a hand to grab the kitten out of danger.

'No, it's fine,' Anders said. 'Rat will not hurt him. He has met cats before.'

'But what if the kitten tries to pounce on him?' It was already waggling its little tail ready to jump.

'It's playing. Rat knows that.'

It seemed that Rat did, for as the kitten attempted to pounce, he leapt nimbly over it and turned to face it again. The kitten turned, overbalanced, slid down the wooden fiddle in a slither of claws, and landed on the bench cushions. Rat followed, dodged again. Within a couple of seconds they were chasing each other happily around the cabin floor.

'Of course the rest of the litter were black and white,' I said. I wasn't totally convinced until the kitten suddenly fell asleep in a corner of the bench, like a wind-up toy running down, and Rat curled up beside it, with the air of a parent on guard.

'He's adopted it,' Anders said. 'It will be fine now.' He rose to put the kettle on; I lifted the cushion under me for the biscuits. We'd just got settled when the VHF crackled.

'Yacht *Khalida, Khalida, Khalida*, this is Shetland Coastguard. Channel 23, over.'

I reached over to the radio, and changed channels. 'Shetland Coastguard, this is yacht *Khalida.* '

It was Hilary's voice. 'Cass, the chopper's done a sweep. There's no sign at all of your people. Do you have any other news of them?'

'No,' I replied. 'No sign here either. Their boat's exactly as it was.'

'Okay,' Hilary said. 'The chopper boys seemed pretty sure that if your people were in trouble anywhere in that area they'd have seen them.'

'They would,' I agreed. 'It's as clear a day as you'd get.'

'Then I think we have to assume they've just gone off for an extra day, maybe to a B&B somewhere. Inconsiderate not to let anyone know, but people are like that.'

'Thanks anyway,' I said.

'Get back if there's still no sign tomorrow morning.'

'I'll do that,' I said. 'Bye.'

I looked at Anders and shrugged.

'Strange,' he said.

'I suppose that as a skipper you get used to doing your own thing, not constantly telling people where you're going,' I said.

Anders shook his head. 'The opposite, rather. Look at the way you inform the coastguard when you are going any distance. You don't think twice about it – it's a sensible safety measure. He, Peter, would think like that. He told you where he was going.'

'I know,' I said.

The wind didn't fall that evening, but veered to the east, causing a white-topped chop against the outgoing tide in the marina mouth, and slapping small waves against *Genniveve*'s sides. It was colder too, a raw air that breathed cold mists, deserted moorlands, the wave-smashed beaches of the selkie wife who'd deserted her child. *Khalida* snatched at her bow-rope and her fenders rubbed at her sides like the creak of a ghost's rocking chair. The moon was a cold grey penny, with the flattened face giving it a secretive look. It was one of these nights where sky and forecast were agreed there wouldn't be any great change, yet my instincts said watch, stay awake. I tightened all warps and went to bed, uneasy.

I was woken by movement on the pontoon, a person walking past, and the jetty rocking. It was at the darkest point of the night, near-twilight – one, one thirty. I took a couple of seconds to register that Peter and Sandra must have returned, and by that time their engine was fired up, put straight into gear, and *Genniveve* was backing towards the turning space. I slid out of my berth and swung into the cockpit. Anders was only seconds behind me, pulling his jacket over his bare chest. *Genniveve* was already sideways on to us, her nose pointing to the marina entrance, her hull gleaming white in the marina lights. The

69

red-jacketed figure in the cockpit leaned down to put her into forward gear and she moved smoothly forward. The figure straightened, looking ahead, then glanced over its shoulder to see us watching. It raised a hand, and a woman's voice shouted, 'Bye!' Then she looked forward again, away from us, the hood screening her face.

We watched the yacht go through the entrance and behind the rock wall of the marina. The masthead light shone red, green, white above it, moving further away, and further; the chug of the engine dwindled, diminished but still audible on so quiet a night.

'That's them, then,' Anders said softly. His tanned face was pale in the white of the lights.

'I suppose,' I agreed. 'Who was it steering, could you see?'

'Sandra,' Anders said. 'It was not tall enough for Peter.'

'But muffled up in sailing gear it's hard to tell,' I said. 'The jacket looked wrong, as if she was wearing Peter's. And why go like that in the middle of the night?'

'Tides,' Anders said promptly.

I tried to think that one through. The water glinted black two-thirds of the way down the dinghy slip, meaning it was two hours to low water here, two hours to high water Dover. 'Yes, they'd do Papa Sound at that,' I conceded, 'but they'll have the full force of the tide against them from halfway to Sumburgh.' I couldn't remember the Muckle Flugga tides off-hand, but they'd just come from north-over, so I couldn't see why they'd go back that way.

Anders shook his head. 'I don't know. There's probably some simple reason.'

'Probably,' I agreed, with equal lack of conviction.

We stood a moment longer, listening to the engine sound in the distance. I was about to turn the gas tap and suggest a cup of tea when the note changed. The faint echo of the engine cut to idle, then was switched off. There was a long moment of silence, and then another engine noise: 'The Bénéteau,' Anders breathed. I didn't ask if he was sure, just as he wouldn't ask me why I'd confidently identified *Genniveve* as a Rustler. Each to his own.

Whatever the meeting was, it didn't take long. The Bénéteau's engine idled for less than five minutes, then we heard it go into gear and purr off, out towards the open sea, I guessed, for we'd have heard it for longer if it had gone south to Aith or eastwards to Voe. After it had gone, the silence closed in again. We stood there listening under the neon-white lights of the marina, but there was nothing. *Genniveve*'s engine didn't start again, nor was there the rattle of sails being raised, or the sharp whirr of a jib being sheeted in on the winch. Only the masthead light burned steadily, visible at two miles, as per Col Regs.

I didn't understand it. Sandra and Madge had certainly behaved as if they'd never met, and there'd been no mention, in that chat in the cabin, of 'I see the Bénéteau's got in here before us. We were moored next to her in Cullivoe ...' as would have been natural. So why were they leaving like that in the middle of the night, for a secret rendezvous? Perhaps Peter was service, as I'd thought; perhaps *Genniveve*'s visit here was cover for a meeting with equally undercover colleagues. Magnie had insisted David and Madge were service too – Customs officers, maybe. My do-gooding might have mucked up all sorts of Secret Service planning.

The distant masthead light went out. *Genniveve* must have been further west than I'd thought. I tried to make out the shape of the hills in the darkness. If she'd turned into the Rona, it wouldn't take long for her to reach the open sea: half an hour.

'That's her, then,' Anders said. His voice rang out slightly too loudly above the slapping waves.

'Cup of tea?' I said.

He shook his head, and was just bending down to swing back into the forepeak when he froze, and straightened again.

'What?' I said.

He shrugged it away. 'I am being affected by your Shetland ghost stories.'

Now I heard it too, in the dimness under these summer stars, with the misshapen circle of moon shining cold on the black water. A cold shiver tingled up my spine. Faintly, far out in the water, a baby was wailing desolately.

3

Gotta taka gamla mana ro.

(Proverb in the ancient Norn language: take the advice of those older than you.)

Chapter Seven

Thursday 2 August
Tide times for Brae:
Low Water 03.41   *0.3m*
High Water 10.06   *2.1m*
Low Water 15.52   *0.5m*
High Water 22.11   *2.3m*
Moon full

'Did you hear anything odd last night?' I asked Magnie when he came to join me in the rescue boat.

He shook his head. 'I'm suffering that much from insomnia the doctor's had to give me sleeping tablets.'

'Insomnia?' I repeated, surprised.

Magnie went red. 'See, I'm given up the drink.'

Now I really had nothing to say. Magnie, on the wagon? 'What, given it up totally?'

'Altogether. See, lass, I canna forget that woman that died, the film wife. She died because I was too drunk to look to her.'

'You don't know that.'

'She's on my conscience yet. That was the drink that made me do that.' He took a deep breath, and became as intimate as an older Shetland man goes. 'I dinna want to be that kind o' a person – the sort to leave a body in trouble. So it's never going to happen again.'

'And are you managing – to give it up, I mean?'

'That very next day, after you told me what I'd done, I took all the drink that was in the house, and poured it down the drain. I'm no' touched a drop since, and I won't either.'

He'd been one of the last of the whaling men, Magnie. He'd endured cold and thirst in South Georgia, and even the rum rations running out on one trip. If he put his mind to something, it would be done.

'I don't much like the sleeping tablets, though,' he added. 'I'm thinking I would maybe take up a hobby, you ken, something to do in the nights.'

'Jigsaws.'

'Na, na. Fiddly things for women, they are, and besides, I don't want fifteen years taken off my eyesight. And don't you suggest patience neither. The only cards I play is five hundred.' Five hundred was the Shetland version of bridge, and the boating club was one of the venues for the winter '500 nights'. 'No, I'm had an idee. I thought I might make a model o' the *Oceanic*, the liner that went ashore on Foula. You mind, me faither was one of the rescue team when she went ashore, and I helped with the dive in the seventies. I'm even got some copper wire from her.' He glanced down at the marina and changed the subject. 'So when did the yacht leave?'

'In the middle of the night,' I said, and told him the story. He rubbed his bristly chin and considered. 'They'd come from the north, so south's more likely, and she'd make six knots. Seven hours to Scalloway. Let's get these bairns going, then we can do some investigating.'

I gathered the bairns up for the pre-sail briefing. We noted that the tide was coming in, and was going to be a high one, then checked out the wind, still more east than south, and between 2 and 3, with the occasional gust that set white horses tumbling on the blue water.

'So,' I said, 'what problems might that cause?'

'Getting out,' Alex offered, with a look at the entrance, flowing in like a river with tide and wind behind it. I gave my pal Inga's lass, Vaila, an old-fashioned look when she suggested the best way round that was for the rescue boat to tow them out, although it might come to that. We did a bit of slick tacking practice on shore, then hovered in the rescue boat as they fought their way out into the voe and began going round their triangle.

'Not bad,' Magnie commented. 'Nobody on the rocks – that's progress. You get them started, lass, while I do a bit o' phoning.'

I organised my bairns into pairs for tacking round each other, and listened while I did it. Magnie was talking to someone called Joanie, and there was a good deal of chasing up news before he got round to asking about the yacht, and a bit more news after, ending with a 'See dee, boy' before he ended the call and shook his head at me. 'They didn't end up in Scalloway, and there's no strange yachts moored up in Burra or Trondra. Well, let me think. They coulda gone straight west, to Foula.'

He made another phone call. 'No sign o' them there either. I wonder now –' He frowned and called again. 'Robbie, boy, it's Magnie here. I'll no' keep you. I was joost wondering if you'd seen a green yacht going past your way, heading sooth ... sail or motor, could be either, a dark green hull, and a fair height o' mast ... thirty-five foot ... no, no, dir naething wrang. Thanks ta dee, boy.'

He put the phone back in his pocket and shook his head. 'She didna go soothwards, that's for certain. If Robbie o' the Heights didna see her, she wasna there.'

Eight hours, forty-eight miles; they could be anchored up in Ronas Voe, to the north, or in Cullivoe, in Yell, the next island up from mainland – except that another couple of phone calls established that they weren't. Nor had they been seen passing through Yell Sound towards Lerwick; nobody had seen a dark green yacht anywhere. Among boat-watchers like Shetlanders, that was nothing short of remarkable.

We left it there, to focus on the bairns, but I didn't like it. That baby wailing in the night had set up an uneasiness that lingered still. There was no reason why Peter and Sandra shouldn't go in the middle of the night like that. There'd been no sign of a stranger fumbling with unfamiliar ropes, or having difficulty starting the engine, and I couldn't be sure that it wasn't Sandra who'd called 'Bye' as *Genniveve* had left the marina. The stealthiness of the footsteps on the pontoon, the quietness of their casting off, could be consideration for our sleep.

I didn't want to bother the local police. My suspicions were all too vague, and, besides, if it was a big international operation, making a noise in Lerwick might scupper it entirely. However, there was another policeman I knew, from the Inverness CID, and I thought he'd listen to me. His name was DI Gavin Macrae, and he'd been up here just over a month ago, investigating the murder Magnie had just talked about, the death of the film wife. For a time I'd figured as chief suspect, but in spite of that we'd taken to each other, or agreed on a truce, at least. I'd accepted he had a job to do, and he'd accepted my past. Me, Cass, the selkie wife. He'd listened to the story of Alain's death and still liked me afterwards.

It was his face I'd seen in my dream.

I thought about it for the rest of the morning. For a start, it was such a trivial thing to bother a busy DI with. For another, I didn't want him to think I was finding an excuse to make contact. I could wait until we met at the trial, ask him then –

And Peter and Sandra?

We seafarers needed to look out for each other. I'd been alone and scared out at sea, with nobody knowing when and where I'd make land. I'd been in frightening situations on land, with only *Khalida* tied at a pier to tell anyone I'd ever existed. When you have the freedom of the sea road, it's easy to disappear. In case there was something wrong, I would do for them what I hoped someone would never need to do for me. Once I was alone in *Khalida,* at lunchtime, I scrolled down my contacts list and found Gavin Macrae. Ignoring the thumping of my heart and my suddenly dry mouth, I pressed the green button.

He answered on the third ring. 'Cass?'

He must be alone; the Highland lilt in his soft voice that ebbed and flowed like the tide, depending on whether he was in the policeman's world or his own, was as pronounced as it had been when we'd been out in *Khalida* together. He'd said my name like this then, with the 'a' clear, the 'ss' soft and lingering. I couldn't read anything other than polite efficiency in his tone.

'Hello,' I said briskly. 'Listen, I'm sorry to bother you. There's something here I'm a bit concerned about.'

'What trouble have you sailed into?' There was a smile in his voice.

'None,' I retorted. 'Magnie and I are being good as gold, teaching sailing to the bairns here. No, I'm worried someone else is in trouble.'

I told him the whole story, and he listened patiently. It was the first thing I'd noticed about him, the way he sat there as if he had all the time in the world, particularly, he'd told me later, if the suspect he was questioning was eager to get away. If he was extra doubtful about them, as he had been about me, he tied sea-trout flies. 'Nobody ever watches their words when they're being distracted by my fingers.' I could see him now as he'd sat then, grey eyes intent on the invisible line and glinting hooks. His brown hands were deft, made for work, not beauty.

79

There was a long pause when I'd finished. 'So,' he summed up, 'the couple went, their yacht's now gone too, but into thin air. Why do you think it wasn't Sandra who took her out?'

'It was the jacket,' I said. 'It was the right sort, scarlet Musto, but it didn't fit her – I saw the sleeve flopping over her hand, and the body seemed long in proportion to her.'

I was glad he took my word for it, instead of making a crack about my fashion sense. 'Might she have picked up her husband's?'

'She might,' I agreed, 'but I don't think she would have. You just don't, aboard a boat. You look for your own, because otherwise you're risking accidents by over-long sleeves flopping about, or not being able to reach something vital because it's too tight under the arms. It's just more comfortable, even for silly things, like your own hood adjusted to fit you. I'd never put on someone else's jacket if my own was aboard. And then, if they'd just come from – wherever they'd been – they'd each have been wearing their own, surely.'

'Who do you think it was?'

'I wondered if it might have been Madge,' I said, 'the woman from the motorboat. The height was right, and she was plump, too plump to fit Sandra's jacket. If she had to look like Sandra, she'd have had to take Peter's jacket.'

'Then she met up with the motorboat, and …?'

'I suppose Peter and Sandra got back aboard from the motorboat – or put her back on to it – and they all headed off to sea. *Genniveve* could easily have gone straight to Orkney or Faroe, without stopping anywhere in Shetland.'

'What would you like me to do?'

'I want to be reassured that they're okay,' I said. 'I know each little thing could have a separate explanation, but I have an uneasy feeling about all of them together.'

'Well, for a start,' he said, 'I'll find out if Wearmouth

really was ex-service, and check what he was doing in Shetland, in case it was official rather than holiday. I can check up on the boat, too, I expect. I don't suppose you noticed if she was on the small ships' register?'

'She was,' I said. Like *Khalida*, *Genniveve* had her number carved into the bulkhead, and stuck on the outside of the hatch. 'SSR90 – something. Another three figures.' I heard him scribble it down.

'Give me as full a description as you can.'

'Rustler 36, dark green with wooden trim, green sail covers and dodgers with her name, *Genniveve*, a Navik wind vane, and a grey dinghy on the coachroof,' I said promptly. He laughed aloud.

'The people, Cass, the people.'

I did my best, and added the cat for good measure.

'Now the motorboat that they seemed to be meeting.'

I obliged.

'Good. I'll text or phone you the minute I have any news.'

I wasn't going to prolong the call with chat. 'Thanks,' I said. I snicked the phone off, relieved, and picked my lifejacket up, ready to get back to the bairns before I could start getting maudlin. All the same, his image stayed with me: not tall, topping my five foot two by maybe half a head, but there was a compact, durable strength about him. I could easily imagine him hefting a ram into a pen, or shoving a boat down a beach. His hair was dark red, the colour of a stag's ruff in autumn, his eyes the grey of the sea on a clouded day, and he had a nose that looked as if it had been broken, and mended squint – damn it, I wasn't going to fall for a policeman.

I stamped on myself wondering if he'd come up to investigate, and went to gather up my bairns from their post-lunch game of throwing jellyfish at each other.

I'd just swung onto the pontoon when I became aware of an engine roar from the voe, a motor boat approaching at speed. The racket was familiar. It was my least favourite marina people, Kevin and Geri, who owned a dark blue Apreamare 9 m. In theory it was a gentlemen's motor cruiser, but in practice this one was shabby outside and in, filled with plastic buckets of fish, creels, and tangled with orange nylon line. The engine noise made Anders shudder.

I was biased against them right from our first meeting. I've had the pleasure of meeting up with whales from time to time, from the brief escort of a blue whale's vast, curved back off Nova Scotia, to a swarm of pilot whales all around me off Shetland, and while I wouldn't go for the 'mystic sages of the world' stuff, I've counted it a privilege every time to meet the ocean's biggest denizens going peacefully about their lives. When Kevin announced that he'd just gone across to Faroe specially to take part in the whale kill there it didn't make me feel I was going to like him; but then, I'm not sure I'd have liked him anyway. He was a fair Shetlander, with sleek, fine hair drooping over narrow-set eyes that darted here and there, as if taking notes, thick red lips, and a general air of thinking he was the cat's pyjamas. I'd taken against Geri straight away too. She was one of these ice blondes, with hair polished to a glassy sheen, and upright as a herring-gull on a pole. She had sea-gull eyes too, that cold, narrow look that measures up the distance between the exhausted sheep and its new-born lamb before swooping for the kill. If there was any softness in her, it was well-disguised. Myself, I wouldn't voluntarily have gone nearer her than sixty paces.

Besides, as Anders and I had learned over the three weeks since they'd got their boat launched, they were just noisy, the sort of people who have to have their radio blaring, and who fire up a barbecue that wafts smoke downwind on everyone else. Kevin and his pal Jimmie went out on night fishing trips, and since the only engine speed they knew was full, they'd wake us up returning. There'd be the engine roar, then the wash, shaking *Khalida* up against the sides of the berth, no matter how tightly we'd tied her up. Their engine leaked diesel which lay in a rainbow sheen over the water and crept in a scum-brown smear up *Khalida*'s sides, and no doubt did nothing for the terns and sea-scallops either.

I couldn't be bothered being polite today. They could sort their own lines out. I slid back below and waited. There was a throaty roar as the big motorboat backed into its berth, water churning all round it. *Khalida* rocked, then steadied as the motorboat cut its engine. Kevin got out to tie the bow lines while Geri fished for the aft ones with a boathook, then Kevin went back on board. I expected him to switch the engine off, but it kept throbbing. Maybe they'd be going back out again, you never knew your luck. The music blared, one of those groups with a thump, thump, thump beat. Rat twitched his whiskers in disdain and disappeared back into his nest; rustling noises suggested he was re-making it. Cat slid into my sleeping bag.

I kept watching. Kevin appeared with a red bucket, one of those rectangular ones, with a lid. He was carrying it oddly; it wasn't particularly heavy, I could see that, but he was treating it with great care, as if it was valuable, or breakable, yet at the same time holding it away from him, as if he wanted nothing to do with it. Geri appeared right after him, and I could see straight away that whatever it was in the bucket, she wasn't having it in the house. Her face was stony under the ice-blonde hair, and she gestured for it to go back on the boat. Kevin's reply included a face, and a gesture at the cabin. He wasn't having it in his boat either. Geri didn't pause for a moment. It was going in the cockpit, then. Kevin tried to reason with her, glancing across at the main town of Brae then making another gesture at the cockpit. Geri shook her head but didn't seem totally convinced. Kevin tried again, a bit more persuasively this time, and at last Geri nodded. Kevin picked up the bucket and took it to their car, Geri followed him, and off they went, leaving their music and exhaust fumes for the rest of us to enjoy. Not for long, though; Kevin must just have been putting Geri home, for he was soon back, jolting his state-of-the-art black pick-up (with roll bars and double headlights) down the gravel drive to the marina. He got out and hauled a box out of the boot. It looked heavy, and something about the lettering, even at this distance, said Scandinavia. I waited until he'd got half-way along the pontoon, then walked towards him, buckling my lifejacket back on.

'Afternoon,' I said cheerfully. 'Did you have a good trip to Faroe?'

His sandy head dipped; he pursed his red lips and edged sideways away from me like a crab making for the sea. 'Oh, no, we're no' been to Faroe. Just away on a fishing trip.' He hefted the box to his other arm, so that his body was between it and me.

'And heading off on another,' I said, nodding at the box.

'Oh, just stocking up on stores,' he replied, and slid around me, changing hands with the box again, so quickly that I didn't get a chance to read what was written on it, and swinging himself onto his boat. 'See you later.'

I had a look into the back of the pick-up as I passed. It was filled with boxes and buckets, all covered over with a tarpaulin. I was just about to reach in and lift it up when Kevin came out of his boat again, and I had to keep walking.

If all that was stores, he had to be planning a round-the-world voyage; or maybe I just wasn't making enough allowance for men who needed a six-pack each just as a mid-afternoon whistle-wetter. He stowed the rest in record time, then the pick-up roared off.

I was left wondering just what was in the bucket. If they'd been to Faroe it could be whale meat – but surely Geri would want that at home, if they were really going to eat it. Some sort of bait? No, that would be left on the boat as a matter of course. I even wondered if it might be some sort of specimen that Kevin wanted stuffed, an outsize skate or something like that, but the bucket wasn't big enough for that – an outsize trout, maybe, but as far as I knew Kevin didn't do loch fishing and besides, that would be something he was proud of, not something he wanted rid of. Ah, well, no doubt all would become clear in time.

Chapter Eight

We had a happy, wet afternoon, playing a sailing version of water-polo, and ending with the inevitable capsize practice inside the marina. The bairns were just hosing down the boats, their splash suits, and everything else within range when a tall, sandy-headed man came over to me. I couldn't remember his name off-hand, but he was Kevin of the noisy motorboat's best pal. He was wearing a red boiler suit and yellow rubber boots, in traditional crofter style, but I had a feeling he wasn't a full-time crofter – he worked in an engineering firm in Lerwick somewhere.

Everything about him was sandy: yellow-brown hair, flattened as if the tide had just smoothed it, a pale tan that matched his freckle. Even his eyes were an indeterminate light brown. His manner was sandy too, a shiftiness that reminded me of slithering down sand-dunes. He didn't look at me as he spoke.

'Cass, aye aye.'

'Now, then,' I responded. Jimmie, that was it. He'd been in the same class at school as Kevin, just going into primary seven when I'd left, which made him four years younger than me, twenty-five. He didn't look it, and he definitely didn't look old enough to be getting married. 'How are the preparations for the big day going?'

He made a face. 'Oh, you ken, a lock of fuss. I do my best to keep out of Mam's way ee now. She and Donna's mam – Donna an aa come to that – are in a permanent spin o' housework and phone calls.'

I dredged up the memory of Inga telling me about it. 'Next Saturday?'

'A week on Saturday,' he said. 'The spree's this Saturday, Voe Show day.'

Getting married in Shetland seemed to include a day of pub crawl, preferably in fancy dress. Shetland men were lucky; in Orkney, your mates tied you to a chair on the back of a lorry, covered you with the most disgusting things they could think of, like rotting sheep guts, and drove you round the streets. 'What's the theme?'

'Fishing,' Jimmie said, 'for our bus, and Donna won't tell me what the lasses' bus is. She says we've to wait for we meet.'

'Oh,' I said, 'I thought the whole point was to have a last spree without the future wife.'

'No these days,' Jimmie said gloomily. 'Nowadays the weemin make sure they come to the same places as us, or at least cross over and end up at the same place, to make sure we don't go home wi' anyone else.'

I wondered if this was feminism or just the AIDS generation.

'You could likely go on Donna's bus if you'd like.'

I shook my head. 'I don't think I would like.' A drunken evening with fellow sailors from a tall ship was one thing, but I'd rather be keelhauled than go in a bus round pubs with drunken lasses in fancy dress. Jimmie sighed and changed tack.

'I wondered if you'd seen Kevin around. I was trying to get hold of him, but his phone's switched off.'

'He was about earlier,' I said. 'You've tried the boat, yeah?'

'It's all locked up.'

Locked up, here in Shetland? I remembered the package Geri wouldn't have in the house. Something they'd brought from Faroe. I said, casually, 'You didn't go over to Faroe with them, that hidmost time?'

He turned his head, a little too quickly. 'Faroe?'

'Yeah, wasn't that where they've just come back from?'

'I didn't ken they'd been over there,' Jimmie said, and frowned, as if he didn't much like the idea. 'Whereabouts, did he say?'

I shook my head. 'I don't think he said, it was just an impression I got.'

'Well –' Jimmie said. He gave me another intent look, with a glint of malice in it. 'It's ower early for the whale cull.'

I wasn't going to rise to his needling. 'So it is,' I agreed.

He laughed at that. 'I didn't like it ower muckle myself,' he confessed. 'The boat reeks o' it yet. I was noticing it just ee noo, the smell o' the guts.' He turned away. 'I'll likely catch up with him later. If you see him, you could maybe say I was looking.'

'I'll do that,' I said.

When I went back along the pontoon, I gave a quick glance at Kevin's boat. The faded brown curtains were drawn, and there was a padlock on the washboards.

I suddenly wondered how heavy a bronze would be, how big. *They've recovered one of the Epstein bronze heads in Faroe,* Madge had said. If it was, say, a portrait head – what did they call it, a bust – then presumably it would be life-size, the sort of thing that would fit neatly in a fisherman's bucket. Cover it with fish, and nobody'd notice.

I wondered how often Kevin and Geri went over to Faroe.

I'd left Cat and Rat together while I was sailing, and when I looked in after the boats were put away they were both sleeping, glossy black and white and fluffy grey fur curled together on my bunk. The kitten had used the litter tray, but the movements were loose and smelly. Maybe he needed special food. I put the last of the mackerel in a dish on the floor and headed off to consult Inga. We'd been at school together from nursery, but while I'd been off messing around in boats, she'd married a local boy, Charlie Anderson, and now they had three children. She was envious of my adventures, and at times I envied her domesticity, but not so much that I was eager to settle down. I babysat her toddler, Peerie Charlie, on occasion, and was always glad to give him back.

Settle down ... I felt the shore world close around me again. College: a whole year in the same place; I could find a boyfriend, have a relationship. My heart contracted in panic. Someone telling me what to do, quarrels and a negotiated life, instead of being as free as the wind could take me –

I walked along the shore rather than by the road, swinging my flip-flops from one hand. The tide was just starting to recede from the black seaweed of high water mark, water sucking around crunching weed, and pebbles rattling as the wave ebbed. A tirrick dived and came up with a twisting fish in its beak. Just off shore, a young guillemot bobbed on the water. A smell of frying drifted down from the chip shop to mingle with the iodine squelch of the seaweed by my feet.

I'd just reached the centre of the beach when my phone rang. It was Gavin. I put a finger over the speaker at the back to baffle the wind noise. 'Hey.'

'I have some information for you,' he said. 'Are you where you can talk?'

'Bang in the middle of a lonely beach,' I said. I went over to a boulder, and sat down. The water swirled towards my feet; I edged my toes towards it, and felt its cold foam curl around them. 'It may be shared with a young guillemot.'

'Guillemots can hold their beaks,' he retorted. 'Okay. Well, I had no difficulty tracing the Wearmouths. Peter is indeed services – he's just retired from being a Chief Inspector in the Newcastle CID.'

'Interesting,' I said.

'Wait. I phoned their HQ, and that's where things did indeed become interesting. Normally, you see, we forces work well together. You explain what you want, and they'll do their best. Not this time. I got thoroughly stalled by an officer who behaved –' his soft voice sharpened – 'as if Inverness was the wilderness. CI Wearmouth was currently on leave, and no information could be given. His cases would now be handled by other officers, and were of course confidential. He didn't quite tell me to get back to my stray Highland cattle and drunk fishermen, but it was close.' He laughed. 'So I investigated further.'

I knew he was a man after my own heart. 'Good for you.'

'I did a bit of digging among the police lists, and a phone call or two got me to one of Wearmouth's working partners. He was reluctant to talk too, and stressed that the operation's on-going, so he could only give me hints to follow up. I'll tell you what they told me, but you need to keep it to yourself.'

'Understood,' I said. Tall ships had confidentiality too.

'Wearmouth was working on one case which he thought was an operation that might be centred in Shetland. It involves stolen goods which go missing on mainland Britain, and subsequently turn up abroad – in Faroe, Iceland, Denmark, and Norway, and even in north Germany.'

I didn't need to look at a map. These were the countries

of the medieval Hanseatic League, in the days when Shetland was the crossroads of northern trading. 'All convenient distances from Shetland, with a fast motorboat.'

'Yes. Wearmouth wondered if items were being brought to Shetland by sea and stored there before being transported further, again by sea, as their value was required.'

'I don't suppose,' I said, 'that the 'stolen goods' included missing art work?'

'It does indeed. The houses being stolen from are all minor stately homes, and all conveniently near a harbour – hence the deduction that the goods are being moved by sea. There's been a bit of spot-checking of vessels by the coastguard, but without any results.'

'And then once they're here, it's easy.' In my mind's eye, I saw Kevin and Geri of the noisy motorboat arguing over their red bucket. 'Stick your contraband in a bucket or a box, and just carry it ashore, to your byre or wherever.' Your lonely cottage out below the trowie mound, with a nice new mooring bouy, and no other house in sight?

'Unfortunately, if you haven't a suspect, then you don't know where to start searching. To make matters worse, Wearmouth suspected there was information being leaked. Forces hate admitting to a mole, so that explained why the first officer I spoke to gave me the brush off.'

'Did this partner know what Wearmouth was up to now?'

'He's genuinely on holiday, and he knew some sort of sailing trip was planned, but not where. I tried for a photograph of Wearmouth, but his colleague was too worried about jeopardising the operation, if he was following a lead.'

'That's a pity.'

'Then I tried him with a description of your other

couple, but that rang no bells at all. I'm still working on their boat – it's a new one, and not that many have been sold, so I'm hoping for a lead there. It'll take a few days.'

'In terms of stowing goods, there's this cottage.' I described it to him. 'I can't think of anything handier placed to hide stuff. You wouldn't be seen coming or going. It's supposed to be empty, but I'd swear someone was watching me from inside.'

'It doesn't have a reputation for being haunted, by any chance, as a bit of extra cover? Customs people always look in haunted houses first.'

I sighed. 'Not more ghosts.'

'Oh?'

'It's just one of Magnie's stories, about a selkie wife who abandoned her baby to go back to sea. You're supposed to hear it crying, and Anders and I did, last night, just after *Genniveve* set off seawards.'

'A crying baby?'

'Wailing. It was a horrid noise, desolate. I've still got the shivers from it.'

'Hmmm ...' There was silence for a moment, as if he was considering something. 'Did you have a pet, as a child?'

'Me? Maman wasn't keen on animals. Inga had a collie.'

'Yes,' he said, as if that confirmed some idea in his head, the 's' lingering softly in the air.

'I have a cat now, though,' I said. 'A kitten. I found it.'

'Black?' His voice teased. 'I can see you on a lonely hill, in the wind, with your hair streaming out behind you, and a black cat at your heels.'

'It's grey,' I said firmly. 'And what has that to do with the price of fish?'

'Just an idea I'm having. Keep listening for your ghost

baby, and tell me if you hear it again.'

'You're doing a Sherlock Holmes,' I said. 'You just want to surprise the weak-minded Watson.'

'I wouldn't dare to call you weak-minded. How's the college plan doing?'

'I've signed up. I got through the interview, and I start in August.'

'Cass, you sound like you're preparing for your own funeral.'

'It's just going to be strange,' I said. 'Ashore, in the same place, for a whole year, day after day in a classroom. I'm not sure I'll know myself.'

'You'll still live aboard *Khalida*?' He had the French trick of turning statements into questions.

'Yes, but she's just going to be a houseboat. By the time I've finished school then it'll be too dark to take her out, and there'll be homework too, likely.'

'Think of the end result – a skipper's ticket. Your chance to belong on a tall ship.'

'Yes.' He'd told me that my voice gave me away, every time I tried to lie to him. 'I know, I need to grow up. I can't stay footloose for ever. It's just – being settled isn't me, you know? I've never been settled. I can't imagine a Cass with a mortgage and a steady boyfriend, going to the pub every Friday and the cinema every second Saturday.'

He laughed. 'I'll be very surprised if that fate overtakes you.' He switched back to business. 'Listen, this cottage –'

'I could sail round and have a closer look at it, if you like. I suspect it'd be easy to get inside.'

'No.' It was a captain's voice. 'This is my ship, Cass, and you have to obey orders. There's an idea that the stolen goods are being exchanged against drugs to be brought into this country, and that means you're dealing with ruthless people. Don't ferret around, don't try to find out anything. You've put it in my hands. Trust me. I'll do what I can.'

'As far as I can,' I said slowly, 'I will. If something else crops up I'll phone you before doing anything.'

'Do that. Have you got paper there?'

I looked down at the damp sand at the tideline. 'As good as.'

'Okay, here's my home number.' He dictated it, and I wrote it with a sharp stone. 'The mobile doesn't work there.' He was smiling again. 'I live at the back of beyond, with my mother and my brother Kenny. We have a farm at the head of a loch. Don't worry if he answers in Gaelic.'

I dredged the remnants of Erse out from my voyage with Irishmen on the *Sea Stallion*. 'Go raibh míle maith agat.' A thousand thanks to you.

He answered with a flood of soft syllables and rang off, laughing. I copied the number carefully into my mobile, tucked it away in my back pocket, and stood to watch the waves smooth the number away.

I thought about that all the rest of the way along the beach. I'd known he was brought up a countryman, but I'd assumed he was now a city-dweller, with a neat house in Inverness, near the police station. *A farm at the head of a loch* ... So he was still a countryman, who woke up to hills, and sea, and silence. My picture of him hefting rams and working with a boat had been spot-on. *My brother Kenny* ... there were brothers like that in Shetland too, who'd stayed on at the family home when neither had married, first with their ageing mother, then as a pair, growing more solitary, more dependent on each other. I wondered how old Gavin's mother was. Unless they'd been very late babies, she'd be only in her sixties.

That was old enough to object to her policeman son taking up with a footloose sailor woman.

Besides, folk wisdom had plenty of warnings against taking up with a man who'd never left home. I switched my attention to Kevin and Geri. Kevin had been out last night too; but then, Anders had said the motorboat we'd heard was the Bénéteau, and he wouldn't have mistaken its engine for Kevin's, not even at low revs. All the same, they went over to Faroe pretty regularly, more often than most. It was odd, too, that they'd locked the boat up so thoroughly, with the packages he'd off-loaded from his pick-up inside. I'd maybe try and look more closely later ... I stamped that thought down. *This is my ship, Cass* ...

4

A holl ida sheek and a dimple i da chin,
Der little grace i da face at der baith in.

(Old Shetland proverb: beware of someone who is too good-looking.)

Chapter Nine

Inga's house was at the far end of the beach, and had been built in the late seventies by her husband's father. One of the things the council had done with the oil disturbance money was to offer 90% grants to any crofter whose house was so dilapidated that a new one would be a good idea, and old Charlie was one of many who suddenly found his roof was unsound. He'd built a large, square house, grey-harled and red-roofed, with a grandstand view of the voe from its picture windows. He'd been a keen Maid sailor in his day, and when he wasn't able to sail at the Brae regatta any longer, then he parked himself in a chair on his lawn, spyglasses in hand. Martin and I used to make sure our gybes at the bouy just below his house were impeccable; any rocked boat or untidy spinnaker work, we heard about it the next time we met him at the club. '*Now, bairns, you would need to make sure you took your sheet in more before gybing that pole ...*' There was a rugosa hedge around the garden, the last magenta flowers opening to show their yellow-crowned hearts, and the first green hips forming. I clicked through the gate and up the flagged path. One side of the garden held a circular blue trampoline; the other had a plastic slide and playhouse. There were no signs of life outside. I pushed the door open and called 'Is anyone home?'

There was a utility room to the left of the lino-clad passage. Inga must have been working in the peats, for there was a row of muddy rubber boots along the hall: big yellow ones with reinforced toes for Charlie, neat green ones for Inga, two pairs in neon-pink for the girls, and

Peerie Charlie's Spiderman pair, lying on their sides, just as he'd kicked them off. I called again and went into the kitchen.

I had to push my way in through the smell of hot fat. Inga was presiding over the cooker, dark hair ruffled and cheeks red; the older two lasses were spraying ketchup over fish fingers and arguing over whose turn it was to have the front seat going in to swimming in Lerwick, and Peerie Charlie was sitting up in his high chair. He had a scarlet trail of sauce on his chin. He waved his spoon at me and tried to stand up. 'Dass!'

'C-c-c-cass,' I corrected.

He gave that shrug and blank look that would become a teenage 'whatever.' 'Dass, I got fish fingers.'

'So you have,' I agreed.

'I eating them.'

'Keep going,' Inga said. 'He doesn't actually like them,' she added, 'but the girls do, so he has to have them too.'

I sat down at the table beside Charlie, and picked up one of his chips. 'How about one of these?'

'I not,' Charlie said. He pushed his golden curls back with both hands, leaving a smear of Ruskoline down one cheek, and went back to playing engines with the head of his fish finger.

I ate the chip myself and looked around the kitchen. It was a strange environment to me, with the shelves of china dishes marching up the walls, and the wide windows framing the voe. It was spacious and tall, and yet so cluttered too: Charlie's plastic tractor parked in a jumble of badminton racquets and roller-blades, a litter of blocks spread in front of the pale wood units. Tilt this five degrees and the bowls and mugs would cascade from their shelves to smash on the floor, the copper-edged pans on their rack would become missiles. I was used to a world

100

that was permanently tied down for action.

'So,' Inga said, 'what's doing with you? Where were you off to yesterday afternoon? I wondered what you were up to when I saw the chopper going over, but as it was sweeping the hill I knew it couldn't be you they'd lost.'

'No,' I said, 'it was folk from the marina.'

'I know,' Inga said. 'It was on Radio Shetland.'

It would have been.

'They turned up, though?' Inga added. She jerked her chin at the rocky walls of the marina, with the masts rising above them. 'The mast's gone.'

'The boat went out last night,' I said. You can't fool someone you went to school with. She gave me a quick look. 'I suppose it was them,' I said, 'but it was all a bit odd. Never mind that, though. I wanted to consult you about a kitten.'

'A kitten,' Inga repeated.

'You know, a really little one,' I said. I glanced across at her cat, a football of black and ginger fur that was curled up by the radiator, ignoring the chaos around it. 'Well, hand-sized. It can eat by itself, but it's got a touch of diarrhoea, and I wondered if it was too wee for fish and mince. Should I be feeding it milk, from a bottle?'

'Are its eyes open?'

'Yes.'

'Colour?'

'Still that opaque blue colour.'

Inga gave me that 'what are you *doing*' look. 'Under six weeks, and you're feeding it mackerel? At least I assume it's mackerel.'

'It was,' I admitted.

'A little white fish,' she said, 'and mince should be okay, but not oily stuff. You can get special kitten food, but don't give it milk, that would be really bad for it,

101

unless the Co-op has suddenly started taking in goat's milk, or soya, that might be fine.'

'Kitten food,' I repeated. 'I'll try for that, and hope Rat doesn't eat it all.'

Charlie suddenly included us under his radar. 'I want to see ditten.'

'It's too little,' I told him. I'd seen the way he handled his teddy.

'You'd have to be very gentle,' Inga warned him. 'You'd have to stroke it with one finger. Like you do with Rat.'

Charlie stuck an orange finger in the air. 'One.'

'What's Rat saying to it?' Inga asked.

'Adopted it, thank goodness. I left the pair of them curled up asleep together, all peaceful and domestic.'

'You and Anders are getting more and more settled.' Inga gave me a sideways look. 'You'll be a couple yet.'

Settled ... 'Heaven forbid.'

Inga laughed, swapped Charlie's plate for a yoghurt tube, and took the plate to the sink, then turned. 'Oh, I knew there was something I was wanting to speak to you about. How are you off for cash? Would you want a part-time job?'

'Yes,' I said.

Inga gave me a dubious look. 'It's cleaning work.'

'I can clean,' I said. 'You haven't seen the brasswork on a tall ship.'

'Cleaning *houses*,' Inga emphasised. 'Well, one house, Barbara Nicolson's, Barbara o' the Trowie Mound. Do you mind Brian Nicolson, who was at the school the same time as us, lived way out the back of beyond, off the Mangaster road? She's his mother. She's wanting a bit of a hand around the house, and I thought of you.'

'I mind Brian fine,' I said. I remembered the empty

cottage that hadn't been empty after all. 'He was the one that said he'd found skulls in the trowie mound.'

Inga began to laugh. 'Oh, yes, I mind that! Him and Olaf, trying to scare us with their talk. I bet it was a sheep's skull all along. They never took it out of the carrier bag to let us look properly.'

'What happened to Brian?' I asked. 'Is he living at the back of beyond house – what was its name?'

'Staneygarth. Brian trained as an electrician, then went off south, working for some security firm, you know, guarding houses, stately homes, that kind of thing. His wife goes to your kirk, you likely ken her. What's her name again? She doesn't mix much with us Magnies, when they're here. Blonde, with a permatan, like a football WAG.'

It didn't ring any bells. I cast a mental eye back over the pews around me of a Sunday, but couldn't envisage anyone of that description.

'Cerys,' Inga said suddenly. 'That's her name. She was pals with Kirsten that's married to Olaf, she's one of yours too, and they used to go on double dates. You must ken Kirsten, she's a regular. Dark hair and green eyes, and she wears dresses.'

'Oh,' I said. 'Yes, I know who she is –' and with the image came memory, the two women coming up for communion together, the smooth dark head and the sleek fair. They'd been just ahead of me. The fair woman had taken communion on her tongue, and shaken her head at the chalice, and the dark woman had her arms crossed in front of her, for a blessing only.

'You don't see Brian down at the marina?' Inga asked. 'He's got a motorboat, used to be his father's.'

'Oh, which boat?' I asked.

Inga rolled her eyes. 'I have a vague impression it's an old dark-blue one, on the middle pontoon.'

I thought through the pontoon and ID'd it without difficulty. 'Old, but it's not a bad boat, sea-going. He's had it out several times in the last couple of weeks. I didn't particularly notice him, though. Does he still live at the back of beyond place?'

'He lives south, I told you that. He only comes home for the holidays, and to help his mum out with the sheep.'

'Well, does she live at the back of beyond?'

'She lives,' Inga said, with emphasis, as if I was Peerie Charlie, 'up in Toytown, one of the council houses. She's the last one after the garage, looking up at Voxter voe there. I can't remember the number. I don't ken whether Brian and his wife stay with her when they're up, or if they go out to Staneygarth. I wouldn't think it. The wife, Cerys, doesn't look the three miles to the road end type.'

Someone had been in the house, though. I remembered that furtive flash from a pair of binoculars. 'I'm not sure I'd know him now,' I said.

'Naa, Brian's no' changed,' Inga said. 'Tell you, go to the rifle range at the Voe show. That's his yearly task while he's up here, he's in charge o' that.'

The rifle range. Shots up at the trowie mound – I felt as though I was doing a jigsaw, finding pieces that were starting to fit together. I'd need to phone Gavin again – no, a text would do for this. I didn't want to look as if I was chasing him.

'Anyway –' Inga finished, tacking abruptly, 'it's his mother that's looking for a cleaner, four hours a week, in two hour blocks. Are you interested?'

'Yes,' I said.

Inga crossed to the phone and picked up the Shetland directory. 'I just hope she bothered to fill in the postcard – yes, here she is. Toytown.' She dialled and leaned back against the wall. 'Barbara? This is Inga o' Cruister here. Are you found someen to give you a hand about the house yet?'

There was a prolonged squawking from the phone. Inga made a face at me over it and cut in smoothly. 'I hae someen here, my pal Cass, you ken her, Cass o' Finister, Dermot Lynch's lass. She was wanting a part-time job – yea, her that lives on the boat in the marina.' There was more squawking, and Inga mouthed at me, 'Wi' the young Norwegian wi' the rat.' She returned to normal volume. 'No, she'll no' bring the rat with her. Why not give her a try this week, and if you're no' suited she'll no' take offence.' She steamrolled the next bit of squawking with the ease of practice; her mother-in-law was easily the fastest talker in Brae, against stiff competition. 'Tell you what, I'll send her along now, and you can see when would suit for her to come. She'll be with you in ten minutes. Bye.'

She put the phone back and rolled her dark eyes. 'It's the last house on the second road. Good luck.'

'Thanks,' I said, and headed off.

Chapter Ten

Inga hadn't added the ominous words, 'You can't miss it –
' but the house was easy to find. I headed left along the
main road, past the Co-op, forked left at the Citroen
garage, and found the little houses of Toytown spread
along my right, grey harled and uniform. They'd been built
for oil workers, then turned to local housing when the
construction phase was over. Now, walking among them, I
could see how each had been individualised: a hanging
basket of neon-pink petunias in the pokey grey entrance, a
front door gleaming aqua, a child's sandpit in the centre of
a postage-stamp lawn.

Barbara's was, as Inga had said, the last of them, facing
out towards the toe-end of Sullom Voe on my right. You
couldn't see the terminal from here, the hill behind Voxter
House was in the way, but there were the first indications
of its presence in the two boom ends that would be used to
protect the seaweed-fringed shore in the event of a spill.
The sea between them glinted dull blue.

This house remained just as it had been built: plain grey
walls and a white concrete overhang jutting out from the L
of wall, with the front door underneath and the shed door
opposite. The shed door was battleship grey; the house
door was half glass, half dark-brown wood, with a bell-
push in the centre. All the windows I could see were
shrouded with net curtain, the heavier sort, with a
knobbled pattern in the centre, and a lacy fringe. This one
was of a little girl holding a watering can; the kitchen had
a sunflower, and the bathroom a design of sailing boats

that would have turned turtle instantly if anyone had been unwise enough to put them anywhere near water. Myself, I'd have torn the lot down and let the sea-clear sunshine in.

I was just lifting my hand to the bell when the door was pounced open from the inside, and Barbara stood there, looking at me. She was a little, thin woman with beady eyes like a shore wading bird, darting at me, a glance at my bare feet in flip-flops, away to the voe, another glance at my plaited hair, a look up at the sky, a glance at my red cotton-knit shore-going jersey. Each glance took less than a second, but I was left with the impression that not much escaped her. By the end of the ten seconds I'd stood on the doorstep, I reckoned she could have given an exact description of me to anyone who cared to ask for it.

My first impressions weren't encouraging. I remembered her as being an older mother than my glamorous Maman; she would be in her sixties now. Her hair was its natural iron-grey, clipped short; her mouth was a thin, disapproving line below those gimlet eyes. She wore a traditional yoke jumper and one of those square tweed skirts, not quite long enough to hide the elasticated tops of her tights-look socks, and grey plastic court shoes.

'Come in then,' she said at last. 'Come in through.'

The porch was a metre square, with a ledge for the post, although the postie'd have to wedge any letters in between pots of flourishing busy lizzies. I wiped my flip-flops on the 'Welcome' mat, and followed her into the house. The hall was a space at the stair-foot. One wall was solid with coats, including a batik creation in black and white which I presumed was the WAG wife's. The door on my right was the kitchen, a quarter of the size of Inga's, and if tilting Inga's would have created a mess, tilting this one would be a catastrophe. Every inch of every surface had stuff on it. The table was piled high at one end with letters and magazines, the work-surfaces had disappeared under bowls of fruit and jars of pasta, and the walls were covered entirely with pictures, or little shelves of dinky china ornaments. I realised, gloomily, why she needed help with keeping it clean.

She showed me into the sitting room opposite. 'Would you take a cup of tea?'

'Yes, please,' I said, and she bustled off to clank kettles around. I sat back against the sandpaper-harsh velour and contemplated my doom. A square, black stove squatted on the hearth, radiating dust on all the plethora of knick-knacks around it: a big china carthorse pulling a wicker dray, an ornate vase with a small forest of artificial flowers in toilet-paper peach, a tabletop's worth of photos in curlicued frames. This window too had net curtains, with a natty border of dahlias, and their curved-up centre was filled with more pot plants, African violets this time, interspersed with little ceramic bowls of dead-looking cactus, the sort with spindly spider arms. It was the sort of house that reminded me why I kept living afloat. Just keeping this place free of dust would take a couple of hours a day, let alone cleaning – and it was clear from the gleam on the brass fire-irons and the glass of the innumerable pictures that a high standard of cleaning was expected.

Above all, I noticed the smell of enclosed air, thick with that pot-pourri made of over-flavoured, over-coloured bark slices. The window opened inwards, against the African violets and cactus, and it didn't need the classic spider web, if any spider had dared to be so presumptuous, to tell me it hadn't been opened in a decade.

I was just about to rise and look at the pictures when there was a step at the door, and the WAG strode into the room on spindly heeled sandals. She was the woman I'd remembered from Mass: a good foot taller than me, with what seemed yards of smoothly tanned legs below a short, flower-patterned dress – or perhaps it was a long top. I hadn't quite made sense of this summer's fashions.

Sunglasses hitched her sleek, blonde hair back. Her arms, legs, and face were a uniform sapele-wood brown. There was a bloom of powder and blusher overlaying the tan on her cheek. She looked so artificial that I couldn't tell what age she might be, but guessed early thirties. She moved with a suppressed irritation that didn't surprise me at all; I could see this mother-in-law and daughter-in-law not getting on.

'Oh,' she said, looking me over, and dismissing any pretensions I had to looks or fashion sense, 'not more interruptions.'

'This,' said Barbara, coming in behind her and banging her tea-tray down smartly on top of the latest *Shetland Life* and *iiShetland* on the coffee table, 'is the lass who's coming to give me a hand with the house. Cass Lynch o' Finister – you ken, the house very nearly at the end of the Muckle Roe road.' She busied herself with pouring the tea, her every movement so brisk and determined that I wondered why she needed a hand; perhaps she was having bother with her heart, or just wanted more time to go to swimming classes, or arrange flowers, or do charity work.

She took the thought out of my head. 'No' that I'm needing help in the house, you understand, but I'm that busy with organising the charity shop rota and the work I'm doing in Lerwick just now that I don't have the time, so Brian said, "Well, Mam, why don't you see if you can get a girl in to give you a hand?" He's a very good son to me.'

The WAG – what had Inga called her, Cerys? – let out an irritated breath. 'Do you take milk, Cass?' She had a flat, bored-sounding voice, with a Liverpool accent.

'No, thank you,' I said. It was only since I'd been living at Brae that there'd been in-date milk aboard *Khalida.* She made a grimace, presumably at the strength of the tea, as she passed it over.

'Now then,' Barbara said, sitting down in one of the two armchairs set square on to the TV, 'what experience have you of cleaning?'

'Only on ships,' I said, 'but I'm a quick learner, and I know how to follow instructions.'

She gave a dry cackle of laughter. 'Well, that's something these days. Those girls in the Co-op, well, I don't think some of them have anything in their heads beyond painting their faces –' a sideways glance at Cerys – 'and as for following instructions, well, I don't think any of them could remember an instruction long enough to obey it.' She had one of those thin, aggrieved voices like a saw working through wire. 'I don't ken what the world's coming to. Too busy talking to their pals on the phone to serve you, half the time. I'm telling you, if I get one like that I just put the goods on the counter and walk out of the shop.'

'And the police officers are getting younger,' Cerys said, with a malicious sideways glint of her eyes under the thick mascara.

Barbara rose straight to that one. 'Policeman! I'm telling you, if that blonde Peterson lass so much as puts a foot back on my path I'll be straight on the phone to Lerwick.'

I'd met Sergeant Peterson over the film murder. She'd made me think of a mermaid, with long pale hair tied in a pony-tail, and ice-green eyes that looked detachedly at the follies of humankind. I wondered what she'd been doing that had annoyed Barbara so much.

Cerys shrugged and added fuel to the flames. 'She was just doing her duty.'

Barbara snorted. 'Duty! I'll duty her. I remember her in her pram, and if her late mother could have seen her coming in here and asking about what my Brian was doing, well, she'd have got the makkin belt out faster than my lady could run, I'll tell you that.'

The Shetland makkin belt was a leather belt with a padded section, for sticking the ends of the knitting needles in, and it was the motherly weapon of choice in the days when you were allowed to hit children. Every Shetland housewife wore one, for idle moments when she might take up her knitting, and the faster shots could get it off the waist and across the back of a recalcitrant child's legs in under five seconds. It'd gone out of fashion with mothers by the time I was growing up, of course, but everyone else's granny was still a dead shot with it in a case of suspected misbehaviour. My schoolmates envied me my French and Irish grannies.

And why, I wondered, was Sergeant Peterson chasing up Brian? I couldn't ask, and Barbara was back on track again. 'Seven pounds an hour, if we're suited, and two hours twice a week.'

Twenty-eight pounds, for just four hours' work. I could live on thirty pounds, just, although I could see it was going to be hard-earned. I agreed to that one, and we settled hours: Tuesday and Friday evenings, seven till nine, which left my days free for sailing.

'And that rat doesn't come in the house,' Barbara stated. Cerys jerked her blonde-streaked head up.

'What rat?'

'It's my shipmate's rat,' I said. 'Don't worry, I won't bring him here.' I didn't add that Rat was very particular about where he went, and wouldn't have been impressed by this house with neither air nor crumbs.

Cerys was still staring at me. 'You're the girl who lives with Anders, at the marina?'

'We share my boat,' I said clearly.

She didn't like that. I couldn't tell why; I was surprised she'd ever come across Anders, unless she was an undercover intergalactic warrior queen. She rose, twisting

112

the strap of her clumsy leather bag between her fingers. 'How come you're cleaning houses, if you live on a boat?'

There was no point in making up an impassioned spiel about my mission to keep china horses shining. 'Money,' I said simply. 'Do you know Anders, then?'

'No,' she retorted. 'No, how should I? I'd just heard about the rat, that's all.' She turned her back on me, and Barbara rose.

'We'll see you on Friday, then. And if either of us is not suited, well, we'll just say so, and that'll be that, with no hard feelings.'

We shook hands on it, and I edged into the postage-stamp hall. She went before me to open the door. As she was showing me out I asked, very casually, 'Do you ever use the old house, Staneygarth is it?'

I was looking her straight in the face. She took a step back. Her thin-lipped mouth snapped, 'Never! I told that policeman, I've not been there in years!' then set like a trap. Behind her, Cerys made a startled movement, then was still, staring at me, eyes blazing with fury.

'I just wondered,' I said mildly, and made my way to the door. Just before the porch, I stumbled forwards on one of the dozens of rugs scattered round and had to catch at the doorjamb to steady myself, which brought my nose up almost against the line of paintings hanging down the fifteen-centimetre strip of wall between the inner porch door and the bathroom door.

The top two were hideous daubs: a little girl with an oversized grin holding a watering can, and a boy, equally toothy, hiding a bunch of flowers behind his back. The third was different. It had a thick frame of dark wood, with an inner border of what looked like gold leaf, and in the centre was a painting of an old man with a long beard. St Nicholas, I'd have said, but I'd have needed longer to look at it to be sure. His robes were a rich purple-pink, his raised hand ivory-pale. The writing below it was in Cyrillic script.

Now what, I wondered, among this jumble-sale of bric-a-brac, was Barbara Nicolson doing with what looked like a centuries-old Russian icon?

She didn't mind me looking at it, but Cerys had raised a hand to her mouth. I pretended not to see, and walked jauntily down the path, turning at the gate to wave. Barbara waited to make sure I'd closed it properly, then went back inside, clicking the door shut behind her. I vaulted back over the gate and slipped to the door, easing it open to listen.

'How did you ken his name, then?' Barbara asked, tack-sharp. 'Anders, you said his name before she did.'

'Someone spoke about him having a rat.' There was a clicking as she fiddled with the clasp of her bag. 'I can't remember who.'

'Someone at the old cottage, maybe.'

There was a long pause, then Cerys' voice came again, clear and cold. 'If you were to spread lies about me, you'd be forcing Brian to choose between his mother and his wife. Are you sure enough of yourself to do that?'

There was a long silence, then a slammed door. I scarpered, just in time, for I was barely out of the gate when a red pick-up slammed to a halt in front of the house, and Brian jumped out.

If I hadn't been at his mother's house, I'd never have recognised him. He'd been a slim primary bairn who'd grown upwards like a weed through secondary; he'd certainly not had the muscled shoulders and chest of the man confronting me, nor the bandit's moustache. He was a 'black' Shetlander, with the colouring of seamen from the Armada ships known to have been wrecked here: blue-black hair curling crisply around his ears and neck, and a swarthy complexion that took a tan with the first blink of spring sunshine. There was something piratical about him, even in his crofter clothes of boiler suit and yellow wellies, an independent tilt to the head, a sharp look to the brown eyes. I wasn't sure I'd want him as a hand aboard any ship of mine. He'd be brewing trouble.

Furthermore, he looked to be in a furious temper, black brows drawn so hard that they met above his nose, mouth hardened to a thin line. His hand was clenched around something. I couldn't see what – a rectangle of metal. Then he glanced over his shoulder and saw me. There was a flare of surprise, then his face lightened. He smiled, and took three steps towards me. His boiler suit reeked of sheep and Jeyes fluid, but as he moved I got a whiff of wood smoke too, as if he'd been working with a bonfire.

'Hiya, Brian,' I said.

'Hey, cool Cass. Good to see you again. You've had a few adventures since we shared a classroom.'

Since the adventures included Alain's death and last month's shenanigans with the film crew, I suspected he was being malicious. Living south had smoothed some of the Shetland from his voice, but I'd no doubt it returned during the holidays. It was a smooth enough voice to listen to, resonant in his chest.

'So have you, no doubt,' I replied. 'You're working south, aren't you?'

'Yeah, I'm an electrician. So much for old Taity chucking me out of the techy class.'

'Someone said you were working with security systems in stately homes,' I said. *My ship, Cass ...*

He grinned. It made him look more like a pirate than ever. A gold ring glinted in one ear. 'Amazing places. Not right posh stately homes, du kens, more the kind o' houses that's belonged to one laird's family for twa or three hundred years. Just lived in. The kind o' house that money can't buy. They even make me wish I'd listened to more history at the school.' His mouth thinned again. 'Me wife hates them. She likes everything modern.' He cast a dark look at the curtained windows and his hand clenched on the metal rectangle. Then he focused on me again. 'So, Cass, what're you doing here? Never say me midder's roped you in for stewarding her fancy work at the show.'

'Not yet,' I said. 'I heard she was looking for a cleaner.'

His reaction was the same as Inga's. 'Cleaning houses? You're no' lived in a house for ten years.'

'You seen the brass aboard a tall ship?' I retorted.

'I'll warn Mam no' to let you sluice down the kitchen floor.' His hand clenched on the metal object again, then turned it over, and this time I got a chance to see what it was. 'See you, Cass.'

He strode off up the garden path. I turned away and headed for the Co-op.

The object he'd been clutching as if he was about to throw it in someone's face was the rectangular innards of an ordinary, old-fashioned mortice lock.

Chapter Eleven

I struggled against the impulse to phone Gavin with those snippets of information all the way back to the main road. An icon hanging on a wall wasn't enough to link Brian with the missing art works. He could have had a suffragette great aunt who'd gonè to Russia with Dr Inglis's Women's Hospital unit, or (more likely) a great-grandfather who'd been a seaman in the Baltic.

All the same, he was working south, with a security firm, which all linked in a bit too neatly. Who would know better how to circumvent security than the man who installed it? I wondered if the police had worked that one out too, and sent Sergeant Peterson to check it out. If that was the case, there was definitely no need for me to be phoning any other policeman. Stick to your own ship, Cass, where you belong.

And just what was Cerys up to at the old cottage, and how did Anders come into it? I tried to remember what he'd said when I'd mentioned the old cottage, and he'd got so uptight. Something about me being too young – *If you were to spread lies about me,* Cerys had said. The answer was pretty obvious, I supposed, as obvious as Cerys herself – and I rather suspected she'd have to be really obvious to get Anders into bed, unless she'd lured him with promises of an engine. He could do a good line in courtly phrases, but they never came out quite right, and I'd never actually seen him with a girl. We had an amiable relationship going, and I was sorry to think he'd got entangled with someone as fake-looking as Cerys.

But it was none of my business.

I went into the Co-op on the way past. They didn't have kitten food, but I got a piece of haddock for just now, and some stir-fry vegetables for tea. I'd try dropping a line from the inflatable tomorrow, and see if I could get some whitefish instead of the ubiquitous mackerel.

Anders was already on board, sitting back in the cockpit with his feet up and Rat curled around his neck. His skin was pale under the tan, and there was a grease smear down his cheek.

'Hi,' I said. 'Good day?'

He shrugged, making Rat wobble like a dinghy on a swell. 'We had to get the engine out of an old wooden fishing boat, and start installing a new one. It meant a lot of heavy lifting – the hatch was a size too awkward to use the hoist properly.' He looked at the bags I'd swung over the guard rail. 'Is that tea?'

'I got some stuff,' I said.

'Good. I was just wondering if I should be going along to the garage for some meat.'

'Can you wait five minutes?'

He nodded, and I sat down on the opposite side of the rail from him. *Very domesticated*. There was a scrabbling from behind the washboards, and an indignant mew.

'I was unsure that you wanted the kitten to come up into the cockpit yet,' Anders said.

'He has to learn not to fall overboard sometime,' I said. I raised the washboard and Cat swarmed out. I lifted him onto my knee and stroked his bony back. He purred obligingly, but was too interested in this new environment to settle. He whiffled his way around the cockpit floor, poking a paw into each drain, clambered up onto the tiller and swung from it, and finally jumped onto the seats and swarmed his way onto the side deck, to peer with interest down into the dark water.

'Don't try it,' I said, retrieving him, then, to Anders, 'I

have a job. Twenty-eight quid a week, for four hours.'

'That is good. What have you to do?'

'Clean an ornament-infested house,' I said with feeling. Anders laughed. 'The woman who owns it is the woman from the cottage round under the trowie mound,' I added. I was tempted to say something about Cerys, but anything she and Anders might be up to was none of my business, and I hoped I wouldn't be seeing much of her.

He flushed red at the mention of the cottage and went straight into Neanderthal mode. 'I do not think you need to go out to work. I am earning a good wage now.'

I stared at him, aghast. 'But –'

'I have enough to keep us both, if the money you got from the film has run out.'

'It's not that,' I protested. 'I can't have you paying for all our food. That's not fair.'

'I do not think they are the sort of people you should associate with,' Anders said. I could see generations of black-clad Lutheran ancestors lining up at his back. 'They are not good company.'

'I won't be keeping company with Cerys,' I said, forgetting my resolution not to mention her. 'I'll be cleaning her mother-in-law's house.' I jutted my chin at him. 'And I've never lived on anyone else's money, and I'm not starting now.'

'You are going to take money from your father for your college course.'

This was a sore point which I preferred not to think about. 'If I can earn a bit more now, maybe I won't need to.'

Anders sighed. 'Cass, I would rather not explain, but I think you should not go to this woman, and you should definitely not go near that cottage, whoever asks you. It is not a good place.' He shook his head. 'And now I have told you not to, of course you will go.'

'I'm not that stupid,' I said.

'Think of it as a pub you have been warned against, in a strange port,' Anders said.

'Can't you just tell me why not?'

The tide of crimson rose up from his neck again. 'I would rather not. But I wish you would let me use the money I have earned to keep us both.' He shrugged, and retrieved Cat from where he was making his way along the side-deck, then gazed at me, blue eyes earnest. 'Please, Cass.'

I didn't quite get why it mattered so much to him, but I could see that it did. For these three months he'd been my friend, my companion, who rarely asked anything of me. I wished that he wasn't asking this, but I couldn't see how to say no.

'I've said that I'll do it, so I'll have to go for this week, then I'll say I'm just too tired after a day on the water. Will that do?'

He nodded. 'Thank you, Cass.'

We didn't talk of Cerys or the cottage any more. After tea, Anders went off to conduct his next bit of interplanetary war, the green-baize roll of painted figures under his arm. I fed Cat his haddock, then took him and Rat across to the shed to play in a half-rigged Mirror while I messed about with boat repairs. Although the Pico hulls were pretty indestructible, their fixings weren't, and we had several boats whose bow-ring was gone, leaving a small hole for water to ooze into the hollow shell. I took out the bungs at the aft end, and propped the boats up to drain. They sailed badly enough without adding several litres of interior water. I glued in new bow-rings, then began searching for decent bits of rope to use as painters, to replace the tatty string the current painters had become. I was just on my knees fishing out a likely piece from underneath an ancient Wayfarer when a pick-up rumbled down the gravel drive, booming eighties rock for a three-mile radius. Rat and Cat froze, then dived under the folded red sail. The shed darkened, there was a door slam, and I heard footsteps behind me.

It was Olaf Johnston, looming out of the bright evening. As his broad shoulders filled the doorway, the light blanked out, turning him into a dark, menacing shape. I'd always been a bit wary of him at school; he and Brian were too swaggering, too almost-leaving full of themselves. I wriggled out backwards, feeling caught at a disadvantage, and turned to face him as I rose. 'Hi.'

He came closer in to me than I liked, not a hand's length away, and he'd grown taller than I remembered, so that my head barely reached his shoulders, and I had to tilt my head back to look at him. He was looking me up and down like a killer whale eyeing up a plump seal. I wasn't going to give him the satisfaction of making me retreat.

'Noo dan,' he replied in a tone that was on the neutral side of friendly. 'Is this you fixing up the bairns' dinghies?'

'Just a few odd repairs,' I said. I lifted the rope to show him. It was an old halyard, gritty with cement dust from the floor, but sound enough. 'I don't ken what the bairns do to their painters. Use them for chewing gum, I think.'

He smiled at that, a sideways smile which made him look like a Viking planning a raid on a rich monastry. Norman hadn't got his colouring from his dad; Olaf was the traditional Norse-descent variety of Shetland man, tall and broad-shouldered, with a ruddy outdoor complexion and a bushy head of hair coloured somewhere between fair and red. His eyes were the same narrowed grey-green as Norman's, though, and he had the same hooked nose. He reeked of Lynx, and was wearing an all-over Fair Isle like Magnie's, hoops of blue pattern on a white ground. He and

Brian had always worn all-overs to school, in spite of them being well out of fashion by then, and totally impractical in the sauna-heat classrooms, and they'd both spoken the broadest possible dialect. It was part of their hard-crofter image. His jeans looked straight from the wash, and he was wearing black shoes rather than rubber boots or trainers. That was reassuring; he looked more like someone on his way to an evening class or a five-hundred night than someone who was going to give me grief about being mean to his bairns.

He took the rope from me and began coiling it. 'That's a fine piece, should do you several painters. Alex is fairly enjoying the classes.'

'He's a natural,' I said. 'I can't remember you sailing when we were at school, but he's definitely got it in the blood.'

Olaf shook his head. 'Me late father was the one for sailing. I crewed in our Shetland model for a bit, before the class collapsed here at Brae, but I'm no' done much since, just crewing for Peter o' Wast Point. That was a fine race the other night. We thought we'd caught you until you got the spinnaker up.'

'I enjoy working the kite,' I agreed. He handed me the rope back, and I took it out into the evening sunshine, slanting down between the yacht masts and catching the dust on the water lapping at the top of the slip. A boat length was plenty for a painter. I measured it against the nearest Pico; yes, I'd get three from it. All the time I was waiting to hear what Olaf had come about. The silence stretched uneasily out as I laid the rope in a triple line along the tarmac.

He broke it at last. 'I'll tell you what I'm come about. I was wondering if you were free on Saturday, you ken, Voe Show day.'

It was the last thing I'd expected. The local agricultural

show was a big day out, with competitions for every kind of farm and domestic animal, garden flowers and produce, knitting, photography, and craft work, as well as a griddle frying fish and minute steak, and teas, sandwiches, and fancies in the hall. Anders and I were planning to be there, along with everyone else in the show catchment area.

'I was certainly thinking to go,' I said.

'Kirsten's working with the Lifeboat stall,' Olaf said. It took me a moment to remember that Kirsten was his wife, the dark woman who'd refused communion. 'You ken, it's in aid of the Aith Lifeboat, and I thought you might be willing to spell her for a bit, if you were going to be there. It's a long day, she'll have to set the stall up for nine o'clock, so that folk have something to look at while the judging's going on, and then it doesn't close till four in the afternoon. She'd be blyde of a hand, and I thought, well, I was coming down the marina anyway, and it would be worth trying to see if you'd maybe help, with your interest in boats.'

They are not good people for you to associate with. It wasn't done to wonder about other people's sins, but I wondered now why Kirsten had refused communion, yet still gone up for a blessing. What had she on her conscience? Whatever it was, I'd have betted my last anchor rope on Olaf having coerced her into it. *It would have been divorce if she'd no' been religious ...*

'That would be no bother,' I said. 'I don't know if I'd manage the whole day, but I could easy give a hand for a couple of hours. When would she like me there for?'

'Oh, now, I forgot to ask that.' His voice made it a dead give-away. He saw me hearing that, and covered smoothly. 'I'll get her to come down and arrange that – or do you have a mobile?'

'I do,' I said, 'but I can never remember the number offhand.' I wasn't going to give my number to Norman's family. *I ken how you got that scar* – 'I'll be seeing Alex tomorrow. Just tell Kirsten to tell him what time she wants me.'

'That's fine of you,' he said. 'I'll tell Kirsten that.' He indicated the rope I'd laid out with one broad hand. 'Are you going to cut that? I have some whipping twine in the pick-up. I'll gie you a hand.'

'Thanks,' I said.

We settled together on the bench outside the changing rooms. All the time I was conscious of his eyes on me. W hatever he had come to say, it wasn't said yet. I cut the rope in three and swittled it in the sea, so that it smelt of salt rather than of dust, then we whipped the ends. 'It's a few years since we shared a techy bench at the school,' Olaf said.

His tone made me uneasy all over again. We'd never been mates, and we'd never shared a workbench.

'You were a bit older than I was,' I said. 'You were left by the time I got to woodwork stage.' I'd enjoyed technical; it gave me a chance to make bits for the boat. I wouldn't have enjoyed it with Olaf and Brian swaggering about the classroom.

'I mind you fine,' Olaf said. 'Cool Cass, that's what we called you between ourselves, Brian and I.' He gave an abrupt laugh that seemed to have nothing to do with merriment. 'We got Inga screaming wi' that trick wi' the bones from the trowie mound, but no' you. You didna turn a hair.'

'I'd seen plenty of sheep skulls out on the hill,' I said.

He grinned, like a Viking about to throw his favourite enemy to the wolfhounds.

'Well, now, I don't know that I'd say for sure it was human bones. Brian said he'd got them from the trowie mound, right enough, but who's to say whether he did?' The broad-nailed fingers stilled on the piece of rope. 'He was aye a bit odd about that place. When he was peerie it was his secret hide-out. He wasna keen on sharing it wi' me, even. He took me inside just the once, then rustled me out quick, before I had the chance to get a right look.'

'What was it like?' I asked.

He shrugged. 'Joost a space inside a built wall, du kens, no' dat different from inside our lambie hoose. I couldna see the attraction o' it.'

'I expect the archeologists would get all excited about it,' I said.

'I daresay they would,' Olaf said, 'but it's on Brian's land – he owns it, you ken, it's been de-crofted – and he'd never let them lay a finger on it. I mind them trying, oh, twartree years back, when he was home over the summer. That Val Turner and her team were keen to put their noses inside, and he wouldn't have them near the place. He even filled in the tunnel we'd got in – we slid through a gap under one of the big stones, a rabbit hole that went right through.'

The kitten's burrow. I gave a quick look across at the Mirror, where Cat and Rat had oozed out again, and were balancing along a spar playing follow-my-leader.

Olaf changed tack suddenly, sitting up straighter, as if this was what he'd really come about. 'I was vexed to hear Norman had been annoying you wi' the jet-ski. They're all the rage south, you ken. When we were on holiday down aside Brian they were everywhere, and the bairns were just wild to try it, so when we got home I got them one for the voe here.'

'I'm just worried about the safety of it,' I said. 'You ken what bairns are. You can tell them to bide wi' the boat till you're blue in the face, but there's always one who lets go of the sheet, or gets thrown clear, and then you have a head on its own in the water, and it's not always easy to see, especially if you're going at any speed.'

126

'I'm told him he's to keep away from the dinghies in future.'

'Thanks,' I said. I remembered Norman's interest in the motor boat, and thought I'd try a bit of fishing on my own account. 'It's always a problem, with strange boats coming in and out – far too many people seem to have heard of Brae marina, these days. It's been like Piccadilly Circus.' I tried a guileless look. 'Oh, I'm forgetting – that last lot were friends of yours, were they no'?'

The hand winding cord around the cut rope end jerked, then stilled. He gave me a slanted look, like a cormorant on a mussel bouy deciding whether to dive for cover. 'That last lot?'

'The white motorboat, David and Madge,' I said. 'I'm sure Norman said you knew them. They were from … no, I can't remember. The Clyde, maybe?'

'I mind a flash white motorboat,' he said slowly, his hand beginning to make careful loops again, 'but I don't think I saw the folk aboard.' He gave me another quick sideways look. 'Where did we ken them from, did Norman say?'

I shook my head. 'I can't even remember what he said – no, I don't think he said anything specific. He just gave that impression.'

Olaf's face went blank; I could see he was calculating something, but I couldn't tell what. He sat frowning at the piece of rope in his hands for a moment, then the worried parent took over from the prosperous businessman. 'Boys,' he said. 'I ken we were just as bad at their age, but there weren't the same temptations. We went for the drink. Oh, yea, there was drugs around, but it was a soothmoother thing to do, so we paid no heed to it. Nowadays wi' the ideas this internet gives them, they get into –' He broke off at that, then gave me a surprisingly charming smile. 'But you'll ken more about that, being still in the singles scene.

Us old married men don't know the half of it.'

I wasn't going to be smarmed by Olaf Johnson. 'I can't remember the last time I went to a disco,' I said.

'How do you manage, money wise? You'll no' earn much at the boating club here.'

'I manage,' I said. 'I work for my keep, mostly.'

'You should do better for yourself than that. Life's what you make it.' He gave me that considering, predatory look again. 'I could put you in the way of earning.'

I wasn't going to earn anything through Olaf Johnson. 'I'm fine ee now.' I went back to the motorboat, ignoring the voice that said *My ship, Cass* – 'Do you think that boat might be mixed up in drugs, then?'

He shook his head, more in resignation than in rebuttal. 'I do mind the motorboat,' he repeated. 'They arrived fairly late, didn't they, then left again first thing.'

'They didn't bide long,' I agreed. I waited a moment, but he didn't say any more, just looked gloomily out over the ruffled grey water. I tied my last half hitch and stood up. 'That's good, that's three boats we'll be able to tow when the wind dies away without the rope breaking on us.'

'Or when they cowp right over near the shore,' Olaf agreed, 'and break the mast.'

'Heaven forbid,' I said fervently. 'The price of spares for these things …'

He laughed at that, but still in a preoccupied way.

'Thanks for the help,' I said.

'You're very welcome. I'll tell Kirsten to send word with Alex then. See you.' He spun around and swung into his pick-up, slamming the door behind him, and fumbling for his mobile. I could have told him there was no signal right here. The heavy pick-up scattered gravel from its thick tyres as it went up the hill down to the hard standing. I watched it curve round onto the main road and stop again on the verge. His hand went up to his ear.

He could, of course, be phoning Kirsten with the good news that I'd help her out, but I doubted that. I wondered if there was any way that Gavin could trace his calls.

Nowadays wi' the ideas this internet gives them, they get into – He'd broken off there and started talking about the 'singles scene', but I wasn't sure that was really what he'd meant. Norman had been curious about the motor-boat, setting Alex on to ask me questions. I remembered how he'd spoken to me: *I ken how you got that scar.* Was he stupid enough, or confident enough, to try those tactics on international smugglers?

5

**Hit's no' fir da kyunnen's god ta be ower cosh wi'
whitterets.**

*(Old Shetland proverb: It's not to the rabbit's good to be
too friendly with weasels.)*

Chapter Twelve

It was not quite nine o'clock. The sun was still bright on the west-facing hills, but the mist was beginning to creep in, long tendrils that fingered their way over Scallafield, over Grobsness. Even though it was the promise of another good day, I had a sailor's uneasiness with mist. The first ghost of the full moon was silvery over the hills, and the tide was already up to the top of the slip. I rigged the Mirrors for tomorrow, then went up to the bar to yarn a bit, but I couldn't settle. I thought about phoning one or other of my parents, but Dad would be busily wining and dining all his Edinburgh contacts to make sure permission for his firm's proposed wind farm passed smoothly through the Scottish Parliament, and Maman would be in the thick of rehearsals I left a good-luck message on her mobile, then went back to *Khalida*, wriggled into my bunk, and lay on my stomach with my chin pillowed on my arms, thinking.

I knew I was doing the right thing. My parents had tried to get me a good education, and between hurt at Dad leaving me for the Gulf, and stubborn homesickness with Maman in Poitiers, I'd thrown that back at them, and run away to sea. I'd spent the last fourteen years in a hand-to-mouth roving life, making friends with people I'd not see again for two years, ten, never. It was time I settled down, but to get on the promotion ladder at sea these days you needed a commercial ticket. I'd swallowed my pride to ask Dad to fund me through college. After that, I could go to sea again. The course began in September, ended in June. Ten months, and it wouldn't all be in a classroom. There would be hands-on work. I could do ten months. I could still live aboard *Khalida*, only in Shetland's ancient capital of Scalloway, moored right alongside the North Atlantic Fisheries College.

Inside, though, I was howling with protest. I'd be shut in a classroom, on shore, with the hard ground under my feet day after day. I'd not be able to hoist *Khalida*'s sails and just go, footloose Cass. I'd be surrounded by strangers who would look at my scar and wonder, until they found someone who'd tell them the story of how I'd killed my lover out in the Atlantic –

The night was still, but the echo of that baby's wail shuddered in my ear. The selkie wife who'd committed herself to a life ashore, and couldn't keep faith with her promises … I lay as the sky darkened to blue, then grey, and the orange of the street lights blinked on and slanted a thin shadow across the chart table. Cat and Rat did a last mad chase along the starboard fiddles, up to the binoculars holder with a leap and scrabble that did my varnish no good, scampered down the steps that covered the engine, and came up to curl one each side of my neck. Cat went straight to sleep, his lion-sized purr vibrating through his little round belly, but Rat was lightly poised, waiting for Anders to finish his intergalactic war and come home.

He swung lightly aboard at last, barely rocking *Khalida* in her berth, and slid through the forrard hatch. Rat oozed away, leaving a cold airspace. I heard Anders undressing, getting into his sleeping bag, then there was silence again, but I could hear that he wasn't sleeping either. I humped myself out of my berth, like a hermit crab leaving its shell, hauled my jeans on over my night T-shirt, and put the kettle on. If he was sleeping, I wouldn't wake him. If he wanted to talk, he could join me.

The kettle was just starting to boil when he came through, in jeans and a checked workman's shirt, and sat down in his usual corner, fair head against the wooden bulkhead, the planes of his cheekbones lit queerly by the gas flames. 'I can't sleep either,' he said.

I put the mugs of drinking chocolate on the table and sat down opposite him, but facing sideways, across the boat, with my right elbow on the table, my cheek on my hand. 'That boy the other day, Norman …' I said.

His eyes flicked across at me, then away again. '"*I know how you got that scar*,"' he quoted. I could smell the beer on his breath. 'I'd have knocked him down if it would have made him be quiet.'

I turned my face to him. The cabin was in shadow now, lit only by the orange of the streetlights falling slantways through one corner of the long windows; his face was a pale blur. The dimness made it easier to talk. 'Everybody knows the story. It's the first thing they ask, once I'm out of earshot: What on earth did she do to her face?'

'No,' Anders insisted. His voice was loud against the soft creakings of a boat on the water. He repeated it softly. 'No. You must not think of it like that, Cass. They do not say that, truly they do not.' He chuckled. 'I was in my father's yard, remember, when you brought *Khalida* in, that first time. They said, Johan and Lars –' He switched into Norwegian, with Johan's north Trondheim accent, 'Did she really sail that little boat, single-handed, all the way from the Med?' And Lars said – he went into housing estate Bergen – 'she must be mad.'

I took a sip of drinking chocolate and answered in Norwegian: our private language, our language of confidences. 'When did you hear the story?'

I felt him tense. 'I haven't heard it. I don't need to hear it, unless you wish to tell it.' His voice was clumsy in the dark. He went back to the ponderous compliment mode that he had used on me before we'd come to Shetland together, before we'd become friends. 'Beautiful Cass, you don't need to justify anything to me. Don't you think I know you better than that by now?'

'What the boy said was true,' I said. 'I did send him overboard.'

'I'd never have been a sailor if it hadn't been for you,' Anders said. 'Tell me, if you want to.'

I had told the story, re-lived it, with Gavin. It had faded a little since. 'We were crossing the Atlantic, and the boat gybed, and hit him a real whack on the head. I thought he was okay.' I could see him still, swallowing as if he was tasting blood, his face paper-white under the tan. *Don't fuss, Cass* – 'He went for a sleep, and when he got up he was delirious. He thought I was pirates. It was a particular fear of his, that's why he kept the gun on board. He was seeing two of me, and he fired at me. I kicked the helm across, and let the jib fly, and as she tacked, it knocked him overboard. I didn't mean it to do that, but I knew that it might.' The definition of murder was where you did something that could be reasonably supposed to cause death. 'I waited. I searched, but he never surfaced again.'

'When he shot at you,' Anders said, 'when that bullet scored your cheek –' He reached one hand out to me. His fingers were warm on the scar. They moved a few centimetres to touch my forehead. 'If it had been just that to the right, he would have killed you. It would have been you who had died, out in the Atlantic.' He drew the hand back, lifted his mug, drank, and set it down again. Rat sat on his hindquarters to peer into the cup, whiskers twitching. He was fond of chocolate. 'No, Rat,' Anders said. 'I've been thinking about you, Cass. I was thinking that your scar was why you do not want to go to college after all.'

'Partly,' I conceded.

'Would it be easier if your scar was inside?'

I stared at the pale blur of his face. The whites of his eyes glinted silver. 'I don't get you.'

He gestured with one hand. 'Everyone, you see, has

things they have done that they would rather not think about.' It was too dark to see if his fair skin had flushed, but his voice was constricted. 'They try and stamp them down, but the memory thickens, it is still there. Then, when you want a new relationship, the scar is there, but nobody knows it but you, and you have to decide whether to risk telling, or to hope your new friend will not touch it by accident.'

I hadn't thought of it like that. I couldn't escape my past, but if circumstances had been different – if I'd had two smooth, tanned cheeks, if I'd met someone I was serious about – I'd have had to tell them, if only to make sure that the moment would never come when I returned home to someone asking with cold eyes, 'Why did you never tell me you'd killed a man?'

I wanted to look across the table and ask, 'What is your scar?' but it seemed too intrusive. I left the silence, in case he wanted to talk.

His head lifted. He spoke in English. 'I thought –' He went to the forrard hatch in one fluid movement, lifted it, listening, then shook his head and closed it again. 'Magnie's stories are sticking in my brain.'

'The baby, or the trowie fiddler?'

He stretched, showing off his magnificent pectoral muscles, and shaking his head. He took both mugs and pumped water into them, then added the last of the hot water from the kettle. I took the drying cloth. 'Did you win tonight?'

'It is not that easy,' Anders reproved. 'It is like real life. You have to learn skills, and make allies. But we will soon reach the big battle, and then – then, when it is over, I'll have to go back home. There is always a fishing boat going that way.'

'It's going to be strange.' I suddenly imagined *Khalida* without Rat balancing along the fiddles, tail at an angle, without Anders sleeping in the forepeak. 'It felt so odd at first, you being aboard, but it's going to be odder still without you.'

His hand stilled in the act of passing me his mug, the dark blue one, then moved again. He sighed. 'Cass, you are so young.'

'I'm three years older than you,' I retorted, and held out my hand for my own mug.

'Ah, but you did not grow up in Bergen.'

'I don't see what that's got to do with the price of fish.'

'And you will have Cat with you, for company.' He ducked under the bulkhead towards his bunk. 'Komme, Rotte. Goodnight, Cass.'

Friday 3 August
Tide times for Brae:
Low Water 04.22   *0.2m*
High Water 10.49   *2.1m*
Low Water 16.32   *0.5m*
High Water 22.53   *2.3m*
Moon full

I woke to a greyer morning, with the wide sky covered
with mottled clouds. Anders hauled on his overalls,
deliberately brisk, and headed for work. I was just
brushing my teeth in the cockpit before going to get the
rescue boat when a red Bolt's hire car turned into the club,
scrunched down the gravel, and drove along to the marina
gate nearest us. It parked there, and Gavin got out.

I nearly choked on my mouthful of toothpaste. I spat it
over the side, laid the brush down on the teak seat, and
went forward to let him in. He stood there, watching me
walk towards him, and the pontoon had never seemed so
long. I felt like a fish being reeled in, dragged inexorably
from the familiar green depths of ocean towards the
dangerous air.

He looked as I remembered him. Even at this distance I
could see the alertness of him, the way he stood like an
sea-eagle in its eyrie, stone-still, seeing everything around
him. It was the first thing I'd noticed about him. He wore
his green kilt and a plain leather sporran, for use, not for
show, and a grey-gold jumper with a round neck: good
working clothes, like a crofter about to walk the fences,
but not expecting to do anything dirty. As I came forward
he reached into the car and brought out black rubber boots
and an olive-green oilskin jacket.

I came up the sloped gangway to the gate. He was a

metre back from the meshed gate, not crowding me as I opened it. Our eyes met while the diamonds of wire were still between us, and suddenly it was all right. The first time I'd seen him, I been shocked by seeing his eyes the shape and colour of Alain's, but now they were his own, sea-grey, fringed by dark lashes, smiling at me. The wind ruffled his dark-red hair, cut just short enough to try and get rid of the curl.

'Hi,' I said. My voice sounded too casual. He'd told me it gave me away. I tried for a natural tone. 'I didn't expect to see you so soon.'

'I had three days of holiday to take.' He clanged the door shut behind him. 'Any chance you could run me out to where the yacht's light went out?'

'I've got a gaggle of bairns coming to go sailing in fifteen minutes, but we could easily take them out that way.' I gave him a sideways look. 'Any particular reason?'

'I'm riding a hunch.'

'It'll take most of the morning. I can't leave them to put you back, once they're out.'

'It's a bonny day to be out on the water.'

'Okay. D'you want to start up the RIB?' I nodded at the grey rubber rescue boat. 'I'll just get my fleece and life-jackets.'

'An initiative test,' he agreed. I'd only just reached *Khalida* when I heard the RIB's engine roar out, then throttle back. I grinned to myself, flung on my fleece, and returned, life-jackets in hand. He was busy undoing the ropes.

'D'you want to steer?' I asked. I passed him the spare life-jacket.

'On you go. You're the instructor here.'

'While you've only had thirty years of messing about in boats.'

'Thirty-four,' he corrected. 'According to Kenny, whose memory is better than mine, our mother used to use the boat as a play-pen.'

'I never had a chance to phone Kenny. I couldn't think of an excuse.'

'Any old message would have done.'

'Oh, no, I did think of an excuse. It's maybe nothing, though.' I bumped the rubber side of the RIB against the pontoon and reached over the side for a ring to tie to. 'It was this icon –' I told him, rapidly, about the Russian St Nicolas.

'Interesting,' he agreed, 'but I think you're right, the seaman grandfather is more likely. The security firm thing is interesting too, but I'm sure Wearmouth's team would have picked up on something as obvious as all the burgled houses having used the same security firm.'

There was the sound of tyres scattering the gravel above us. Magnie's ancient mustard-coloured Fiesta swerved round the corner and slid down the drive to the hard standing just as we reached the dinghy slip above the pontoon. He abandoned it by the caravan utilities cage and came over. He was dressed for going on the water: yellow rubber boots, jeans, an ancient grey jersey, and his council issue oilskin jacket.'Now then, Cass.' His eyes narrowed as he recognised Gavin. 'Now.'

'You remember Gavin Macrae, don't you?' I said.

'I don't mind us actually meeting,' Magnie said, aimiably enough. 'What're we done now?'

'It's Cass's missing yacht,' Gavin said. 'She's got me intrigued.'

'Ye, that was an odd thing, right enough,' Magnie said. He turned to me. 'Olaf o' Scarvataing wasn't giving you grief yesterday, was he? I saw his car as I came along the road, but I hadn't time to stop.'

'He was being helpful,' I said. 'Our problem parent,' I

added to Gavin. 'Norman's to keep away from the dinghies, and he whipped a couple of painters for me.'

'There'll be something in it for him,' Magnie said darkly. 'He's no' one to be helpful when he doesn't get an advantage from it.'

'I said I'd help Kirsten out with the lifeboat stall at Voe Show.'

Magnie shook his head. 'He'd no' be bothered about that. He's like the old fishermen, get the wife to take the kist on her back all the way to Lerwick, while he swaggered along beside her.'

'A kist?' I repeated. 'Do you mean the old-fashioned seaman's chest?'

Magnie nodded, grinning. 'Great, heavy things they were.'

'Aye,' Gavin said. 'I mind that was the way in the western isles, as well.'

Now I had two of them baiting me. 'Are you seriously telling me the wives carried them for their husbands, all the way to Lerwick?'

'They carried the husbands too, if there was a burn to ford,' Gavin said. 'To keep their feet dry, for them going to sea.'

'Piggy-back, I suppose,' I retorted.

'I suppose so too,' Gavin said gravely.

'I mind seeing it happen, as a bairn,' Magnie added.

I gave him an old-fashioned look. 'Come off it, Magnie. In the 1950s?'

'Well, maybe no',' he conceded. 'But my faider used to speak of it.' He and Gavin exchanged a look over my head. *Men.* And if Magnie was going to take to match-making, he could just mind his own business.

'Gavin wants a look at where I last saw the Rustler,' I said, 'so we'll take the bairns up that way.'

141

I turned to look down the voe. The wind was still from the south, gusting up to 3, making pronounced waves with white-fretted tops. It was a beautiful sailing day, with enough wind to be fun, yet not so much that they'd have trouble with the spinnakers. The sky would clear; already the mottled clouds were separating out to show the blue behind them. The sheep had got over their panic and were spread out again, white, rust, brown, black dots moving against the dark green heather or lime-green moss patches. It was two hours yet to high tide. The water rippled up the boatclub slip, each new wave pushing a hairsbreadth further.

'They can get the spinnakers out again. It's a touch more of a dead run than it was, but they can't knock themselves out with the boom in this.'

'Never say "can't",' Magnie said. We looked up as we heard the roar of a quad coming along the road. 'That boy could damage himself in a flat calm.'

The quad swerved into the boating club drive at the last minute, in a splatter of gravel. I was surprised not to see a pillion-rider, then I realised it was Alex himself driving, even though he had to be well short of the legal fourteen.

'Are you supposed to be driving that thing on the roads?' I asked, as he sauntered over. Given my own record of illegal driving over the summer, I didn't dare look at Gavin.

'Dad said I could take it,' he said. 'Norman wasn't around to run me, he'd gone off somewye. Dad wasn't very pleased with him.'

'Mirrors again,' I said. 'Let's see how well you remember hoisting the mainsail.'

'Where are we going today?'

'Along to Weathersta.'

His eyes lit up. 'Cool! Did you know it's haunted? There's a baby that cries and cries, because its mother

murdered it.' He put a gruesome emphasis on *murdered*.
'She wasn't married, and she killed it by hitting it with a
stick until it died, but it screamed and screamed, and the
neighbours heard and came and arrested her.'

Yuck! I preferred Magnie's selkie wife who found her
skin again, and couldn't help herself. Alex took my silence
for disbelief. 'It's true,' he insisted. His lavender-blue eyes
went round and solemn. 'See, I was over playing with
Robbie last night, he lives just at the back of the point, and
we were messing about on the shore. We heard it, clear as
clear, crying.'

'What time was this?'

He went pink, deliberated within himself for a moment,
then decided I wasn't a parent, so would be safe to tell.
'Well, see, we should've been in bed, but – well, we'd
been to bed, and then I'd climbed out of my window and
he'd sneaked out of his back door, and we met up. It was
the middle of the night.'

'What colour was the sky behind this hill?' I asked,
pointing eastwards. 'Black, or grey, or dim blue, or first-
light blue?'

He frowned, visualising. 'Dim blue.'

That meant it had been between one and two in the
morning. I could feel Gavin's intent silence behind me.
'Did you see any boats about?'

He shrugged. 'But we heard the baby crying, Cass,
really we did. Do you suppose, if you saw it, it would be
all covered in blood, with a muckle gash in its head, like
the dead people in *The Sixth Sense*?'

I didn't have the heart to spoil his fantasies. 'I suppose
it might be.'

'But then,' Alex said, 'maybe it's like those light
things, you know, Magnie's stories, the closer you get,
then it moves. Because when we heard it, we crept over
the hill and towards the beach straight away, but then it

sounded like it came from the island, Linga.'

'There were lights up at the trowie mound dastreen,' Magnie said. He gave me a sideways look, to see how seriously I'd take him. 'Likely another trowie wedding. They minded me o' the old Lea lights, in Aith – do you ken that story? The house called the Lea, well, it had earth lights apo the hill. We used to stop on the way home from dances to watch them. It was a regular thing. They'd just move up the hill, for all the world like someen walking up carrying a lantern. You could only see them from far off, though. The old man that lived there, he never saw them.'

'Lights?' I said. 'Alex, you'll notice what you've done wrong with that tiller the first time you try to tack.'

'Oh, yeah,' he said, and got the helm out over the traveller instead of tangled under it.

'Moving up and down the hill ida mirkening,' Magnie said. 'I couldn't sleep, so instead o' taking them tablets, I went for a walk up over the hill.' He slanted a quick, intelligent look at Gavin. He wasn't going to help the police, exactly, but he didn't mind passing on information he thought they should know. 'I could see them clear as clear.'

Gavin looked at me. 'The trowie mound, that's the cairn your sailors were going to?'

I nodded. I wondered, I wondered very much, if the inside of the trowie mound might be a good place to store things. Reasonably small, portable things, like paintings, well wrapped up against the damp, and little statues. I'd been concentrating on the cottage, but now I came to think of it, that wasn't such a good hiding place. It was too accessible by land. All you needed for the loot to be discovered was a group of young boys daring each other to break in via a window, or a tramp looking for shelter. The trowie mound, by contrast, was an enclosed space with no obvious break-in points, and it was a stiff climb up the hill, to deter the casual passer-by. To retrieve your hidden objects, all you had to do was moor to the bouy at the cottage and go up the hill. To keep them safe, all you had to do was keep the nosy archeologists away. What had Olaf said? *That Val Turner and her team were keen to put their noses inside, and he wouldn't have them near the place.* You didn't even need to be seen, if you had a fast boat and plenty of fuel. You could arrive at the bouy from Norway, from Faroe, from Iceland, pick up your cargo, and be away again.

Gavin was watching me. He said, 'My ship, Cass. You focus on your bairns.'

Chapter Thirteen

I focused, gathering them around me for the usual briefing at the whiteboard in the shed: where the wind was coming from, what the tide was doing, how would that affect getting out of the marina, knowing when to tack going upwind. There was the usual confused flurry as they trundled boats to the pontoon and set off, then once the last set of red sails had made it past the wind-shadow of the marina entrance, we led them up the voe. We started towards Busta, went around one of the mooring buoys there, zig-zagged back towards Weathersta, across to Muckle Roe, and back to the near corner of Linga. I steered, Gavin sat upright on the port side, looking forward, hair lifting in the wind, and Magnie settled comfortably on starboard, booted feet stretched across the boat.

We dropped the anchor just off the north end of Linga. I cut our engine, then turned side-saddle on the padded seat. A hundred yards behind us, Alex had his boat nicely balanced, but all the others were either sailing too close to the wind, or miles off it. I leaned over the side of the rescue boat and let the wind carry my voice back to them.

'Kevin, Ali, you're both pinching. Come off the wind a touch.' They obeyed; I did a thumbs-up. 'Cheryl, you could go closer.' She looked blankly at me. 'Push the helm away a bit,' I said, then, as she did the opposite, 'no, the other way. Away from you.' I gave her a thumbs-up too and leaned back. 'Wouldn't you think,' I said, 'that push it away from you would be a simple instruction?'

'You should use the approved touchy-feely phrasing,'

Magnie said. 'What do they say we should call the helm, the "steering stick"?'

'Creator Lord,' Gavin said devoutly. 'What do you call the sail?'

'I've heard it called the flappy thing,' I said. I was pleased to see Gavin shuddered. 'I won't do it. Children can learn six new words a day. How can they possibly work their way up to a tall ship if they're talking about steering sticks and flappy things? Peerie Charlie's not three yet, and he could name his way right round *Khalida*.'

Peace descended, temporarily. The water tricked around the stones of the shore; a tirrick dropped into the sea and came back up with a fish glinting in its beak. 'I should have brought a flask,' Magnie said.

'What amazes me,' Gavin said, leaning an elbow against the grey rubber side and looking back at Brae, 'is the prosperity here. All that you've done with your oil money – you've got employment, the best of social care, that school and leisure centre – and the roads! When I compare it to the Highlands, I can't believe they're both Scotland.'

'That's a matter of debate,' said Magnie.

I intervened hastily, before we could get into the rights and wrongs of Scotland retaining this former Norwegian archipelago. 'What are the Highlands like, then?'

Gavin's grey eyes, long-lashed and clear as the sea on a winter morning, dimmed like a cloud going over. 'Tourist country. That's all there is. There's nothing for locals, none of these centres, and the roads are worse than you have to the most remote cottage. And your young folk stay here – ours can't. The land could be worked, but the minute a house comes up for sale the big letting agencies buy it up for a price no local could ever raise, and there's another holiday cottage.' His eyes sparked. 'Don't get me started. Do you know how much of Scotland is owned abroad?' His chin went up. 'But the first Act our new Parliament passed was the buy-out act, and I was over in Assynt, no' long ago, they were the first crofters to buy the laird out. Now they've got plans – jobs, houses for local folk, making the moor productive again, and no' just with wind turbines either. They're going to get our way of life back.'

He stopped abruptly, as if this was getting too personal, but I was left wanting to ask more. The wind stirred the kilt on his brown knees, fluttered the little ribbon on each sock, just visible above the green wellingtons. He turned his head and shielded his eyes from the sun with one hand. 'And where did your boat's lights go out, do you think?'

'I tried to look and see,' I said, 'but it's hard to be sure. She could just have gone behind that headland there, on her way to the open sea.'

'Think to before you assumed that. Where did you think she was as she was meeting the motorboat?'

'Here,' I said. I jerked my chin towards the circular expanse of water between Linga, the voe of Grobsness, the island of Papa Little, and this side of Muckle Roe. 'Cole Deep.'

'How deep is deep?'

'*Khalida*'s echo sounder goes off its scale. Over 90 metres.'

Gavin gave the water a sweeping, speculative look. '90 metres. And being this close inshore, nobody'd have nets down. How about darrows?'

He meant a long hand-line with half a dozen hooks at the end; it was a Norse word, *dorrow*. The west coast Scots were descended from Vikings too.

Magnie shook his head. 'Nae fish to catch in here. You'd go out into the Rona for that.' He was watching Gavin with sceptical interest, as though he was a seaside pier conjurer about to produce a rabbit.

'So this island, Linga, or that other one – Papa Little, is it? – would be the nearest land?'

'I suppose so,' I agreed.

Gavin fished out a pair of hand-sized binoculars, the old-fashioned sort with brass rims and brown leather around them. They looked like they'd belonged to his grandfather. *A farm at the head of the loch* – the spy-glasses conjured it up, a stone-built building at least a century old, with faded curtains, well-worn carpets and three generations' worth of jackets, caps, and walking-sticks in the hall; a comfortable house where you'd feel at home. He turned his head and gave me a rueful smile. 'I told you, I'm riding a hunch here.'

The first Mirror was approaching us. It tacked with a rattle of sails and halted using the simple method of ramming the rescue boat. Magnie fended it off and held it while Alex and Robbie sorted themselves out.

'We were first by miles,' Alex said.

'That was because you weren't pinching,' I said, 'and you remembered about trim. Well done. Wait for the others, then you can race back, gybing around the bouy off Busta.'

'The one we came round?'

'Any of them,' I said.

I went back to watching the approaching Mirrors, ignoring an altercation in the one behind me. Alex had some ploy on that he wanted Robbie to join in, but Robbie was still in trouble after last night's exploit. The next-door neighbour had been out checking sheep, and seen the pair of them, and he'd told Robbie's mum, who'd grounded him for a week. After five minutes the second Mirror thumped against us, quickly followed by the next two and finally the fifth.

'Okay, guys,' I said. 'Now you're going to race back, and the race ends at the pontoon, with the boat tied head to wind, and the crew ashore.' I went quickly through spinnaker drill with them, checked they were all set to operate the various bits of kit required, then set them off with the one who'd come last going first, and Alex kept until last, in spite of his protests. After five minutes of flapping and shouting, all the spinnakers were up and we had peace again.

Gavin lowered his glasses and shook his head. 'Maybe I was wrong.' He gave me a sideways grin. 'Now I'm going to feel really stupid.' He stood up in the boat and cupped his hands around his mouth. 'Puss, puss, puss. Puss, puss, puss.'

The call echoed off the rocky beach and around the water, then died into silence. Gavin shrugged, and sat down, but his hands were tense on the binoculars, and his eyes still roving the island.

'Here, what's that?' Magnie said. His head tilted, listening. For a moment, I thought it was a seagull, then I realised it was what we'd heard last night, that thin, wailing cry of a baby. A tingle crept down my spine. It was coming from the island, just as Alex had said.

'We heard it last night, and thought it was your ghost baby,' I said. 'It must have been a seagull after all.'

Gavin lifted his binoculars again. He scanned the island, then gave a grunt of satisfaction. 'Got him.'

'That's no seagull, lass,' Magnie said. He turned his whole body, his yellow jacket creaking. 'I don't know what he's doing here, but – my mercy.' His head stilled; he leant forward. 'Well, now, there he is.'

Gavin lowered his glasses and nodded.

The wailing cry was getting louder. I saw a flash of dark back like a wet otter slipping between the heather stems towards the shore.

'What is it?' I said.

'You'll recognise him in a minute,' Gavin said.

'Don't you worry,' Magnie called to it, 'we're not going to leave you. Haul the anchor up, Cass, and let's get ashore for him. The Good Man alone kens how he got here but his folk will be glad to get him back.'

The creature had reached the shore now and come right to the water's edge, waiting for us. Now I could see the white front, the chocolate brown paws, the black mask and ears, although it was too far off for me to distinguish the cornflower-blue eyes.

It was Sandra and Peter's Siamese cat.

I lifted the outboard up and paddled the boat to the shallows. Magnie sploshed over to pick the cat up. It stopped its unearthly wailing once it saw we were coming for it, and paced back and forward on the pebble beach instead, eyes fixed on us. I couldn't tell if it looked tired, as if it had swum ashore. Its coat was as immaculate as it had been when we'd met it aboard *Genniveve*. I was certain that whatever Sandra and Peter were involved in, they wouldn't have thrown their cat overboard to drown, or marooned it on this uninhabited island.

It came to Magnie straight away, and he picked it up and sploshed back with it in his arms. He put it on the padded seat while he made a dry nest for it with his jacket in the fish box where we stored the bouy-anchors and rope, then coaxed the cat into it, soothing it with his gnarled hands. He brought out a bottle of water and tipped some into his palm. The cat drank thirstily, then relaxed in the jacket, blue eyes fixed on Magnie. He sat back, shaking his head at me.

'Now, Cass, ghost babies indeed! You're been listening to too many of my yarns. Haven't you heard a Siamese yowl before?'

'Never,' I said. So that was why Gavin had asked whether I'd had a pet as a child. I turned to him. 'Did you guess that, just from what I said about the noise?'

'A horrid, desolate wailing noise, you said. We had a Siamese when I was a child, and I remembered the minister's wife coming in once.' He leaned forward to let the cat sniff his hand, then scratched it under the ear. 'She wondered where the baby was.'

'Ah, they have good voices,' Magnie said. 'They're talking cats too, you can have a conversation with them just as if they were Christian souls. I'll be glad to look after this one for a day or two, until his folk get back for him.'

If they were alive to come back for him ... I'd been thinking in terms of *Genniveve* sailing away, but I saw now that if you were going to scuttle a yacht with a fifteen-metre mast this wasn't a bad place to do it. There was a fish farm with a floating shed behind Linga, and various lobster pots around the shore, but nobody would be dragging for scallops in the deep itself; no fishermen's net would snag on a mast. A boat could sink into the bottom in peace.

I could see that Gavin was following my thoughts. His mouth was grim; he nodded as our eyes met. 'Put me ashore when you can,' he said, 'and I'll get things moving.'

I looked at the cat curled in Magnie's jacket. 'When we came aboard,' I said, 'he vanished into the locker at first, and only came out once he'd decided it was safe. If it hadn't been Sandra who'd come to take *Genniveve* away, that's what he'd have done, slipped down into his favourite hiding-locker, and stayed there.' Until the intruder had gone ... until the water began to come in, and he'd had to take to the cockpit first, and then to the cabin roof, and finally to the sea. The wailing we'd heard had begun after the light had gone out, after the rising water had taken out the boat's electrics. He'd been calling for help, and nobody had come. At last he'd have had to swim for his life to the nearest shore. Most animals can swim, if they have to, and the light breeze would have blown him shorewards. Yes, he could have made those two hundred yards.

'You'll not be able to have him and yon boy's rat in the same boat,' Magnie said. 'I'll tak him home wi' me, give him a feed and somewhere to sleep. You'll manage fine without me for the afternoon, a day like this.'

We putted back to the pier, reaching it just ahead of Alex and Robbie. Magnie carried the cat ashore, and headed off in his car with it sitting beside him in the front seat. I hoped it would get on with his other cats.

'I'll come back later,' Gavin said, 'or phone to tell you what's happening.'

'Okay,' I said, and turned back to order the chaos at the pontoon.

We did another beat up the voe, this time with me throwing coloured balls astern for them to pick up as they zig-zagged behind me, then a spinnaker run down to the club again. I couldn't focus, though. I kept glancing over my shoulder at the ruffled steel waters of Cole Deep, and wondering what lay in their depths. Magnie joined me again at lunchtime, and reported that his visitor had eaten ravenously, then fallen foul of his top cat, Tigger. He'd left the Siamese shut in the spare room, exchanging menaces with Tigger through the closed door.

'But I doubt,' he said, glancing over at Cole Deep, just as I had been all morning, 'that the pair of them had better get used to each another. Have you heard back from yon kilted policeman yet?'

I shook my head. 'I think he has to deal with Newcastle as well as Lerwick.'

'Aye, they were Geordies.'

The past tense echoed in a little silence. I took a deep

breath and fished my whistle out from the neck of my lifejacket. 'Well, what will we get them doing this afternoon?'

We did 'follow my leader' in pairs, and a rather sploshy game of 'tag' and ended with a couple of races. Once the boats were put away, I left the bairns to shower and went up into the clubhouse, where there were log-books to be signed, and biscuits and hot juice to distribute. There was a parent rota for that, and this time it was Kirsten's turn. 'Uh-huh,' I thought, and waited to see if she'd mention the lifeboat stall tomorrow.

She did, straight away. 'Thanks, Cass, for offering to come and help out on Saturday. It's good of you – you're doing so much with the children you mustn't get much time to yourself.'

'Oh, it's no bother,' I said. I touched wood. 'I've never needed to call the lifeboat out, but I'm glad it's there.' I hadn't offered, though.

'I'll be there from eight, but you just come when it suits you.'

'I won't be there as soon as that,' I said. 'I was thinking to bring the boat round, so say ten, ten thirty.'

'That'd be plenty early,' she said. 'Thanks. D'you want some hot juice?'

'I'll make myself drinking chocolate,' I said. 'I'll have a biscuit, though.'

'You'll not need to slim, you're so active,' she said.

'You're not needing to slim yourself,' I said. This was the kind of female conversation that always left me feeling awkward. She was slim almost to the point of scraggy, one of these nervous women that couldn't sit still for worrying. Even now, when all the bairns had had their juice, she was dabbing at the table with a cloth, and collecting tumblers almost from their hands. Her collar-bones jutted out above the neck of her pale blue vest top, you could see the bones in her shoulders, and her hipster jeans hung loose below the nobbles of her pelvis. I wondered again about all that had gone wrong in her life that she had to control her body so rigidly. Maybe it was the last area of herself that she owned; Olaf was one to take over everything else. She was pretty in a modern film-star way, with a long, thin face with high cheekbones, and green eyes smudged into their sockets. Her dark hair was super-sleek, and curved round her face in one of those symmetric cuts, the two sides touching her chin.

'Thanks for doing the hot juice,' I said, and went off to get my drinking chocolate and the box of log-books. I went through them one by one, calling the child over and noting what they'd done: *Mirror, 3 hrs helm, 2 hrs crew, down-wind sailing, CL.* I was only halfway through them when Kirsten went, calling 'See you on Saturday.' She must have taken Alex home with her, for when I got to the bottom of the pile, his book was there, but he didn't answer to his name. Good. I was glad one parent had the sense to keep him off the road. I put the books back in the box, and the box back in the cupboard, washed up my mug, and headed home.

There was no sign of Anders yet. Rat and Cat were flatteringly pleased to see me. I hung my drysuit from the backstay and sat down to let them scramble all over me, Rat whiffling his whiskers and Cat purring like the rumble of water in a sea-cave. I propped my mobile up in the corner of the chart table, where it sometimes got a signal, but Gavin didn't call.

I'd just switched off Radio Shetland and the six o'clock headlines, and was thinking about making some kind of tea, when I heard the marina gate clang. Naturally I wasn't going to rush out and look. There were footsteps, then somebody called my name from outside – not Gavin. I went out to see Olaf standing on the pontoon.

'Cass,' he said, 'I was wondering if you'd seen Alex

about after the sailing, or if he'd mentioned going anywhere else. Kirsten took it he'd come home already, when she left, and then we thought he'd likely gone with one of his pals somewhere, but he hadn't said, and so we phoned around, and though he'd left the sailing with the others, nobody'd seen him after that.'

It was too soon to push the panic button, here in Shetland, but I could share Olaf's concern. 'No,' I said, 'he's not still around here. He doesn't have a mobile?'

'It's switched off,' Olaf said. He rubbed a hand over his chin. 'He didn't mention anywhere he was going?'

'Not to me,' I said. 'He was sailing with Robbie – he didn't say anything to him?

Olaf shook his head. 'We tried Gary and Peter too. Nothing. Ah well, I'll just keep looking.'

'Can I do anything to help?' I asked. 'I could go along the shore.'

He shook his head. 'He'd not have gone that way, he had the quad.'

'He'd not come to any harm, here in Shetland,' I said.

'No' the south sort of harm,' Olaf agreed, but the thought didn't seem to comfort him much. He strode away along the pontoon, leaving it rocking.

I sat down in the cockpit, disquieted. It was, of course, entirely likely that Alex should have gone off on some ploy without telling anyone. All the same, bairns didn't usually head off on ploys without another bairn to share the adventure, and his friends had been collected by their parents or gone blamelessly home on their bikes.

Then I remembered what finding the Siamese cat had driven right out of my head. He had had some plan in mind, for he'd been trying to persuade Robbie to it, while they'd hung on to the RIB, waiting for the others to come. Robbie had refused, because he was grounded for sneaking out the night before. Now what might Alex have had in mind?

It was obvious, now I'd worked my way back there. He'd been there and listening while Magnie had talked about lights up at the trowie mound. He could easily get up there with the quad, going along the road to the end, then up over the hill. I frowned. It was a steep hill, and he was too light for the quad. Perhaps he'd overturned or had some other misanter. I tried to see the simple, the plausible, not letting myself think about a yacht slipping below the waves, then went back below and unearthed the phone book from where it was acting as insulation below Rat's sleeping box. Johnston … Johnston.

It was Kirsten who answered. I was sorry to dash the hope in her voice.

'Kirsten, it's Cass. I had a sudden thought. Magnie and I were talking about him seeing lights up at the trowie mound, you know, the chambered cairn up the Hill of Heodale, the hill at the back of the Nicolson cottage, and Alex was listening. I wonder if he might have gone up there to investigate?'

She grasped at the suggestion. 'He might. It's the sort of thing he'd do. I'll phone Olaf straight away and tell him to look there.'

'I'll go round by sea,' I said, 'and look from that side.'

This is my ship, Cass … I tried Gavin's number, but either he was in a 'no signal' area or he'd switched his phone off. I tried to compress my message. 'Gavin, it's Cass. There's a boy gone missing. I think he's gone up to the trowie mound. I'm going round by sea.' I sent Anders a text: 'Taken RIB to old cottage.' He'd know what I meant.

I'd refuelled the RIB before putting her away. I put my fleece and lifejacket back on, clipped the kill-cord round my leg and set off at planing speed. In less than ten minutes I was turning the corner into the Rona; ten more, and I was out in the Atlantic, heading straight for the red cliffs below the trowie mound.

I didn't know it then, but Alex's body had already been found.

6

What's forborne sood aye be forsworn.

(Old Shetland proverb: what's been warned against should be kept clear of.)

Chapter Thirteen

It was seven o'clock now, and the wind had fallen away completely, leaving the water clear and still, a pale silvery blue stretching to the Atlantic horizon. The sun made the cliffs translucent fire-orange, but this hill was in shadow, the cottage crouching dark behind its sheltering arm of hill.

The tide was flowing. I put a kedge out astern, paddled the RIB in, sploshed ashore with a running line, then hauled the boat back out. I paused, looking over the cottage, then took a deep breath and walked slowly around it, starting at the nearest side. It was ill luck to go round against the sun in Shetland. The window panes were dark, but clean; someone had washed the salt of the winter storms off them since spring. Even without staring I could see that the house wasn't deserted. The curtains at the windows were clean, the floor of the living room carpeted, a rug by the fireplace and another by a little chest of drawers, but there was an odd space in the middle, as if the room had been used as a bedroom, and the bed had been taken away. An armchair was pushed back from the fireplace as if someone had just risen. I scanned it without turning my head, and walked on. The porch roof was in good condition, the blue paint on the door only slightly cracked. The Yale lock was gleamingly new. I remembered Brian's hand clenched on an old lock, his black brows twisted together, and Jeemie's voice: *Robbie o' the Knowe let his mouth open a bit wide* – Brian hadn't bothered asking for his keys back; he'd changed the locks to stop Cerys' games.

The drainage ditch around the cottage gave off a smell of damp moss, and I could hear water trickling in the bottom of it. The roof was edged with moss too, as if the rain sat at the skews and worked its way into the attic. A blackbird shrilled his alarm call from the twisted sycamore at the back of the house.

It was darker around the back. I remembered the flash of spyglasses I had seen, and didn't like the thought. Suppose the somebody who'd pushed the armchair back had crept out of the house to wait for me as I turned the last corner? I froze and listened. No, there was nothing but the wavelets tapping the stones of the shore, the rustle of wings as the blackbird changed branch to watch me better. I walked on. The tarred roof came down to a foot above my head, and the rough walls were bulged under their patchy coat of whitewash. The back extension had plastic curtains and a modern gutter running down into the earth. I came slowly round the second corner and stopped dead, breath-held, at the dark bulk looming in front of me, but it was only a pile of wood, cut branches from the sycamore and dismembered palettes. It smelt faintly of mildew, as if the lowest planks had been there a long time. I slid around it and on to the last corner.

The kitchen window had a net curtain across it, a cast-off of Barbara's, I guessed, for it was in the same style, with a pattern of large flowers bordering an upwards curve. A cup and plate were upended on the stainless steel draining board. There were two chairs at the bare wooden table. I came back to the shoreline and paused to examine the track leading to the end of the road, a smudged line worn by generations of feet trudging to school, to the shop, to a neighbour's house. In winter it would be a guttery pick-your-way; now, it was an earth trail between blue pincushion scabious and the first bog orchids, pyramids of blush-pink petals above brown-spotted leaves. You'd get a pick-up along it, and someone had, for there was a clearly worn double set of tyre tracks ending in a turning place.

On the beach below, someone had had a bonfire. I'd been right about the missing bed. Here were the black remains of mattress springs, a wooden frame, even a corner of what looked like a black satin sheet. I grimaced. Cerys' taste, I supposed. Flung on the remains was a broken metal tripod, twisted as if someone strong had wrenched it apart. So Cerys had been videoing her games too. Yuck. And Anders? *It is not a good place* ...

I was searching for a missing child. I looked at the path again, but there were no tyre tracks that suggested Alex had been here. I let out a relieved breath that I hadn't realised I'd been holding. I didn't like this place. All the instincts that kept me back from rocky shores or mist-filled bays were kicking in now: go back, stay well clear.

I headed up the hill of Heodale. My feet scrunched among the heather stems, releasing their honey scent. The grass was starred with yellow tormentil like miniature Tudor roses. Above me, the cairn crouched like a waiting trow on the hill's top, the front of it grass-greened and bright in the sun, the back a dark shadow. I could hear a boat engine in the distance, but it was too close in to the cliff for me to see who it was.

I paused at the top to get my breath back. I was standing in the flattened space overlooking the water, looking out just as the Neolithic people who built this must have done. The sun was still well up in the sky, but turning from gold to whisky-amber, and the water was tinted like a prospector's stream. The three shelves of Foula, seventeen miles away to the south-west, lay clear on the horizon, sharp-edged, with the isle filled in a misty grey. Where I was looking, due west, was the Vikings' road to Greenland and North America. We'd been returning from my first Atlantic crossing when Alain had died. It had taken me ten years to come to terms with the knowledge that I'd killed him. I remembered Anders: *Would it be easier if your scar was inside?*

I shoved the thought away. Looking down from above, the cliff wasn't as sheer as it looked from the sea. There was a series of narrow ledges slanting down it, like a zig-zag ladder; I'd have taken a bet that the Shetland Climbing Club would have wanted to try it. *Brian wouldn't let them near the place ...*

I began strolling around the stone and grass mound. There was no sign of the quad here either, and no movement on the green hill, no sound of roaring, bumping engine. Whatever Alex was up to, he wasn't here now.

A dozen steps on, and I knew he'd been here. On the far side of the mound there was a trampled tyre mark where the grass had fallen away to expose the soft peat. I knelt down beside it. Yes, it was a quad mark sure enough, with the tyres wider than a motorbike's. A metre away was a torn-out bit of heather where the other wheels had gripped harder to compensate for the sudden loss of traction. I ran my fingers over the indentation in the clinging mould. I didn't need police training to see how recent this was. He'd heard us talking and brooded over the trowie mound during the sailing, then headed up the minute he'd changed.

When I came around to the front again, I stopped. Somebody else had been here recently. I'd come straight up the steepest part of the hill, but there was a sheep path leading down the gentler way down to the cottage, and beside it, just below the mound itself, there was a clear footprint. It wasn't the man's rubber boots that I'd seen below, but a smaller, neater foot, wearing trainers. I put my own foot beside it and considered the two outlines. It was just bigger than my size 5: a small woman or a child. Furthermore, the prints weren't from any old trainers, but from ones which had been designed to grip. The die-cut running the whole length of the sole, and the second one round the ball of the foot, stood proud in the damp peat mould. A sailor had come up here, a child or a female sailor not much taller than I. I grimaced at that. Most people were taller than me. Sandra had been around five foot four, and Madge had been taller again, nearer five foot six. I'd guess these neat feet were Sandra's, rather than Madge's, because I'd expect someone plump to have broader feet, but that didn't necessarily follow.

That meant Sandra and Peter had been here, and had gone again. Alex had been here, and gone again. Gavin needed to know about this. I took my mobile out, and got him this time. He sounded tired, with an undercurrent of distress running below the soft 's' he gave my name. 'Cass, where are you?'

'At the trowie mound. Alex has been here – there are quad prints.'

'We've found the boy,' he said. His tone made it an elegy. 'He seems to have come off the road just at Mavis Grind and gone down onto the beach. The quad turned over on him.'

The breath left me as if I'd been punched. I couldn't manage a word.

'Are you still there, Cass? Get yourself home.'

I put the phone away and came back to the platform. As I moved away from the wall of stones facing the sea, the sun picked out a vertical crack between two slabs. I froze, looking at it. A long, deep fissure ran down from the hanging heather, as if this stone could be moved, and there, on the other side of the great stone, another dark line, like the crack each side of a doorway. Those Neolithic people had had to get into the mound to lay the bones of their dead inside, and of course the doorway would be here, looking out over their territory. I thought of the Tomb of the Eagles, in Orkney, built high above the bay. You entered that one via a low passage, half underground. Why shouldn't this cairn be the same?

Now I'd spotted the doorway I looked more closely at the heather above it. It wasn't growing between the stones here, as it was on the rest of the tomb, but hanging down from above the horizontal stone above, the stone which I could see now as a lintel. The stone with the crack each side was a massive plug, and for me to be able to see that so clearly it had to have been moved, and recently.

I kept looking at it, and ran my fingers down each edge. Was there a slight dent, a sharper chipped edge, just here, in the centre of one side, exactly where I'd have placed a crowbar to get it open? Perhaps, perhaps. If something this size had been prised out, it would fall just by where I was standing. I looked down and saw the indentation's curve highlit by the setting sun. The edges of it were still slightly rough, and at the far side a yellow tormentil flower was crushed over on itself, the heraldic rose petals just beginning to brown at the edges.

They must have followed me up from the cottage, coming quickly over the brow of the hill while I was at the far side of the mound touching Alex's tracks, then played hide and seek around the mound itself. They would have listened while I talked to Gavin. I heard feet shifting on my right, and turned to see a shape looming over me, an upraised arm. My head exploded in a splintering of stars which dissolved into darkness. With the last rags of consciousness I felt myself falling and stretched out my hands to save myself, only to feel them rag-limp as I went down onto the grass-lined platform. My cheek landed on cold moss. I felt my shoulder thud after it, then there was darkness.

Chapter Fifteen

I wasn't dead, but they were shoving me, ready to fling me overboard. The deck planks were wet with blood; it was smeared on my cheek and smelt sickly in my nostrils. I couldn't see their faces, although I was striving to open my eyes, and the no, no that I was trying to say was silent. They rolled me over, and I was falling, falling, then I was lying on Marielle*'s deck, the cold fibreglass under my back, except that it was covered with grit, I hadn't had time to sweep the decks, and it wasn't Alain but Anders who was lying beside me, one arm across my breasts, and he was kissing me, his neat beard rough on my cheek. In the dream I wanted him to go on, but not now, my head hurt too much, and I was trying to tell him that, turning my head away from him even as my body was arching against his. The scrape and thud of the great stone being eased into place echoed dully round me ...*

I awoke then. My cheek lay on grit that smelt of things left to rot, long forgotten. It was my own arm that lay awkwardly doubled across me, fingers brushing the earth. I reached a little further and felt the hard grains below my fingers. My body was aching and cold. Worst of all, the darkness pressed around me. I hadn't realised that I was afraid of the dark. Even on the blackest night with the ship's lanterns glimmering through shafts of rain, it was never truly dark at sea. Now I felt it as a presence, drawing closer to suck the breath from me. It lay over me like a shroud, and however much I strained my eyes, hoping for one friendly pinprick of daylight, there was no variation in its thickness. Pain-heavy eyelids open or shut, it made no difference. Above the darkness was the weight of stone and peat and heather. I could feel it pinning me down until the last breath was crushed out of me and my bones decayed with the others. How would my ghost communicate with the Neolithic ghosts of so many centuries ago? If I died here, would my spirit be shut up under the earth, unable to ask Alain's forgiveness?

My head throbbed, and I wanted to be sick. My body hurt all over, arms, legs, wrists, ankles, as if I'd been stretched on a rack. Whoever had flung me in here hadn't bothered to handle me like a living person. They'd just rolled and dragged me inside the doorway and left me.

They didn't expect me to be a living person. It didn't matter what you did to someone who was going to die of thirst in the next couple of days. Maybe they'd meant me to die sooner than that. It had been an efficient clout over the back of the head. I wanted to raise a hand to feel the bruise, but it was too much effort. I knew it hurt.

I clenched my teeth. I wasn't going to die. I'd just told Gavin I was here. The minute I heard noises from outside, I'd shout until they heard me. I said it out loud to myself, to break the silence that pressed in on me, and the weight of centuries that hung above me echoed it derisively: *shout shout shout shout* until the word died in the whimper of a caught throat. No noise would escape through this solid bubble of stone and earth. Had someone said that, as they'd dragged me? A voice in my head whispered like a memory: 'It doesn't matter. Nobody'd hear her through these walls.' I couldn't tell whether it was a man's voice or a woman's; the words dropped into the silence and curled in my aching head. *It doesn't matter ... doesn't matter. Nobody'd hear her ...*

I was nearer to panic then than I'd ever been in my life, nearer than when that tropical storm had swept the Caribbean and we'd stayed crouched on deck all night, making our anchors hold, nearer than when Alain had gone and I had to go on alone. I made myself relax on the cold ground and took ten long, counted breaths. They were going to hear me. I'd find a loose stone and bang with it. I'd yell as if I was hurling orders to the top of the mast in a force 10.

I took ten more breaths. I wasn't going to lie and wait for rescue either. I'd try to get out. If I couldn't move the great stone from within, I'd find the entrance that Brian had used. I wasn't much larger now than he had been then. If he could get in and out, so could I. If he'd filled the hole, I'd clear it.

The first thing was to find out if I was injured. I eased my right arm from across my breast and laid it by my side. It felt stiff, but it wasn't damaged. I lifted my other hand, slowly, and felt my head. There was a bonny bump and a crusting of blood, but the skull was intact, with no dangerous indentations. Sore but not fatal. I lifted my head and turned it gently from side to side. No neck injuries. Nothing else hurt as it would if it was broken. I stretched my arms out cautiously. My wrists hurt where I'd been hauled by them, but otherwise I didn't seem to be injured. Legs, ditto. Your mistake, guys.

I needed light. I felt for my mobile, but the pocket was empty. They wouldn't risk me getting a signal in here. It didn't matter. One useful function of my otherwise very basic Timex was that it could go luminous by pressing the winding-handle. Peerie Charlie was fascinated by it, and one of his shipboard treats was burrowing down into my bunk and seeing it light up – and on the thought, I took my hand away from the button. I didn't need to know what time it was, and I'd see much better if I didn't look at the green disc. It would be my torch to help me get out of here. It worked by stored light, so it wouldn't last a huge number of flashes, perhaps eight, and they wouldn't throw the light far, but if I used them carefully that might be enough.

If you had a tricky manoeuvre to do on a boat, you thought it through first, because the sea didn't give second chances. Now I knew I could control the darkness that pressed on me, I wasn't afraid of it. I'd save my light until I was ready to use it. I groped upwards with one hand. There was nothing there to bump my head on. I inched both arms out, as if I was making a snow-angel, the way Inga and Martin and I had as children, and met only empty space to their furthest extent. Good. I eased myself up to a sitting position, ignoring all the protests from muscles that had lain in one position too long, then began to stretch and flex. I rubbed down my arms, massaging the wrists, then did the same to my legs and ankles. I focused on getting my body working for me again, leaving my subconscious to consider options and gather the evidence and memories I needed.

Once I was warm and loosened up I hugged my knees to me under my fleece, and thought. I was inside a circular mound ten metres across, and two high. If it was like the Tomb of the Eagles, there would be little cells all round the walls, with niches for the bones, and the doorway facing the sea. It would be worth looking at that door stone; perhaps I could lever it out from within. I could put first one, then a second, then more stones in the cracks, easing it forward. Archimedes: give me a lever and a place to stand, and I could move the world. Sailing ships were designed for strong men, and small women got very good at using levers.

If it wouldn't shift – and I wasn't hopeful – then I needed to find Brian's entrance. It wouldn't be through the walls; that would be so obvious that others would have found it too. What had Olaf said? I visualised us sitting together on the wooden bench outside the club house, with his hands making careful loops of twine around the grey rope. *A gap under one of the big stones, a rabbit hole that went right through.* Yes, he'd called it a tunnel: *He even filled in the tunnel we went through.*

When the kitten had crept out to eat my sandwiches, I'd been sitting against one of the big stones on the left of the entrance, and the kitten had come from a metre further. If it was the same entrance, if I was lucky, I might be able to find this end of the burrow, somewhere between two and three metres from the entrance, to show me where to dig.

Which was my better bet? Which must I spend my light on, the entrance stone or the possible tunnel? If I used the light to locate the entrance, then I could work around the inside of the walls to the tunnel, searching for a dent in the earth, a dim glimmer of light, a current of outside air.

In Brittany, as in seafaring communities the world over, the men used to go for a last Mass dedicated to Our Lady for her blessing before they went to sea. I needed a blessing on this enterprise. I sat straighter, crossed myself, and breathed a fervent prayer for help to think clearly, to use my strength wisely, and for luck or God's grace to give me a way out. *In the name of the Father, the Son and the Holy Spirit* ... I took a deep breath, turned my watch away from me, and pressed the winder in.

Instantly the tomb was bathed in green light, sickly and flaring to my dark-dazzled eyes. I saw evenly spaced stone piers corbelling up to the roof, as though I was the hub of a great stone wheel, with dark voids between them where the light couldn't reach. I turned my head to the wider gap between two piers, the entrance stone, then let the button go. The blackness closed in again, stifling as stale air. Keeping my head very still, I sat for a moment, loosening the green glare from my eyes, then swivelled my body around until I was facing the entrance. The piers were a metre from me. I had to crawl forward for two metres and I would touch the great stone. As I went, I'd feel out for stones I could try to lever it with, and if I didn't find any, I could then work my way round the perimeter, looking for Brian's entrance. I wasn't hopeful about loose stones. That walling had been built to last. Those Neolithic men and women who had brought their dead here would have been proud of it – I shut that thought away. No need to conjure the ghosts of four millennia ago, although I feared their presence all around me. Cool Cass, Brian and Olaf had called me, practical Cass. Don't imagine bones, torchlit processions, long-dead men and women whispering you to join them, think about escape. I wasn't going to try pulling stones out of the piers, but there might be a place where some had fallen. If there was, I'd find it as I went round. For the moment, I needed to go forward those two metres to the entrance stone.

It was much harder than it sounded, to shuffle forwards into the dark. I inched forward on one hand and two knees, the other hand stretched out in front of me, expecting every moment to bump into the wall, or worse, some unseen *thing* which had crept towards me in the darkness. I concentrated on calculating: the wall was two metres away, and I'd moved my hand forwards ten times – fifteen – seventeen – twenty-one, before my outstretched hand met the smooth stone. Ten shuffles made a metre. Okay. I eased myself into a sitting position and felt the floor around me, as far as I could reach. There was no sign of any stones, just the grit, and that was no good. I put my shoulder against the entrance stone and pushed. There was no give at all. The stone felt as though it slanted inwards, which would make sense from the shape of the outer wall. That meant that what was holding it in place was its own weight, and gravity. I turned around and braced my back against it and put the full strength of my legs to the earth floor, pushing until my muscles began to tremble. Nothing. I mustn't waste my strength on the impossible. I gave it one more try, this time in short, rhythmic bursts of pushing, as if I was part of a watch heaving a heavy yard round, but there was still no movement.

If I had to, I'd come back to it. Now I'd try for Brian's

entrance.

To feel around the perimeter wall, I'd have to go into each pier, where the bones had been laid. There was no need to be afraid; dry bones couldn't hurt me. All the same, I'd look before I touched. I shuffled back, reached out for the pier on my left and crawled to the opening of the space, then held my watch up again and pressed the button.

The tightly packed stones sprung up once more, in their green light, laid out like a brick bookcase. Grey dust lay over the shelves, over the bones laid in neat heaps, with a skull beside each pile of long bones. Hazed by cobwebs, the eye sockets confronted me.

I let the button go and crawled forward. Here, between the piles, the floor was two inches deep in powdery dust that stuck to my hands and swirled up to my face. Even as I coughed it away, I realised that meant something. There had been no dust in the centre of the mound; someone had cleared it. So the mound had indeed been used as a storage place. No wonder the person who had coshed me didn't want me investigating the entrance. Before I left, I'd use my last light in a final look right round.

I found the wall and felt carefully along the bottom of it. The floor was even under the soft, clinging dust. The burrow should be in the next cell. I crawled round the pier and began wiping my hand along the join between floor and wall, then drawing it backwards to feel the earth before the wall. I was beginning to think Brian must have filled his tunnel in completely when my knee went down, and I fell forwards, catching my hands with a scrape on a shelf. A smooth cane of bone was under my fingers. I snatched them back, pulled my knee up, and set my hands to explore what I'd found.

It had to be Brian's tunnel. It felt like a rabbit hole, as wide as my shoulders, and when I lay down and stretched my hands into it, they sloped down a little way, then began to go towards the wall. I stretched further, and my hands touched a tangle of stiff fibres: heather stems. *He even filled in the tunnel* ... From what Olaf had said, Brian had filled in the tunnel to stop the archaeologists; it was an adult job of filling in. I felt around the heather stems until I found an edge, and another. Yes, he'd taken fells from casting peats, breeze-block slabs of heather tussocks and roots, and pushed them down. I wriggled my fingers into the sides of the first block and pulled until it began to give, then took a firmer hold and hauled it out, my mind exploding in triumph. *Thank you, God* ... I was going to get out of here.

The second block came as easily. I stacked it on top of the first. For the third, I had to wriggle half into the tunnel, and it was at an awkward angle to pull. It came in a slither of earth and small stones, as if he'd bunged a couple of bags of loose earth on top to camouflage his fells. With the fourth came daylight, a dim film of grey that I'd used to help me place the fell on the others before I realised that I could see the pale blur of my hands on the dark block.

I couldn't see the sky yet, but the light filtering through was becoming clearer. The smell of things dead and rotting seemed to enfold me. I couldn't wait to get up to the air. When I began clearing the loose earth, I realised how much my hands were scraped by the tough heather. I took off my fleece, knotted the sleeves, and used the arms as gloves to scrabble out the loose earth, digging quicker and quicker as freedom came within my grasp. I knew I had to make it large enough for me to slip through without too much shoving. Although the lowest course of stones was slabs of boulder which had stood solid for four thousand years, no foundation likes being undermined, and the tunnel was almost the width of the great rock that formed its lintel.

I flung the last of the earth out and put my fleece back on, pulling the hood up and tightening its drawstring under my chin. It might protect my head from the scrape of rock. Then I turned back to the tomb. The cleared space in the middle, the thick dust at the sides – I wanted to know.

I shone my watch round in a slow circle until the light faded and died. There was no doubt now that this place had been used for storage. Opposite me, the green light had cast black cage shadows from a wooden frame, designed to hold paintings upright and separate. Beside it had been five wooden crates, each divided into four compartments of around thirty centimetres square. There was an arm's-width roll of bubble-wrap, and a litter of smaller pieces, with an incongruously domestic pair of scissors lying on top.

I was going to get out, to tell Gavin what I knew. I stretched both arms in front of me, like a diver, and went into the tunnel. It was tight around my shoulders, but not dangerously so. Earth trickled over my hood and down into my neck. The stench of something rotting filled my nostrils, making me want to gag. A dead rabbit in the hole, perhaps? I'd just said it to myself, pushing my shoulders onward like a weevil in a biscuit, when the first true daylight blinded my eyes, and my groping hand came down on cold fur, with the inert flabbiness of death under it.

I couldn't bear to crawl over it. I pushed it ahead of me through the last metre, and turned my face away from it, although I felt the dead fur touch my cheek, as I shoved the earth of the narrowed entrance forwards. I rolled it out of the hole and hauled myself after it into the light.

Chapter Sixteen

I collapsed against the stone I'd sat at to eat my mackerel roll, only the day before yesterday, although it felt like years ago. I must have sat there for half an hour, back against the stone, legs stretched, smarting hands on my belly, face turned to the sun, drinking in the heather-sweet air, the blessed warmth, the gold of light on my closed eyelids. I hurt all over, and I was as tired as if I'd done a full day's rope hauling in a Cape Horn gale. Soon, I'd go down, get into the RIB, and take it home to Brae, but I needed to rest first.

Now, with the first shock over, the death of Alex hit home. Poor Kirsten, poor Olaf – he'd been so young, so alive – he'd had the makings of a good sailor. I saw him as I'd last seen him, flushed and triumphant at having got to the RIB first, and then in that last spinnaker run home. Robbie had been helming, and he'd crouched forward on the gunwale, concentrating on keeping his yellow and red spinnaker a perfect curve. Once they'd got ashore, he'd de-rigged the boat and washed it down so thoroughly I'd had to tell him to bale it out before he put it away. That was the last time I'd spoken to him. 'Alex, Robbie,' I'd said, lifting the red sail to show them a foot of water in the boat, 'you've maybe overdone the wash-down a touch?'

'Oh,' Alex had replied, and given me his broad grin. 'Sorry, Cass. We'll bale her out.' They'd set to with the shovel baler, and most of the water went over each other, to shrieks of indignation and threats of revenge.

It was such a trivial exchange, to be the last time I'd speak to him, yet it seemed important to remember it. I remembered his intent face as he'd trimmed his spinnaker, and grieved. He'd been lively, and daft, and done no harm to anyone. Had somebody feared harm from him? I remembered how he'd asked me about the people in the motor-boat. *I ken them, see ... I'm seen them afore, anyroad, when I was down at Brian's.* I'd thought then it had been Norman who was asking. Norman was Alex's big brother, his hero. If Norman wanted to know, Alex would do his best to find out. I'd stonewalled him, but then he'd heard Magnie talking about the trowie lights, and decided to investigate. The quad track by the mound showed he'd been here. He'd seen something or met someone, and they'd killed him. Then what?

They'd hit me on the head and slung me in the mound, but I could be made to disappear very easily. All they had to do was tow the RIB out to sea a bit and leave it loose. Everyone knew I always wore a life-jacket, but lifejackets can fail, and though they'd search for my body it wouldn't be that unusual if they didn't find it. One of these accidents at sea, case closed.

It wouldn't be so easy to make Alex disappear. There'd be a huge search the minute he was officially missing. No, for Alex they'd have to engineer an accident. *He seems to have come off the road just at Mavis Grind and gone down onto the beach*, Gavin had said. *The quad turned over on him.* Mavis Grind was just north of Brae, south of where I was now, a narrow neck of land between two voes, one reaching in from the North Sea, on the east, and the other a finger of the Atlantic on the west. If you were good at throwing stones, you could chuck one from the North Sea to the Atlantic, and tourists often tried. I tried to see the lie of the road in my mind's eye, and couldn't see anywhere that you'd accidentally bounce a quad off the road to land on the beach. Gavin must have meant that he'd apparently driven down to the beach, and overturned the quad there. Then I visualised the chart. Yes, the virtue of Mavis Grind was that it was the nearest place to here where you had both main road and sea access. It wouldn't take long, by quad, to get back down to Mavis Grind, half an hour maybe, and then a boat could pick you up. There were headlands by the beach where even a sizeable motorboat could nose in, to let someone jump aboard from the hill.

If they'd hit Alex as they'd hit me, one person could prop him before them on the quad, holding him as if he was still alive, then drive down over the hill to Mavis Grind. If you went direct to the beach, you wouldn't need to go on the road at all. Then – thinking of it made me feel sick. Then you finished off your inconvenient witness, and upturned the quad over him, to look like an accident.

I needed to talk to Gavin. If that was how it had been, Forensic would find traces. I opened my eyes and prised myself to my feet, joints protesting. The sun was almost at the horizon now; half past nine. The water dazzled like new-polished brass, and every grass tussock on the hill cast a shadow twice its own size. Beside me, the hump of inert fur I had pushed up from the depth had gold stripes ... I looked at it in the daylight. It wasn't a rabbit, as I'd thought, but a cat – Cat's mother, whose death had forced her kittens out onto the hillside.

I realised what had killed her as soon as I turned her over, ready to put her back into the quiet earth of the burrow. Someone had been shooting on the hill, Magnie'd said, the evening before David and Madge, and Peter and Sandra had arrived at the marina. It hadn't been rabbits the marksmen had been after. Cat's mother had been shot; one back leg was shattered, with splinters of bone sticking through the fur, and the leg contorted in an agonised spasm, and her belly was swollen up as if with injury there too. A trigger-happy teenager, or someone who wanted to protect their hiding place in the trowie mound even from a cat?

I grimaced at the irony. If they hadn't killed Cat's

mother, I wouldn't have found that starving kitten, wouldn't have known where to look for Brian's tunnel. I wouldn't have survived to tell what I'd found in the trowie mound, to be evidence for what might have happened to Alex. If I had any say in it, their casual cruelty was going to be their undoing.

It was time to go. I'd just taken a step away from the mound when I heard more than one someone coming up the hill below, climbing silently and fast towards me.

My first reaction was indignation. I'd had enough. Yet even as I was thinking a reproachful, '*Oh,Lord!*' I was backing across the cropped turf of the platform, to get to the other side of the mound. It might be rescue, but I'd heard no boat arriving in the time I'd sat here recovering. No, these were people who'd already been here, in the cottage, maybe, and the first thing they'd see, as they came up over the brow of the hill, was the enlarged tunnel entrance. They'd know I'd escaped, and they'd be determined to finish me off now.

I couldn't play hide-and-seek around the mound, and the hillside here was too open. I'd get a good start on them, and I'd be running downhill, but I'd be seen. I didn't want to be a target for people with a gun. If I crouched behind a knowe, I'd be flushed out of cover as they came to search, and I'd just be a closer target. There was only one other possibility, and I'd have to take it fast: that cliff ledge some two metres below the platform. I'd be a sitting duck there, of course, if they looked. I was taking a chance on them thinking I was long gone, across the hill to Mangaster, and already well along the main road towards the police station at Brae.

I slipped to the cliff edge. Shutting my mind to the drop to the sea, I half-slid, half fell, dangling for a moment from my hands while my feet felt for the ledge below me. The trampling feet were almost at the brow of the hill now. Any moment, my enemies would be able to see over onto the platform. I dropped the last two feet, and landed with a jar that had me staggering outwards. I clung to the sharp cliff-face with my hands, and managed to keep my balance.

My fleece was dark green. I hauled the the hood over my head and hurried to the furthest end of the ledge, where a knobble of rock cast a Cass-sized shadow. I crouched down and froze, like a novice skipper caught in a tanker-filled shipping lane, hoping stillness is safety. If I was lucky, if I was very lucky, I might escape a cursory glance. If they looked harder – well, I hoped they'd shoot to kill, and get it over with quickly.

There was a shout overhead, a flurry of speech. Crouched under here, I couldn't distinguish words, or recognise voices, but I could hear the anger. They'd found the end of my tunnel. Footsteps scuffled from one side of the mound to the other. A woman's voice spat out, 'She can't have gone far!' A man replied, 'Look!'

I could hear the scrunch of heather, the give of the turf, as they moved, feel the vibration of the earth. It seemed forever that I crouched there, hearing the hunt go on above me. At last the feet came to the platform.

'Nothing.' It was a woman's voice.

'If he doesn't come soon, I'm not waiting. They'll find the boy soon.' The man's voice crackled with anger. I was pretty sure it was David speaking. 'I can't see what he'd want that would be so urgent.'

'That's him.' There was relief in the woman's voice. Madge's? I couldn't be sure. I could feel the vibration in the hill, then there was the sound of a vehicle approaching, a pick-up or 4x4, driven fast across the uneven ground. I heard it stop, not very close. There was a surprised exclamation from the man, then a shot, a scream from the woman, another shot. The double crack bounced across from hill to hill until the echo diminished into silence.

The cavalry wouldn't come out shooting. I waited in stillness as a single set of footsteps came around the mound above my head. There was a dragging sound, grunts of exertion, and then with a slither of little stones, something was shoved from the platform edge above me, thudded on my ledge with an inert weight and fell on downwards to the sea. I opened my eyes too late to see what it was, but heard the splash and saw the ripples. Something dark surfaced on the gold water far below.

The second body was thrown over from the direction I was facing. I saw the cartwheeling of arms and legs, clad in a dark jacket and trousers, the heavy thud as it bounced against a ledge lower down. I recognised David's face, mouth open beneath the thick moustache, eyes glaring blindly. I heard the second splash, then there was a long silence, as if the person with the gun was standing there, waiting. I closed my eyes once more. *Lord, protect me.*

The relief when the footsteps moved away left me shaking. The pick-up started up with a roar, and drove away over the hill. I waited until the last rumble had died away before I lifted my head, stiff muscles protesting, and gradually straightened up to stand on the ledge there, hands splayed against the red stone, feet planted on the grass ledge. Below me, the two dark backs hung heavy in the water. Already they were beginning to separate from each other, tugged away from the shore by the undertow. The police would need to retrieve them soon.

I turned to face the cliff. I'd had to drop maybe two feet onto the ledge, so I'd need to climb back up. I didn't want to do it. I was too tired, too scared of the long drop below me. I turned my back on it again and dropped onto the grass tussocks. Someone would come looking for me. They'd throw a rope over to hoist me up –

I must have sat there for a good half hour, watching the bodies in the water drift seawards, and feeling sorry for myself. I hurt all over. My hands were black with earth, and criss-crossed with tiny scratches which I'd have to disinfect. I had a sizeable graze showing through a tear on one knee of my jeans. The blood showed dark red among the earth. My ankles hurt where I'd jarred them, dropping down here, and I didn't want to think about what I'd done to my face.

It was the drone of the Coastguard helicoptor that galvanised me into action. Gavin must have got back to Brae, seen that I wasn't there, and called them out. The red and white chopper came up from the south, quite high, then went round in a circle as if it had spotted something. The RIB, I betted, drifting with nobody aboard. Then, under the rotor-blade whirr, I heard the roar of a high-speed engine. They'd called out Aith Lifeboat as well. It came out of the Rona in a plume of white water. I was never going to hear the end of this ... and the thought of dangling helplessly on the end of a rope, in full view of the combined rescue services, galvanised me into action. I turned my back on the drop to the shimmering sea, and looked properly at the cliff. All I needed was a foothold at knee height, and another at the same height again. That would get my shoulders above the cliff edge, and I could haul myself from there. If the ledge I stood on had been solid ground, I wouldn't have hesitated for a moment.

It didn't take very long to find the holds I needed. I took a deep breath, then swarmed upwards, giving myself a good shove upwards from the second hold, and wriggling my torso forwards on the viewing platform while my legs kicked wildly in the air. It wasn't elegant, but I'd made it. I didn't need rescued any more. I staggered to my feet and stood there, swaying.

Yes, they'd found the RIB. I could see it now, drifted out from the cottage bay. The lifeboat was taking it in tow while the chopper circled, looking for my body. I unzipped my fleece. The T-shirt beneath it had been white when I'd put it on after sailing, but it wouldn't pass any Persil test now. I hauled it off, put my fleece back on, and began waving the T-shirt as a signal flag. My watch wasn't quite big enough for a signal mirror, but it could give off a flash. I tilted it to the sun, away again, towards them again, several times, then went back to waving the T-shirt.

They'd spotted me. The chopper turned and came straight for me. It hovered, the red and white chevrons right above me, then tilted sideways, moving to the open hill just past the trowie mound, hovered again, and sank to rest. The ear-splitting noise continued for a moment longer, and the wind of the blades whipped my hair across my face and buffeted my body. Then the blades slowed, drooped and stilled, and the noise ceased. The door in the side of the chopper opened, and Gavin got out.

I wanted to run to him, to be hugged and soothed, but we weren't on those terms. I waited, casual as I could be with my dirty face and torn jeans, until he was within earshot. 'Doctor Livingstone, I presume.'

'Ms Stanley.' He gave me a quick, comprehensive look. 'Superficial grazes but no real damage?'

'Nothing a shower won't cure,' I agreed. 'If you can give me a lift back to the RIB, I'll take it home.'

'The lifeboat had it in tow.'

'Then if the winchman can put us down to the lifeboat, I'll save them the journey to Brae.'

'They're halfway there already,' the pilot said. 'They set off as soon as we recognised you, and knew we didn't have to look for a corpse.' He grinned. 'We might have known you'd turn up safe and sound.'

'I have,' I said, 'but I'm afraid you do have a corpse to deal with – well, two.' I gestured over the cliff. 'Someone shot two people and rolled them over, about an hour ago. Dark jackets, but they were still floating.' I grimaced at Gavin. 'I've had an interesting evening. Let me tell you about it on the way home.'

Chapter Seventeen

The chopper landed on the football pitch in Brae. Gavin stayed with it, to get back to the police HQ in Lerwick, and I had only to walk along the road to the boating club. This being Shetland, the second car that passed was Magnie. He stopped to pick me up.

'Lass, you look as if you've been digging.'

'I have,' I agreed wearily. 'I got stuck inside your trowie mound – Magnie, I'm knackered. I'll tell you the whole story once I've had a shower.' My belly was reminding me I hadn't eaten either. 'Are you busy this evening? I couldn't get you to drop me off at the club, and then go and get me a fish supper from Frankie's? I've just realised I haven't had any tea.'

'No problem, lass.'

The shower was magnificent. I lathered the earth out of my hair, soaped all over, wincing a bit, then just stood in the hot water for five repeat presses of the 'on' button. When I came out, I was pink all over. I dried myself, slathered my cuts with Savlon cream, anointed the rest of me with strawberry-smelling cream from Shetland Soap and headed back to the boat. In passing, I had a quick look in the RIB, and was pleased to find my mobile stashed in the under-seat locker. A nice touch.

Magnie was there before me, and Anders with him, both tucking into fish suppers. Mine was still in its blue and white box, with a cup of tea steaming beside it. Rat whiffled disapprovingly at my strawberry and Savlon smell, but Cat swarmed straight up my clean jeans and jumper to curl around my neck, purring like a steam engine. Magnie and Anders each glanced up, then returned to eating. All the same, I knew what they'd seen; a network of scrapes and grazes across my face and hands, with the occasional bit of earth still ingrained.

'Aaahh,' I said appreciatively, sitting down on the engine box and leaning back against the cabin doorway. My box contained a slab of haddock that wasn't far off the size of *Khalida*'s doorstep, and perfectly cooked chips. The fish was sea-fresh, with moist white flesh in crunchy batter. I put a piece down for Cat, then polished off every last crumb, including the inevitable final hard chip in a pool of vinegar.

'I got some ice-cream too,' Magnie said. He produced three white chocolate Magnums from a swathing of newspaper. 'You looked as if you could do with it.'

People who live on small boats don't have a freezer to keep ice-cream in. An unexpected Magnum was bliss. I ate it very slowly, giving Rat a piece of white chocolate. He nibbled it from his front paws, sitting up like a squirrel, whiskers twitching appreciatively. Cat finished his fish, then sat in my lap to wash his face.

'So,' Anders said, 'what have you been doing?'

I launched into the story. I added what Gavin had yelled at me in the chopper, that Alex's death was being treated as murder, because of suspicious circumstances in how he was found. He hadn't given further details, and I hadn't asked for them. I kept seeing his face, the lavender blue eyes, the straggle of fair hair … He hadn't suffered, Gavin had said. A blow on the head had killed him outright.

'And it was yon David and Madge that shut you into the mound, you think?' Magnie said.

'It must have been,' I agreed. 'They knew I'd escaped – ergo, they put me in there. But then who shot them?'

'And where do the other pair fit in?' Anders said. 'Peter and Sandra, who owned the yacht?'

'And how did my visitor come to be left apo Linga?' Magnie added.

'Gavin seems to think he swam there,' I said. 'He thinks the boat was scuttled in Cole Deep, that night we saw it leaving.'

'There's serious money in an operation that can afford to sink a boat like yon,' Magnie said. 'What'd she be worth, would you say? Seventy thousand?'

'Nearer a hundred,' I said.

'Peter loved his cat,' Anders said. 'You could see that. He would not have left it to drown, any more than I would leave Rat. So if the boat is in Cole Deep, it was not Sandra who took her out, that night.'

'But someone shot David and Madge,' I said. 'They were waiting for a *he*. Someone they weren't afraid of.'

'Someone from here who is involved in what's going on,' Anders said. 'You said it was a pick-up.'

'It sounded like one,' I agreed, 'and you couldn't take a normal car up there.'

'Well, then,' Anders said, 'you wouldn't hire a pick-up from a garage. They have small run-abouts, or comfort cars, or vans. A pick-up means it was someone local.'

'Yes,' I said slowly, 'I suppose it does.' Kevin of the noisy motorboat had a pick-up. Brian of the cottage did too … but then, so did ninety per cent of the Shetland rural population. It wasn't much of a clue.

There was another thought knocking at the back of my head. I jerked upright. 'Oh, murder! It's Friday. I was supposed to be cleaning for Barbara o' Staneygarth. Looking for Alex drove it clean out of my head.' I looked at my watch. 'Eleven o'clock. I can't phone now.' Realising how late it was made me give an enormous yawn that cracked all the starting-to-heal scratches on my face, and Magnie rose.

'Lass, I'll leave you to have an early night.'

An early night sounded a good idea. Even after the shower, I was aching all over. Sleep wasn't so easy. When I'd wriggled myself into my berth I couldn't switch off, even with Cat purring in the crook of my neck. My eyelids were shut, but the eyes under them were wide open, gazing at ordered stone walling lit by green light. When I did sleep, I was plunged into a nightmare about being buried alive: *Khalida* had turned sideways, and earth was pouring into her like water. I could feel the weight of it on my legs, and smell it in my mouth –

I was woken by Anders shaking my shoulder. 'Komme ut, Cass, you are having a bad dream.'

I was too shaken to argue, filled with that sense of foreboding that you get from a nightmare. I crawled out and immediately he wrapped a fleece blanket around me. He sat on my side of the table, and pulled me up against him, one arm warm around my back, my head pillowed comfortingly on his shoulder. I tucked my bare feet up into the fleece and let myself relax into being held. It had been a bad day, and although this was only Anders, the Warhammer nerd, for a moment it was good to believe in his Norse god looks. He felt strong, and safe.

'See,' he continued in Norwegian, 'you are home now.' I could feel the warmth of his breath on my hair. His other arm came up to curve me to him. 'You do not need to be SuperCass, who can dare anything. You are in your own *Khalida*, and you are allowed to admit that you were frightened, shut in that tomb.'

'It was so dark,' I said. I wasn't going to wail; I kept my voice low and drowsy. 'It was like there would never be any light ever again, as if the sun and moon had been snuffed out at the end of the world. And it smelled of earth, and cold, and forgotten things. The walls were of thin stones, laid together, perfect. It was built to last till the end of time. I could see myself lying there always with their dead. I couldn't shift the entrance stone from inside. After that I was afraid I would never get out, even though I knew that Brian had once got in. I had to believe I could, but deep down I knew he could have filled up the hole once and for all, concreted it in. And then I'd only just got out when they were hunting me again.'

His arm shifted and tightened. 'I could not have let myself drop down onto the cliff edge like that.'

'You would have,' I said, with conviction. 'There wasn't an alternative.'

'I would have taken my chance on running.'

'I knew they had a gun.' My eyes were starting to close properly. I let his shoulder take the weight of my head. 'They'd shot Cat's mother. If they hadn't done that I wouldn't have known where to get out. If they hadn't sunk the Rustler and left the Siamese to swim ashore, Gavin wouldn't be dragging Cole Deep tomorrow. Bast's revenge.'

'Sleep, Cass.' I could hear the smile in his voice.

'The motorboat must be moored up by the cottage.'

'The Inspector will find it, or the Coastguard, or the lifeboat.'

The cottage … My brain had had a chance, now, to sort out what was going on there, with the bed and tripod. *What are the laws about films of sex in this country?* Not bringing in pornography, but making it. Cerys must have approached Anders, asked if he'd be in a movie. I couldn't see many normal, healthy young men turning that one down, but once he'd done it, it must have lain on his Lutheran conscience. No wonder he'd had that air of combined bounce and misery. The prohibition on the cottage made sense too. He didn't want me being tricked into her games.

'I looked inside the cottage,' I said. 'I saw the set-up. It doesn't bother me.' It did, a little. I didn't want to visualise Anders making love to Cerys.

The warm arms tensed. 'I went only once,' Anders said. I could hear in his voice that he was blushing. 'She asked me, and I thought it would be a laugh, you know, and then when he offered to pay me, I thought, well, why not, although I was nervous, because I had never done such a thing before. But I did not like it. It was not right, and I knew that. That was why I did not want you to go working – I thought that at least the money would buy us food for two weeks.' Confession over, his arms relaxed. 'But I would not do it again. I felt ashamed. It was not nice.'

'Did Olaf work the camera?' I asked.

He nodded. 'That is why I did not want you to have anything to do with him. He is not a nice man.'

'I did something as bad,' I confessed. 'I heard Alain was thinking to set off across the Atlantic, so I chatted him up, became his girlfriend so I could go too.' Was that why it had ended as it did, because I'd begun with the wrong motives? Yet we'd become good friends as well as lovers. The loss of his death swept over me again. We could have had such fun exploring the world's oceans together –

'Think about something else,' Anders said. 'Why do you not dress up and come dancing tomorrow night?'

It was warm against his chest. 'I look silly dressed up.'

'I don't know how you know. You have not dressed up for years, only once, for that press interview. The pretty dress your mother brought you for it is hanging in the locker.'

'Maman. *Joue avec tes poupées, chérie, sois sage.* Be a little girl.'

'I would like to dance,' Anders said. 'I have not tried

192

your Shetland dances yet. I would like to see if they are descended from the Norwegian ones.'

I considered this for a moment. He was being so comforting that it seemed churlish to refuse. 'Do you mean going in to one of the Islesburgh tourist evening things?'

'I meant the Show dance, tomorrow night.'

The sleepy mood was broken. I sat upright. 'Oh my mercy, Voe Show tomorrow! I said I'd go round and help out with the lifeboat stall. That is, I suppose it's still happening – after Alex. Maybe they've cancelled it.'

'It would be too late,' Anders said. 'We only heard about the boy here after eight o'clock, from the owner of *Renegade*. He had joined Olaf looking, until they found the boy, and the police took over.'

'But it was Kirsten, his mother, who was doing the stall.'

The arms around me jerked. 'His mother is called Kirsten?'

'You wouldn't have met her,' I said. 'She doesn't often come after the sailing.'

'I did not know –' Anders said. 'The poor lady.'

'Do you know her?'

'Be a good girl,' Anders said, 'and stop asking questions. I think you are half-mongoose, like the old English stories by the grandfather of the man who makes the cakes.'

I didn't bother to disentangle that. 'She wouldn't take communion,' I said. 'And now this. Poor Alex. He would have made a good sailor, and it would have kept him out of mischief too. He was so young –'

The spell was broken. I pulled back against Anders' arm, and he let it fall. I clutched the fleece blanket around my nightshirt, not looking at him, and sat back on my engine box. 'Do you want to come to the show too? I'd likely need to set off straight after breakfast.'

'Are you sailing around?'

'I was thinking to.'

'Then set out as soon as you like, and I will wake to help moor up in Voe.'

'Okay,' I said. I wriggled my way back into my bunk and curled into my sleeping position. 'Goodnight –' and then I added, self-consciously, 'Anders, thank you.'

He sat for a moment longer, then sighed, and rose. *Khalida* rocked as he moved forward and undressed; I heard the nylon rustle of him wriggling into his sleeping bag, then there was silence.

7

'Hit's a fine day in Voe.'

(Shetland saying from the times of prohibition: Voe was one of the few places where alcohol could be bought.)

Chapter Eighteen

Friday 3 August
Tide times for Brae:
Low Water 04.22   *0.2m*
High Water 10.49   *2.1m*
Low Water 16.32   *0.5m*
High Water 22.53   *2.3m*
Moon full

I woke just after half past six, and lay for a moment, feeling the events of the last days rushing back at me. Gavin's arrival, and he and Magnie winding me up about trowie lights. Finding the Siamese cat. Alex winning the race – Alex's death. Jimmie looking for Kevin, and the boat still locked up. The dark cottage, with the tripod broken over the charred remains of the bed. The earth smell of the mound, and the raw stone of the cliff. Anders, comforting in the night.

That memory sent me wriggling out of bed. I felt stiff all over, and the cuts hurt each time I used my hands. Once I'd got dressed and pulled my boots on, I found the tube of Norwegian hand cream and rubbed it in thoroughly.

The wind was soft, in keeping with Voe Show tradition. Those in the know took their oilskins to Walls Show, for the morning at least, but their suntan cream to Voe. The first Saturday of August had been glorious summer for every childhood year I remembered, and judging by the fret of cloud around the horizon and the burnished blue above, today was going to be the same again. I left my oilskins hanging in the locker, and hoisted the mainsail while we were still in the berth. No need to wake Anders by putting the engine on; I cast the ropes off, flinging them to lie neatly on the pontoon, then pushed the boom out to edge *Khalida* backwards. Once we had the wind on the quarter, I unfurled the jib, and we slid silently out of the marina and set our noses to the south. Naturally, that was the direction the wind was coming from; I sheeted in, and we tacked across to the old Manse, back to Busta House, across to short of the underwater Cuillin and back to the Burgastoo, that odd volcanic plug at the mouth of the canal separating Muckle Roe from the mainland. That should make sure we'd clear the cluster of rocks just off Weathersta Point.

I wasn't the first out on the water. I'd heard Inga's Charlie's boat going out just as I'd woken, and now I saw her red hull out in Cole Deep, with a varnished fishing boat that was usually kept in Voe sidling out past Linga to join her. Both were all-purpose boats, thirty-five foot long, with a white superstructure jutting up behind the wheelhouse – the winches they used for hauling up a line of creels. As I sailed down Busta Voe, the varnished boat came out into Cole Deep, and the two began steaming steadily across the stretch of water, in line. When they neared Muckle Roe, they turned, as a pair, and went back again. Dragging, I thought at first, but searching the bottom with their echo sounders seemed more likely. These days, even the smallest fishing boat had instruments that could spot a bucket on the bottom, let alone a substantial boat with a mast that would make a distinctive shape on their screens.

I'd just come to that conclusion, off Burgastoo, when my mobile rang. It was Gavin.

'Good morning. I see you're none the worse for your adventure yesterday.'

What had Anders called me? 'SuperCass, that's me.'

'And where are you going, this bonny morning?'

'Round to Voe. Where are you?'

'On the varnished fishing boat.'

'Are you dragging, or echo-sounding?'

'Echo-sounding. If we find her, it will take more than these two boats to lift her.'

'Good luck,' I said. 'I'll hear how you get on.'

'I'm sure you will,' he agreed. 'Would you like the news from last night?'

'If you're allowed to tell it.'

'The local force is in charge of the death of that poor boy, but they're happy to have me liase with Newcastle over the other two. We found one of your bodies, the woman. The helicopter will have another look for the other one today, but it may have sunk faster, or have been more in the current. They won't find him alive, after a night.'

'It won't make any difference,' I said. 'They were both dead when they went over. Hang on, I need to tack here.' I laid the phone down, swung *Khalida* round, changed sides with the jib, and lifted the phone again. 'I'm back.'

'Newcastle is sending somone up to identify the body we found. I would have thought fingerprints and a photograph would do, but they seem determined.'

'Was their motorboat moored at the cottage?'

'It was indeed, but we can't do anything with it until we've identified it as theirs. You could do that for us, then we can get a preliminary warrant. We've not had a chance to talk to the owner of the cottage yet.'

I remembered Inga's talk. 'He's busy setting up a rifle range.'

'Voe Show. I'm a countryman myself, remember. I could only get these fishing boats for an hour, this early. After that, Keith here will be busy frying mackerel and monks' tails on the barbecue, and Tam, on the other boat, has to go and judge cattle.'

'I'm helping with lifeboat souvenirs.'

'The Newcastle officer wants to see all the set-up here, which will mean opening up your mound.'

'Will you be allowed?'

'I'll try to make the case that others have been in there recently. No doubt the county archeologist will want to be present, and probably someone from Historic Scotland too. I don't know how long it will take to get permission from them.'

'I'm not volunteering to go back in and take photos.'

'I've already suggested one of those robot cameras. Chief Inspector Talley, the Newcastle man, insisted on leaving a guard up there too. You can imagine how popular that made me.'

'Especially with the guard.'

I heard a shout behind him, both through the mobile and echoed across the water. The varnished boat stopped, backed a little. 'I must go,' Gavin said. 'I'll see you later.'

I put the mobile back on the chart table, and set *Khalida* on course to slip into Olna Firth, between Weathersta and Linga. I linked the autopilot chain over her tiller, and left her to sail herself while I watched what was going on five hundred yards away. Both boats had stopped now, right in the middle of Cole Deep. I could hear an excited buzz of conversation from one to the other.

They had found the yacht.

I'd been conscious, as we came closer to Voe, of more traffic than usual going along the main road that skirted the voe here, all in the Voe-wards direction, and now as we came between the narrows into inner Olna Firth, it was very clear it was show day. The road was clogged with cars indicating the left turn-off. The marquees were up behind the hall, and the green fields stretching down to the school were covered with busy people, just as they had been when I'd been a child, and the Voe Show was the highlight of the summer holidays.

Voe was a divided village, set around the end of long, thin Olna Firth. On each side of the voe the hills were steeper than usual in Shetland, and on our starboard side was a trail of croft ruins, spaced out along the green hill. The grey stone rectangles had once been ten minutes by boat from the pier, but now that everything had to be accessible using wheels, they were an unthinkable mile's walk. The first still-inhabited houses were by the road that ran over the Camel's Back to Aith, substantial two-storey croft houses with porches and dormer windows, looking chunkily workmanlike below the pale-yellow Georgian elegance of Voe House, restored by BP for its executives to hold receptions. The stone-built Pierhead Restaurant was owned by Keith, who was echo-sounding for Gavin, but about to go and take over the barbecue, then the road curved up to meet the main road north. The houses continued along the shore, a mixture of traditional and new-builds. A west Highlands-style burn tumbled down the hill, wooded by spiky-branched electricity pylons.

The north side was a different world, big business come to Shetland. Down by the shore were the remains of an old kirk and graveyard, with the newer kirk a hundred yards further, solidly whitewashed, but the houses above were single-storey bungalows, painted blue, white, rose, and yellow – Mulla, this estate was called, and it had been built by the oil companies to house its officials and their families. On this side too was the shop, Tagon Stores, with a petrol pump, and behind that was the school, with three wooden extensions around the old school building, and the hall, extensively refurbished in the eighties.

I stuck some bacon under the grill once the narrows

were passed, and buttered two rolls. Rat came out to check for crispy rind, whiskers twitching hopefully. I sent him out to the cockpit with it, but kept Cat below with his. He'd not been loose at sea yet, and he was too small for a pet lifejacket. The Siamese cat would have had one, and I betted he'd have worn it; another reason to be sure it hadn't been Peter and Sandra who'd sunk the Rustler. Besides, it was their home. I remembered the interior, posher by far than *Khalida*'s, but with that same air of being lived in, books open, cushions set ready, mugs to hand. It wasn't some hired boat to be jettisoned. No, they wouldn't have sunk *Genniveve* any more than they'd have drowned their cat.

The sun hadn't quite broken through the mist yet, but the grey was thinning, and you could see it would soon be a glorious morning. The show was laid out as it always had been. Immediately behind the hall there was a mesh of wooden-built pens, filled with black and white Shetland cattle. I could hear them bellowing from here. There was always one bull who spent his day objecting to being penned in a space four metres square. Next to that, there was a green agricultural shed like a giant tin can sliced longways, which housed the plants, and a rectangular shed joining it. Above that, fluttering multi-coloured bunting, was the small white 'admin' caravan where you bought the programme. There was a slot-together stage flanked by huge speakers on this side of the shed, then the battery of small pens with hens, geese, and ducks. The marquee next to that would be pets and fleeces, with the dogs on tethers beside it, and the one after that'd be the beer tent. I'd never been in there, as the bar staff had always included one secondary teacher from Brae High School, who knew to a day when every child in the area became legal drinking age. I'd not quite been sixteen when Dad had gone to the Gulf, and I'd been packed off to Maman in France, old enough to have a couple of tins at a disco, but the show would have been pushing my luck.

After the beer tent came the two trade-stall marquees gable end on to me, with a straggled row of pick-ups, trucks, and horse-boxes parked behind them. The lifeboat stall would be in one of those. The barbecue was in the middle of the field, and already doing good business; I could see the blue reek standing above it, and there was a snake of people waiting for their first bacon roll. My 6.30 rising had been a long lie compared to the people who'd been giving horses, sheep, and cattle a last brush at 4 a.m. before loading them onto trucks. Even from here, I could smell the first waft of fried mackerel, drifting on the air along with the bull bellowing, a dog barking, and the country classics CD that had said 'show day' as long as I could remember.

The pens in the lowest field were sheep and horses. The sheep were just wooly backs within their squares, white, grey, black, brown, like a chessboard. The horses were judged in the ring, and a circle of black, chestnut and piebald was making its way around the field set aside for them, enclosed by a square of spectators. Below that, at the back of the school playground, the green grass was checkered by the first two lines of parked cars, chrome and mirrors glinting as gleams of sun broke through.

I rolled the jib and slipped the mainsail down just below the old kirk, two hundred yards from the pier. Anders appeared at the first turn of the engine, and made the mooring ropes and fenders ready. We motored alongside the pier that once shipped Shetland knitwear all over the world. The long, low building just on the other side of the road, which was now the Pierhead, had once been Adie's Knitwear – as in Kate Adie, intrepid BBC war correspondent – and the jumpers Tenzing and Hillary had worn as they stood on the summit of Everest had come from this factory.

Of course, here in Shetland, Voe had been a fishing

village too. We'd come along the long, sheltered voe that had made it a safe haven for the herring boats casting their nets out to the west. They'd rowed and sailed their sixareens fifty miles towards America, until the western island of Foula was just below the horizon, and dropped their long lines for haddock, cod, turbot. There would have been a haaf station on the beach, for slitting, salting, and drying the fish, and the building just above the pier was the Böd, once the net-shed and sail loft for Voe's fishing fleet. It was turned now into camping-style accomodation, but there were still commercial fishing boats at the pier, along with a beautifully restored fishing smack, and a cluster of little boats moored side-by-side and nose-to-nose in the small marina.

We moored on the outside of the last berth, and sat in the cockpit to eat our bacon rolls. Keith's varnished boat came in just as we were finishing, turned on itself with a roar of bow-thrusters, backed into its berth, and cut the engines. Keith looped his mooring warps over his cleats, then raised a hand to us.

'Your policeman's still out there,' he called. 'Charlie brought his diving gear, and he's going down to take a look.'

'You found it then,' I said.

He nodded. 'No doubt about it. The mast showed up on the echo-sounder, plain as plain.'

I grimaced at Anders.

'I think the idea was to put a rope on any bodies, and bring them up, even if lifting the boat has to wait,' Keith finished. He stepped ashore. 'I'll wedge the gate. There'll be a few coming to the show by boat.'

I hadn't thought of bodies being aboard the boat, but I supposed it was logical. If Peter and Sandra had been killed at the trowie mound or the cottage, then it would have been easy to transfer bodies from the motorboat using the boom as a crane. If she was to be found, in two, three, twenty years time, then the bodies might as well be found inside her, instead of surfacing somewhere else and starting off an enquiry. The brightening day was dimmed by the reminder.

We finished off our bacon rolls, had a cup of tea each, then Anders and I set out for the show, leaving Cat and Rat behind. Shows were only suitable for animals who could be trusted to behave on a lead. The Pierhead car park was empty, but the tables were set out ready for the throng who'd naturally gravitate there once the tent bar stopped selling. They'd be serving fish and chips during the day, too, and the restaurant upstairs with the dormer windows that looked right out over the voe would likely be booked out for the evening, as well as them doing a roaring trade in pub meals downstairs. It was worth coming to Voe just to eat there; Keith grew or caught all his own scallops, mussels, salmon, haddock, and monkfish. The only way you'd get fresher was in one of those restaurants with a pick-your-fish tank.

We came down the steps by the side of the Böd, scrunched along the beach, then cut up the steep, green hill directly for the show. My legs protested as we went upwards again, after yesterday: two hills in two days. If I went on like this my fellow sailors would be volunteering me as a runner in the Shetland equivalent of the 'three peaks' race. The grass was like a medieval tapestry, studded with gold tormentil, the first pincushion-scabious, sky-blue squill, the hooded dusky pink of lousewort. A lark twittered above our heads, and the smell of barbecued mackerel hung tantalising in the air. I reminded myself I'd just had a bacon roll. I'd save the fish for dinner, after a morning selling souvenirs.

We came between two houses and reached the road at last, a two-lane highway, the arterial route between Brae and Lerwick. We crossed it, and headed up through the car park to the marquees.

I'd forgotten that the rifle range was set up between Marquees D and E, in that nice clear space where stray bullets would fall harmlessly into the stretch of grass between the back of the marquees and the line of animal trailers. The stall-holder was still putting the last touches to it. I stopped to stare. *Brian's no changed*, Inga had said. *Go to the rifle-range*.

The range itself was competently home-made, with a high, plyboard back, two sheets of eight-by-four standing upright, and a shelf with pyramids of tin cans ready to be shot at. The plyboard was painted white, and well pocked with missed shots from previous years; the cans stood out in neon orange. There was a counter set up in front, a metre from the targets, with an upright pole bobbing with furry toys in garish colours, smaller toys along the front, and, in the middle, a two-metre space with a business-like rife lying in it. The dull gleam of the metal told me it was well used and maintained. There were several neon posters with slogans like 'Try your luck, pardner!' and 'Show off your sharpshootin' skills!' Above the counter, keeping it steady, was a title board, with Wild West lettering spaced between painted cowboy hats and pistol belts: 'Shooting Range'.

Brian himself was busy hammering a long plank to the ground four metres from the front counter – the toe-rail for his customers. He was dressed in full Western gear, a checked shirt and leather waistcoat, leather chaps over his jeans, and a ten-gallon hat hanging down his back. He lifted his head as we came over, gave the board a last couple of bangs, then stood up and turned towards us. In the cowboy gear he looked like a Mexican extra from an early Clint Eastwood movie, and not one to be trusted either. His dark eyes flickered across at Anders, and his mouth curled in the scornful twist I remembered, then he looked at me and flashed white teeth in a smile.

'Hey, Cass, come to have a shot at being Annie Oakley? How d'you like my stall?' Trying to impress me hadn't worked for him and Olaf at school, but it seemed old habits died hard. I gave the hats and pistols board a long stare.

'It looks really good,' I said. 'Eye-catching.'

He nodded, satisfied. 'It gets brawly popular, especially as folk have a dram or two in the beer tent. All the men want a go then, to show their girlfriends how macho they are.' He picked up the rifle and held it out to Anders. 'Here, have a go for free.'

I could feel Anders almost take a step back, then re-balance himself. He jutted his chin and stepped forward. They stood for a moment like that, eye to eye, a strange pair, like darkness and light, Brian's dark head and Anders' fair one, Anders' pale gold skin and Brian's mahogony tan, and the locked eyes giving off a bristling like two cats on a wall. I couldn't think of any reason why Anders should ever have handled a rifle, except playing cowboys through the forest as a child, but he took it easily enough, weighing the balance of it with his wrists, and lifted it to his shoulder as if he knew what he was doing. Brian noticed it too; the dark eyes narrowed, and his mouth thinned under the bandit moustache. But he'd laid down the challenge, and he had to go through with it now.

Anders took the rifle from his shoulder, and looked down for the marker plank. He stepped behind it, lifted the rifle again, sighted, then gave a contemptuous shrug, and took three, four, five paces back. A quick glance up at Brian, watching him with a look I couldn't read and didn't like, then he raised the rifle to his shoulder again. There was a long pause; the country music jangled in my ears, and I shifted my feet on the dew-slippery grass. Then Anders' finger moved on the trigger, and the centre pyramid of cans clanged to the floor.

He didn't bother to take a second shot, simply walked

back to the marker, rifle held out. 'It is a nice gun.' Brian took it from him in silence. There was no sign of triumph on Anders' face, no expression that I could read. He'd retreated, as he sometimes did, behind impenetrable smoothness. 'Thank you. Cass –' A glance flicked up at Brian. 'I'll head up to the hall. Text me if you need help in carrying boxes.'

He turned on his heel and strode off. The disquieting expression I'd seen in Brian's eyes had gone. Now he was laughing, although it seemed a forced laugh, and shaking his head. 'I should have remembered that there are still bears in Norwegian forests.' He laid the rifle back on the counter and picked up the box of pellets. 'What stall are you carrying boxes for?'

'The Lifeboat.'

'Oh, Cerys will be back soon.' He smiled, but it didn't look as if he was thinking about his wife fondly. Of course; if he knew about her games with Anders at the cottage, that would explain that little bit of one-upmanship which had backfired on him so badly. I decided Anders and I would be leaving Voe before the range closed, before the bar got rowdy. All that muscle suggested Brian might be too handy with his fists. 'My wife, Cerys – you met her at Mam's, the other day. She's doing the stall for Kirsten.' His face shadowed. 'You heard about the bairn, right enough. That was a tragic thing. He should never a been on that quad, he was over light for it. Cerys and I, we feel it like it was one of our own.' He dropped onto the spectator bench at the side of the marquee, and I sat down beside him. 'We dinna hae any bairns, well, no yet anyroad, and Olaf and I have aye been pals, and then we married pals too, so their boys have been back and forward, well, since they were babies.' There were tears shining in his dark eyes. 'I thought maybe they'd cancel the show, but it was just too late the news came. There'll be a lock o' folk not feeling like it today. But we canna make a better o' it.'

He took a deep breath. On the other side of the field, a tractor started up.

'He was one of ours at the sailing,' I said. 'He had the makings of a good seaman.'

Brian nodded. 'Aye,' he said. He took another breath, and squared his shoulders. 'So Cerys said to Kirsten that she'd see to the stall, get it set up, then go back to her. She'll be any minute. I needed the pick-up for shifting this, then she took it back to load up.'

He stood up and turned away from me, as if he'd had enough of the conversation. 'You're in this marquee here.'

'Thanks,' I said.

I took a quick look back from within the doorway of the marquee. He was slamming the fallen cans back with a ferocious energy that made me uneasy. In spite of the jaunty checked shirt and scarlet neckerchief, he was brewing trouble for somebody.

Chapter Nineteen

Since there was no sign of Cerys, I supposed I'd better get the apology to Barbara over with. She'd been a steward in the knitwear section all through my childhood, so I headed up to the hall. The knitwear had always been the first thing you saw, as you came in the back door, and it still was. There were two small rooms, normally used for committee meetings and the like. Each had a large table in the centre, and items pinned up all around the walls. The first room was adult knitting, with cobweb-fine lace shawls on one wall, thicker-wool 'haps' in scallop patterns of natural colours or shades of green and red on another. In the centre were traditional Fair Isle jerseys, the women's yoke jumpers with a round-the-shoulders ring of the fir-cone or star pattern, and the spectacular men's 'all-overs' like the one Magnie wore when he was dressed up, hoops of pattern in three shades of brown, green, or blue on a white background.

The second room was fun knitting, mostly by children. There was a tea-cosy in the shape of a croft house, complete with porch, and another made like a flowerpot with huge crochet begonias tipping out of it. A platoon of knitted scarecrows, soldiers, big-eyed moppets, and flat-faced bears stared at me. The youngest schoolbairns must have been doing 'bugs and beasties', for there was a swarm of knitted ladybirds, dragonflies, and spiders, with two women I took to be the judges conferring earnestly over them.

Barbara was standing apart from them, catalogue in hand should she be needed, but making it clear by her stance that she wasn't influencing them in any way. I was about to back off, thinking this maybe wasn't the time to distract her, but the movement caught her eye. She looked over at me, and nodded. 'Now then.'

She'd aged ten years. The eyes that had been so sharp behind their glasses were reddened, with dark bags under them, and her firm mouth had a tremor in it that hadn't been there before. Olaf's children must have felt almost like her own grandchildren. 'I was expecting you last night.' Even her voice lacked conviction.

I sidled over, and spoke softly under the judges' deliberations. 'Barbara, I'm really sorry. I heard about Alex being missing, and had a sudden idea where he might be. He'd been listening when we were talking about the trowie mound, up above your cottage.'

Her brows snapped together at the mention of the cottage. 'He'd have no call to go there.'

'Magnie was speaking about lights up at the mound. I thought he might have decided to investigate it. I just went chasing off without thinking about what day it was.'

She shook her head. The catalogue trembled in her hands. 'It was an awful thing, an awful thing. I was always faerd o' those quad bikes. That's an accident waiting to happen, I thought.'

I nodded. 'He was a fine boy. He was one of my sailors.'

'Aye, his grandfather was a good hand with a boat. The boy favoured him, with the shade of his eyes.' She drew a hankie out from her sleeve, and blew her nose, then glanced across at the judges, moved on now from the ladybirds to knitted vegetables. 'I'd need to be concentrating on this work.'

'What day would you want me to come now?'

She turned back to me with an apologetic look, and looked away again. 'I was thinking – I had a word with

211

Brian – and he was feeling I'm no needing to pay for any help. He thinks I'd be better applying to the council for a home help, now I'm over sixty-five. So I doubt I'll maybe do that.' Her neck flushed a mottled crimson. 'I hope I'm no' wasted your time.'

'No, that's fine,' I said. Her embarrassment made me feel awkward too. 'No problem. I'll see you later, then.'

I backed away from her, navigated around the tables, out into the fresh air and walked back down the field to D Marquee. So Brian had decided that his mother didn't need help, had he? Was it just because he thought the council would pay (a non-starter in the current financial crack-down, I'd have said), or because he didn't want a nosey-parker noticing unusual items, like a genuine Russian icon among the bric-a-brac? Cool Cass had been a bright one, doing well in tests, tipped for seven Credit Standard Grades if she hadn't been packed off to France …

Oh, well. I was sorry about the money, but Anders would be pleased.

I was passing the stacks of hen-and-duck cages when I noticed Kevin of the noisy motorboat. A glance down at the pier showed me he'd come around in it; it was moored outside *Khalida*. I hoped he'd used plenty of fenders, and taken a line to the pier, rather than to my cleats.

It was the furtiveness of his behaviour that made me notice him. He had something he was jingling in his pocket, and he was standing as if he was admiring the crated fowl, but with constant looks over his shoulder, as if he was trying to spot someone, or avoid them. He shuffled on a metre to the next set of cages ("Cock and two hens, same breed"), turned his face towards them and stood waiting, his eyes still darting everywhere. I stood at the corner of the pens and watched him, eyes as casually turned towards the exhibits as his.

He was getting impatient. He checked his watch, turned to look down towards the pier, then checked his watch again, other hand jingling in his pocket throughout. I was feeling too conspicuous. I slipped around the pens to the other side of where he was, a metre from him, with the tall stack of pens between us. I could just see the top of his head, and his welly-booted feet. I took a step back, conscious of my own feet. Now he wouldn't be able to see me at all.

The yellow boots fidgeted like a pony who's been asked to stand still. Then at last he turned round with a sharp, exhaled breath. 'I was thinking you werena coming.'

A pair of muddy black wellies stopped beside the yellow ones. I tried to peer through the gap between two pens, but could only see Kevin's elbow. The other man had a deep voice, and didn't sound concerned in the least by his impatience. 'The ram was being awkward. It wouldna load.'

The jingling noise came again. Kevin's hand pulled a key-ring out of his pocket. It had a cork ball on it – one of the floating ones, and so probably boat keys. 'Here. It's all on board, ready. Just transfer it to your pick-up.'

'Yeah, yeah.'

'And mak' sure he doesn't see you,' Kevin hissed. 'The place is crawling with fuzz,' he added.

The other man's voice rang out, unconcerned. 'The fuzz are busy out in the voe, with this yacht they'd found on the bottom. The chopper's brought in another body too.' The black boots marched along the stack of pens; I dodged back quickly as they came out around, and watched them go. I didn't know the name of the crony who'd come up to him, but I recognised the face: one of the most persistent of the party-goers.

So whatever had been on board was being moved,

before 'he' found it. Gavin, I wondered, or someone else?

I went into D Marquee, and found two empty tables with a card marked 'Aith Lifeboat' tacked on the nearest. We were right by the door, sharing the tent with someone from the council advertising composting bins, the Organic Food Growers, a stall selling bags of home-made toffee, knitwear, hand-made cards, and bric-a-brac, in aid of the restoration of Gonfirth Kirk, and the Cat Protection League with an array of cat-related items. I looked these over, wondering if I should be getting Cat a hessian-wound scratching-post with a swinging ball, to save *Khalida*'s woodwork.

'I've just found a kitten,' I explained to the stall-holder, 'and so far he's not sharpened his claws on my varnish, but prevention might be better than cure.'

'It's an individual thing, with cats,' she replied. 'Some are awful furniture scratchers, whatever you do, and others only scratch outside. How old's he?'

I was just giving the details when a red pick-up slithered over the grass and swerved to a halt with its rear to the marquee entrance. It had a dozen cardboard boxes wound round in blue and white RNLI tape in the back.

'Speak to you later,' I said, 'that's my stall arrived.'

The door opened, and Cerys got out, dressed today in a candy-pink vest top and the sort of shorts that are just sawn off jeans. Hers were so short that the flaps of the pockets hung down below the fabric. It looked odd to me, but I was willing to accept it as high fashion – what did I know? Her vest top swooped down to show a lacy black bra, and she had huge pink-framed sunglasses stuck on the top of her head. She was more ferociously made-up than ever, but her eyelids were swollen under the frosted powder, and the whites of her eyes were tinged with red.

'Hi,' she said. Her voice was hoarse, as if she'd talked

herself ragged. 'Hope you've not been waiting long.' The flat voice wasn't exactly friendlier, but it had less of a sharp edge. I supposed her mother-in-law didn't bring out the best in her.

I took a step to the pick-up. 'Shall I bring these in?'

She held her hand up. 'Let me just sort out the inside first.'

She was impressively efficient about it. I'd have set her to organising a watch-rota any day. Before I knew it, I was helping to shift the table to a place where it didn't rock that was simultaneously a yard out from the back wall of the tent, yet not sticking in the way of the folk who'd be coming in. She turned the second table around to make an L, with room for people to crowd round and look, and commandeered chairs for us to sit on, then directed me to a smaller, upright box which contained large polythene bags and rolls of that green plastic temporary path. I was set to laying the path out on top of the poly bags between the chairs and our stall, for us to stand on, while she borrowed a table from an as-yet unoccupied stall to lay the boxes on while we unpacked. Only then was it all hands to carrying boxes.

'I've had a lot of practice,' she explained, once we had the ticker-tape boxes in a neat line. 'Kirsten and I do this at each show, through the summer.'

There was nobody close. It was a good time to say it, as much as any time can be good. 'I was so very sorry about Alex,' I said. 'He was one of our sailors, and a real star.'

Her eyes filled with tears that glinted on the lacquer mascara. She shook her head, unable to speak, and pounced on the box labelled 'cloths'. We draped white sheets and a banner with 'Royal National Lifeboat Institution' on it along the table in silence, then began opening the boxes: books about the sea, notepads, decorative thimbles, fold-away hairbrushes, glass tankards with a Severn lifeboat etched on them, packs of cards, tea-towels and dusters, T-shirts and peg-bags, and carrier-bag holders. There was a whole box of pens, pencils, rubbers, and little notebooks, and another box entirely filled with plastic boats. Finally, there was the 'bairnie gear': balls, crocodiles with wind-up arms for playing in the bath, grab hands in the shape of sharks, laser-patterned spinning-tops. I would never have believed so many different items could be squished onto two tables. It took a good hour to get it all set out.

'There,' Cerys said, when everything had been set out to her satisfaction, and the last empty box had been stowed under the table. 'Now there's just the food box, then I can get rid of the pick-up.'

She brought in one more box. She was obviously planning to settle in for the day; a silver flask stood up in one corner, and among the rest were packets of crisps, apples, a bag of marshmallows, and – going native here – a packet of the puffy, powdery biscuits known simply as 'muckle biscuits', a tub of Lurpak, and a block of cheese. Two plates stood end-on beside the flask, held in place by two mugs, a jar of coffee and a plastic bottle of milk. A knife-handle stuck up in the corner.

'Make's a cup of coffee, will you? I won't be a minute.'

She headed off. Now we were set up, people were starting to drift into the tent and look at the stall. I sold the woman from the cat stall a dish-towel, and an old seaman bought a notebook. I'd just set the two cups on the immaculate white sheets, on our side of the goods, when she returned and sank down on the chair with a sigh of relief.

'Thanks, Cass. Once I've had a coffee I'll be able to face the day.'

'What is it you do normally?' I asked. 'At home, I

mean.'

A wry smile twitched at the corners of her mouth. 'I work on and off in a teenage boutique.'

A group of younger children came in. We sipped our coffee while they picked up everything on the stall, showed it to each other, laid it back, and moved on, chattering like a tribe of bosun's monkeys.

'This is a treat,' Cerys said, watching them go. 'They're too young and too honest to shop-lift. The tales I could tell – honest to God, I don't know what kids are coming to. I'm not twenty years older than them, and I'd have said I was streetwise enough when I was their age, but I'd never have thought of half the tricks they come up with.'

'There's nothing to nick at the boating club,' I said.

A teenage lass came in, straight from the riding classes, judging by the immaculate jacket, tie and breeches, and the netted hair. 'Do you have one of these instant shoe polish pads?' she gasped.

I'd laid them out myself. 'These? £1.'

'Thanks.' She paid for it and disappeared at a run.

'They're nice kids here,' Cerys said. 'Mind you, they can't complain. It's a rich place, Shetland, good wages, and the parents spend on them. Her outfit now, we're talking upwards of £300, and the horse and tack to go with it won't have come free neither.'

'It's not just the money,' I said. 'It's the community too.' I thought of the children I'd worked with abroad, in sailing schools, sullen teenagers whose parents just parcelled them from one to another, and who'd decided that their only way forward was to exploit any guilt coming their way. There was no lack of money thrown at them, but that didn't compensate for feeling they didn't have a home any more. 'Here, there's no question about who you are, and where you belong. I felt it too, coming back. One day home and I was Dermot Lynch's lass, her that grew up out along Muckle Roe, that lass that got the sailing trophies. It's like an intricate map, and there you are on it, your place in the community.'

'I think that's the bit I can't stand,' Cerys said frankly. 'It's a spider's web, not a map. I have fun breaking the small town rules for these summer weeks, and winding Brian's mum up, but I couldn't live here. Thank God Brian's given the idea up.'

'The small town rules help too,' I said. 'Teenagers know them. They know that, whatever happens south, up here if you get caught shoplifting your name's in the papers, and everyone knows, and your mum's going to be so mortified.'

Another trio of children came in, deliberated over the exact colour of rubber to buy, and went on to the Gonfirth Kirk stall's toffee. Confusingly, here in Shetland, toffee was what the Scots would call tablet, squares of crunchy brown sugary stuff which were brilliant for instant energy. I remembered enjoying it myself on Voe Show day – the only time I was allowed it, as Maman insisted it would *détruire les dents*. It went like snow off a dyke at shows. The Gonfirth Kirk lady's cardboard boxful of little bags was half emptied already, and I'd need to hurry if I was going to buy some.

'Our mam would've leathered me if I'd even thought of coming home with clothes I'd not paid for.' Cerys shook her head. 'Times is changing. We had the good years, when there was money. Now everyone thinks they're entitled to it all, but the money's gone. Those riots, were you here then?'

I shook my head. I'd been in Bergen then, but I'd watched them on TV, a mob of teenagers indulging in an orgy of destruction and theft. I'd found it hard to believe what I was seeing, areas of London and Manchester turned into a no-go zone.

Cerys shook her head. 'No, I don't know. Sometimes I think maybe Brian's right, in spite of the small-town gossip.' She rose to bag up a handful of assorted pencils and rubbers and notebooks for a middle-aged lady in a yoke jumper. '£3.50, please. Ta. If we were thinking of kids, we should come back here, where it's still peaceful. The old-fashioned lifestyle, with all the mod cons.' She settled herself back in her chair, gave a quick look around to make sure nobody was listening, then slanted a sideways look at me, malice gleaming from between the spider-leg eyelashes. 'And you can still manage a bit of fun. What do you do when you want a man? Or are you into women?'

Her bluntness disconcerted me. 'It hasn't been a problem,' I managed, after a two-breath pause. That wasn't entirely true, but most nights I crawled into my berth too knackered to worry about my non-existent sex-life.

She gave a smooth, shark smile. 'You could do worse than Anders, now I've warmed him up a bit for you, got him over his inhibitions.'

There was no answer I could make to that, and I wasn't going to let this over-dressed Barbie doll wind me up. 'A couple of beers would do for that,' I said.

'Oh, we did better than beer.' Her eyes glinted, veiled by the glossy lashes. 'Not that he knows it.' She rose as an old man came in wanting Christmas cards, served him with a candy-sweet smile, then sat down again. 'You can never tell how well a man's going to perform with a camera on him, so you slip him an enhancer in a beer beforehand.'

This wasn't at all the sort of conversation I was comfortable with, but I wasn't going to show her that. Cool Cass … furthermore, the idea of her slipping Anders some sort of Viagra without his knowledge enraged me. 'Underhand,' I said, as contemptuously as I could.

Her eyes flashed angrily; the sugar-pink lips thinned. 'You'd prefer him to make a fool of himself by shooting too soon, or not being able to get it up at all?' Her tone suddenly went intimate. 'I know which he'd prefer. We had a good night.'

I smiled sweetly. 'Nice to hear about people enjoying themselves.'

Her eyes went to her watch again. 'So which do you prefer?'

I gave her a blank look, as if I'd forgotten the question.

'Men or women?'

'Men,' I conceded. I didn't add my personal view that a good sail was generally more satisfying. The knot of children that had gone straight for the toffee had finished rearranging everything on the Cat Protection Stall; it was our turn now. I stood up and smiled at them.

'Hiya, Cass,' one said. It took a moment to recognise her, out of her black and pale-blue wetsuit. The dark eyes gave her away as Inga's middle child, Dawn. 'Did you ken they've found a yacht near Linga? Dad's boat is one of the ones that was looking this morning.'

'They've found a *body*,' emphasised one of the boys. I knew him by the hat: Shaun, an expert in the art of dry capsizing, but not so good at remembering technicalities like sail trim.

'On the yacht?'

'Yeah, it said on SIBC, at eleven o'clock.'

SIBC was the local 24-hour radio station, with a news bulletin on the hour. I waved them out and sat down, thinking about that one. A body on the yacht. Peter? Sandra? I felt like I'd been rammed in the belly.

'How'd you feel about two at once?' Cerys' voice was as businesslike as if she was asking if I took milk in my coffee. 'I could set you up with, say, Anders and someone dark.' She paused and looked me over, as if it was a serious proposition. 'No, you're dark. Another blond man. How long's your hair, when it's loose?'

Darkness and light ... for a moment, I was too flabbergasted to answer. She continued as if I'd already agreed. 'One on one, you see, nobody's interested. They can do that for themselves. But if you're not into women, it has to be a threesome.'

I wasn't going to lose my temper. 'I think it's a revolting idea,' I said, 'and I'm not interested.'

Another slanted look. 'Sometimes people who aren't getting any sex are glad of an offer. Anders was.' She gave her watch another glance. 'Think about it, anyway. I'd need to get back to Kirsten. Will you be okay on your own?'

'I'll be fine,' I said.

I didn't follow immediately. She'd given me too much to think about. *It has to be a threesome* ... was that why Anders had been so shame-faced? And who had been the other woman? I heard his voice from yesterday: *His mother is called Kirsten?* Kirsten and Cerys, friends married to friends. Dark hair and fair, darkness and light. Kirsten, who was under Olaf's thumb; Olaf, who'd been a swaggering bully at school. I had a memory of him boasting about magazines he'd read, though even he hadn't risked bringing them to school. And the way he'd been eyeing me up, when he'd come to the boating club; had he been wondering how I'd take an offer like this? Had he set Cerys onto me, or did she go fishing for herself? Olaf was the 'he' Anders had mentioned, filming the threesome. *I do not want you mixing with these people ... the cottage is not a good place for you to go.* Now I'd begun, it was obvious what the relationship between Olaf and Cerys was. They were brash enough, both of them, to be lovers, in spite of being married to someone else. Maybe once he got bored of illicit sex with

221

his best mate's wife, he'd got his own wife to join in, his mistress's pal, Kirsten, who'd gone up for a blessing, but refused communion, as if she'd done something so wrong that she couldn't take communion until she'd been to confession.

I thought of Brian, in his gaudy shirt, with his rifle to hand, and that suppressed air of rage. *Robbie o'; the Knowe'd let his mouth open a bit wide* ... and so Brian had found out what everyone else in the place knew, that his wife and best friend were carrying on in his own house. He'd left Olaf with a key, to keep an eye on things while he was south. He'd gone there and found the bed with the black satin sheets and the video tripod. In a rage, he'd burned and smashed. He'd changed the locks so that there'd be no more of it. He couldn't confront Olaf now, not after Alex's death. There'd obviously not been a reckoning with Cerys yet either, with his mother in the same house – but there would be, I was sure of that.

Suddenly I wondered what Norman's part in all this was. What had Magnie said? *The mothers arena keen on their lasses going anywhere near him ... he goes along to the old Nicolson house.* Was Norman, young as he was, taking advantage of the kingsize bed and the video? Or was he part of his father's sleaze empire too? He was nearly sixteen; at nearly sixteen, I was working out how to run away from France, earning money and stashing it in an account Maman didn't know about, booking myself on board a tall ship that would bring me back to Scotland, where sixteen was an adult, and nobody could force me to go back to school in Poitiers, where I'd been a fish out of water, the selkie-wife having to pretend interest in the latest music and fashions. Norman liked knowing what was going on; he'd have found out about his father and Cerys soon enough, and could well have set to turning their set-up to his advantage. They did the threesomes, he invited the young lasses. I wasn't going to under-estimate a precocious teenager.

It was horrid, all of it.

Chapter Twenty

I was just brooding on the nastiness of modern life when there was a scuffle at the door, and Peerie Charlie charged in, gold curls flying, with the air of being propelled by his scarlet trainers. 'Dass, I seed ditten.'

He was dressed today in shorts and a lime-green T-shirt with a T-Rex on it, all slavering jaws, and the sort of thing I'd have thought would have given any toddler nightmares.

'I hope you don't mind,' Inga said. 'We came to the marquee earlier, and there was no sign of you, but we saw *Khalida* at the pier, so we drove down to see if that was where you were, and of course Charlie had to say hello to your kitten.'

Charlie held up a finger. 'I gentle. One.'

'It rather liked him,' Inga said.

Charlie did an imitation of a purr. 'I stuck in cat flap,' he said. He raised one elbow to show me a graze.

'Ouch,' I said, wondering if I'd heard right. 'What were you doing in the cat flap?'

'I stuck,' Charlie said.

'Did I hear that right?' I asked Inga.

She rolled her eyes. 'It was a notion of the lasses. Some TV programme had said burglars south were putting toddlers through cat flaps to open the door, and Dawn said it wouldn't work, and Vaila said it would, so they tried it with Charlie.' She grinned. 'It didn't work.'

I made a face. 'You wouldn't believe parents would do that with their own children, would you?'

'It didn't have to be theirs,' Inga said. 'Remember Oliver Twist, that bit where Bill Sykes took him to go burgling?'

'You're reading Dickens?' I said incredulously.

'Don't be daft. Miss Morrison showed us the film, in S1, as an end-of-term treat.'

I searched backwards in my memory. 'The boy who wanted more and lots of singing.'

'That's the one.'

Charlie had moved on to investigating the plastic boats on the stall. 'Mine,' he said, holding one up.

'You have one the same,' Inga said. 'In your bath. That's not your one, that's Cass's. You can choose a different one.' She sat down on Cerys' chair, her cheery smile dissolving. 'I was just over to see Kirsten. We both play in the netball team, and Alex was in Dawn's class. It's just awful.'

'How is she?' It felt a stupid question; what could you expect?

Inga shook her head, mouth twisting. 'Is that coffee?' She reached into the box and found a mug, added coffee powder, water, and milk. 'Oh, God. She's – she's distraught. It's not just Alex –' She shook her head again. 'I don't mean 'just' Alex. That's enough to send any mother crazy. I don't know how she can bear it. Just the thought of it makes me want never to let any of mine out of my sight ever again.' Now she was crying too, with a quick look to make sure Charlie was intent on trying the boats out on the floor. 'It's so awful. He was such a fine bairn.' Charlie looked up then stood up, toddler muscles shoving him straight up from a squatting position. He came over to give Inga a hug. 'Mummy not cry.' He gave her a kiss. 'I make it better.'

Inga brushed the tears away with one hand. 'Thank you, Charlie. I'm better now.' He went back to playing with his boats, but I could see he was keeping an eye on her. Inga knew it too; she calmed her voice. 'Poor, poor Kirsten. They've got her under sedation, but she was talking wildly, about it being God's punishment on her, and she kept trying to get up. I had to coax her into lying down again.'

'Was she involved in the goings-on at the cottage?'

Inga shot me a sharp look. 'Is this all something to do with your missing yacht?'

'I think it's all linked somehow, but I can't see how.'

'Don't you mess about with it. Leave it to your DI – what's his name, Macrae? It's his job.' She gave me a sudden fierce look. 'You haven't been messing about already, have you?'

I shook my head. 'Hand on heart, no,' I promised. 'I looked for the missing yacht folk, but that didn't lead to Alex's death.'

Her jaw sagged open. She gave me a steady look from her seal-dark eyes, then took a long drink of coffee. 'I hadn't thought of that. It was an accident – wasn't it? Alex.' Her voice was beginning to rise; she took a deep breath, and softened it. 'You're not saying that someone did that to him. Oh, God, poor Kirsten –'

It was Gavin's ship. I didn't know what I could say, and not say, and what harm saying the wrong thing might do. I shook my head. 'I don't know what the police are thinking.'

'He talks to you though, doesn't he, the Inspector from south? You had him out in the rescue boat yesterday.'

'Was it really only yesterday?' I asked. 'It feels like years ago.'

'And what're you done to your hands?'

Charlie looked up at that, stood again, and came round to look, taking my hands one at a time and turning them

226

over. 'Sore,' he pronounced. 'Poor Dass.' His voice oozed adult sympathy. 'Diss it better.' He gave each hand a slobbery kiss.

'Thanks, Charlie,' I said.

He took my hand. 'Now we see horses. Dass, come.'

Inga gave me a look that warned me I'd get the third-degree later, when Charlie was out of earshot. 'On you go,' she said. 'Have a wander. I'll take over here for a bit. If you see either of the lasses, can you tell them this is where I am?'

'I'll tell them,' I agreed, and stood up. Instantly I was towed towards the horse pens. The judging had finished; the small ponies were back in their pens, next to the sheep, and the big horses stood in a line in makeshift stalls. I steered Charlie towards the pens. I'd feel safer if there was a barrier between him and those plate-sized hooves. The grass we walked over had been cropped short by sheep in the weeks before the show. It was dry underfoot, with the occasional skein of wool entwined among the longer tussocks, but you had to watch out for drying lumps of sheep sharn.

Close to, the pens were made out of wooden pallets attached to upright posts with orange baler twine. Each pen was three pallets square, just big enough for three ponies or half a dozen sheep. Charlie clambered up the first pallet as if it was a ladder, and leaned over the top, staring. From below, a moorit ram with rust-coloured fleece and a magnificent pair of horns curling around his cheekbones glared back. Its eyes were yellow, with horizontal oval pupils. I grasped Charlie's T-shirt. Storms at sea were one thing, enraged Shetland rams quite another.

'Beeeh,' Charlie said, and climbed back down. 'Sheep. Beeeh. Not horse. Neigh.'

I steered him past a dozen more pens of sheep to where

the horses began. 'Here's a baby horse.' It was a red and white foal in the pen with its mother, its head no taller than Charlie's, its back still woolly, and its little tail waggling like clockwork. As soon as it saw Charlie's shoes peeping through the pallet, it came over to lip at the front of them.

'No, baby horse,' Charlie said, shuffling from foot to foot. 'Bad.'

'Babies always put things in their mouths,' I said. 'I expect you did too, when you were a baby.'

Charlie climbed down and put his face to the gap between the planks, then jumped back as the foal blew at him. For a moment he was uncertain whether to laugh or to cry, then he laughed and blew back. The foal jumped sideways on stiff legs. The mare, who'd been focusing on her haynet, lifted her head. I picked Charlie up, ignoring the protests from my shoulder muscles. 'Look, these ones are sleeping.'

There were two mares and two foals together in the next pen, and both foals were stretched out flat, totally relaxed, miniature hooves pawing on air, eyes closed. One was black, one black and white. The one nearest us had impossibly long eyelashes. As we stopped to look it opened one brown eye, looked at us drowsily, then closed it again.

'Awww,' Charlie said, with exactly Inga's intonation. 'I touch.'

'Not these ones,' I said. 'Let's see if we can stroke the riding ponies.'

We ducked under the fence and went along the front of the line of ponies who'd competed in the riding classes. The girl who'd raced in for polish was there, giving water to a pair of black Shetlands. Both were the traditional style, with a great froosh of mane between the ears, hiding half of the faces, and falling on both sides of the strong neck. The black coats shone as if she'd used the polish on them, and both had long tails that rippled to just above ground level.

'Hiya,' I said. 'May Charlie stroke one of your ponies?'

'This one,' she said. 'Hiya, Charlie! You ken me, I'm Janette. I'm in Vaila's class at the school. Would you like to sit on the pony?'

Charlie nodded, eyes wide.

'Gie him a pat first,' Janette said. She squatted down beside Charlie. 'He's that gentle. See.' She leaned forward, took a hold of the headcollar and gave the pony a kiss at the end of its black nose. The pony took it without a blink, then stretched its head forward and snorted at Charlie. His hand jerked in mine, but he stood his ground as the pony nosed at his T-shirt, then shook its head and snorted again. Janette kept her grip on its chin. 'Now you give him a stroke. See how soft his nose is.'

Charlie edged his hand forward, just touched the velvet nose and snatched it back, then touched again. 'He soft.'

'He's really soft,' Janette agreed. 'Shall I sit you on his back?' She swung him up, and kept an arm around him, so that she was taking his weight. Charlie held on tight to her shoulders. Gradually she coaxed him into sitting alone, with a chunk of mane held tightly in both hands. 'See, the pony doesn't want you to fall. He's standing still as still.'

To me, the pony had more of an air of 'not another one' than positive benevolence, but who was I to argue? You didn't find ponies on board a tall ship. Janette swung Charlie down again.

'Say "thank you" to the pony,' she said.

'Ta,' Charlie repeated.

'And to Janette,' I added.

'Thank you.' Charlie waved and towed me off at speed again. Pony time was obviously over. 'Ice cream.'

He was heading straight for the Mr Whippy van, parked

just opposite the barbecue. My stomach felt like it might be lunch-time, but my purse was in my jacket, draped over the chair behind our stall, and just because it felt like ice-cream time to me didn't mean it was that time for toddlers.

'Let's ask Mam first,' I said.

I was just leading him back towards the marquee when Charlie jumped and waved. 'Daddy!'

It was big Charlie, sandwiched between his two daughters. Peerie Charlie had got his colouring from his dad: Big Charlie had the same curly fair hair and light skin, weathered to a reddish tan this far on in the summer. It was strange how the boy favoured his father, the girls their mother, yet now I came to think of it, that was the Shetland way. Viking look-alike men weren't that uncommon, particularly in Yell, where there were a lot of tall, square-built men with reddish-fair hair, but you rarely saw that Scandinavian look of radiantly fair women. A lot of Shetland women were small and dark, with blue eyes, the Pictish look they'd inherited from their long-back fore-mothers, who'd been taken as Viking concubines when the raiders had arrived.

Big Charlie had been in charge of the other echo-sounding boat. I gave a glance down at the pier. Yes, he'd moored up there too, among the other fishing boats. *They found a body on board the yacht* ... As he turned to me, the forced cheerfulness he'd been using with the lasses evaporated. His skin was grey under the tan, and his mouth was turned down, as if he was feeling sick. 'Cass. Inspector Macrae asked me to look for you. He tried to phone you, but there's no signal up here.' He bent down to swing Peerie Charlie up onto his shoulders. 'Now, then peerie-breeks, have you seen the horses?'

'I sat horse,' Charlie affirmed. 'I hands tight.' He clenched his fists to show his sisters. 'Now I ice-cream.'

'Better ask Mam,' Charlie said. He swung his son down

again, and handed him to the lasses, then fished a fiver out of his pocket. 'Check with Mam, lasses, then take him off for an ice-cream.' He waited till they were out of earshot, then spoke softly. 'Yon police officer asked me to ask you, Cass, if you'd get a chance to go down to the pier. We found the yacht – you saw that.'

I nodded.

'I had my diving gear, so I went down.' His face tightened. 'There was the body in the cabin. I put a line around him –'

'Him?' I cut in. Peter –

Charlie nodded. 'Once we'd got him onboard I had a bit of an inspection with the flashlight.' He looked quickly around him, as if checking he wouldn't be overheard. 'Whoever sunk that yacht did it deliberately.'

'Could you tell how?'

Charlie nodded. 'One of the toilet pipes was sawn through, just past the seacock.'

'That'd sink her, right enough.' The seacocks were the fittings over the holes in the side of the boat: cooling water for the engine, sink and cockpit drains, and toilet water in and out. They didn't fail regularly, but if they did then you were in trouble, because you had a three-centimetre hole in the bottom of the boat. Every boat carried plugs for each seacock, just in case.

'The seacock was open – it was one of those lever ones, you could see it was open. The pipe just past it, one of those green plastic hose ones, the toilet intake, it was sawn right through, as if someone had taken a hacksaw to it, then opened the cock.'

'No sign of anyone trying to plug the leak?'

He shook his head. 'A bonny yacht, for someone to scuttle like that.' He glanced around him again, face grim. 'They've got the bodies in a white van down there, the one from the yacht, and one the chopper picked up this morning. The Inspector wanted you to name them for him, if you could, before they take them to Lerwick.'

'I'll go right now,' I said.

8

He's da main string o' da fiddle.

(Old Shetland saying: he's the most important person in an enterprise.)

Chapter Twenty-one

Gavin must have seen me coming, down the green slope of hill, against the grain when everyone was climbing up it, for when I got down to the beach he was waiting there for me. He was wearing a blue shirt, with the sleeves rolled up to the elbow to show brown, muscled arms; his kilt hung square above grey-green socks. 'Good afternoon,' he said, and fell in at my shoulder.

'Is it really that late?' I said. I glanced at the sun, and the short shadows; not far off one o'clock. A look at my scratched watch confirmed it, ten past one. No wonder I was hungry. I wished I'd eaten before I came down. I might not fancy food, after.

'We got a body in the yacht,' Gavin said softly, 'and another was found floating at sea, just where you'd expect it to be if it was thrown over the cliffs last night.'

'The Coastguard has a computer programme,' I said. 'You put in where the object was lost, factor in the tides, the wind and the size of the object, and it tells you where you can start looking.'

'The programme was bang on. The helicopter found her this morning, and the lifeboat picked her up, just about the time we found the yacht, so I told them to bring her to Voe.'

'Madge,' I said. 'The woman on the motorboat. And Peter on the yacht. So where's Sandra?'

Gavin spread his hands in a 'don't know' gesture. 'There's no sign of the motorboat. It was moored up at the cottage while you were being rescued, I saw it below us, but when the lifeboat came back it was gone. We've put an alert out.'

'But why should Sandra be taking David and Madge's boat?'

'The yacht was scuttled. The diver had a look around. He said there was a broken pipe in one of the seacocks.'

'He told me,' I said. 'Even a broken pipe'd only sink her if the person on board wasn't able to stop the leak. They'd have had plugs aboard, or a broom handle with a towel wrapped around, anything would do. You should be able to get the boat home.'

'If you were alive to sail it,' Gavin agreed.

'Was he alive?'

Gavin shook his head. 'Forensics will have to confirm it, but he was lying below, in the cabin, and there was no sign of locked hatches to trap him there. I think he was dead when the yacht was sunk.'

We'd come to the road now, and the background of music from the Pierhead had become a boom, boom, from chest-height speakers placed one each end of the pub front. The tables were busy with folk enjoying a pint and chips. Gavin led me past them and round into the car park. The white van was backed up to within a half-door width of the shed opposite, so that the back doors could be opened just enough to look in without anyone else being able to see inside. A policeman in uniform was waiting beside it, just to make sure everyone around knew what this was.

'This isn't going to be very bonny,' Gavin said. His voice was matter-of-fact, a warning, not sympathy.

I nodded. My hands had clenched at my side; I forced the fingers to uncurl.

'The man we picked up last night is already in Lerwick. You don't need to see him again. You'd already identified him as the man calling himself David Morse, who you saw falling dead, and as there aren't likely to be two moustached men falling off cliffs into the sea, we're taking it that that's who he is. We've got prints and a photo, so if he had any kind of record we'll soon get his real name.'

He opened the van door until it touched the wall behind, and motioned me into its space. Inside the van were two long parcels in black plastic, like dolphins washed up on a metal shore. The heads were at this end. I took a deep breath, bracing myself. One body had had a night at sea, with the salt water swelling the skin. The other had had three nights down on the bottom, among the crabs and lobsters.

Gavin came into the alcove of the van door and wall beside me. I could feel the warmth coming off him, through his blue shirt. He opened the other door, so that we stood in a triangle of metal, close as lovers. I could hear his breathing, the rustle of his shirt-sleeves as he leant forward to unzip the first bag. 'This is the one from the yacht.'

I closed my eyes for a second, summoning up my courage, then opened them again. Gavin had opened the bag down as far as the waist, but tucked one corner back over the head. I was looking at a man's torso, clad in a jumper which had been baggy, but which was now moulded to the contours of the body, a body blown out by gases so that the gansey was stretched tight. Fishermen's wives used to knit their men's initials into the square underarm gusset of their navy ganseys; they wanted to be able to identify their own. This jumper was knitted in eye-hurting stripes of dazzling colour, darkened by the water, but when it was dry it would be neon yellow, pink, lime green. *I put my foot down about the Phil hat, didn't I, pet?*

Gavin's eyes were intent on my face. 'You recognise it?'

I swallowed. 'Peter Wearmouth had a jumper like this.'

'I'm sorry about this,' Gavin said. His hand moved to

the triangle of black plastic which covered the head.

It was more unpleasant than I could have imagined. The underwater creatures had been busy. The face was a blur of ragged, whitish flesh, with pale bone sticking through along where the cheeks had once been, and around the eye-sockets. A piece of bony cartilage marked where the nose had jutted out. One eyeball lay in its socket, complete, but squashed out of shape; the other was a trail of colourless tubes. I saw more than I wanted to in that brief glimpse before my eyes found his hair, a ragged cap of silver, water-darkened to grey, and plastered in lines across the bony scalp. It was barely a face, yet I recognised the proportions. I nodded, feeling too sick to dare open my mouth.

'Can you tell who it is?'

I clenched my teeth and took a deep breath. 'Peter. It's Peter Wearmouth. I can't recognise the face, but the look is right, the hair and the proportions.' Nausea welled up; I turned away, battling for control, and didn't turn back until I heard him zip the bag again. He spoke gently.

'Can you bear another one?'

I nodded.

I watched his hands ease the zip down the black plastic. What was underneath was black too, the black jacket and trousers I'd seen spinning in an endless cartwheel. It was only when he'd taken the zip to waist level and withdrawn his brown, sure hands that I looked upwards at the head, expecting to see Madge's crab-orange hair and plump face.

The face was plump enough, swollen by the water, and completely colourless. It was more horrible than the other. That had hardly been a face at all, but something from a special effects studio. This was a dead person, with all that had made her alive wiped away to leave cold clay, the mouth slackened, the expression gone. In a way she was harder to recognise, now that what had made her human was gone. The staring eyes were grey-green beneath the fair brows, and blank as the eyes of a fish on a slab. Then I looked again at the hair. It was fair as the neat brows, cut in a long bob. I didn't understand how she had come to be with David on that cliff above my head, but I knew her. I nodded, and turned away again until Gavin had covered her once more.

He shut the further door, and took my arm to lead me into the sunshine. I was grateful for the warmth that fell like a caress on my bare arms. I stood, clutching it to me, as Gavin nodded to the policeman. 'Off you go now.'

His hand came up under my elbow again. He led me forward along the pier to *Khalida*. 'Let me make you a cup of drinking chocolate.'

I sat down in my own cockpit, shivering. Cat scrambled forward into my lap, a purring circle of warmth. Even this light wind was cold on my cheek, and the slatted seat was hard under me. I heard Gavin below, the familiar sounds of water being pumped into the kettle, the flare of the gas, the chink of mugs being taken from their compartments, the spoon rattling in the cocoa jar. I hugged Cat to me, and leant my head against Rat's warm curve, and shuddered until the kettle whistled, and Gavin came out of the cabin and put a mug into my hand. 'Don't try to talk, just drink this.'

He'd put extra sugar in it, and a slug of *Khalida*'s emergency whisky. My teeth chattered on the rim of the mug as I drank, but it heartened me. When I'd finished, I set the mug in its holder on the cabin step and looked at Gavin. His grey eyes were steady on me, assessing, heartening. 'Well?'

'I don't understand it,' I said, 'but that woman, the one who fell from the cliff last night, who was there with David Morse, that was Sandra Wearmouth.'

Gavin came out of the cabin and sat down opposite me. He glanced over his shoulder. There was nobody near us, and the incessant beat from the speakers outside the Pierhead drowned our soft speech. Facing each other like this, our knees were almost touching across *Khalida*'s narrow cockpit: my navy cargo trousers, the green and white wool of his kilt. The light purr of wind was just enough to ruffle his russet hair. His grey eyes fixed mine steadily.

'Talk to me, Cass. What sense are you making of it?'

It was all jumbled in my head. I went for the strand I could follow.

'It must have been David Morse and Sandra Wearmouth who put me in the tomb,' I said. 'They were the two bodies found in the sea, the ones I saw falling, and before that they were talking about me having escaped – ergo, they put me there. They meant me to die in there. But … the mixed couples is confusing me. I thought David and Madge were the couriers, in their flash motorboat, and Peter was the policeman following them. But now it looks like David and Sandra were working together.'

'That doesn't mean your first premise wasn't right too. Peter's partner thought he'd gone off sailing, but why shouldn't he be using his holiday to follow a hunch, just as I did?'

'And if Sandra was the mole …?'

Gavin nodded. 'We will do it. It's against all the rules, but you come home and you're tired, but your brain's full of your current case, and you have absolute faith in your wife, your girlfriend, your brother, and so you tell them about it. Creator Lord, the trouble I'd be in if Kenny wasn't reliable.'

'So she told David and Madge what was going on, they thought Peter was getting a bit close, and decided to get rid of him.'

'Someone local's involved too, because of the use of

the tomb. Granted, Shetland's the ideal centre spot for delivery to the places the works have turned up, but surely there must be easier places to stash things away. I haven't been up there yet. What did you see up there that made it a good hiding-spot?'

'It wouldn't be disturbed, for a start,' I said. 'Even here in Shetland, there's no old cottage or byre so remote that somebody might not start poking around in it. A tourist caught in a shower of rain, kids playing – whereas no casual passer-by would be able to lift that stone.'

'A cottage could be locked. Did you try the door of the one you mentioned, below the tomb?'

'It was locked, but I don't think that was anything to do with this. Brian Nicolson, the owner, well, he left a key with his best mate.' I was annoyed to feel my cheeks going crimson. 'I gather there were sex games going on, involving his wife, and he found out and changed the locks. That was on Thursday. The first time I went round, on Wednesday, I didn't try the door, because I wasn't sure there wasn't somebody inside. Coming back down, I saw a flash from binoculars. It wasn't David, he was off fishing, but it could have been Madge. There was no sign of her on the boat. Or I suppose it could have been Sandra.' Threesomes ... 'The cottage was damp too. It had a ditch running round the outside, and there was moss on the roof, around the skylights, whereas that tomb was dry, and still – as near an air-conditioned underground store as you'd get, outside a museum.'

Gavin made a face, unconvinced. 'Is it overlooked by houses?'

'No,' I said, 'and that's unusual too. Nearly everyone can be seen by someone, so normally comings and goings would be noticed, and there'd certainly be comment if people were seen carrying paintings in and out from a boat. You can only see the trowie mound from the sea, or from the Ward of Muckle Roe – 'ward' means peak.

That's how Magnie saw the lights. He couldn't sleep, and climbed the hill. Then there's the mooring bouy below. They could have moored up, climbed to the mound, opened it using whatever leverage gear they used, taken out the artworks they wanted, and gone again, without anyone knowing they'd been there.'

'Unless some hillwalkers interrupted them.'

I shook my head. Rat gripped my shoulders in protest; I put up a hand to steady him. Cat purred in my lap, warm and comforting. 'The opening was on the seaward side, and you've a clear view landward, a good way. If you had a look-out, you'd be able to shut the stone again and be innocent sightseers eating a picnic by the time they got to you.'

'So, someone here stole the items and brought them up, hid them in the tomb, for the couriers to take on from there. Who?'

'The obvious person is Brian,' I said. 'Brian Nicolson. He'd been inside it as a bairn, and it was on his land, so he could keep the archeologists away. Furthermore, he works south, as an electrician with a security firm.'

'Yes, you spoke of him before.' Gavin fished a black notebook out of his sporran. 'Anyone else?'

'Everyone of that age group, and a few younger ones too.' I explained how Brian had tried to scare us with the skull in a carrier bag. 'Any of us could have remembered that, if we'd had things to hide.'

Younger ones ... 'There's a link between Brian and David and Madge. Norman, that's the brother of Alex, the boy who died, he thought he'd seen them before, when they'd been down staying with Uncle Brian. He set Alex on to find out more from me.'

Gavin noted that too. 'I saw the boy. About sixteen, dark-haired? He'd been out searching, and came in just after we'd broken the news to the parents. Okay, so Brian could be your local man. Does he come up and down often?'

'Pretty regularly, I think, to keep an eye on his mother.'

'Mmmm.' Gavin made another note, then flipped to a new page. 'What about the dead boy's father, Olaf? Would he have known about the mound?'

'Yes, he'd been inside once, he said, Brian had taken him in, then rushed him out before he got a right look around.'

'So he not only knew there was a way in, but he'd visited Brian south too. And he had a key for the cottage. That puts him pretty high on my list of local suspects.' He smiled at my surprise. 'You're in the thick of it, Cass. You're too busy sailing and being attacked and escaping to have a chance to think.'

'I'm still confused,' I admitted. 'Sandra seemed so nice, so ordinary, just half of a contented couple. I'd never have suspected her.'

'Stock-in-trade for the professional criminal. You'd be astonished at how nice the really good ones are, how plausible. It's the small fry that show their villainy on their faces.' He had a nice smile, slightly squint, the sort of smile that made you feel he was a friend. He hadn't used it as part of his inquisitor act; it was genuine. I smiled back. 'And that certainly explains why Newcastle was being so cagey. If they had the least suspicion that the wife of a high-level officer was involved in a drugs operation, they'd want to make as little stir as possible about bringing her to book. If there's one thing we police loathe, it's the loss of public confidence and the "told you so" of the press when one of us goes wrong.'

'So ... was Sandra the Ms Big?'

'It's looking like a possibility. She employed Olaf or Brian as the thief, for her art vs drugs trade-offs, and David and Madge as the couriers. Olaf or Brian brought the goods up to Shetland, and stored them in the trowie mound, David and Madge picked them up and took them on abroad. Or perhaps she, David, and Madge ran the operation together. We need to find out the connection between them.'

'I don't suppose –' I began.

He looked at me, waiting.

'Lying dead like that, her face all swollen, and her eyes open, I thought it was Madge for a moment, and then I realised the hair was wrong. When I saw her first, her eyes reminded me of someone's, and I couldn't think who, but now I think it was Madge. I don't suppose … might they have been sisters?'

'It's worth looking at.'

He returned to efficient detective mode. 'Let's do a timeline, using what we now know or surmise. It began on Monday evening, with the arrival of the boats?'

'Before they came, there was shooting up at the trowie mound. Magnie told me about it, the next morning. He blamed Norman, but that was the night Norman was blasting around the voe on one of those infernal jet-skis. It wouldn't have been Brian either, because he was busy doing sheep things, nor Peter and Sandra – they'd just come in. They and the boat had all the signs of having done what they said they'd just done, sailed all the way along the top and down from Muckle Flugga.'

'You think it was the motorboat pair, then, David and Madge?'

I nodded. 'They were shooting Cat's mother, because she was showing people there could be a way in under the walling. So David and Madge had been up there before they came around.'

'Why should they come into Brae at all? Wasn't that drawing attention to themselves?'

'Fuel,' I said promptly. 'That boat would drink like a

sea-cook. They filled all their tanks up before they left. Then on Tuesday morning there was the conversation in the showers – that could have been put-on, for my benefit, but Sandra also told Madge that they were going up to the trowie mound.' I frowned. 'Somebody searched *Khalida* too.'

'Okay.' Another note. 'On Tuesday, Peter and Sandra headed for the tomb by land, and the motorboat couple went around by sea. Peter was probably killed there, and his body put aboard the motorboat.'

'You seem very sure Madge is still alive.'

'Someone took the motorboat away.'

I shook my head in disbelief. 'They felt like such an ordinary couple, except that she didn't like his cat much.'

'People who love each other tend to extend that to their pets.' His grey eyes flicked to Rat, comfortably curled round my neck, with his tail neatly tucked in, and his whiskers tickling my cheek. 'So the boat sat there all day Tuesday. Did anything particular happen on Tuesday evening?'

I shrugged. 'No – oh, yes. There was a points race, and Magnie was asking me if there was any sign of them. It was one of those moments where I was calling back over the spinnaker flapping, then it went quiet, all of a sudden, so the whole voe heard me say I'd have to do something if they didn't come back soon. Olaf Johnston was crewing. He certainly heard.'

'Wednesday. You went around to the cottage mooring in the evening, and saw David fishing, but no sign of anyone else on board, and somebody was watching you from the cottage. So they were still hanging around then. And that was the night somebody took the yacht out.'

'I thought it wasn't Sandra,' I said, 'but I'm not sure now. I saw only one person, but whoever it was certainly got her started up and out with no fumbling of ropes or searching for unfamiliar gears. Maybe it was Sandra and Madge, with David bringing the motorboat around to meet them.'

'They put Peter's body on board, cut that pipe, and scuttled her, not caring if the cat drowned, and then headed off.' He scribbled another couple of words. He used a black pen, very clear and definite on the off-white paper, and wrote a thin, italic hand. He was left-handed, like me.

'And then, Wednesday night,' I said, 'that was the night Magnie saw lights, moving up and down the hill, in the gloaming.'

'David, Madge and Sandra clearing the mound?'

'It was certainly cleared when I was inside. Thursday. I phoned round to see where the yacht had ended up, and drew a blank, so I phoned you. Then I visited Inga – oh, Brian's mother. The lady with the icon, I told you. She was wanting a cleaner, and I applied.'

He didn't look at me, but the smile quirked the corner of his mouth again.

'I've been sacked already,' I said. 'She told me this morning that Brian had talked her out of having me.'

'And then on Thursday evening you got shut into the trowie mound.'

'Thrown, more like. I've got a wonderful collection of bruises.'

'We found the boy just after six. He must have gone straight up to the mound, and been killed there, either because he saw something suspicious, or because he recognised them. Had he seen the two couples close enough to know which man belonged with which woman?'

'Yes,' I said. 'He was hanging around on Tuesday morning – that's when he asked me about them.'

'So perhaps he simply saw David and Sandra together.

Or maybe he came on them as they were taking the last items out of the mound. Who knows? But they killed him.'

'They were very ruthless. Peter, Alex – did they need to leave such a – a trail of blood behind them?'

'Once you get into the drug game, people are ruthless. I've heard stories, even in the quiet Highlands.' Gavin closed his notebook. 'One young man, he'd got deep into debt to them. They kidnapped him and held a knife to his throat as he phoned his parents, begged them to find the money.'

'And did they?'

Gavin's mouth twisted, wryly. 'They were an ordinary middle-aged couple who couldn't believe the nightmare world he'd catapulted them into. They re-mortgaged their house to pay that set of debts, and sold it entirely the next time.'

'What I don't understand,' I said, 'is why they should still have been hanging around. They'd cleared the mound, they'd sunk *Genniveve*, so there was no reason to stay.'

'They were meeting someone. You said that, in the helicopter. They were waiting for someone who came over the hill in a pick-up – the person who shot them. You can't give me any clue, however small, as to who that was?'

I shook my head. 'It was just a pick-up. It came over fast, and stopped, the shots were fired, and then the person hauled the bodies to the edge. I could hear they didn't find it easy, they were rolling as much as dragging.'

Gavin shook his head. 'Dragging a heavy body would take two, but rolling it could be done by one, especially on level ground like that cleared space in front of the mound.'

'There was no sound of it being two.'

The sun was warm on the back of my neck. I stretched backwards and found myself leaning against the rope from Kevin's noisy motorboat. It reminded me of this morning's conversation among the hens. 'Are we sure that David and

Madge were the couriers?'

'It looks that way, certainly.'

'It's just there's this other couple, in the marina, who've been acting oddly.' I described Kevin and Geri to him, and jerked my chin at the dark-blue boat tethered alongside. 'That's their boat. They go off to places like Faroe and Iceland too, and the locked boat's really odd. Even Kevin's best pal Jimmie didn't seem to be allowed inside.'

'Ah.' Gavin grinned. 'I watched the boat being unloaded while I was waiting for you to come down.' He flicked a glance over at the Pierhead. 'I think you might be about to get that mystery solved.'

Chapter Twenty-two

I followed his gaze. While we'd been speaking, a bus had parked opposite the Pierhead, where the white van had been, and the group of T-shirt clad drinkers around the tables had been joined by men in fancy dress. Some were in fishing waders and green oilskins, while others had exaggerated Edwardian plus-fours in neon check and tweed hats with flies stuck all round. They were all laughing with the raucousness of youngsters who'd begun drinking just after breakfast. Jimmie was in the centre of them, festooned with badges and a sash that no doubt said something like 'Last day of Freedom'.

'I was at a pre-wedding do of one of my colleagues, in Orkney,' Gavin said, shifting round on his seat so he could see better. 'It was enough to persuade you to do the bride-and-groom-only wedding in Thailand. Here's the bride's bus arriving.'

You couldn't have missed it. It was fluttering blue, white and yellow balloons from every possible tie-on point, and blaring steel-drum music from the open roof-hatches. It lurched to a halt just before the narrowing of the Pierhead road, and Donna and her pals shimmied out.

They'd gone for a tropical island theme. There were grass skirts in neon colours, bright bikini tops or short-sleeve shirts twisted in a knot just below the bust, black wigs surmounted with wreaths of flowers, and tans that glowed in the sun. You could tell they were going all out to have a memorable day. Donna's skirt was silver and white, and her bra was two heart shapes. I was glad she was too far away for me to read what was written on them, as I was pretty sure I wouldn't appreciate it. Her blonde hair was back-combed, Amy Winehouse style, and she wore a tiara that glinted in the sun.

The men greeted them with cheers and whistles, and there was an instant mingling of the two groups, with dusky maidens swarming all over their Edwardian fishing gents and vice versa. 'I still don't see –' I said.

Gavin was looking to the left, where the road swooped around to upper Voe and the showground. I followed his gaze, but didn't see anything special: a pick-up, a couple of cars, another pick-up with what looked like a couple of plastic chairs in the back. He stood up. 'Shall we get a little closer?'

'I'm not sure I want to,' I said frankly, looking at the mingled costumes and hearing the shrieks of laughter. 'I don't much care for drunken gatherings.'

'My highly tuned detective senses tell me they'll be heading off soon.' He turned to smile again, his tanned cheeks reddening. 'I didn't tell you last time how a mere DI got sent up here, to such a high-profile case.'

'No,' I agreed. I put Cat and Rat below, and shut the washboards.

He pulled *Khalida* to the pier and stepped ashore with a swirl of green pleats. 'Something got lost in translation. The message that ended up at Inverness HQ was just that a body had been found on a boat up at Brae.' He went into a clipped imitation of a Chief Constable. 'What's that man from the west, Macrae? Send him up there, he's good with the crofters. He's one of them, dammit.' The corners of his mouth turned down, ruefully. He held out a courteous hand from the pier. I ignored it. If I couldn't get from my own boat to the pier over a four-foot gap, I'd take to cleaning china carthorses for a living.

'So there I was, in the middle of the highest-profile case the Highlands had seen since the murder of the Red

Fox, and with a line-up of equally promising suspects.'

'With me at the head of them.'

'Yes,' he agreed. 'At one point you were the width of a bracken leaf from being arrested.' His eyes were grave, his voice matter-of-fact. 'You had form.' Alain's death.

We'd reached the parked buses. I lifted a hand to the driver, and stopped level with the bumper, a road's width from the unruly mob at the tables. 'Now what?'

'There,' Gavin said. He nodded at the pick-up that was rattling around the curve and along towards us. My guess had been right; it was two plastic chairs in the back, that hard, institutional, red plastic type, with rusted metal legs. They were attached side by side with orange baler twine to a wooden beam across the pickup. When the pick-up pulled up, I could see inside. A familiar red bucket stood in one corner, and a couple of boxes. It was all beginning to make horrible sense. I glanced over my shoulder at Gavin. 'The smell should have told me. Whale guts, from Faroe?'

'That'd be my guess. Do you want to see the whole process, or shall we cut along the shore ahead of them?'

'The shore,' I said, and threaded the way between buses and store, alongside the converted fishing boat and to the stony beach. Behind us, the shrieks of laughter intensified, mixed with yells of protest. I risked a glance over my shoulder, then turned to look properly. It reminded me of the first time I'd crossed the Equator on a tall ship. No amount of arguing that I'd done it in a small one was going to persuade my shipmates not to do the whole Neptune ritual. Jimmie was being man-handled into the pick-up by a dozen of his mates. Three held him down in the chair while another two tied him up firmly. Beside me, Gavin nodded. 'They're doing it properly.' The water chuckled half-way down the shore. An irridescent shag bobbed not six metres away, long bill tilted towards the noise. I could just imagine it going home to its nest: 'And you'll never believe what those humans were doing ...'

Donna was going for dignified acquiescence. A throng of her hula-skirted mates helped her up into the pick-up. It was hard to recognise any of the women under their black tresses, but I was pretty sure the one tying Donna to the throne beside Jimmie's was Geri. She flicked her hanging hair back, raised the bucket, grimaced, and handed it to Kevin. He lifted the lid. There was a disgusted, gleeful roar from the crowd, and when the stench reached us, a few seconds later, I recognised it. Whale guts, two days riper than when I'd smelled them in the marina. I'd have gagged if anyone had hung something like that around my neck. Jimmie and Donna yelled in protest, but their friends weren't bothering. Kevin looped up a length of slippery, glistening intestine and hung it round and round Jimmie's neck, then did the same to Donna. For good measure, he tipped the red-tinted water over their heads.

The second bucket contained what looked like an oatmeal mixture, that trickled down their faces, and sat in their hair and on their shoulders in mealy lumps. After that, Kevin handed out one of the boxes, then jumped down. It was eggs, and the crowd were drunk enough to make a fun throwing match of it, like Tudor villagers tormenting a couple put in the stocks. The aim was mostly at their bodies, but I saw Donna wince as one smashed across her cheekbone. It had been a whole cardboard box of egg boxes, maybe twenty dozen, and by the time they'd finished throwing them, Gavin and I were half-way up the green hill, looking back at them.

'It's a very good argument against marriage,' I said.

'They wouldn't do it to you,' Gavin said. 'You don't move in those circles.'

'I'm beginning to,' I said. 'I've got settled back here now. I know all the faces again.' *Settled* ... 'Inga's trying to talk me into joining her netball team, once the summer's over. That'd make me one of the lasses.'

Far away, below us, the pick-up was enveloped in a white cloud. 'Flour next,' Gavin said. I sat down on the grass to watch. My thigh muscles had definitely had enough of this land-climbing lark. Gavin sat down beside me, spread hand ten centimetres from mine.

'My leg muscles hurt,' I explained.

The little figure that was Kevin was back in the truck, ripping open bags of flour and scattering the contents over the snowmen pair. Four of the hula maidens were tying bunches of balloons to the corners of the truck. I didn't need to be closer to know that the pink ones, on Donna's side, would be festooned with slogans like 'Hen party – no cocks', or 'naked hunk' cartoons, and the blue ones on Jimmie's would say 'sexy male' or 'the party's here'. There were cheers as a couple of shaped balloons were added to the front corners of the cab. From here, they looked like a scarlet penis and a blow-up woman.

Gavin sighed. 'It all makes me feel as if I'm somehow missing out on the modern world. I can't imagine how this is supposed to be fun. I don't even like getting drunk, particularly, though I'd never refuse a dram of a decent whisky at the end of the day.'

'You and me both, boy,' I agreed. 'Luckily drink's just too expensive in Norway for them to want to go there, but there were loads of stag parties on the Med. They were awful. They'd get boozed up all night, men and women, and be a real nuisance. The whole bar area would be a no-go zone until they'd gone. They'd each spend enough for me to live on for a fortnight in one night's getting smashed, then remember nothing about it the next morning. I just couldn't see the point.'

'Being police, we had to stay sensible at that Orkney one. Well, at least we kept it within the hotel. There was no parading round the streets.'

Below us, the last box was being opened. From the sounds floating up, it contained a selection of what Maman would not have called musical instruments. The squeal of plastic penny-whistles, trumpet-squeakers, the choked sound of kazoos and the rattle of maracas shrilled up to us. The steel band tape blared out again, the pick-up turned around in a ripple of foil curtain and swaying balloons, and the crowd fell in behind. The hula-skirts swayed as the lasses waved their arms in the air, and the men raised their cans and fired off party-poppers. As it passed closer to us I saw Jimmie and Donna, sitting up straight as though for a coronation, but encrusted in flour that was already drying with the egg in the sun to make a hard, grey paste. Jimmie was drunk enough to be taking it as a joke, but Donna's smile looked forced, and the gunge-encrusted tiara sat squint on her powdered head. The clamour swelled towards us as they came along the road and up the curve, and died away as they went around the hill. Above us, a lark was singing. The wind rustled gently in the grass beside us, and for a moment it was beautifully peaceful. Gavin lay back, crossing his arms behind his head, and closing his eyes. The sun picked up lines of strain on his forehead and running from nose to chin. I remembered that even although it wasn't his case, he'd been up a good part of the night, and then early this morning. Then the noise came around the road again, mixed with hooting of horns from passing cars. I sighed, and rose.

'I'd better get back to my stall. I must have been away an hour. Inga'll be tugging at her mooring lines.'

Gavin rose too. 'I'll get back to Lerwick, and liase with Newcastle. See you later.'

He went off down the hill, and I began scrambling upwards again. When I looked down from the road, he had already reached the shore.

The pick-up with Jimmie and Donna was doing a

triumphant round of the showfield as I reached it. I dodged behind the laughing crowds, feeling snooty. I could almost hear my voice sounding like Maman's, '*Vulgaire* ...' and felt ashamed. Their mates had gone to a good deal of bother to make sure their impending big day was celebrated with the maximum fuss, and just because it wasn't my style of fuss didn't mean they weren't having fun. The laughter from the crowd was a mixture of sympathy and affection.

Inga was at the door of the marquee, clapping and laughing with all the other stallholders. I stepped over the guy ropes to the side and slipped in beside her. 'I'm sorry that took so long. Did Charlie tell you?'

She nodded. 'Was it bad?'

'Horrid. Gavin fed me extra-sugared drinking chocolate after it. Then we got diverted by this lot.'

Inga grinned. 'Geri's been planning this for weeks. You wouldn't believe the choice of hen party balloons and banners on the internet.'

'Netball team too?' I couldn't imagine the immaculate Geri doing anything that would get her flushed and sweating, except maybe a heads-down bicycle run in the gym, clad in black lycra.

'Hockey.' Ah, now that I could imagine; a killer game if ever there was one. 'Okay, if you're fine to go back on the stall, I'll go and round up the bairns. Peeriebreeks is with his dad, and the lasses are around somewhere. So long as they're not winning more goldfish ...' She rolled her dark eyes. 'Either you find them belly up, or they eat each other.'

'Really?' I said. I'd never heard of cannibal goldfish.

'Really. We got four one year, and by the end of September there was only one left, three times the size he'd been. Have you eaten? D'you want to get yourself a bacon roll before you're trapped?'

I shook my head. 'I don't feel like it.'

'Must have been bad. See you later, then.' She gathered up her russet jacket, hoisted her bag over one shoulder, and headed off. There weren't any customers in the tent, so I stayed in the sun, leaning against the pole that held the marquee door flap back.

The show was in full swing now. The traditional tape had been replaced by a live band consisting of three fiddles, an accordion, and a bass guitar, all played with expert panache by T-shirted youngsters. The leader looked fourteen, but she leant and swayed to the music as if this stage was her home. Behind her, the bass player grinned as he thumped his backing notes. The flowers had spilled out of their half-can green hut behind the stage, great pots of scarlet begonias that were as big as roses, and hanging baskets of pale blue lobelia and silvery fern. I couldn't grow things aboard *Khalida*, but I enjoyed looking at flowers ashore. Sometimes, I'd sneak a gardening catalogue on board a tall ship where I'd be out of sight of land for weeks, although I made sure nobody saw me reading it.

The tethered dogs slept in the sun. A child came out of the pet tent carrying a ginger kitten as small as Cat. She took it to a clear patch of grass by the marquee and let it run around, catching it back when it went too far. The hens settled in their pens, making that broody noise. The sun dazzled off chrome and warmed my face.

Everywhere, there were folk: men in T-shirts and jeans, and women like summer butterflies in shorts and vest-tops, white, candy-pink, sky-blue. Toddlers staggered across the warm grass, and were retrieved by older siblings; teenagers gathered in clumps, passing coke bottles between them, and sharing pictures on their phones. The older women showed off their best summer frocks, sprigged navy and sage green. Even the older men had left their jackets in the cars, and went shirt-sleeved, although they didn't risk taking their caps off. The barbecue and ice-cream queues snaked separately towards each other, then joined in a double line, with people from one chatting to people from the other. The two heading the queues turned away together, and did a complicated swap of steak rolls and swirl-topped cones. My head didn't want food, but my stomach considered the smell of barbecued minute steak with onions, and approved.

Behind the food stalls, a long line of old engines had been set up. There were a few truly vintage tractors (in Shetland, most tractors are relatively vintage), the old grey sort whose registration numbers run to only five figures, a rattling steam traction which looked like something from *Tess of the D'Urbervilles* and various contraptions set up on plank tables. Some were marine engines, with buckets of water and hoses leading to what would be a raw-water intake. Naturally, Anders' fair head was among them; he and an old man were leaning over a great, square lump of metal piping. When it came to engines, his hands were sensitive as a lover's; one caressed the injector pipes, the other smoothed round to indicate the fan belt. The old man jerked his head sideways, considered, prodding his pipe with a match, then nodded. Anders fished in his pocket for his multi-tool, and the pair of them bent over the machine again.

I was just reckoning I had zero chance of getting away without a full run-down over our evening meal when I spotted a familiar maroon Clio being jolted recklessly over the cattle grid into the parking area behind them, and spinning into a space. The driver got out, leaving the door to swing to behind her, and walked forward in that careful, drunken way, as if the daisy-studded grass was ice beneath her feet.

It was Alex's mother, Kirsten.

Chapter Twenty-three

Cerys said they had sedated her, but sedation didn't always knock people out. I'd seen that on board ship. Kirsten looked as if it had wired her up instead of calming her, set her brain scurrying down whatever track it was fixed on so that she had to act, even though her body would barely obey her. It was a miracle she'd managed to drive the five miles from Brae without sliding into the ditch.

She'd just reached the outermost row of cars, swaying and supporting herself on the sun-glinting roofs, when there was a blare of music and a roar of applause from the gate beside the hall. An open-backed truck swept in, decorated with flowers in cream, lemon, ochre, and buttercup. In the middle of it, dressed in yellow bridesmaids' dresses and sitting on flower-woven thrones, were the Voe Show Queen and her two princesses. They were chosen each year from among the oldest lasses at Olnafirth Primary school, and this was their big moment. Every head was turned towards them as the truck made its round of the showfield.

Kirsten looked at them as if she couldn't remember what they were. She made a helpless gesture, then her head turned slowly, her eyes searching among the crowd. I scanned the people too, for someone who might come and lead her away from here: Cerys, Barbara, Inga, anyone who would be able to pet her and soothe her and get her back lying down, so that sleep could take the burden from her. At his stall behind my shoulder, Brian gave a sharp intake of breath, then came to speak softly in my ear. 'She shouldna be here. Go you and get her over, sit her down, and keep her calm. I'll try to get hold of –' His face darkened, his mouth hardened, but Kirsten's state overrode his own feelings. 'I'll get Olaf.'

Going to her was the last thing I wanted to do. I was no good at touchy-feely. I did plotting voyages and giving orders, calculating tides and riding out ocean storms. What could I say to a poor woman who'd lost her child?

Brian's hand was on my back. 'Geng du, Cass, afore anyone sees her.'

The truck had stopped in the middle of the green for the show president to do a speech. Somebody had to go, and it seemed the somebody was me. I cut across the soft turf to intercept Kirsten's wavering track towards the crowd. She wore pink patterned leggings and a long T-shirt, like pyjamas, as if she'd been coaxed to bed, and had risen just as she was. Her feet were thrust into pink canvas pumps. Her handbag dangled from one hand, and the other was stretched forward, as if to catch at somebody's shoulder. Her dark hair was tousled, and her eyes stared in her white face, the pupils dilated. She brought the stretched hand back to shade them, screwing her eyes at the brightness of the sun, and took slower steps, swaying as if she could barely stand.

I caught the handbag arm. 'Kirsten, it's too bright for you out here. Come into the tent.'

It took her a moment to react to my touch. She stopped walking, but didn't look at me. 'Cass. I need to find –' She frowned, bloodless mouth closing and opening again. 'I need to find –'

'Come with me,' I said, drawing her away from the crowd. 'Come and sit down.'

She let herself be drawn, but slowly, her eyes still searching. 'I don't see him.'

'Come and sit,' I said, 'and if you tell me who you're looking for, I'll find him, while you rest.'

'Rest –' she echoed vaguely.

I slipped my arm under hers, and took her weight as she stumbled beside me. Her feet were sliding along the grass as if it was too much bother to lift them, as if the will which had brought her here was almost exhausted. My fellow stall-holders knew her of course, and stood aside to let us through, the woman from the Gonfirth Kirk nodding in approval. 'I'll make a cup of tea,' she murmured, and headed towards her stall.

I eased Kirsten into one of our chairs. 'You just sit down here,' I said, keeping my voice very steady. She nodded, but I wasn't sure she'd understood. My jacket was draped over the back of her chair; she fumbled for a hold of it, and tugged it to her. 'Cold –' I eased it from under her clutching fingers and draped it over her shoulders, tucking it around her. For all it was a fine day outside, she wasn't dressed for sitting in the cool shadow of the marquee. She needed a doctor. There had always been a St John's Ambulance tent, up behind the hall. Maybe I could send someone for help.

She was sitting still now, eyes half closed. The Gonfirth Kirk lady came over to me with a mug of tea, milky, so that Kirsten could drink it straight away. I took it and held it in Kirsten's lap, clasping her hands around it. 'Here, drink this.'

She lifted it obediently, and sipped. The warmth brought colour to her lips. She drank about half of the mugful, then handed it back to me, like Peerie Charlie when he'd had enough. Her eyes opened. The pupils were still too large, but at least they focused on me. 'Cass.'

I nodded. 'Just sit still.'

Her thin hand gripped my wrist. There was surprising strength in it, and the nails cut into my skin. 'You go to our church. I've seen you there. You *know* –' Her eyes were the green of sea over sand, and filled with a desperate earnestness. 'Confession.' Her other hand groped for mine. 'I can't sleep.' Her voice sank until I could barely hear it and became a rapid mumble; her hand clutched my fleece. 'I need Father Mikhail. I thought he'd be here. I want to go to confession. Olaf wouldn't let me. I escaped, I took the car when he thought I was asleep. You know Father Mikhail. Is he here? I want to go to confession, before I sleep.' She looked around, quick, furtive glances. 'You'll hide me, won't you, if Olaf comes before Father?'

I needed someone I could trust here. I wanted someone to go for the St John's Ambulance worker, but I couldn't deny this appeal for a priest. I had no right to judge the depth of her need, and refuse her on my grounds that she needed a doctor more. She was one of my fellow Catholics, and she was asking for a priest; that was all I needed to know. I had a vague feeling I'd noticed Father Mikhail's black robe earlier. It was strange, I thought irrelevantly, how the 'Sacrament of Reconciliation' reverted to the old name of 'confession' when it was needed. I wouldn't think about what she wanted to confess, a sin grave enough to keep her from the Eucharist. That was none of my business. My task was to find Father Mikhail for her, and make sure she was allowed to talk to him. I could put an appeal over the tannoy, asking him to come to D Marquee. I didn't want to leave Kirsten, nor to draw attention to her, but Brian was looking for Olaf, so I had to act quickly.

I grasped Kirsten's hands in mine, and looked straight into her haunted face. 'Kirsten, I'm going to go and look for Father Mikhail. I'll bring him to you here. You just stay here and wait.'

She gave a gasp of alarm. 'Suppose Olaf comes? He won't let me talk to him.'

'I'll be very quick,' I said. 'I'll go straight to the tannoy, and ask Father to come here, then I'll come back and wait with you.'

She shook her head and struggled to her feet. 'I won't wait, he'll come, he'll take me away.' Her arm slipped around mine, and clamped it to her. 'I'll stay with you.'

I could see there was no point in arguing. 'Then let's be quick.'

I gave the Gonfirth Kirk lady a quick glance. 'Can you mind the stall?' I mouthed at her, with a glance over my shoulder at our array of red, white, and blue goods. She nodded. I mouthed 'Thanks' and led Kirsten away.

The president's speech was finished now; the queen and princesses had come down from their flowered thrones, and were doing a ceremonial tour of the showfield, the president and queen together, the princesses arm-in-arm behind. The crowd was beginning to disperse. I saw people glance at Kirsten, and then look down at the grass, or away across the voe, shy as otters flipping away into the water, too kind to stare. Only those who didn't know her looked twice at us, walking steadily across the grass.

It felt three times the distance. Adapting my stride to her sleep-walker's pace, I felt as if every hollow in the grass was the trough of a wave, every bump an ocean roller. The band had begun again – no, it was a different group, school pupils in a line with a dozen recorders in varying sizes, and their parents and relatives filled the space between us and the caravan. I steered Kirsten to starboard a little. We could cut through the flower hut and come out by the cattle. The bull was still bellowing indignantly. It would have a sore throat by the time the day was over. We were in luck though, for there was no sign of Brian and Olaf, not yet.

Twenty metres from the flower hut door, Anders' fair head was still bent over the engine he was tuning with deft hands. Now, if only he would look around – I willed him to see us, but he was twisting a nut with his adjustable spanner, too intent to lift his head. I thought for a moment of leaving Kirsten by the pots of scarlet begonias, but her weight was heavy on my arm, and I wasn't sure she could stand unaided. I paused for a moment, looking at him, then called: 'Anders!' My voice was lost under the final flourish of recorder tune. I raised my free hand to cup around my mouth, but Kirsten caught at my wrist.

'Don't call, Olaf will hear, he'll come –'

'I'm calling Anders,' I said. 'He'll help us. You know Anders.'

It was the wrong thing to say. Her white skin crimsoned. 'No, don't, don't call him. I can't face him. Please.'

I didn't want to upset her more, but I needed Anders. I was skipper here, and this was my call. He would get the St John's Ambulance person for me while I stayed with Kirsten. In this crowd, there'd be someone I knew who would go to him for me. I lowered my hand and led her into the flower hut. It was cool and scented like a hot-house, that mossy smell of damp green leaves mixed with the sweetness of rose and gardenia, and the sound of the indignant bull faded to a hush in the gentle hum of people admiring flowers. We threaded our way among them. On our right was a central isle of flower specimens, vases with three perfect blooms in each: roses, honeysuckle, marigolds. Along the side of the hut was a line of tables heavy with miniature gardens: a tiny crofthouse, a Japanese ravine with bonsai trees, a pebbled beach. Pansies smirked mascara'd eyes at us as we passed, and hanging cactus stretched out spider arms to catch our hair. The ten metres felt like so many cables against wind and tide, but we came at last to the the bottle-neck between the half-can shed and the square one joined to it. There luck came at last, in the form of one of my sailors, pointing out his volcano garden creation to his mates. It was Drew, with the bottle-blond Mohican, as mad as a south-sea mate, but I knew he'd do what I asked. I ushered Kirsten ahead of me through the doorway, and put my hand on his shoulder. He turned his face to mine, surprised. I made a 'sssh' mouth and spoke softly in his ear.

'Drew, it's an emergency. Anders is by the engines. Can you tell him to come to me, at the caravan?'

His eyes went round as pebbles. I glanced at Kirsten, and he followed my gaze, and understood. He nodded his head emphatically, and twisted off among the crowd.

Help was on its way. I came beside Kirsten again to pass the sheaves of green oats and jars of jam. A wooden wheelbarrow filled with one enormous kale plant, its roots still dark with earth, half-blocked our path. Beyond it, a man in black breeks and a blue and white Fair Isle gansey was sitting in an upright restin-shair, demonstrating how to weave straw to make a traditional kishie, the Shetland back-basket that was supported in place by a band around the forehead. He looked up, and I saw by his face that he knew Kirsten; he leaned forward and drew in his half-finished basket to let us pass. I was beginning to feel the space behind my back was filled with people watching, and wondering.

We reached the hut doorway at last, a double-door rectangle of bright sunlight. Kirsten flinched again as the light hit her, and raised her forearm against it.

'Close your eyes if you like,' I said. 'I'll lead you.'

It was a dozen steps to the admin caravan. I steered Kirsten towards it. 'Open your eyes now,' I said, 'for the steps.' I helped her up them and into the caravan. Sanctuary.

The girl behind the table was Kirsten's age, a cheery, ruddy-cheeked crofter lass in a Voe Show T-shirt. She took one look at Kirsten, and brought round a chair for her. 'Kirsten, lass, sit down. You shouldna be out today.'

Kirsten folded into the chair. She looked at the end of her strength.

'Can you put out a tannoy for me?' I asked. 'We need Father Mikhail, if he's here still.'

I'd have had that lass on my watch any day. She went straight to her intercom, without any questions or fussing, and sent the message out, clear as daylight. 'Father Mikhail, if you're on the showground, could you come to the caravan immediately, please. Father Mikhail, Father Mikhail, to the caravan, please.' Then she went to fill the kettle.

I went to the door of the caravan, and stood there, scanning the people. Bless Drew, here he was, weaving his way through parents collecting their recorder-playing children with Anders in tow, pointing to the caravan. I scurried down the metal steps. Drew gave me a thumbs-up sign and squirmed back into the hut. Anders greeted me in rapid Norwegian: 'What's wrong?'

'Kirsten's here, doped up. I need the first-aid people, the green and white tent, over behind the engines.'

'Here?'

I nodded, and he turned on his heel and began to run through the crowd. Again, I blessed the ship's habit of obedience. The cavalry was coming. On his way he passed Father Mikhail, striding towards us. I went to meet him.

'Father, thank goodness.'

'Cass.' Scotland was a missionary country now; Father Mikhail was Polish, and none of us tried to pronounce his second name, let alone try to write the complicated sequence of ys, cs, and zs. He was barely thirty, and not long ordained; we were only his second parish. He gave me a quick look-over, brown eyes crinkling in his square, tanned face. 'What is up?'

I motioned him before me to the caravan. When I came in after him, Kirsten was already on her feet, both hands stretched out to him. 'Father, you'll hear my confession, quickly, before Olaf comes? He'll not allow me –'

Father Mikhail flicked a look at me. 'She needs a doctor.'

'First aid is on the way.'

He kept his eyes on Kirsten, but pulled his car keys out of his pocket, and held them out to me. 'You know my car? It is just the other side of the hall, a red Fiesta. My black case is in the boot. Bring it.'

I raced out, past the cattle pens, through the gate by the hall and to the parking area. Why did so many people have to have red cars? I ran up the boots of one row and down the bonnets of the other, found the right one at last and thrust the key into the lock. The little black case was there. I grabbed it, slammed the boot shut, and ran back to the caravan. Father Mikhail had Kirsten seated again; I gave him the case, and the crofter-lass and I came out, shutting the door behind us. We waited there in silence, guardians of their privacy, while the soft murmur of voices came from the tin wall behind us.

Then the door opened, and Father Mikhail came out to us.

'I will drive her home. She should be in bed. Her friend Cerys was there this morning. I will phone her.'

The St John's Ambulance woman arrived then, and Father Mikhail took her straight in, while Anders and I remained outside. 'She is well?' Anders asked softly.

'She should be home,' I said, 'with someone looking after her.'

Father Mikhail came out again. 'I will drive her home, and this lady will stay with her until her friends come. Cass, you will help her walk to my car.'

Kirsten's eyes were closed now, her face at peace. Soon she'd be fathoms deep, but for now she responded to our urging and stood up, with the St John's Ambulance woman on one side of her, and me on the other, arms around her waist, her weight heavy on our shoulders. As we eased her down the steps the show queen's truck went past, with the girls waving from their thrones, and we moved into the space left by its passing.

Kirsten had taken only four faltering steps when Brian and Olaf strode around the end of the truck, and came straight towards us.

9

Mad folk is aye waur as mad kye.

(Old Shetland saying: Angry people are worse than angry cows.)

Chapter Twenty-four

Olaf looked as if he'd dressed by guess this morning, in an old pair of jeans and a grey jumper, rather bagged around the elbows and stomach. His face was tired, drawn, with lines running from nose to mouth-corners. His tanned cheeks were pale, and his Viking-red hair stood out around his head. He walked as if every step was an effort.

It was Father Mikhail that he saw first. His face closed down to wariness. Then he saw Kirsten, between the first-aid woman and I, and then Anders, walking at my side. His grey-green eyes narrowed. He looked from side to side, but there was a row of cars backed by a fence on his left, and the wall of the hall on his right. He took a step backwards, but retreat was blocked by the queen's truck, which had stopped to let the queen and princesses clamber down for their tea and cakes in the hall. For a long moment he stood there, sizing up his options, then he ran two steps towards us and darted into the alley between the cattle pens.

What he hadn't realised was that it was a u-shape, with the alleyway blocked at the far end by the biggest pen. He bolted in, then swung around to confront us. Brian took a step towards him, and Anders came forward too. I saw Olaf realise that he was trapped. He looked at them, then behind him, put a hand on the pallets and vaulted over, countryman style, into the pen. A crofter in a navy boiler suit shouted a warning, and another came running from by the water hose. The cow in the pen lifted its head and shifted uneasily, and I saw that it wasn't a cow but the bull who'd spent his day complaining, broad of face and chest, with long, lethal horns. Olaf wrenched at the metal latch and swung the gate open, towards us, then dodged behind the bull and slapped it on the rump. He was swinging himself into the main showfield as it turned towards him, catching the bottom of his jeans with one horn, and then it turned back to face us.

It seemed to move in slow motion at first, one cloven foot lifting and stamping. It gave a majestic sweep with its horns, then began lumbering towards us. The crofter flattened himself against the other pens, and it passed him by, mad red eyes fixed on us, this triple person of Kirsten, the First Aid woman, and me. Kirsten had no awareness of the danger, she was too slow, and it was going to be on us before we could drag her to safety. Around us people were shouting, and I heard running feet from behind us, then Anders shoved me aside, a swift push that had me stumbling towards the other side of its path. I fetched up against the pallets and clung there, and smelled the animal heat of it as it passed by me.

I looked around then. Anders had grabbed Kirsten by the waist and was spinning her towards the outside of the pens when it caught him in the back and tossed him. I couldn't see his face, but I felt the jerk of pain as the horn went into his back, as his feet left the ground. It hurled him two metres through the air, tossing him as if he was an unwanted coat, and he rolled as he fell, with a cry of pain. I leaped away from the sheltering pallet and flung myself on my knees beside him.

I didn't see how they managed to trap the bull. I heard the shouts behind me, but I was concentrating on Anders. *Please, God, please, God* – Already his white T-shirt was blotched with red blood pulsing out. I dragged my fleece over my head and bundled it up to clamp over the wound, leaning on it with both hands. Anders groaned, and tried to pull away from the pressure.

'Lie still.' I said it as if I was on deck, matter-of-fact,

giving an order. 'Stille, Anders, stille. I've got to stop the bleeding.'

There were people crowding around now. The blood was seeping through my fleece. I could feel the wet stickiness of it beneath my palm. The First Aid woman had a walkie-talkie; I could hear her talking to her colleagues, requesting assistance, an ambulance. 'Urgent,' she said. I pressed down on Anders' back as he lay on the ground, face turned towards mine, eyes closed in pain, his colour draining away. The blood was oozing between my fingers now, and although I didn't feel as if I was crying, tears were running down my cheeks and dropping on my hands. Then there were more running feet. Black polished shoes under dark-green trousers appeared on each side of me. Hands came in over mine, sure, experienced hands, lifting Anders from the rough ground and winding white bandage around and around the fleece. The first layer was scarlet instantly, and the second, but they kept winding, pulling tighter, and at last the layers remained white. They'd brought a stretcher, and they laid him on it, on his front. He opened his eyes then, and I bent over him. I took his hand, and his fingers clenched around mine. 'Stille, Anders. Hjelpe komme.'

One of the first-aid men bent over me. 'Does he speak English?'

I nodded. The scarlet was seeping through the bandages again, but faintly, a seaweed-rust smudge. Anders spoke with an effort. 'I speak English.' He managed a smile, and I felt my heart twist. 'Better than Cass speaks Norwegian.' His eyes returned to mine, and he murmured, in Norwegian, 'Det gjør vondt, Cass.' It hurts.

I nodded. 'You saved Kirsten and me.'

'Good.'

There was another burst of sound from the walkie-talkie, and a different voice replying. Around me, the feet

274

were clearing backwards. There was an official voice over my head: 'Stand back, please. Stand clear – thank you.' Someone was putting screens around us, green canvas screens with splayed silver feet. Anders closed his eyes again, lips tightened to a thin line, his hand tight around mine. I couldn't bear to think about how much pain he must be in.

I tried to remember what I'd seen. The horn had caught him high up, the point slicing upwards, and it had spun him around rather than piercing him through. There hadn't been any blood on his front when they'd lifted him. The gash I had leant upon had been just below the shoulder-blade, and I'd not noticed foam in the blood on his T-shirt. Please God, it had been above the lung. It hadn't touched his spinal cord, or he wouldn't be able to move his hands, although the arm on that side was lying limp. That might be the pain, that he was instinctively keeping that side still, or the horn might have caught a key muscle. I bent my head to his. 'Kan du bevege ditt armen?'

He gave that faint smile again. 'Lege … Kapitain.'

He was right. The medics were the captains now. I had to leave them to do their job.

I raised my head to look around me. They'd caught the bull. Half a dozen crofters were man-handling it back into a trailer, still stamping those splayed feet, but held in check by a stick attached to the ring in its nose. On the other side of the pens, Olaf was being marched away by two policemen. The First Aid woman was still with Kirsten and Father Mikhail, and now Cerys had arrived as well. They were coaxing her towards the exit. A blonde police officer tried to stop them, but Father Mikhail said two sentences to her, authoritative, and she let them pass. The queen's truck was being moved, in preparation for the ambulance coming.

'Cass Lynch?' It was a woman's voice, a woman's polished shoes at my knees. I lifted my head, and

275

recognised her straight away: Sergeant Peterson, with her smooth, fair hair clipped back at the nape of her neck in a pony-tail, and her ice-green eyes detatched, like a mermaid's eyes watching the follies of mankind. She looked down at Anders. 'It's Anders, isn't it?' She frowned, consulting the card-index of her memory. 'Anders Johansen.' I nodded. She flicked out her notebook. 'Is his address still with you, aboard *Khalida*?'

I nodded again. 'His home address is in Bildøy, just outside Bergen. He lives with his parents there, off the Døsjevegen, just by the marina.'

'I'll need a contact number, and a statement from you, about what's happened.'

I fished out my mobile with my free hand and thrust it at her. My fingers were blood-stained. 'It's under contacts, Anders home.'

Inga came over then, bag flying. 'Cass!' She looked at my face and didn't ask stupid questions, but rummaged in her bag, found a pack of baby wipes and pulled out a handful. 'Here.' I held my hand out, like Peerie Charlie, and she wiped it, then gave me two more. 'There's blood on your face too.'

I wiped obediently.

'Cerys has gone off with Kirsten, so I'll clear up the stall,' Inga said. 'You'll likely do good business for this last hour. Everyone'll want to know what happened and how Anders is.'

'Sore,' I said, 'and lost a good deal of blood, but I don't think it's touched anything vital.' He was drifting away from consciousness, I could feel it. 'I hope an ambulance comes soon.'

'The only ambulance,' Inga said. 'Cuts. If you're lucky, it's in Lerwick, waiting to go.'

Lerwick to Voe would be twenty minutes, with the blue lights flashing. I felt like I'd been kneeling on this gritty ground for a lifetime, but it would have been less than ten minutes. Ten more to wait.

If we were unlucky, the one ambulance could be delivering a mostly recovered old lady with a broken thigh back to Baltasound, two ferries away. Oscar Charlie could come, though, and land on the showfield. Inga echoed my thoughts.

'If it's half-way to Out Skerries they'll send the chopper. They'll come soon.' She turned to go, calling 'Phone you later,' over her shoulder.

Sergeant Peterson closed her notebook again, gave me back my mobile, looked at my face, and turned away to bother somebody else. Anders was becoming paler, as if he was cold; the shock of sudden injury, of losing so much blood. One of the first-aiders leant in to tuck a blanket around him. I curled it under his chin. His beard prickled the back of my hand.

The helicopter lived at Sumburgh. Sumburgh to Voe, even if they scrambled in less than two minutes, would still take half an hour. I sent up a prayer that we'd be lucky. I wanted Anders safe in the hospital, with new blood being pumped into him, and antibiotics being dripped into his system, and clean, starched sheets in place of this gritty, animal-trodden ground. While I listened for a distant siren, or the first hum of rotor blades, I willed my strength to flow into him through our joined hands. My thoughts fell into the rhythm of the rosary that had comforted me in my exile in France: *Hail Mary, full of grace, the Lord is with you* –

Father Mikhail came back then. 'Cerys has taken Kirsten home. She'll stay with her.' He looked at Anders. 'Is there anything I can do here?'

I shook my head. 'Pray.'

'Of course. The young man is not from our church?'

'He's a Norwegian Lutheran.'

'We are all one in the Christian faith,' Father Mikhail said serenely, and took a step behind me. I could feel his willpower joining mine. Inga's Vaila came running up with my jacket clutched to her. She stopped by the stretcher, staring solemnly, then remembered her errand and thrust the jacket at me. 'Mam said you'd need this if you were going to Lerwick with him. Your purse is in the pocket. She said we'll go and feed the kitten and Rat.'

Bless Inga's practical sense, mother of her family, used to organising the universe. *Khalida* would be fine. She was tied up properly. I'd get back later, once Anders was in safe hands, and sail her back to Brae. Dear God, why didn't they come?

At last there was the rumble of a heavier vehicle in the car park behind the hall, and the reflection of the blue flashing light on the curved white roof of the caravan. I heard the rattle of rubber wheels on the gravel, the metallic creaking of a trolley, then the ambulance men arrived, their trolley between them, and even as I was moving back to let them in, they had Anders on it, and were trundling him away. I grabbed my jacket and ran after them. They loaded him into the ambulance, and I clambered in after, before they could tell me I couldn't come. Anders turned his head. 'Cass?'

I took his hand again. 'You're in the ambulance now. Det er ... ambulansen.'

He gave that faint thread of a smile again. 'Sykebilen.'

'I've never needed to call an ambulance in Norway,' I retorted.

I could rest now. The paramedic in the back with us was ready with an oxygen mask, and checked Anders' temperature every five minutes with an ear-gadget, his blood with a velcro collar round his arm, and his pulse with a clothes-peg on his finger. At the hospital, they did the same smooth process in reverse, and then I was left to fill in forms in that smelled of disinfectant and polish, while they rushed him through a double door into the bowels of A&E. I was just wondering when he'd last had a tetanus jab, if ever, when there were steps in the corridor, and Gavin came in and sat down beside me.

'They reckon the honours are about even,' he said. 'He threw you out of the path of the bull, you stopped the bleeding straight away. It's on the Shetland News website already.'

I made a face.

'"Dramatic escape at Voe Show." He grimaced. 'Along with "Third body found"' He glanced up, making sure the nurse behind the desk was intent on her papers. 'Now, if this had been even five years ago, it would all have been *sub judice* by the time Friday's paper came out, and we'd have had no coverage at all.'

'Will it be *sub judice*?'

His glance flicked back to the nurse. 'When did you last eat?'

'Breakfast.' It seemed a different world. 'Anders and I, we had bacon rolls when we arrived in Voe.' We'd been sitting in the cockpit, slightly shy of each other after the night before, with the sun still hidden behind the mist, and the tide coming in. It would turn again soon, flooding its strength into the world. I hoped that would help Anders, fighting behind those closed doors.

His brows drew together. 'Breakfast.' He shook his head, rose and went over to the nurse, flipping out his warrant card. 'Detective Inspector Macrae. I'll take Ms Lynch for some food. We'll be back within half an hour.'

'I have to fill this in,' I said. 'Two minutes.' I looked at the nurse. She was in her twenties, with light red hair, and an oval face on a long, slim neck. Her eyes flicked between me and her computer screen even as I was speaking to her. 'I've filled in all the factual and contact details. As far as I know Anders has no food allergies, but I just can't tell you about medical ones.' I handed the sheaf back to her. 'I'm not next of kin, just a friend, so I can't sign the consent form, but when I last saw him Anders was clear enough to be able to give his own consent, or you could phone his parents.' I stopped being efficient, and gave her a pleading look. 'Please, could you just tell us how he is, before I go anywhere?'

She pursed her lips, considered me, then frowned and looked again properly, distracted from her electronic world. 'Here, I ken you. Aren't you that lass that was in charge of that film boat? I mind your picture in the paper.'

It was the last thing I wanted to be reminded of, but if it was going to get me through to Anders, I'd use it. 'I was the skipper,' I said, 'and Anders was the engineer.'

'And you met Favelle and all them?'

I nodded.

'Cool,' she said. 'I'll go and ask what's going on.' She gathered the papers together. Her blue overall rustled as she disappeared through the swing doors.

'Interesting,' Gavin said. His voice was amused. 'When I came in you were looking wiped out, then you suddenly got a new lease of captainly life when I tried to be in charge for half an hour.'

'I'm used to being a captain.'

'I know. I'm that way too. That's why I prefer being sent out to deal with crofters. It's just me and my sergeant, and no complicated hierarchy breathing down my neck.'

There was low-voiced speaking behind the double doors, then footsteps, and the nurse returned, with an older woman in ordinary clothes with the doctor's badge of a stethoscope round her neck. She carried a clipboard, with the form I'd just filled in at the top of it. 'Ms Lynch?'

I stood to attention. *Lege ... Kapitain.*

'Anders has lost a good deal of blood. He's got a broken shoulder-blade and a torn muscle, but there's no damage to any organs. We've got him under sedation. You could phone later to see how he's doing, and you'll be able to see him tomorrow.'

'Has someone phoned his parents?'

She glanced at the nurse, who shook her head. 'You could do that. Tell them he's doing well, his condition is stable, and they're welcome to phone the hospital for news at any time. If they ask for Dr Goodwin I'll give them more details. We'll see you tomorrow.'

She nodded, turned away and strode back into the safety of her ward. I picked my jacket up. 'What's the hospital number?'

'Oh, I'll give it you – here.' The nurse scribbled it down on a post-it. 'That's reception, then this is the ward he'll be in.'

'Thanks,' I said.

I wasn't allowed to use my mobile in the hospital. I sat on the bench outside, and weighed it in my hand. After Alain's death, I'd chickened out. I knew I should have phoned, but I didn't know what to say. *This is Cass, who killed your son* – I would do it this time.

The police must have already phoned, for Anders' mother pounced at the first ring. 'Ja, Elisabet Johansen –' Then she switched to English. 'This is Anders' mother.'

'This is Cass.' I tried to compress the important bit. 'Anders is in hospital here. I have just spoken to the doctor, and he has lost blood. His shoulder blade is broken, and he has a torn muscle. You have to phone the hospital. Here is the number.' I waited for her to snatch up a pen, then read out the numbers from the post-it the nurse had given me.

'I have it written.' She read it back to me. 'But how did he come to be injured?'

'A bull was loose, and he saved a woman from being hurt. He pushed her out of its path, and it caught him instead. He was very brave.'

'I told him to come home.' Her voice rose. 'He has a job here, he cannot just stay on a boat with you like a hippy. His father needs him. Now we will come and fetch him home. He should not be with you, getting mixed up in murder.' The venom in the 'you' stung like a snapped rope lashing out. 'I told him not to go with you. You are older than he is, you are not interested in him, and there was the man who died at sea, but he would not listen. I have seen on the internet already, there are more deaths.'

I had deserved this tongue-lashing for Alain. Now I realised that I deserved it for Anders too. I hadn't thought of myself as Elisabet Johansen saw me: the older woman, the footloose, uneducated hippy, leading her moonstruck son astray. I'd been blind, wilfully blind, accepting his care for me as friendship, because that was all I wanted. He'd come at my asking on the film-boat adventure with me, and he'd stayed afterwards, in spite of my condescending to him as a nerdish younger brother. I hadn't deserved him. *You are so very young, Cass...*

There was a click on the phone, and it was taken from Elisabet. Anders' father's voice boomed in English over the wires. 'Cass, is that you? What is the news?'

He didn't apologise for Elisabet, and I didn't expect him to. 'Anders is in hospital here in Lerwick. The doctor says that he's stable. She is Dr Goodwin, you can speak to her. I'll come back in the morning.'

'I will phone this doctor. We will come. There is a direct flight from Bergen. You must phone again if you have more news, or when you have seen him.'

'I will,' I promised.

Chapter Twenty-five

I put the phone away, and walked over to Gavin's car. He was already seated behind the wheel. I climbed in beside him. His grey eyes flicked up at my face, then looked back at the dashboard. He put the car into gear. 'He's an adult, you know. He chose the risk of being hurt himself to make you and Kirsten safe.'

'I know,' I agreed. I didn't feel guilty about his being hurt. I knew he'd weighed up the risks. He had lightning-quick reactions, Anders. I felt guilty about not having seen him.

Gavin let the car roll towards the exit. 'Fish and chips, Indian or Chinese?'

'Chinese would be exotic.' Chinese was a once-every-two-months treat – there was a team of chefs who went round the country halls in turn, preceded by a hand-painted notice, and one of their 'kitchens' was the boating club.

'Eat-in or takeaway?'

'Takeaway. I need to get back to *Khalida*.' She was my home, my security, and right now I wanted her. I turned my wrist to look at my watch, and could hardly believe it was only twenty to five. 'There's a five o'clock bus.'

'My B&B's up near Brae, remember? I was going to give you a lift back.'

'Oh –' I was annoyed to find myself blushing. 'Thanks.'

He pulled out across from the Clickimin Leisure Centre, an oyster-shell building coiled around with flumes for the swimming pool, and flanked by a double football pitch and a red asphalt running track, and negotiated the roundabout by Grantfield Garage.

'I can't believe how much you're paying for petrol up here. I thought we were bad in Glengarry, but you're fully 10p a litre more.'

'I know,' I said. 'Especially since most of it arrives here, up at Sullom Voe. I suppose it has to go south to be refined before it comes back, but all the same, someone's getting rich on it.' I cast him a sideways glance. 'Anders and I were even thinking we'd have to get rid of the car.'

He sighed. 'No licence yet?'

'I've applied,' I said defensively. 'I presume that means you don't want to sail to Brae, and then let me run you back for your car?'

'Only if you'll accept me driving it on my own third-party insurance.'

I considered that one as he pulled in across from the Red Dragon Takeaway and parked above the council houses. He was, after all, a police officer, and in rural Scotland that meant a lot of time talking to teenagers about the importance of a proper licence to make sure you were insured, for the sake of everyone else on the road.

'I hardly ever drive it these days,' I conceded. 'Most places, I can walk or take the boat, and there's a good bus service to Lerwick, so long as you don't mind hanging about.'

We crossed the road to the Red Dragon. It was a tiny shop on the street corner, with two wooden benches and a counter, and tantalising smells filtering from the kitchen beyond. A hanging lantern made of plastic jade and red cloth jingled as Gavin closed the door. 'Nearly legal in someone who's not naturally law-abiding counts as a success story.'

'I'm naturally law-abiding at sea,' I retorted.

We leaned companionably together over the counter

and considered the menu. 'What do you call those little parcel things, with the red sauce,' I asked, 'and may I eat them in the car?'

'Crispy won tons. Can you manage not to drip the sauce over Bolt's seat covers?'

I gave him a withering look. 'I've drunk soup at sea in a force 7 without spilling a drop.' He grinned, unwithered. 'I'll have those as a starter, and a chicken satay with egg-fried rice.'

'Mmmm. I'll go for the prawn toast, then a chow mein.'

We took the white plastic bags of foil trays back out to the car and munched our starters companionably along the highroad back to Voe. The road passed the field of coloured foals chasing each other around their grazing mothers at Gott, and cut between the hills to skirt the loch of Girlsta.

'Did you know,' I said, crunching the folds off the top of one won ton parcel, 'that the Vikings used ravens to find the nearest land, like Noah with his ark?'

'Floki the Navigator,' Gavin said. 'I've seen the model in the museum in Reykjavik.'

'His daughter Gerhilda was buried on that island in the loch,' I said. In the back seat, Gavin's phone shrilled. I was pleased to hear he'd opted for a simple ring. He glanced at me. 'Can you get that, while I pull over?'

I reached behind and fished out the phone out from his green tweed jacket pocket. It felt too intimate, like a lover's gesture. 'Hello, Gavin Macrae's phone.'

'It's his brother, Kenny.' His voice was older than Gavin's, with a much stronger accent, as if he habitually spoke Gaelic. 'Is that Cass?'

'Gavin's driving.' The car swerved to the left, into the gravel verge, and stopped.

'Ach, I'm no' needing to speak right now. You could be telling him to phone me later.'

'He's just pulled over.'

'Have you found your missing boat now, Cass?'

'I'm afraid so. Here's Gavin.' I handed the phone over and listened as Gavin broke into a flood of Gaelic, musical as water running over pebbles. His whole face softened, talking to his brother, lost that wary look he gave me, and livened into expression; he gestured with his other hand as he spoke, as if his brother could see him. I concentrated on my won tons, dipping them into the chewing-gum red sauce, and looking out across the water buttercup swaying at the edges of the lochan below us. I was trying not to listen, but I caught my name a couple of times. Gavin ended the call with a laugh, tossed the phone behind us, then started the car again.

'Our ram is giving bother. He's found he can get out of his field, if he charges the posts, and so he's having to live on a tether. He doesn't like it.' His square brown hands were steady on the wheel.

'Is he much older than you, your brother?'

'Ten years. My mother was already in her thirties when she had him, and then I was even more of a late baby. She'll be seventy-nine next year.'

We came past the peat banks opposite the Half Way House, and into the wide moorland valley between the East and Mid Kames. 'So this,' Gavin said, looking round at the heather hills, 'is where your father's windfarm is to be. How is that going?'

'Stalled. The Shetland Islands Council made a lot of noise about consulting the people, then passed the buck to the Scottish Government.' Inga was strongly anti-windfarm, and her group hoped for a public enquiry so that the issues could be aired properly. 'Dad's down in Edinburgh just now, lobbying.'

'Have you decided where you stand yet?'

I made a face. 'It's getting more and more difficult. These hills look so barren and empty, but it's a whole eco-system out there, with rare birds nesting, and the peat storing carbon. The folk who're going to have to live with a hundred huge turbines on their horizon are unhappy too.'

'They're springing up all over the Highlands,' Gavin said. 'People are discovering health problems the developers kept quiet about.'

'Dad's firm promised a health survey, but they've not done it yet. And that's another thing,' I said. 'As you say, wind farms are springing up everywhere. Why will people buy our more costly electricity, with the interconnector to repay as well as the turbines, when they can get it from somewhere nearer? If it doesn't work out, we've got an unsightly white elephant, and we've ruined acres of pristine moorland for nothing. But then –'

'There's always a "but then".'

'I read last year's seabird breeding figures the other day. They made awful reading. Birds I thought were common, like the black shags you see out in the voe, and standing on Papa Little, I knew there were fewer of them here, but on Fair Isle there were forty per cent fewer. Forty per cent! And I went to the museum one day when they were showing film from the thirties, and there was just a cloud of seabirds around every cliff. I've never seen that many gulls here – no, I've never seen that many gulls anywhere. I don't know what's killing them, but if it's climate change then we've got to do our bit, whatever it costs.' I brooded for a moment, looking out at the smooth sweep of heather-green hill sliding past. 'Imagine Peerie Charlie going out in a boat round Papa Little and there being no guillemots popping up to look at you, no eider ducks going, 'whor' as you pass, no shags on the cliff, no kittiwakes. We can't let that happen, if we can stop it.'

'Onshore's not necessarily the answer, though,' Gavin said. 'Look at your tides in Yell Sound. You could run a dozen turbines with them.'

'Yes, and I'm not sure big's the answer either. Surely it would make more sense if each community generated its own electricity, like they do for each hall.'

'Not everywhere's got as much wind as Shetland.'

'So we need to share with those who've got none.' I sighed. 'I'm sitting on the fence at the moment. I think my head's with dad, and my heart's with the objectors.'

The long road continued round the smooth curve to Voe. I could hear a flutter of music from the showfield. The beer tent was still open, and there would be a dance later. Anders had asked me to dance with him …

We turned off down towards the pier. It was busy here too, with every table filled, and a waitress running from hatch to customers with plastic boxes of fish and chips. Gavin parked beside the restored fishing boat, and we headed for *Khalida* with our foil boxes. I switched on the gas as we climbed aboard. 'Cup of tea?'

'Please.'

Rat swarmed out as soon as I lifted the washboards, and Cat followed him. I scooped Cat up and put the lower washboard back, to keep him coralled while we ate. Rat whiffled at Gavin, then perched on the washboard, head moving, eyes bright and interested. Cat scrabbled up and over in a scraping of claws. I gave them each a chicken piece on the cockpit floor. A young man of Anders' build came down the hill, and Rat sat up taller, watching him, then settled again, whiskers drooping. I got out two plates and cutlery, and we settled on each side of the table, Gavin in Anders' place in the corner. He looked at home there, his hair blending into the red-brown of the mahogony bulkhead, the light from the window highlighting his cheekbones.

'Well?' I said.

'I'm starving,' he replied. 'Can I eat first?'

We launched in. He ate neatly and quickly, like someone who was used to meals being squeezed in between other activities. I didn't believe he'd manage to keep quiet right through, and he didn't. Once his plate was half-cleared, he laid the fork down and began.

'Well. A lot of what we'd already surmised was right enough. Newcastle's still being tight-lipped, but I think we're safe to take Sandra Wearmouth as the police mole. They seemed relieved it wasn't Peter. She, or she and David, or the three of them together, could have been the Mr Big who dealt in art for drugs using David and Madge as couriers, but that's not certain. Maybe she just supplied information to the real Mr Big.' He took a forkful of chow mein. 'This is good.'

'But,' I said, 'if David and Madge were in cahoots with Sue, how come they thought Anders and I might be the police spies? Why search *Khalida*? Why draw attention to the burglaries the way they did?'

He answered that question with another. 'If you were really running an operation using the trowie mound, would you draw attention to it the way they did? Shots, lights, coming into Brae, taking the boat out at midnight –'

I hadn't thought about that. 'They almost went out of their way to draw attention to the whole operation. Talking about it, the motorboat coming in to Brae, the trip to the trowie mound, leaving the boat overnight – Madge taking her out, when it would have made more sense, surely, for Sandra to take *Genniveve* and David and Madge the motorboat.' I narrowed my eyes, concentrating. 'So what were we meant to think?'

'Sandra'd taken off, remember,' Gavin said. 'They'd killed Peter, and presumably she was all set to leave with David and Madge.'

'Yes,' I agreed. 'When Peter and Sandra didn't return, someone would ask questions. They'd find us and Magnie, nice respectable residents –' His eyes crinkled at the corners. I ignored them. '– who could tell how they'd set off up to the trowie mound. If they looked there, if they got in – and an investigation would soon find Brian's tunnel – they'd find the crates and boxes, and the birds flown. If they asked a bit further, we'd tell them how *Genniveve* left in the middle of the night, and we couldn't swear it was Sandra or Peter at the helm. They'd think that Peter, the good guy, had fallen foul of the bad guys up at the trowie mound. They'd killed him and Sandra, and stolen the boat to sell. If they'd investigated further, and found the yacht, well, there was Peter's body aboard.'

'It was only the cat that made us find the yacht.'

Peter's cat. *She doesn't talk to me* ... jettisoned, left to drown.

'Killed by the nasty art thief couriers, who'd headed off in their unmarked motorboat to parts unknown, on a full tank of diesel.'

'Or killed by the local man.'

'Was it Olaf?'

'He's admitted to having had connections with your motorboat pair over his sex videos, in the days before you could just whizz everything over the internet. He says he's had nothing to do with them for the last five years, and knows nothing about any art theft, and now can he get back to his wife, who's in great distress over the loss of his boy.'

'If he's that innocent, what was he doing setting a bull on us?'

'He saw Kirsten with your priest and panicked, thinking his porn enterprise was about to be public knowledge. His lawyer agrees that that's a perfectly reasonable way to think. The Lerwick Inspector's thinking of what they can charge him with.' He smiled. 'Apparently there's an offence of releasing a wild animal to the danger of the public, which has never yet been used in Shetland, but he and one of the sergeants got technical as to whether a bull was a wild animal exactly, so they may just go with breach of the peace.'

My answering smile was a feeble effort. 'It was pretty wild at us.'

'They reckon they can do better, though. These art thefts, they were simply done. The perp went straight in, ignoring any ringing alarms, through the nearest window to the painting or whatever most worth taking, took it, and scarpered. Most of the places were small operations, but one of the owners heard about the thefts through the lairds' grapevine, before it hit the headlines, and installed an amateur version of CCTV. We've got a good portrait of Olaf in action. Even in dark clothes and a pull-down knitted hat, he's pretty unmistakeable. Even better, Northlink Ferries are already working on a print-out of his boat trips down south to visit his best pal Brian. If the dates don't match the robberies, I'll eat my sporran.'

His face sobered. 'There's one drawback, though. When David Morse and Sandra Wearmouth were shot on the platform above you, Olaf was at home. He'd just had the news of Alex's death broken to him by two officers, and his wife had collapsed. He didn't leave the house for as long as ten minutes, let alone for the time it would have taken to drive the pick-up to the trowie mound. Their murderer's still out there.'

A cold shudder ran down my spine. Gavin continued, in that neutral voice, 'He might think, you know, that you can identify him. It's an outside chance – it's far more likely that you'd have told us everything you know.'

'We've certainly been seen together by half the west side,' I agreed cordially. He'd treated me like a partner, dammit, and now I was going to be sent behind the firing lines -

'All the same, I'm not sure you should be staying on the boat on your own in the marina.' The carefulness of his voice made it clear he knew he was pushing his luck. 'Espcially with the whole place at the show dance. Would you consider going to your father's?'

I'd sailed to America in a 32-foot boat. I'd seen more dangerous corners of the world than he'd had hot dinners. 'I had to sleep ashore during the film murder,' I said. My inner three year old rose up; I borrowed Peerie Charlie's phrase, and said it with his air of gentle finality. 'I not.'

'No,' Gavin said. 'I didn't think you would.' He hesitated, his eyes looking round *Khalida* as if he was considering hiding-places. 'I could leave an officer on board.'

I jutted my chin at him. 'I don't need protected.'

There was a long silence. I could see in his eyes that he was considering making it an order, and I had no doubt that he could see in mine that coercion would do serious damage to whatever tentative relationship was between us. In the end he said, mildly, 'If the murderer believes you can identify him, then he may try to silence you.'

'You keep saying *he*. Do you know who it is?'

Gavin spread his hands, palms up. 'We have a suspicion, but no proof.'

'If I'm surrounded by officers,' I said, 'he can't try.' I leant back against the shelf, stretched my legs out to the opposite berth, and looked sideways at him. 'You can't charge him with anything.'

I saw him think about that; think about whether I could be relied on as a colleague. Then he nodded, and gave in. 'Do you have any idea of what will happen to my official head if I set you up as a tethered goat, and the tiger gets to you before I get to him?'

'Then make sure he doesn't,' I said.

10

Seldom comes a doo fae a craw's nest.

(Old Shetland proverb: A dove rarely comes from a crow's nest.)

Chapter Twenty-six

It took an hour to sail up to Brae. The wind had fallen away, but it was still nicely on the beam, so I hauled up *Khalida*'s red, blue, and white geneker, a half-balloon of a sail which crinkled and rustled like tissue paper as the wind came and went. It was a slow sail down long Olna Firth between the sea-serpent humps of mussel rafts. Voe House, the noisy pier, the fluttering bunting of the show, receded behind us until we came through the narrows at the Point of Mulla, and they were hidden behind the curve of headland. The tide was against me, a mid-tide stream with the full moon thrusting the water shorewards. On the sun-catching side of Souther Hill, there was already a purple tinge to the heather, and the clouds were building up away to the west, piled high like the stern of a ship of the line. Tomorrow, the moon's face would be flattened to the other side. The end of summer was on the horizon, the colder days, the autumn gales, the equinox.

Rat was anxious. He'd watched as I'd prepared for sea, looking from me to the shore, then once we'd cast off he stayed in the cockpit, staring back. He knew we'd left Anders behind, and I hadn't any way of reassuring him. I picked him up to curl around my neck, and he sat there for a bit, but once Voe was out of sight, he squirmed below to his nest. Cat wriggled after him, stubby tail gesticulating as he squeezed down between the cushions. I wished I could explain to them.

I sighed, and made myself a cup of drinking chocolate, then settled back on my seat in the cockpit. The green shore slid past us, the ruined houses, open boxes of walling standing in rectangles of brighter green, where tatties and kale had once grown, and tethered cows had grazed. The tangle of rusting metal above a stone pier had been Shetland's last whaling station. Crofting and whaling, once major Shetland industries, gone now. Maybe Dad's windfarm was all we'd have left to keep us in prosperity once the oil ran out.

As *Khalida* sailed herself onwards towards the heather-dark curve of Linga, I tried to think. I had to work this out, for word would have spread round the Show, with the whole of the west and north mainland meeting together, of how the Lynch lass, you ken, her that lives on the boat, had been rescued by helicopter from a cliff. There'd been two bodies shot – no, no her doing the shooting, someen else, but she'd been there.

If I was the killer, I'd want to know where the Lynch lass had been during the shooting, and what she'd seen. Gavin had wouldn't give me a name, but if he could work it out, so could I. I needed to know who to be afraid of.

There had been too much going on, too many strands confusing the plot. Kevin, Geri, the mysterious bucket, the locked boat, that was clear now. The cottage, and Olaf's sex videos, with Kirsten bullied into taking part, and Cerys drawing new people in, to amuse her when Brian brought her up to the dull country for the summer, I understood that part of it too. It would make sense that Brian's best pal Olaf would have a key, to keep an eye on things – and if Olaf had a key, then he could have given one to David, so that they could use the cottage in their visits. The watcher of my first visit could have been Madge, making sure I didn't come near Peter's body, if it'd been stored in the cottage before being transferred to the motorboat. Robbie's gossip had made Brian suspicious. He'd gone there on Thursday, the day I visited his mother, driven along to the old cottage. He'd flung the sexy bedding and camera tripod out on the shore, and changed the locks.

There'd be no more goings-on there.

I frowned, and sat up straighter. This timing didn't work. The cottage locks had been changed on Thursday, so David, Sandra, and Madge couldn't have been using it after that. The trowie mound had been cleared, I presumed, on the night Magnie had seen the lights going up and down. That had been Thursday night, the night after *Genniveve* had been scuttled. It had been empty, except for the crates, when I'd been thrown in there on Friday. Yesterday. Had it really only been yesterday? I felt I'd lived a year since then.

They'd killed Alex yesterday, after Peter's body had been sunk and the mound cleared. *So what had he seen?*

The question stopped me short. I'd been working on a vague assumption that he'd gone up there and seen them moving art works, or otherwise behaving in a suspicious fashion, but that didn't make sense. The loot had been shifted, Peter's body disposed of, a day before he came along on his quad. Like I'd reasoned before, he wasn't an easy person to dispose of, and there would be ten times the hue and cry about a child that there would be for an adult. Unless he'd been a serious, direct danger to them, then he was a stupid person to kill, and Sandra hadn't been stupid. So what had made him so dangerous?

Now I'd thought it through, it was obvious. I heard Alex's voice: *See, I ken them. I'm seen them before, anyroad, when I was down at Brian's… we were haeing a holiday down there, where he lives, and that's where I saw them.* Talking to his father Olaf, perhaps, arranging the next robbery. Then he'd paused, and I'd thought he was just making up detail, but if it had been true it would be fatal: *I mind the man.*

He'd seen David Morse, with his bulky stomach and walrus moustache. He'd even half-remembered his name: *It began with a B … No, no, an M.* He'd watched them, in the marina. He'd have known that slim, ash-fair Sandra

298

wasn't the motorboat woman. Him identifying the mixed-up couple, David and Sandra, would spoil their nicely set up scenario of the good guys killed by the bad.

I kept thinking from there, as we slid smoothly past Linga, past where *Genniveve* lay ninety metres deep. I remembered Olaf as a boy; I remembered the way Brian used to withdraw from him when his bullying got too much. *Always a bit secretive* ... Kirsten had withdrawn that way now. I hoped she would be all right. I thought about Cerys' games at the cottage, and Barbara's sharp voice.

Most of all, I thought about peerie Charlie, playing engines with his fish fingers, and comforting Inga in her own voice.

I poled the geneker out and put a protector to stop the main swinging back, and we drifted goose-winged up Busta Voe towards the marina. By the time we reached it, I'd a pretty good idea of who'd shot David and Sandra above my head on the trowie mound ledge, and why. *An outside chance*, Gavin had said, but this murderer might not think that rationally. For a moment I wondered what my pride had got me into, when I could have been safe at Dad's, with a policeman guarding *Khalida*. The thought jolted my courage back. I'd crossed oceans. I'd keep myself safe.

The marina was quiet as I ghosted in. I couldn't be bothered starting the engine, so I drifted outside for a bit, getting the geneker and pole stowed, then went in under mainsail, taking a wide curve around the inner pool to slow *Khalida* down before steering her into her berth. I slung a loop of the stern rope over the aft cleat and left her like that, with the start battery on, and the key still in the engine. I might need to make a quick get-away.

It was almost ten o'clock, an hour and a half yet to high tide. The dusk was gathering in the curves of the shore, and the moon was scattering silver light across the glassy ripples. The tirricks gossiped as they settled down for the night. There were clinking sounds from the caravan park that ran around the shore side of the marina, a biker working underneath an old-fashioned Triumph. Saturday night or no, it was still as death, no cars moving around, no noise of television or radio blaring out from open windows. Even the club was closed tonight. Those who felt up to it were at the Voe Show dance. It seemed a hundred years ago that I'd talked of dancing with Anders.

My heart was thumping unevenly. An outside chance. I hung up my sailing clothes, and put on a T-shirt, jeans, and light canvas shoes. I was still thinking of exits. They were clothes I could swim in, if need be. I went along the pontoon to the RIB's berth, just below the marina gate, and checked the key and kill-cord were in place, just as the lifeboat men had left her. I untied her ropes too, except for the bow line. It was a still night; she'd come to no harm. The biker raised his head and watched me for a moment, then went back to his mechanics.

Rat swarmed out as I came back aboard, and sat for a bit on the cabin roof, looking around, then went back below, and into the forepeak. Cat curled around my neck and purred. Above me, in the green park around the standing stone, a ewe called her lamb home for the night, and it answered in a high bleat. I thought of Kirsten, lying sedated in her bed. Her child wouldn't ever come home. David and Sandra had paid for that. Surely that was enough?

Their killer had been watching for my sail coming up the voe. I'd only sat in the cockpit for five minutes when I heard the pick-up scrunching down the boating club gravel. A shadow came out from it, unlocked the marina gate and slipped through, leaving it open behind him. He came walking steadily down towards *Khalida*, along the pontoon and paused by her berth, seeing me in the cockpit. His hands were empty. I was glad of that. I have an understandable dislike of having a gun pointed at me.

'Hello, Norman,' I said.

Norman, Olaf's son. Just as Peerie Charlie copied Inga's voice and gestures, Norman had grown up to imitate his father. I could hear Olaf's philosophy, *Life's what you make it. I could put you in the way of earning* ... I didn't think Norman had been actively involved in the thefts, though I wouldn't have liked to bet on that one either. He was quick, Norman. He could have squirmed in a narrow window, grabbed the chosen object, and been out again before the alarm bells had time to warm up. Fagin teaching waifs to pick-pocket wasn't just a Victorian exploitation. *I stuck in the cat flap* ...

He paused beside me. 'Bonny night.'

'It is,' I agreed.

The silvery light of the pontoon lamps shone on his face. He looked bleak and young and lost, and his breath caught in his throat as if he'd been crying, but I wasn't going to let that get under my guard. Olaf had done a good line in repentence too, when trouble loomed over him. I gestured to the cockpit seat opposite me. 'Come aboard.'

I let him get settled before I moved to make a cup of tea. I was careless of my safety, Gavin reckoned, but not so careless that I'd go out of sight with Norman. 'Sit still,' I said. 'I'll put the kettle on. Tea?'

He nodded.

'Milk, sugar?'

'Yeah.'

I could feel his eyes on me as I lit the gas, put the kettle on, brought out the mugs, teabags, and milk, and gave the hardened sugar an experimental dunt with a teaspoon.

'It's cool,' he said. 'Living aboard like this. You have everything you need. Nobody bothers you. You can just take off and go.'

'Wouldn't you miss the widescreen telly and full-speed broadband?' I asked.

He shrugged. 'I'm no' sure I would. I watch stuff but I never really get into it. Games, I like games. I like the stuff where people play tricks on people.' His eyes travelled up the mast. 'How far've you sailed in this?'

'I bought her in the Med and sailed her to Norway, but that was coast-hopping. The crossing from Bergen to here was the longest ocean-crossing I've done in her.'

'Cool,' he repeated.

I handed him his mug, and clambered out into the cockpit beside him. 'Your wee brother had the makings of a good sailor,' I said.

'He liked it,' Norman said. He jutted his lower lip, determined not to show feelings. 'He wouldn't miss it whatever.'

'You usually ran him along,' I said. *Inga's lasses, taking Peerie Charlie's hand to lead him back to Mam.* I'd always wanted a brother. I'd have looked after him. He'd have looked up to me, the way Peerie Charlie looked up to Vaila and Dawn – the way Alex had looked up to Norman. If Norman had asked him to do something, however dodgy, Alex would have done his best.

He gave a 'whatever' jerk of one shoulder.

'How's your mother now?' I asked.

He would have learned to disregard anything his mother said from the way his father ignored it. He shrugged again. 'She's doped to the eyeballs. Cerys is with her. The pigs have dad down at the nick.' He glanced sideways at me. 'They say he's mixed up in art theft. Up at the trowie mound.'

For his father, the law wasn't important. *The pigs, the nick.* You did what you wanted, made money the way that

302

seemed best to you. If the chance came up to make big money, money that would mean you didn't have to kow-tow to anyone else, then why not? I could hear Olaf's schoolboy voice as he pocketed another pencil, or helped himself to a video from the library: 'Why no'? They've got loads.'

Olaf's son shifted in his seat again, and took a breath. His voice was too casual. 'Didn't you get stuck up there? Yesterday?'

This was what I knew he'd come to ask, while I was alone here in the twilight, with everybody else at the dance in Voe: *Did you see me?*

'When the shootings were,' Norman pursued. 'You got rescued by the helicopter. Everyone was talking about it, at the show.'

I knew they would. My record of never having needed to call out the lifeboat was ruined. I didn't have thoughts to waste on regretting it.

'I was on the cliff, on a ledge below the grass in front of the trowie mound.' I looked him straight in the eye. 'I heard it all, but I didn't see anything. I couldn't identify the killer. I told the police that.'

I sensed rather than heard the relieved breath. He leaned back against *Khalida*'s guard rail. I waited in silence. He looked so vulnerable, with the gold earring dangling towards his thin cheek, and his grey-green eyes, Kirsten's eyes, narrowed in doubt. Perhaps I was making too much of his resemblance to Olaf. Perhaps the conscience, the principles that Kirsten would have tried to instill into her sons was struggling to free itself. Eventually he set his cup down and turned to face me again. I saw that he hadn't believed me; that he wasn't just going to go away and forget me. His voice had lost its aggressive edge and become tentative, young.

'I was wondering, see, if you ever get used to having

killed someone. If you ever forget.'

'No,' I said simply.

He jerked backwards at that, as if it wasn't what he wanted to hear, but now wasn't the time for kindly lies. They wouldn't help him, or me.

'There's nothing you can do to make it better,' I expanded. 'You can't say sorry, and bring them back to life. You can't change what you did that killed them. If you could, you would, ten times over, but it's too late.'

Norman had wanted money. *I know how you got that scar* – The rumour was that I'd been well paid for the film job, because everyone knew there was big money in film, but Anders had warned him away from me. Then he'd seen the shadowy figures his dad had dealings with. There was money there all right, if you could find a way to touch it.

'It was my fault Alex died.' He said it aggressively, as if I'd disagree. 'I set him to spy on them, the couple with the flashy new motorboat. If I'd not done that, they wouldn't have killed him.'

The police would have told Kirsten that they were looking for someone else in connection with Alex's death, that they weren't satisfied it was an accident. Norman must have understood what he'd done as soon as he heard the news. He'd have phoned the couple to make them wait, saying he was his father perhaps, and gone out like a fury, bouncing the pick-up over the rough hill to meet up with his brother's killers, and exorcise his guilt and anger with revenge. A young person's fury –

I nodded. 'He wouldn't have been up at the mound if he'd not been spying for you. But it was them who killed him, not you.'

'It was my fault,' he repeated. He turned the anger on me. 'Do you tell yourself it was the water killed your man?'

'No,' I admitted. Across at the caravan site, the man under the motorbike gave up chinking and stood up. He stretched, looking out across the marina, then went into his mobile home. A rectangle of pale gold light marked the doorway. 'It was what I did that killed him. I didn't mean it to, but I was responsible for his death.'

Olaf had been worried about what his son was doing. *Young eens these days, you never know what they'll be up to ...* He knew Sandra, David, and Madge weren't to be messed about with. Quietly, I leaned back and draped my left arm over the guard rail, by the horseshoe bouy. I kept my gaze on his as my hand stole down to the whistle that hung from it, a snail-shape of hard plastic wound round by cord. Behind the bouy, my fingers untwisted the cord and turned the whistle so that one movement would have it to my lips. He'd already said too much to let me go.

'Did you get their mobile number from your dad's phone?'

He slanted a startled look at me, then looked away, mouth twitching. 'Yeah,' he conceded, 'but I phoned from a mate's phone. I asked for money not to shop them to the pigs.'

'They wouldn't have been happy with that.'

'My dad got on to me.' He took a deep breath, as if he'd decided something. 'Then, when I heard about Alex, I nicked Dad's phone. I texted to say I had to meet them, up on the mound. Then I switched it off so's they couldn't phone back and find out it wasn't him. I took the pick-up up there, and Dad's gun.' He looked sharply at me. 'You're not surprised. You knew it was me.'

'Not then,' I said. 'I worked it out later. The people in the yacht were dead, and Brian and the cottage had nothing to do with it. Cerys is too self-centred, and she couldn't drive a pick-up up that hill. Your dad was at the house with your mam, after they'd heard Alex was dead. That left you to avenge his death.'

He sat up straighter, so that he was taller than me, and broader. 'You told your policeman pal this yet?' I'd heard Olaf sound like this too, in the playground. I hadn't been frightened of him then, and I wasn't going to be intimidated by his son now.

'They killed your wee brother,' I said. 'Alex. He's dead, and now they're dead too. Can't it stop there?'

He shook his head, and leant towards me. I swung my arm round, quick as thought, and put the whistle to my mouth. It was one of those ear-splitters with a pea inside, and I gave it all the breath I'd got. He flinched, and before he began moving towards me I dropped the whistle and sprang to my feet, vaulting over *Khalida's* guard rail. Instead of going up the walkway as he'd expected, I took a running dive from the pontoon-end straight into the calm inner pool of the marina, a racing dive that turned into a fast crawl which had me halfway across the fifty metres of water before he'd registered what I was doing.

The water closed over my head like an ice-cold shower. My clothes held out the water briefly, then it came through them. I wouldn't be able to stay in here very long, but I'd banked on the natural reluctance of a dressed person to leap straight into cold, deep water. The gamble had paid off. There was no second splash.

I came up in the middle of the pool and brushed the water from my eyes. Norman was standing in *Khalida's* cockpit, staring after me. I saw him realising that I had the advantage of him now. If he came after me by water, I'd be ashore, up the slip and in the clubhouse with the door locked before he reached the dinghy pontoon. If he came around by land, I'd be back on *Khalida* with my single rope cast off before he got back to me. I sculled slowly on my back to the end of the dinghy pontoon, and waited.

Then the blue dusk split open with light, a blaring white

searchlight from the open caravan door that caught Norman first, then swung back to me. The cavalry were here, as we'd agreed, fifty yards away, with a grandstand view of everything that happened on *Khalida*. I wondered if there was a police marksman in the caravan. I turned and began to swim for the slip, around the dinghy pontoon, ignoring the shouting and running feet, until I realised that under the shouting and the banging was a sound I knew, the clunk, clunk of *Khalida*'s engine. I lifted my head and looked.

He'd thought fast, Norman. They were coming for him by land, so he'd go by sea. *Khalida*'s was a simple engine, he'd have used a dozen like it. By the time the police had got down the pontoon, he was backing out of the berth. He didn't waste time turning her, just kept her going stern forwards towards the rocky entrance.

My thought for haste had helped him, the single rope and the key in the engine; now his haste helped me. He was looking ahead at the entrance, ignoring the shouting behind him. *Khalida* never got up to full speed straight away, so her progress must have felt painfully slow. His hands were clenched on the tiller, his eyes fixed to the narrow gap between the rocks as if he was willing her forwards. I hoped he'd remember Gibbie's Baa, the single rock awkwardly placed just outside.

I struck out towards my boat and stretched up to catch two of the uprights that held her guard-rails as she passed me. Her bow was higher out of the water than I'd realised. I hauled myself up so that my elbows were on her deck, then reached further with one hand and grabbed the forrard cleat. My other hand caught the rounded anchor-pipe cover, and that gave me enough purchase to get one knee aboard. The wash and sway as she turned gave me the impetus to get my other leg aboard. I ducked my body under the wires and slid rapidly forward to huddle behind the rounded front of her cabin. He'd have seen me if he'd taken a proper look forward, but I was banking on his either looking far ahead, to the sea horizon, or over his shoulder at the pursuit. Furthermore, he'd shoved the gear lever forwards to full throttle, and below the water the propeller wash was hammering full on her rudder, forcing her to turn to port. He was struggling to keep her on course, and I thought for a moment I was going to have to leap up, because we had to be almost on Gibbie's Baa. Then he managed to get control of her, and turn her seawards. Now was my danger moment, as he looked forwards. I lay still, crouched in the curve of salt-washed fibreglass.

The shouting in the marina had stopped. Now, roaring out over the thunk, thunk of *Khalida*'s engine, was the sound of the RIB. Glory be, the cavalry was still on its way. I wondered if Gavin himself had been inside the biker's caravan.

Norman heard it too. *Khalida* swerved again as he turned to look. I took the moment when the RIB's nose edged out of the marina to lift the forehatch and swing down into the darkness of Anders' bunk.

Chapter Twenty-seven

Blessed respite. Within the forepeak, behind the blue and yellow curtain, I felt safe again. Rat squirmed out of Anders' sleeping-bag and inspected me, whiskers twitching at the cold. I hauled my wet T-shirt over my head and fumbled in Anders' kitbag for another, and a fleece. Cold meant you made stupid mistakes. Anders' clothes smelt of Imperial Leather soap and engine oil. Dear Anders, safe in the Gilbert Bain Hospital with the brisk doctor looking after him. 'I'll see you tomorrow,' I promised myself. His jeans would be no good on me. I felt for a pair of sailing thermals, edged my canvas shoes off, eased my clinging jeans down and pulled the long johns on. The dry warmth enclosed me like a blanket.

Khalida was still bucking her way seawards, the engine revving and clunking, the tiller fighting against Norman's hold. She knew she was being taken hostage. It was only then that it occurred to me I'd given him a more valuable hostage, when the police came. My first instinct to go out and tackle him was over-ridden by sense. The RIB would catch up with us in a matter of minutes.

I risked a glance out, in the crack between the curtain and the bulkhead. He was looking behind him at the approaching RIB, then he turned to face forwards again, frowning. He glanced to his left, and I saw the thought as clear as a tide-wave: if he ran *Khalida* ashore, he could leap clear and run, take the first car with keys in the ignition, and make his getaway. He wasn't thinking of after: the known number-plate, the need of ID to get off the island, whether by ferry or plane. His immediate impulse was flight.

The shore outline behind his head wheeled, the Co-op, the Building Centre, the boating club, and settled with the standing stone clear behind his shoulder. He was heading across to the hall and the streets of council houses behind it. Below the hall was a pebble beach, with seaweed-covered rocks at low tide. If he ran *Khalida* ashore at this speed he would take the keel right off her.

I could hear the RIB approaching. Norman didn't look around. His gaze was fastened on the shore, teeth gripping his underlip. He bent down and touched the gear-lever, reassuring himself that she was at her top speed. From the way the far hill was receding behind him, the shore must be less than five minutes away. The RIB wouldn't go in front of her to be rammed. *Khalida* was twice its size. They'd go ashore – even in my anxiety, I hoped Gavin would remember to lift the engine so that the propeller didn't touch bottom – and grab Norman as he came off.

I took a deep breath. It was no good trying to be stealthy. The minute I came out into the cabin he'd see me. I took ten seconds to think the manoeuvre through, then slipped off the berth and stood upright, ready. I made a dash for it, left hand flinging the curtain aside, right foot over the hanging locker area, and through the cabin between the sofa on one side, the cooker and chart table on the other.

Norman saw me as soon as the curtain moved. His mouth opened wide. He took a step back, then his mouth closed, and he squared himself, ready for a fight. His hands clenched on the tiller.

That suited me. I came slowly forward, through the cabin. 'You're not going to get away, Norman.' I kept my eyes steady on his. 'There's no need to run my boat ashore.'

Then, swift as thought, I dropped down beside the

cabin steps, my left hand grabbing the engine box cover which made the top step of the companionway, right hand reaching in to pull the lever that would stop the engine, left hand flicking the start lever so that he couldn't just turn the key to make her go again.

The thunk, thunk of the engine slowed. He made a grab forwards but the moment he let go of the tiller, *Khalida* swerved violently. He stumbled forward and had to grab at the guard rails to stop himself falling head-first down into the cabin. I held the lever until there was silence, then let it go. Then it was just the two of us aboard *Khalida*, with the sound of the waves against the hull. He raised his head and looked at me, and before he could move, I reached up and pulled the sliding hatch closed over my head.

He rose like a fury, cursing me in a torrent of repeated 'Fucking bitch –', and shoved it aside. It was stiff enough to slow him down, and I'd left the engine step open, so by the time he'd come below to grab at me, I was already out of the forehatch and on deck ready to fend the RIB's grey rubber off my white topsides. Norman didn't try the hatch, but came back out into the cockpit. I retreated to the foredeck as two police officers clambered aboard to get hold of him.

'A bit late,' I commented to Gavin, who was watching critically from the RIB below me.

'On the contrary,' he retorted, 'a very neat operation. You didn't actually need to go with your boat. You could easily have watched from on shore.'

'Someone had to stop the engine, to let you catch up.'

'I take it you didn't think about how a hostage could hamper us.'

'Not till it was too late,' I admitted.

Behind me, the police officers had managed to quieten Norman down. They kept a hold of him as he climbed down into the RIB, the handcuffs making him clumsy. I left Gavin reciting the 'suspect's rights', and got my engine re-started before we drifted ashore.

Sunday 5 August
Tide times for Brae:
Low Water 05.40   0.3m
High Water 12.06   2m
Low Water 17.48   0.5m
High Water Monday 00.10   2.2m
Moon waning gibbous

I went to see Anders the next morning. It was Sunday, so I'd had a lift organised in for Mass, but I went earlier, hoping some kind driver would pick me up. I was in luck; although the stillness of a community hangover lay over most of Brae and Voe, I got a crofter driving to check lambs from just past the boating club to Voe, then a Sullom Voe worker coming off-shift and heading for Lerwick.

I got him to drop me off at the garage to buy grapes and a large bar of chocolate, Anders' favourite Green and Black's white, then I walked slowly up to the hospital. It was a sixties block, harled fawn, with white window-frames. It looked over the 'sooth mooth' – the south entrance to Lerwick, the Aberdeen ferry's way in and out, hence the local name of 'sooth moother' for anyone who wasn't a native. It was a spectacular view in sunshine: the high white cliffs of Noss, with its wheeling gannets constantly in motion around it, and the sea horizon (next stop, Norway; Anders would be looking out towards home). In front of Noss was the green hill of Bressay, the island that had sheltered the Viking fleet before the battle of Largs, the Dutch fishermen of the seventeenth century, the herring smacks of the nineteenth, the battleships of both world wars. Then there was the sound, with seals sunning themselves on the rocks, and closest of all, the south end of Lerwick itself: the Health Centre, the roundabout, the 21st century AD Tesco facing the grey stone tower of the 2nd century BC Clickimin Broch.

The hospital doors slid open reluctantly to let me through into a blast of warm air and cleaning fluid smell.

'I was wanting to visit Anders Johansen,' I said to the girl behind the glass panel labelled 'Reception'. 'He was admitted yesterday. Ward 1.'

'It's on the first floor,' she said. 'Follow the signs.'

I followed through the pale green corridors with their photographs and paintings – mostly of Shetland, as if patients might forget where they were – up the echoing stairs, and into the ward.

I don't know what I'd expected: Anders looking as I'd seen him last, with the colour drained from his face, rigid with suppressing pain, bandaged, fettered by drips of scarlet blood, of colourless solution. It was a shock to see him pillowed upright, by the window, with his face turned towards the ward. The only sign of injury was the bandage around his shoulder. He had his colour back, and he was relaxed and smiling – he'd obviously just made some joke at the young nurse in the pale-blue overall, for she was telling him off with mock-severity. A pang I didn't want to recognise squeezed harsh fingers around my heart. He was younger than me, and so handsome, and I'd a scarred cheek, and a wardrobe of jeans and sailing gear –

Then he turned his head and saw me. His face lit up; he launched straight into Norwegian, forgetting the pretty nurse. 'Cass! I'm glad to see you. You couldn't bring Rat, I suppose, but is he okay without me?'

I dumped my contribution to his five-a-day in his lap, and put his kitbag with a selection of clean clothes on the floor. 'He's missing you. He's either going to ground in his nest or watching for you.'

He held his brown hand out, and I put mine in it. His fingers closed warm around mine. I looked down at it, the smooth skin, the faint blue of the veins running up the back of it. The colour and texture of the two hands matched. I couldn't look at his face.

'How are you?'

'Sore. But the doctor says it is not serious, the muscle and shoulder-blade will heal, and the horn did not go too deep. I was tossed rather than gored.'

Relief swept through me. 'Good. I was worried about your arm.'

'You are okay?' he asked. 'The bull did not touch you? I did not manage to ask, yesterday.'

'You're a hero,' I joked. 'You got both me and Kirsten out of the way. It's all over the Shetland news website. I should have brought my laptop, to show you.'

'And last night? I was worried about you.' I looked up then. His eyes were the blue of the sea out of the window behind him, fringed by his long, fair lashes. 'I didn't like the idea of you being alone on *Khalida*. The killer might think you could identify him.'

'He did,' I said, and forgot my shyness in telling him the end of the story. 'Luckily *Khalida* hadn't touched ground,' I finished, 'and so she's fine. They drove the boy off in a police car, and I've heard no more of that.' Poor Kirsten, waking to this second disaster.

'But the cavalry were there all the time. Your policeman.'

'Him too.' I smiled. 'He wasn't very pleased that I'd risked being taken hostage.'

Anders snorted. 'A landsman. I would have done the same as you.' He grimaced. 'I phoned my parents, this morning, as soon as I was awake enough. They are coming, today, by plane, and they want me to go home.'

'You'll need to rest for a bit,' I agreed.

'I cannot take Rat home on a plane.' His hand tightened on mine. 'You would let me mend on board *Khalida*.'

I thought about that for a moment. I could see it so easily, us continuing our gipsy life, with meals at odd times, and evenings together with the lamp shedding its candle glow over us. Then, when he was healed, before the winter set in, we could forget about college and regular work, and go adventuring, across to the Caribbean, where the warm water was aquamarine over yellow sand, and the night stars hung so low you could reach out and touch them. We were two of a kind, Anders and I. The selkie wife should have stayed with her own kin, instead of trying to make a life ashore ... except that I'd tried that already, with Alain, and it hadn't worked. I wouldn't steal this son from his parents.

'Of course I would,' I said, 'but I think you'd be better at home, in a clean bed, with real sheets, and a shower next door.'

Anders pulled a face. 'And regular meal-times, and my mother watching everything I do, and the neighbours calling.'

'Sometimes you need that.'

'And you will look after Rat, till I can come back for him?'

'I'll bring Rat to Bergen,' I promised. 'The first fair wind, I'll bring him over.' I drew my hand out of his and stood up. 'You keep getting better, now. Is there anything I can get you, in town?'

He shook his head. 'Although I have not tried hospital food, yet.'

'Then, if I don't see you before, I'll see you in Bergen.' I leaned forward to kiss him on the cheek, but his head turned, as I had known it would, and his mouth found mine, warm, clinging, and I felt giddy as I felt myself respond, it was only a kiss – and then I pulled myself back from him when I was wanting to lean forward, to crouch down beside the bed so that we could hold each other, never let go. I tried to keep it casual.

'Keep taking care of yourself. If the forecast's good, I'll see you in a few days.'

I turned to wave as I left the ward. He was leaning back against the immaculate pillows and smiling.

I'd a dozen things to do before I could leave. Both the short-range and long-range forecast were clear. I could go tomorrow, with a southerly force 4-5 to give me a fast reach each way, a day to Out Skerries, then a thirty-two hour passage. After that, a low was heading for us, with gale force winds and rain. If I didn't go now, I wouldn't go at all. Maybe it was just as well. The next time I saw Anders, he'd be his mother's son again, bandaged and scrubbed, not fit to go adventuring, safe under her eye. Returning would be in the lap of the weather gods.

I sent him a text: *Weather good now see you in Bergen.*

There was one more week of the sail training, but twarthree phone calls got the other instructors to cover that. I checked *Khalida*'s rigging and made sure the autopilot was working properly. I went through the lockers and made a list of stores for the voyage; I stowed all the loose items and put the little table away. Rat watched intelligently; he knew what we were doing. I hoped Cat wouldn't be seasick on his first proper voyage. A trip to the shop, and we were ready for sea.

I had just spread my North Sea chart, tide-tables, pencils and paper out on the table when I heard footsteps on the pontoon. Rat looked up hopefully, then dived into the forepeak as Gavin's voice called my name. I stood up and stuck my head out of the hatch. 'Kettle's about to go on. Come aboard.'

He swung over the guard rail. 'I can't stay long. My flight's at 18.20.' He came down into the cabin. I moved my heavy-duty oilskins forrard.

'Have a seat.'

Gavin put the cushion between his back and *Khalida*'s wooden shelf and leaned back, looking at the spread charts, the streamlined grey autopilot. Silence fell as I made the coffee, only partly the comfortable silence of friendship. I was too conscious of his physical presence. Anders had once said, *You know how it is, at the end of a voyage, you have become close, and perhaps for that last night you become lovers. Even you, Cass who walks by herself.*

Suddenly I wasn't Cass who walked by herself any longer. It was the end of this voyage, and I couldn't look at his face. I watched his hands instead, a countryman's hands, weathered brown and made for strength, but with beauty in their deftness. They were hands for lifting sheep, for mending fences. Land hands, that would hold a selkie wife ashore. I avoided touching his fingers as I handed him the mug which was close to becoming his, and kept a careful distance between us as I sat down. 'What news?'

'They caught Madge in Bergen – though only because a sharp-eyed policeman spotted that she was a woman alone on the right sort of motorboat. She must have had her disguise all ready aboard: a long, dark wig, with brows and lashes to match, shoes to make her two inches taller and clothes to make her look slim, rather than plump. The art works stowed aboard were a giveaway, though. Your 'sisters' guess was bang on. She's insisting, of course, that she was an innocent partner in David and Sandra's shady dealings. They met through her, fell for each other, and worked out this scheme. David had already had dealings with Olaf, and they decided to exploit his connection with Brian to find out about security in likely houses to rob.

317

Sandra of course could find out about drug dealers through Peter, and she did those negotiations, with David passing the actual selling down the line. A very nice earner.'

'And was the clumsiness of this deliberate?'

'It was indeed. Sandra was planning just to leave, but when Peter insisted on coming up to Shetland, with these burglaries particularly in mind, David took fright and decided he had to go. If anyone in Newcastle was worried, well, Sandra had her mobile and could reassure them for a bit – then, when there was a suitable nasty storm forecast, she'd do a last call from that area then drop the mobile overboard. Meanwhile, she and David would be living it up abroad. If there were more investigations, well, it was as we figured, there could be a conclusion that Peter had uncovered something, and those responsible had eliminated them both. I'm pretty sure we'll have no trouble convicting her. Norman's a juvenile, of course.' He looked at the chart spread on the table. 'Where are you off to?'

I lifted it to show him. 'Bergen. I have to deliver Rat home.'

'Anders is going by a more conventional route?'

'By plane, with his parents.'

I felt him withdraw from me. 'So you're giving up your college plan.'

'No,' I said vehemently. I spread my hands, trying to conjure the thoughts I couldn't quite articulate. 'I don't know if I'll fit in there or not, but I need to grow up. I can't stay a footloose hippy all my life.'

'People do.'

'I don't want to.'

He smiled. 'That's different.'

'There's a weather-window now. I'll take Rat over, then I'll return as soon as I can.'

His grey eyes were steady on mine. 'What about Anders?'

'I'm coming back,' I said. 'I don't know what he'll do.' It wasn't quite what he'd asked, and he saw that. He shook his head.

'For a woman who rules her own life, you're leaving the initiative open.'

'I've never been good at this part of it,' I confessed.

'If you come back from Bergen, call me.'

'I'll come back,' I said.

A note on Shetlan

Shetland has its own very distinctive language, *Shetlan* or *Shetlandic*, which derives from Old Norse and Old Scots. Magnie's first words to Cass in *Death on a Longship* are:

'Cass, well, for the love of mercy. Norroway, at this season? Yea, yea, we'll find you a berth. Where are you?'

Written in west-side Shetlan (each district is slightly different), it would have looked like this:

'Cass, weel, fir da love o' mercy. Norroway, at dis saeson? Yea, yea, we'll fin dee a bert. Quaur is du?''

Th becomes a *d* sound in *dis* (this), *da* (the), *dee* and *du* (originally thee and thou, now you), *wh* becomes *qu* (*quaur*, where), the vowel sounds are altered (well to *weel*, season to *saeson*, find to *fin*), the verbs are slightly different (quaur is du?) and the whole looks unintelligible to most folk from outwith Shetland, and *twartree* (a few) within it too.

So, rather than writing in the way my characters would speak, I've tried to catch the rhythm and some of the distinctive usages of Shetlan while keeping it intelligible to *soothmoothers*, or people who've come in by boat through the South Mouth of Bressay Sound into Lerwick, and by extension, anyone living south of Fair Isle.

There are also many Shetlan words that my characters would naturally use, and here, to help you, are *some o' dem*. No Shetland person would ever use the Scots *wee*; to them, something small would be *peerie*, or, if it was very small, *peerie mootie*. They'd *caa* sheep in a *park*, that is, herd them up in a field – *moorit* sheep, coloured black, brown, fawn. They'd take a *skiff* (a small rowing boat) out along the *banks* (cliffs) or on the *voe* (sea inlet), with the *tirricks* (Arctic terns) crying above them, and the *selkies* (seals) watching. Hungry folk are *black fanted* (because they've forgotten their *faerdie maet*, the snack that would have kept them going) and upset folk *greet* (cry). An older housewife like Barbara would have her *makkin* (knitting) *belt* buckled around her waist, and her *reestit* (smoke-dried) *mutton* hanging above the Rayburn. And finally ... my favourite Shetland verb: *to kettle*. As in: *Wir cat's joost kettled. Four ketlings, twa strippet and twa black and quite*. I'll leave you to work that one out on your own ... or, of course, you could consult Joanie Graham's *Shetland Dictionary*, if your local bookshop hasn't *joost selt* their last copy *dastreen*.

There are a number of grammar constructions which are Scots / Shetland. One I've used is *needs + ed* – for example, something in the fridge *needs used*.

Adults using the diminutives Magnie (Magnus), Gibbie (Gilbert), and Charlie may also seem strange to non-Shetland ears. In a traditional country family (I can't speak for *toonie* Lerwick habits) the oldest son would often be called after his father or grandfather, and be distinguished from that father and grandfather and perhaps a cousin or two as well, by his own version of their shared name. Or, of course, by a *peerie* in front of it, which would stick for life, like the *eart kyent* (well-known) guitarist Peerie Willie Johnson, who recently celebrated his 80th birthday. There was also a patronymic system, which meant that a Peter's four sons, Peter, Andrew, John, and Matthew, would all have the surname Peterson, and so would his son Peter's children. Andrew's children, however, would have the surname Anderson, John's would be Johnson, and Matthew's would be Matthewson. The Scots ministers stamped this out in the nineteenth century, but in one district you can have a lot of *folk* with the same surname, and so they're distinguished by their house name: *Magnie o' Strom, Peter o' da Knowe* ...

Glossary

For those who like to look up unfamiliar words as they go, here's a glossary of some Scots and Shetlan words.

aa: all
an aa: as well
aabody: everybody
ahint: behind
allwye: everywhere
amang: among
anyroad: anyway
auld: old
aye: always
bairn: child
banks: sea cliffs, or peatbanks, the slice of moor where peats are cast
bannock: flat triangular scone
birl, birling: paired spinning round in a dance
blootered: very drunk
blyde: glad
boanie: pretty, good looking
breeks: trousers
brigstanes: flagged stones at the door of a crofthouse
bruck: rubbish
caa: round up
canna: can't
clarted: thickly covered
cowp: capsize
cratur: creature
crofthouse: the long, low traditional house set in its own land
darrow: a hand fishing line
dastreen: yesterday evening
de-crofted: land that has been taken out of agricultural use, e.g. for a house site

dee: you. **du** is also you, depending on the grammar of the sentence – they're equivalent to thee and thou. Like French, you would only use dee or du to one friend; several people, or an adult if you're a younger person, would be 'you'.

denner: midday meal

didna: didn't

dinna: don't

dis: this

doesna: doesn't

doon: down

drewie lines: a type of seaweed made of long strands

duke: duck

dukey-hole: pond for ducks

du kens: you know

dyck, dyke: a wall, generally drystane, i.e. built without cement

ee now: right now

eela: fishing, generally these days a competition

everywye: everywhere

fae, frae: from

faersome: frightening

faither, usually **faider**: father

fanted: hungry, often **black fanted**, absolutely starving

folk: people

gansey: a knitted jumper

geen: gone

greff: the area in front of a peat bank

gret: cried

guid: good

guid kens: God knows

hae: have

hadna: hadn't

harled: exterior plaster using small stones

heid: head

hoosie: little house, usually for bairns

isna: isn't

joost: just

ken, kent: know, knew

kirk: church

kirkyard: graveyard

knowe: hillock

Lerook: Lerwick

lintie: skylark

lipper: a cheeky or harum-scarum child, generally affectionate

mair: more

makkin belt: a knitting belt with a padded oval, perforated for holding the 'wires' or knitting needles.

mam: mum

mareel: sea phosphorescence, caused by plankton, which makes every wave break in a curl of gold sparks

meids: shore features to line up against each other to pinpoint a spot on the water

midder: mother

mind: remember

moorit: coloured brown or black, usually used of sheep

mooritoog: earwig

muckle: big – as in Muckle Roe, the big red island. Vikings were very literal in their names, and almost all Shetland names come from the Norse.

muckle biscuit: large water biscuit, for putting cheese on

na: no, or more emphatically, **naa**

needna: needn't

Norroway: the old Shetland pronunciation of Norway

o: of

oot: out

ower: over

park: fenced field

peat: brick-like lump of dried peat earth, used as fuel

peerie: small

peerie biscuit: small, sweet biscuit

peeriebreeks: affectionate name for a small thing, person,or animal

piltick: a sea fish common in Shetland waters

pinnie: apron

postie: postman

quen: when

redding up: tidying

reestit mutton: wind-dried shanks of mutton

riggit: dressed, sometimes with the sense dressed up

roadymen: men working on the roads

roog: a pile of peats

rummle: untidy scattering

Santy: Santa Claus

scaddy man's heids: sea urchins

scattald: common grazing land

scuppered: put paid to, done for

selkie: seal, or seal person who came ashore at night, cast his/her skin, and became human

shalder: oystercatcher

sho: she

shoulda: should have, usually said sooda

shouldna: shouldn't have

SIBC: Shetland Islands Broadcasting Company, the independent radio station

sixareen: double-ended six oared boat, around twenty-five foot in length

skafe: squint

skerry: a rock in the sea

smoorikins: kisses

snicked: move a switch that makes a clicking noise

snyirked: made a squeaking or rattling noise

solan: gannet

somewye: somewhere

sooking up: sucking up

soothified: behaving like someone from outwith Shetland

spewings: piles of vomit

splatched: walked in a splashy way with wet feet, or in water

swack: smart, fine

tak: take

tatties: potatoes

tay: tea, or meal eaten in the evening

tink: think

tirricks: Arctic terns

trows: trolls

tushker: L-shaped spade for cutting peat

twa: two

twa-three (usually twa-tree): a small number

vee-lined: lined with wood planking

voe: sea inlet

voehead: the landwards end of a sea inlet

waander: wander

waar: seaweed

wand: a fishing rod

whatna: what

wasna: wasn't

wha's: who is

whitteret: weasel

wi: with

wir: we've – in Shetlan grammar, we are is sometimes we have

wir: our

wife: woman, not necessarily married

wouldna: would not

yaird: enclosed area around or near the croft house

yoal: a traditional clinker-built six-oared rowing boat.

For more information about **Marsali Taylor**
and other **Accent Press** titles
please visit

www.accentpress.co.uk